"It gives me great satisfaction that many times people have written to me to tell me, in varying terms, that I have made them feel better, not worse, about being human. That's all the acknowledgement I need."

Edith Pargeter

EDITH PARGETER ("ELLIS PETERS")

Edith Pargeter was born in the small village of Horsehay, in the English county of Shropshire, on September 28, 1913. She attended Coalbrookdale Country High School for Girls in Ironbridge Gorge, and after leaving school in 1930 worked for seven years as an assistant in a chemist's shop in Dawley. She published her first novel, *Hortensius, Friend of Nero,* in 1936; five others (three of them pseudonymous) followed in the years prior to the Second World War.

Throughout the war Ms. Pargeter served in the Women's Royal Naval Service and continued to write. Among the novels she published during this period, *She Goes to War* appeared in 1942, and the three volumes of her wartime trilogy *(The Eighth Champion of Christendom, Reluctant Odyssey, and Warfare Accomplished)* in 1945-47.

In 1951, *Fallen into the Pit,* the first of her mystery novels featuring Detective Sergeant George Felse, was published. It appeared under her own name; ten years later, the second Felse mystery was published under the name "Ellis Peters," as would be the eleven further installments in the series.

Ms. Pargeter's best-known creation, Brother Cadfael, made his first appearance in Ellis Peters's *A Morbid Taste for Bones: A Medieval Whodunnit,* which was published in 1977. Nineteen other volumes of The Chronicles of Brother Cadfael, as well as short stories, were issued during the next seventeen years; they have been translated into twenty-three languages. Sales of the Cadfael Chronicles are in the millions worldwide, and they have been adapted for a popular series of television programs starring Derek Jacobi.

In all, Ms. Pargeter published more than eighty books, including many translations into English of Czech novels and stories. Among the numerous honors and awards bestowed on her, she received the British Empire Medal, the British Crime Writers' Association's Silver Dagger and its Diamond Dagger, the Mystery Writers of America's "Edgar," the Gold Medal and Ribbon from the Czechoslovak Society for International Relations, and in 1994 she was awarded an OBE by Queen Elizabeth II.

Edith Pargeter died in 1995, in Shropshire.

Also by Edith Pargeter in A COMMON READER EDITION:
The Coast of Bohemia

By the same author in
A COMMON READER EDITION:

The Coast of Bohemia

EDITH PARGETER

The Marriage of Meggotta

A Common Reader Edition
The Akadine Press
2001

The Marriage of Meggotta

A COMMON READER EDITION published 2001
by The Akadine Press, Inc., by arrangement with the Estate of Edith Pargeter.

Copyright © 1979 by Edith M. Pargeter.

First published in 1979 by Macmillan (London) and The Viking Press (New York).

Cover design by Jerry Kelly; woodcut illustration by Albrecht Dürer, from
THE BOOK OF THE *Ritter von Turn*, Basel, 1493.

A Common Reader Edition and fountain colophon are trademarks
of The Akadine Press, Inc.

ISBN 1-58579-029-X

10 9 8 7 6 5 4 3 2 1

THE MARRIAGE OF MEGGOTTA

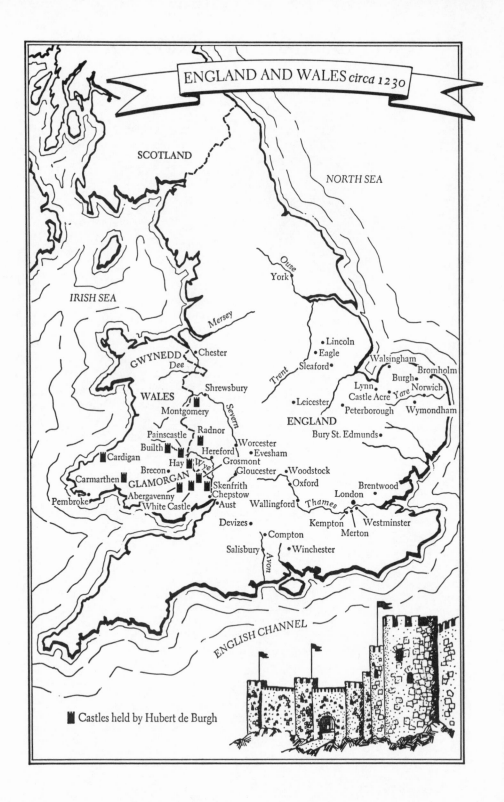

ENGLAND AND WALES *circa 1230*

SCOTLAND

NORTH SEA

IRISH SEA

Ouse

York

Mersey

GWYNEDD • Chester

Dee

WALES   Shrewsbury

Montgomery   *Severn*

Radnor

Painscastle   Worcester

Builth   Hereford • Evesham

Cardigan   Hay   Grosmont

Brecon   *Wye*   Gloucester

Carmarthen   Skenfrith

GLAMORGAN   Chepstow

Abergavenny

Pembroke   White Castle   • Aust   Wallingford

Devizes •

Compton

Salisbury   • Winchester   *Avon*

Lincoln
• Eagle
Sleaford •   Walsingham
Burgh   Bromholm
Lynn   • Norwich
Castle Acre   *Yare*
• Leicester   Peterborough   Wymondham

ENGLAND

Bury St. Edmunds •

Woodstock
Oxford   Brentwood
London •
Kempton   Westminster
Merton

Thames

ENGLISH CHANNEL

THE PEOPLE

THE ROYAL HOUSE OF ENGLAND

King Henry III.

Richard, earl of Cornwall, his younger brother.

Eleanor, his youngest sister, wife and then widow of William, Earl Marshal of England and earl of Pembroke.

THE ROYAL HOUSE OF SCOTLAND

King Alexander II.

Margaret of Scotland, his eldest sister, formerly betrothed to King Henry III, now wife to Hubert de Burgh, earl of Kent.

Marjorie of Scotland, his youngest sister, later wife to Gilbert, Earl Marshal and earl of Pembroke.

THE NOBILITY OF ENGLAND

Ranulf de Blundeville, earl of Chester.

William Marshal, Earl Marshal of England and earl of Pembroke.

Richard, his brother, and successor in both titles.

Gilbert, third brother, successor to Richard in both titles.

Isabella, their sister, widow of Gilbert de Clare, earl of Gloucester, later wife to Richard, earl of Cornwall.

Simon de Montfort, of the French house of Montfort l'Amaury, later earl of Leicester.

John de Lacy, earl of Lincoln.

Hugh d'Aubeny, earl of Arundel.

Hubert de Burgh, earl of Kent, justiciar to King Henry.

Gilbert Basset and Richard Siward, barons of England.

RICHARD DE CLARE, heir to the earldoms of Gloucester and Hertford, son of the late Gilbert de Clare, earl of Gloucester, and Isabella Marshal, his wife.

MARGARET, or MEGGOTTA, DE BURGH, daughter of Hubert de Burgh, earl of Kent, and Margaret of Scotland, his wife.

CLERICS AND OFFICIALS

Edmund Rich of Abingdon, treasurer of Salisbury and later archbishop of Canterbury.

Luke, archbishop of Dublin, confessor and friend to Hubert de Burgh.

Peter des Roches, bishop of Winchester, Poitevin by birth.

Peter des Rivaulx, his nephew, treasurer of the royal household.

Stephen Segrave, successor to Hubert de Burgh as justiciar.

Geoffrey de Craucombe, steward of the royal household.

Roger Niger, bishop of London.

Robert Bingham, bishop of Salisbury.

Lawrence of St. Albans, Hubert's attorney.

1

November, 1230:
Burgh-next-Aylsham;
Westminster.

*R*ichard came to Burgh in the steely twilight of a November day, blown in at the gatehouse on a withering east wind that scoured torn wisps of blacker cloud before it across a vast, forbidding marbled greyness of wintry sky, and stung the lips and eyelids with salt spray even at this distance from the sea. There was no ground, in all those nine or ten miles between, high enough to ward off the flaying cold of it, only the open coastal plain and the leaden mirrors of the pools that the tides shaped and reshaped almost every spring. And then the wilderness of the sea, and beyond the sea lands as flat as these, and nowhere any shelter from the blistering cold.

Meggotta was used to the East Anglian winds, and well wrapped up against them. Alice had bundled her into her furred cloak and hood before she would let her run loose in the baileys, for there was no keeping the child indoors now that she knew her father was coming home. Ever since his herald had ridden in at noon, with word that the earl's company were only a few hours behind him, she had been in and out like quicksilver wherever the bustle and excitement ran highest, through kitchen, buttery, bakery, stables, and mews, in and out of the armoury, where there would soon be work enough for every hand, after a summer campaign in France, and, after every foray, back to her mother or to Alice, whichever had more time to answer her endless questions.

"Do you know about this boy my father's bringing home with him? Do you know what he'll be like? Shall I like him?"

"Of course you will, my duck. He'll be a playmate for you, like a brother of your own."

Meggotta wondered why Alice, even preoccupied with hauling out the best hangings from the wardrobe-chests, should suddenly check and chuckle when she said "brother," but that was one question she had no time to ask; there were so many more urgent.

"How old is he?"

"Why, no more than a few weeks ahead of you, chick. He's eight last August."

That sounded reassuring and right. "Will he be a nice boy, do you think? As nice as Peter?" Peter was the head groom's son, twelve years old, and a reliable escort for a child almost too bold and fearless on a pony.

"Now, how should I know that before I so much as see the lad? I daresay he'll turn out very well, you'll see. He's as well born as any boy in the kingdom, and he'll be an earl like your father when he's grown, and gets seisin of what's his. So I don't doubt he's been taught nicely, and will deserve you should be pleasant to him, miss. He'll be a great man some day."

"Then why," asked Meggotta reasonably, "is he coming to live with us, if he has such great lands of his own?"

"Because the poor child's lost his father, dead in France, and the king's given him to your father to bring up like his own son. And to look after all his lands for him, until he's grown and can do the like himself. It's a great honour, mind, to have the rearing of him, and there's many a lord and baron must be envying your father the charge."

It was already known to Meggotta, through sharp ears and a thoughtful intelligence, that there were many other things the magnates of England envied her father. She did not understand the reasons, but she had sensed the slight unease that formed a dark reverse to his pride in his own grandeur, and recognized it, curiously, rather through her mother, the countess, who viewed rank and eminence only from above, being born royal. But this was one subject on which Meggotta had never asked questions, having a sure instinct for those that would only proliferate disquiet, rather than allaying it. So she asked only, frowning, "And has he no mother, either?"

"He has, my duck, but for such a great young gentleman it's needful he should be in the charge of a proper guardian who can teach him all he needs to know. This isn't Wat from the stables, you know, he'll be learning to bear arms, and manage his estates, and all the craft of a great barony, so it needs a proper man to mind all those matters, and see him ready for his earldom. A mother's very well, but not without a man's guidance."

Meggotta was not sure that she wanted to share her mother and father with anyone else, though it was certainly hard that a boy should be left without parents, and the prospect of gaining a brother had its decided attractions. True, she already possessed a half-brother, the son of her father's first wife, but John was a grown man, married and with lands and manors of his own through his wife, and Meggotta had seen him only two or three times in her life, so he hardly counted. She thought of him as belonging to her father's generation rather than her own. And there was something else to be considered, before she decided to give these important changes her approval.

"And what if we all get to like him," she demanded, "and then when he's ready for his earldom he has to go away and leave us? That would be worse than if he had never come."

And Alice laughed, and said, in the knowing way of someone in possession of a joke Meggotta did not know, "I shouldn't worry about that, my duck, if I were you. By that time—who knows?—he'll be setting such store on you that he'll take you away with him."

It seemed to Meggotta a silly answer, since it would mean leaving her father and mother behind, which of course she would never consider doing. But she had no patience with the smugness of grown-ups, in this mood of keeping secrets from the children, and so never went on to ask the further questions that would gratify them. Instead, she left her nurse busily shaking out the tapestries for the solar walls, and went off at a run to watch Peter forking fresh litter into all the empty stalls in the stables, ready for the twenty or so tired horses they would soon be housing, and thence to the bakery, and the brewery, and then out through both baileys to see if there were any sign yet of horsemen along the road.

They came with the dusk, turning the drearest hour of the day into the brightest and most joyful. As soon as the outriders came clattering up the causeway to the gatehouse, the whole household came flooding out, grooms running with torches to meet the cavalcade and bring them in, the Countess Margaret appearing in the hall doorway with her maids behind her, the seneschal emerging from the armoury, and the falconers from the mews. Hooves clashed on the cobbles of the outer bailey, and the fringe of torches fumed and crackled with resin on either side, streaming crimson flames along the wind. Through the gate into the inner bailey, hunched, cloaked figures on tall, tired horses shouldered their way and clattered to a stand, their breath cloudy on the cold air. Grooms ran to take the bridles, and one of the pages came scurrying importantly with a pitcher of mulled wine.

Meggotta, who had run in and out a dozen times in the day, grew grave and responsible now that they had really come, and went to take her stand beside her mother, clinging to the shelter of her skirts and reaching up to take her hand. The darling daughter she might be, but her mother was the wife and chatelaine, and no one had the right to be before her in welcoming the earl home after six long months of absence. A year ago the child would have run headlong, with open arms, and without asking leave of anyone, but she was beginning to glimpse the mysterious uses and properties of ceremony. All the same, she was one stair ahead of her mother as they came down to the bailey from the hall door, and her hand was tugging at the strong, cool hand that clasped it.

"Go, then, run!" said Margaret, loosing the clasp, and urging her daughter forward with a hand behind her shoulders. "You know you want to, he'll look first for you."

And Meggotta ran, very willingly now that she was bidden, leaping down the steps like a puppy, and rushing across the bailey to where her father had just set foot to ground. Halfway to him she launched a joyful, wordless cry, and he swung to meet it gladly. Even in the flickering, smoky glow of the torches she saw his face kindle into joy like a lamp newly lighted. Then she was in his arms and hoisted high, hugging him and being hugged, her arms tight round his neck, and her cheek against his bearded cheek.

"Father, I've missed you so, you've been away so long! Don't go again, don't go!"

"My Margery-pearl, Meg, Madge, Meggotta!" He was a grave man, burdened with affairs and taking them heavily; she was the only creature who could make him laugh, and for her he laughed even without reason, for pleasure and gratitude. His hard, commanding voice grew soft and playful for her, even his big hands, browned by weather and callused by weapons, accustomed to bear down heavily on all with whom he had to deal, and gnarled with the onset of years, handled her as lightly and tenderly as Alice had handled her in the hour of her birth. "We're home, my dove, and Christmas is coming, and who knows what I have in my saddle-bags for you from France? There, I'll not leave you yet, not this year, and never for so long, I hope. We've done with French campaigning, pray God!"

"You're cold," she said, nestled against his cheek.

"I shall get warm, here at home. And have you been good all this time I've been away?"

She said, "Not always." It was whispered serenely into his ear, where her hood and his made a secret place.

"But enough! I know! Always good enough for me, my heart!" He hugged her, and brushed his lips against her round cheek, cold as frost to the first touch, warm the next moment, and set her down. Her hand he kept in his as he turned to greet and embrace his wife, who had been standing by serenely while they communed without her. She watched their mutual love, and was content.

"My lady. . . ." His kiss was fervent and hungry, a much younger man would have been proud to match it.

"Welcome home, my dear lord," said the Countess Margaret.

She took the wine from the page, and presented it. It was hot and strong, welcome after the cold ride. He drank, and waved it on to his escort. They were down from their saddles now, and the grooms were leading the first horses, steaming and jaded, to their earned rest. Hubert loosed his hand from Meggotta's, and turned to where the last of his cavalcade stood pawing and heaving, heads drooping to the cobbles.

"And here is Richard de Clare. Our new son!"

The horse was tall and noble, an earl's mount, but it was a groom who had been riding him, a thickset fellow in a strange livery who was just leaning down from the saddle with a cloaked bundle in his arms. One of the de Burgh grooms stood to receive the burden, lowered it to the ground, and set it gently on unsteady feet. The feet, however feeble, gripped and held, the boy stood up and put aside the shrouding folds of the cloak that wrapped him, shrugging back the hood upon his shoulders, and standing to be seen.

He was in no case to be proud of what he displayed. The first part of the journey he had made in good heart, rigid with pride, a princeling well mounted and well taught, fit to be shown to any countess. But the way was so long, and so tiring, and the ever-increscent pain and loneliness had eaten into his resolution, until he had been direly sick, and submitted to being carried on his groom's saddle-bow, wrapped in a cloak and cradled in the rider's arms. He stood now, stiff and weary and defiant in his despair, soiled and crumpled and speckled with his own vomit, a solitary waif somewhat over eight years old, heir to two earldoms, newly orphaned and bitterly aware of his situation among strangers. In particular he bled for his mother, young and pretty and richly endowed, who had cried a little, and smiled a little into her mirror, and let him be taken away from her to this alien place. He had thought she loved him. He knew he loved her. But she had let him go without a murmur, and told him sweetly that it was his duty to go where the king directed. The king had directed, it seemed, that he should be given to the earl of Kent, to be brought up and instructed according to the earl's wish. And Richard had obeyed, not understanding at the time much of what was said to him, though it had been said very gently and considerately; and he was here. It seemed that the long ride was over; they had arrived.

He was so tired and still so sick that he could hardly see or hear, he could only stand erect, the least he could do for his lost, loved father, and make some gallant pretence to respond to whatever was said to him by way of welcome, or excuse, or whatever this might be. He stiffened his back and stared, prepared for enemies. Since those he knew as friends were gone, long left behind, what could these be but enemies?

"My lord Richard," said Margaret, stooping to his cheek, "you're more than welcome." He felt her lips touch him, and was stung by unbearable memories that started him shaking like a man with ague. To him this woman was hugely tall and terribly beautiful, far more daunting than his fair, kind, soft mother. She had a generous bosom and a slender waist, a long, lofty neck and a head that reared above splendidly erect, a small head if it had not been for the great burden of coiled hair that weighted it down, hair of a brown so dark that it seemed almost black, until the flickering light of the torches caught the coils in its fiery play of radiance and shadow, and startled flames red as rubies among the darkness. Her eyes were the colour of bracken in autumn, and her mouth was wide and imperious and warm. Richard marvelled and was mute. With all his courtly training, it took him a long moment to recover himself in the face of such authority, and lean forward to raise and kiss her hand. It was vital and large, and retained his hand firmly when he would have loosed it.

"They've tired you out," she said with compunction. "Never fret, you'll have time to rest now. This is your home."

"And here's my daughter to greet you," said the earl. "Meggotta, make Richard welcome."

He had not even noticed her until then, but now he recalled that there was a daughter, and remembered her significance. And there she was, barely a yard away from him, a creature at least on his own level, even somewhat smaller, so that he could look at her without feeling menaced. For a long moment they stared at each other with the candid, unflattering curiosity of hound pups unexpectedly encountering nose to nose, and with the same suggestion of imminent hostilities if the inspection failed to satisfy.

Meggotta saw a boy rather well grown for his years, a good hand's-breadth taller than herself, but slender. He was in one of the shooting-up stages of his growth, at present having difficulty in managing a frame run all to arms and legs. Later he would fill out and rediscover the balance and grace that were surely his right. He had an oval face, grimed with travel and tiredness at the moment, and even smeared, she realized, with the traces of some furtive weeping, no doubt hidden inside the cloak and scrubbed away in its folds. When clean, this would be a suave, pale face, ivory and bright instead of pinched and taut with cold as now. He had fine, fastidious features, proud and vulnerable, loftily lidded blue eyes that stood her off like lances, and yet had something of fright and something of appeal in their challenge. He was very fair, his curling hair the colour of wheat-stalks, and his lips were set like steel to keep them from quivering. All this Meggotta took in gravely, before she remembered her manners, and said, in a wary voice, "You're very welcome, Richard." It sounded obedient but not enthusiastic. On the whole she was disappointed. A future earl should have looked more impressive.

Richard saw a trim, well-rounded little girl, clean, glowing, comfortably warm in her hooded furs, and very neat in her person, everything he did not feel at that moment. The tresses of hair that burst from under her hood were of a brown only a shade less dark than her mother's, and showed the same glinting sparks of red. Her face was round but delicately moulded, perhaps even a shade broader than its length, with a wide, resolute mouth, and the very-wide-set eyes that stared at him so intently were huge and clear, and the deepest, most luminous grey imaginable, fringed with long lashes almost black. He found it an unencouraging face, as fearless, innocent, and aloof as a cat's, and as indifferent to the impression it made. He resented her obvious well-being. Well for her, she was at home here, these were her people, her lands, her servants, she could afford to dispense with any good opinion of his, there was no harm he could do to her, and no good. He felt even more alone as he said, with hurt, arrogant dignity, that she was very gracious, which was the last thing he felt about her then.

"Come in, out of this cold," said Margaret, undisturbed by the stiff wariness of children, and ushered them before her, one in either hand, up the steps and into the hall. There Richard was borne away to the chamber prepared for him and his tutor, and the earl withdrew into the solar to shed his travelling clothes for a woollen gown. There was great running about with hot water and towels for all the new arrivals, and Meggotta was at leisure to consider what she had seen of her new brother, and a little to reconsider it, for he was, after all, at a disadvantage. There was a great deal yet to be discovered about him, and she was willing to suspend judgement. It seemed he had brought with him only a small personal retinue, his tutor, his own groom and manservant, and one clerk, who would return to the household at Gloucester as soon as all the details of Richard's wardship were established. With so small an entourage to deploy between him and the household into which he was being adopted, he would not be able to hide away from her.

He looked better when he was led to the high table in hall and seated between the earl and countess, in the place of honour. The stains of his journey were washed away, and he had changed into tunic and hose of fine wool, and with the pinched blue of cold warmed out of him he was seen to be a presentable child enough. But he did not look any happier, and he had almost nothing to say, for all the gentle efforts Margaret made to draw him out. He ate very little, and seemed to have difficulty in swallowing anything at all, and before supper ended his eyes were drooping shut over his trencher. There was nothing to be done with him, in kindness, but put him to bed, though it was still much earlier than Meggotta's bedtime, and she took care to disappear from sight, in case it should be taken for granted that she, too, had had a tiring day, and ought to compensate with an early night.

She had a great deal to think about, and much of it was puzzling. Richard's tutor had returned to the hall, and the manservant was there among the grooms at the lowest table. Now the newcomer was really alone for a while, and surely as lost among the implications of the day's experiences as she was. She tried to imagine what it must be like to lie lonely in a strange bed, in a strange house, surrounded only by people never seen before, but the effort was too great for her; all it did was fill her with a curious unease, as if in some way she had failed to change something which manifestly ought to be changed. She knew her way here, and he did not. She was secure and happy among these people who were strangers and formidable to him.

There was music now in the hall, and those of the household who had stayed at home and those who had returned from the campaign in France were mingling merrily, with much to tell on both sides, and much to hear. For the moment no one was noticing her. She slipped out by the door behind the screen, and along the passage past the chapel. There was a small chamber beyond, much like the one she shared with Alice, and that was where Richard and his tutor were accommodated. The tutor, she knew, was still sitting at table in earnest conversation with her father's chaplain; two learned men would naturally find much to talk about. It was not that she had any reason to fear being observed; she was Meggotta de Burgh, and could do what she pleased here. It was rather that she had need of privacy for her own soul's sake, and could not have gone on if anyone had violated her secrecy. But here, outside the door, left ajar in case the occupant should call for anything, there was only silence and stillness.

No, the silence was not absolute. Small, infinitely small, sounds, pinpricks in the hush, came from within the room. At first she thought she was listening to nothing more than deep-drawn, sleeping breaths, but then she was caught into their broken, spasmodic rhythm, and knew that no sleeping creature ever made sounds so troubled or so suppressed. Not even in bad dreams. She had had bad dreams, though very rarely, and shrieked her indignant terror to bring Alice to her. This was no such matter. The stranger-boy within was weeping with a desperation that chilled and dismayed her, and moreover, he was muffling his misery under covers and pillow, to shut out the world from ever glimpsing it. She felt, rather than heard, the great, shuddering convulsions that passed through him, for they were almost silent, and yet went pulsing through her small body and into her heart. Nothing in her experience matched this intensity of grief.

If she had been older she would have gone away silently and left him alone, but she was eight years old, and knew no reason why she should not move in upon any need or any challenge. She pushed open the door and went in. There was a light burning on a press beside the smaller of the two beds, a wick afloat in a dish of oil. It was enough to show her her way, and to illumine the slight huddle of rugs and furs stretched rigid along the upper half of the bed. The boy was invisible but for a thin hand, not at all like her own plump little paw, that dragged the pillow down over his head, to smother the immense, sighing sobs that were shattering him.

Meggotta went on her knees beside him, with no care at all for silence, for she knew that he knew someone was there, and better he should know at once who it was. She laid a hand on the hand that gripped the pillow, and her cheek against the hand, and whispered into the hollow where he lay hidden, "Don't cry, Richard, please don't cry! I can't bear you to be sad. It's me, Meggotta! No one else is here, only me. No one else knows. Don't cry! I'm here! I don't want you to feel sad. I love you!"

She said it not at all casually, but of blunt design, knowing what words mean. All she wanted then was to comfort him, and what you want to comfort, you love. She was superbly sure of that. Children cry, and you humour them, and they hop up in a moment, as soon as their spleen is over, and begin to play again. But Richard was past playing, and this was more than a game. She felt him stiffen and hold his breath, and reached a hand to ease the pillow away from his tormented face. He lay on his left cheek, she saw but half his countenance, drawn and ugly with pain, but the open eye was levelled upon her, blue as a lance under the folds of its reddened lid. It was looking at her as if it had never seen her before. And still he was holding his breath.

She was a little frightened, and did not know quite how to start him breathing again, so she leaned and kissed him on the cheek. He started violently under her touch, and then began to cry in quite another way, a way she understood, easy and large and very wet, and without the terrible heaves and silences that broke her heart. She slid one arm gratefully under him, and folded the other over, and made little word-less sounds such as Alice had made for comfort when her chick had tumbled and grazed her nose. She hugged him close, half his pillow and all, until the paroxysm passed, and he lay exhausted, she almost as tired on top of him. For some minutes they remained so, and were very quiet.

"You mustn't be sad," she said. "I'm here!" She did not recognize the largeness of the claim, only its validity, so she was not intimidated. She laid her cheek on the crumpled pillow beside his, and his face swam into a distorted, sorrowful beauty, and possibly so did hers to him. "We'll make you happy here," she said, serenely sure because she, apart from this shared distress, was so happy. "My mother will be your mother, you'll see. And my father is the best man in the world, he'll care for you. Don't grieve! I want you to be happy."

"My father's dead," said Richard's muffled voice, more in accusation against fate than in grief.

"I know!"

"Only a day before the king sailed for home! He caught a fever in Nantes. . . . I can't bear it without him!"

But even more bitterly he wanted his mother, who was not dead but who had let him go from her almost lightly. He wept again at the thought, briefly and wearily, and clutched Meggotta's warmth to him in sudden surrender. "Don't go! Stay with me! It's all so strange here!"

"It won't be. Tomorrow I'll show you everything. If it's sunny we can ride. Peter'll come with us, and I'll show you where we go fishing, and hawking. And my father's best bitch-hound has had puppies, and you can choose one for yourself. It's nice here at Burgh; you'll like it once you know it."

It was the music he heard rather than the words, the eager, concerned voice making strangely motherly sounds. The shoulder of her woollen tunic smelled comfortably of the resiny smoke of pine-flares and the warmth of the fire. "Don't go!" he said again in a pleading whisper, resigned for once to his own weakness, and too far gone to resent having it witnessed.

"No, I won't. But it's cold here. Let me into the bed with you, and I'll hold you, and you'll go to sleep."

He lifted the covers, and she clambered in beside him, and folded an arm possessively round his slight body in its linen night-shirt. At first he felt chill to the touch, and stiff, and then he heaved a huge sigh and relaxed into a soft, heavy ease in her arms. She went on portraying for him, low-voiced, all the attractions of Burgh, but before she had touched on half of them he was fast asleep. She lay curled in the warmth of their shared nest, and did not even try to account for the sense of triumphant achievement that filled her, as though she had won a great battle. Very soon she followed him into sleep.

It was not until the boy's tutor repaired to his own bed that Alice found her lost nurseling, for whom she had been turning the manor upside-down an hour or more. Flushed and rosy, sunk fathoms deep in slumber, the two children lay intertwined carelessly and innocently as kittens in the tumbled bed. Alice smiled her knowing smile as she looked down at them and, cautiously turning back the covers, lifted Meggotta out of Richard's clasp. The same smile was on the tutor's face as he covered the boy warmly again, and held open the door for nurse and nurseling to pass through.

"Well, well!" said Alice softly, bearing Meggotta away to her own bedchamber. "Bedded before wedded, eh? A body would think you'd planned the whole business yourself."

The Countess Margaret closed the heavy door of the solar upon the distant, merry babel of the hall, and at last they were alone. Hubert lay back in the great chair drawn up for him beside the fire, and heaved a vast sigh of content as he stretched out his feet to the warmth.

"Well, it's done! We're home, and pray God we can stay home now, and get on with the business of running England."

He was approaching sixty years old, and had had enough of campaigning against the French in King John's time, and shown mettle enough to earn the right now to refrain from heroics. But for King Henry, young, excitable, and romantic, the impractical dream of recovering all the lost possessions in Normandy still beckoned, long after all wiser Englishmen had written them off as debts impossible of collection. Nothing would do but he must mount his great expedition and show himself to the world as a conquering hero. And since there was no preventing, the best his justiciar could do was go with him and see to it that he never provoked pitched battle, or caused enough consternation to bring all the warring nobility of France together in one formidable host against him, for that might well have been the end of his own realm as well as his pretensions to Normandy and Poitou. Those who knew him, and had served him faithfully and without open criticism since his accession at nine years old, knew he was no soldier and never would be, but not the whole company of saints could have persuaded the king of so unwelcome a fact.

So they had sailed for St. Malo at the beginning of May, four hundred and fifty knights and some thousands of men-at-arms, King Henry gloriously provided with the panoply of a conquering emperor, crown and sceptre and silver-gilt baton, mantle of white silk and purse heavy with money. But all that had followed had been a stately progress through Brittany and south into Gascony, all the regions where Henry might wander at will without alarming the formidable queen-mother of France, who would certainly have raised force enough to annihilate him had he seriously infringed her borders. It had not always been easy to steer him away from rash action, when impulsive and discontented Norman barons came promising him easy conquest, or exuberant minstrels sang him into thinking himself Charlemagne; but it had been done, and largely by Hubert de Burgh, earl of Kent, justiciar of England. Hubert had nursed him laboriously but safely back to Nantes, and thence home to Portsmouth, leaving a number of his lords sick of an outbreak of fever, and one, the earl of Gloucester, dead.

"Poor little wretch!" said Hubert, thinking of the boy. "He's had a sad enough time of it. He thinks his father died of his privations, after a heroic campaign, but it was overindulgence cost us most of our losses. Well, if the king's gained little, at least he's lost nothing but his expenses."

"And he's had his whim out," said Margaret. She stooped to raise her husband's face to her between caressing hands, to kiss him with hungry deliberation upon the mouth. "Half a year without you is half a year lost!" Her deep voice acknowledged at last the passion and deprivation she never showed in public. "And will that be the end of it? You can't be for ever restraining him from his own ruin. And be warned, even if you could, it isn't the sort of service he receives with gratitude."

Hubert reached up and drew her down into his arms. "Ah, surely we must have seen the end of it now. Not for years can we afford such another pageant."

"Sometimes," said Margaret seriously, "I think he comes near to hating all those he most relies on. And the more he owes to a man, the more he may hold against him. It's in his nature."

"Oh, no, love, you do him wrong. He has impatient moods, he's easily swayed, but his heart is just. He has given us the boy, has he not?"

"So he should. It was Earl Gilbert's wish for his son while he was man alive. That's simply keeping his word." Still, that was much; they had the wardship of the boy and his future disposal, as promised. Richard, sixth earl of Hertford and seventh of Gloucester, slept in the manor of Burgh for the first time, and had brought with him the administration of all his vast lands, not least important Glamorgan, to add to all the justiciar's southern Welsh holdings, the makings of a great palatinate that might some day take in most of Wales.

"I've never had cause," said Hubert warmly, "to accuse the king of injustice or want of consideration."

Margaret turned her head and studied her husband earnestly in the glow of the fire, remembering with cool wonder, almost with amusement, that once she had been intended as the bride of this very King Henry whom she now distrusted, rightly or wrongly, for Hubert's sake. The compact had been made between her father, King William the Lion of Scotland, and King John, long ago, when she was a girl of about fourteen and Henry was barely two years old. John had taken her into wardship in England, with the promise that in due time she should be married to his heir, but praise God, the compact had never been kept, and she had made a better match in the end, with Henry's full approval. Perhaps he had been as glad to get out of the bargain as she. And here she was, married to this man twenty-five years her senior, instead of an unstable youth twelve years her junior. She had never ceased to thank God for the exchange.

There were others, however, to whom the mating of a royal princess with a new man, not even born noble, the son of this modest manor, had given grave offence. She knew better than Hubert how many among the barons envied him every land and every honour showered upon him by the king, followed with resentment his progress from a country land-owner to a great lord, how the aristocrats by birth doubted, opposed, and even despised him. The princess of Scotland and the earldom of Kent, bestowed together, had been the final aggravation. There were those who would never forgive him for being too successful. And he never courted friends, and never expected enemies.

She owned to herself, with her customary honesty, that he had not the public graces that might have reconciled men to his usurped eminence. And she smiled at him even as she admitted the thought, for he had all the graces that she valued, enough to outbalance the flaws she recognized as well as any. Her marriage had begun with respect and loyalty, had discovered love, and grown into the most absolute of comradeships.

At sixty he was a big, burly, thickset man, above the middle height, with a massive head thatched with thick brown hair laced with grey, and a blunt-featured face framed in a greyer beard, and lit by two deep-set, reddish-brown eyes. There were lines seaming his forehead and hemming in his mouth, and the big hands that clasped her were freckled with the brown patches of encroaching age, and slightly mis-shapen with incipient muscular distortion. In repose they looked tired and lost. Caressing her, or his daughter, they were eloquently tender. She would not have exchanged him for any man on earth. It was why she feared for him, though she was fearless for herself.

"Never?" she said softly. "Have you forgotten October of last year, at Portsmouth? When he drew on you?"

He was astonished and disturbed. He had never given a thought to the incident since. He opened his deep eyes wide at her, marvelling. "Dear God, from whom did you ever hear of that?"

"Not from you," she said, and smiled. "But I do know. I know the king laid all the blame at your door, when his Cinque Ports bailiffs failed to provide him with ships enough for his venture. I know he called you traitor, and drew on you, and Ranulf of Chester, who claims to hate you, plucked you by the shoulders away from a thrust that might have killed. Why did you never tell me?" she said gently. "Do you think it would have surprised me? I knew a great deal about King Henry by then."

"I thought no more about it, once it was done. Should I put you in anxiety, my heart, over a child's tantrum?"

"A child of twenty-two years," said Margaret, "who might have killed you. Who meant to kill."

"Not he, never! It's true he leaves go of his self-control too easily, but that's all it was. He was sorely disappointed, and he hit out at the nearest person."

"The nearest? And by chance? There were many people present, as I heard it. No, he leaves everything to you, and he blames you for everything. It was his officers at the ports had his direct orders about the supply of ships, that was none of your work, and well he knows it. I tell you," said Margaret vehemently, "I only pray God you may always have your honourable enemy Ranulf close by, to ward off this child whenever he chooses to fly into a passion. One enemy like Chester is worth a great many fair-weather friends."

"I doubt I must get along without him for the present," said Hubert, smiling indulgently at her solemnity, "for we've left him behind with the Earl Marshal, in France, to watch the king's interests there. If he's wise, Marshal will hold still and play for a truce. I would not trust Count Peter of Brittany too far, if he sees his advantage in shifting with the wind."

Yet he trusts this shifting young king who makes me so uneasy, thought Margaret. Or is it that he has no choice but to trust, having served the boy loyally since he came to the throne as a charming little knight, nine years old, in circumstances of danger and deprivation that held his officers to him every bit as securely as personal love? The habit is too old and well established to be shaken now. Always he thinks he is dealing with the pretty, passionate little boy, and does not see that Henry is now that terrifying thing, a little boy with a man's stature and a king's power, and no more balance or constancy of mind than he had at nine years old.

But there was no point in saying any of this to Hubert, who would have listened with affectionate courtesy and forborne from comment, granting that she had a right to her own judgement but convinced that she was fretting without cause. So all she said, confirming the un-doubted good, was, "Well, at least we have Richard. Now it's for us to win his heart."

"Meggotta will do that," said her fond father, with absolute faith.

In his palace of Westminster King Henry was writing that same evening to the bailiffs of the earl of Gloucester and Hertford, the late Gilbert de Clare, dead in Perros-Guirec, in Brittany. A felt loss, and a huge and vital estate to take into care, especially in view of the considerable prowess and undoubted ambition of Llewelyn ap Iorwerth in Wales. The Welsh lands of the earl of Gloucester were a strong fence against the great prince, and it needed a firm hand to keep the fence in repair.

The clerk had already taken down his Grace's kindly expressions of sorrow at the loss of his beloved Earl Gilbert.

"Continue: 'In accordance with the compact agreed between the aforesaid Earl Gilbert and our well-beloved and faithful Hubert de Burgh, earl of Kent, our justiciar, concluded with our approval and under our auspices, we have conceded to the said justiciar the custody of the lands and heir of the aforementioned earl of Gloucester.' "

He went on dictating to the end, with his royal compliments and commiserations in their bereavement, and committed the letter to the open rolls for all to understand. Not until it was sealed and sent, and the business of the evening ended, did he look back and reconsider all the words he had used, and the course he had taken.

He was well made and slender, a very comely young man with fair, trimly curled hair, and a light yellow beard that just framed sensitive, petulant lips. He loved fine clothes and jewels, and had excellent taste in both. Only the slight droop of one eyelid marred his debonair appearance by giving him a calculating look, as if he chose always to command an ambivalent view of every situation. The look did him less than justice, for though he might at times close one eye to events he preferred not to see, his outlook on what he did choose to see was invariably single, total, and passionate.

He was tired, and had sent all his people away until he should wish to retire for the night. He did not feel that he had achieved much in France, now that he came to look back in quietude, or learned much. It had seemed the wisest course to withdraw before the winter set in, and he had left his brother-in-law, William, the Earl Marshal, to guard his interests in Brittany and the fringes of Normandy. But somehow this royal progress he had made through the west of France from north to south did not now appear to him the triumph it had seemed at the time.

He had lost an earl he could ill afford to lose, and had only an eight-year-old child in exchange, and he had conveyed all the rights in that child to his well-beloved and faithful Hubert de Burgh. The huge shadow of Hubert had been cast athwart his royal prerogative ever since he had grown old enough to realize what that term meant. He had sheltered beneath the shadow time and time again, and had cause to be grateful. But he was also something of a gardener, loving shapely green things, and they do not grow well in shadow. He had a quick, sensitive, self-dramatizing mind; he had only to conceive of the comparison to feel himself a delicate shrub cramped and starved of growth under the menacing shade of a tree in need of pruning.

Henry lay back in his cushioned chair and sipped his mulled wine, comfort before bed. A solitary bed! He must really get down to the serious business of finding a suitable wife. It was years now since he had got rid of the tall, intimidating, self-possessed Scotswoman bought for him by his father, bestowing her on this very Hubert who was now looming so large in his restless thoughts. That marriage had produced this little daughter, the same age as Gloucester's boy. And here was he, the most eligible match in Europe, still probing and discarding and testing and finding wanting, twenty-three years old and in the best case to get a promising heir. No need, however, to be in too much haste. His bride must reach high to match him; it was not for him to offer the inducements.

Meantime, God had set him in charge of a kingdom, an inescapable responsibility, and he was answerable to God. The thought, reinforced with divine sanction, soothed and warmed him. It would be a dereliction of his plain duty and a profanation of his coronation oath to let any man grow so large as to usurp the royal privileges. And there were others, besides the justiciar, who were showing unseemly growth, now that he came to feel the chill of their shadow. He was beginning to be aware that even his own younger brother, Earl Richard of Cornwall, showed alarming tendencies to assert himself in council, and to enlarge himself in possessions to an unbecoming degree. All very well, so long as he used his powers in loyal support of his king and brother, but of late that was not always the case.

And now there was this matter of the widowed countess Isabella of Gloucester, and what was to be done with her. Young, handsome, well endowed, and representing in her person an alliance with the earldom of Pembroke, as the Earl Marshal's sister, Isabella was a fortune in herself, too valuable to be left unclaimed. So lofty a marriage was a state matter, not to be lightly decided. And here was his brother Richard plainly hinting his interest, and canvassing his claims. The lady, too, had indicated that she was well disposed to the idea. Was it wise to countenance a match that would make Richard a potential power through south-west Wales? And on the other hand, was there a safer candidate, without unpardonable disparagement to so great a lady? On the whole, it might be well to set up Richard in his grand alliance with the Marshal family, to balance the justiciar's gains in the wardship of the boy. There was no love lost between the imperious young prince and the hard-headed old official; thus poised against each other, they might well decide to compete in support for the crown. Yes, on consideration he thought it politic to approve the marriage. Let Richard have the relict and whatever influence she might confer on him, and Hubert take the heir and his lands, and either be a check to the other.

He was sick and tired of old men, eternally holding him back from action, eternally sure they knew better than he did, curbing and criticizing. It was three years now since he had declared himself of full age, but still he felt the weight of the old men hampering his movements at every turn. Certainly they had served loyally while he was still a child, and he had had cause to be thankful, first to the old Earl Marshal and then to the justiciar; and it was well to pay attention to their guidance even now that he was a man, provided they continued to be effective. But had this campaign in France been managed effectively? He was no longer so sure of it. And now that we have time to look westwards towards Wales, thought Henry, we shall see if the earl of Kent is any more effective where his own close interests are concerned.

Richard awoke from the too-deep sleep of exhaustion into sudden sharp panic. The room in which he opened his eyes was the wrong shape, and nothing in it was where it should have been, not even the window, through the wooden lattice of which a light far too limpid and bright for home was falling upon him from the wrong direction. He started up in the bed, staring wildly round him, too drunk with sleep to make sense of what he saw. Then he remembered the girl, and knew where he was, and how he had come there, and all the grief rushed back over him like a drowning wave, cold as the cold and glittering light.

He could not bear it! Kind though she had tried to be, the memory of her was an offence. She had seen him at his weakest and most wretched, and all his male pride rose in outrage at the recollection. He was Clare, and Hertford, and Gloucester, and she had seen him weeping and desperate, ready to cling even to a stranger-child for maudlin comfort. One such lapse he might, in time, forgive himself, but there must be no more. All the weight of his ancestral name and the honour of his forebears dropped heavily upon his slight shoulders. He rose and dressed slowly and grimly, determined to give no ground ever again. Hearing him astir, Master Carrell came in to help him, and to make sure that he washed, and it seemed to Richard that his tutor regarded him with a curious, suppressed smiling, as though nursing a secret amusement at his expense. He knew! He must know! The girl must have told everyone.

He opened the door, and she was there waiting for him, still and expectant. She must have been waiting for a long time, patiently silent, not to disturb him from the long sleep he needed, not to miss him as soon as he did come forth. She was ready and eager to conduct him to his breakfast, and afterwards, since the day was fine, to lead him by the hand round all the delights of Burgh, the kennels, the stables, the mews, the mill and the armoury, to show him the best fishing-pools close at hand, and the coverts where there was game to be hunted. He withdrew his hand from hers, civilly but resolutely, as often as she clasped it, but if she was hurt by the stiff rejection, she gave no sign. The benefited may turn his back in indignation upon his benefactor, but for the one who has reached out to give, impulsively and generously, there is no escape. Meggotta had committed her heart once for all.

He had half expected that she would make some mention of the previous night, by way of establishing her rights, but when she did not, instead of being disarmed he was perversely infuriated, feeling it as an added offence that she should show such magnanimity. It was like being pitied all over again; he would not bear it.

"You told them!" he accused outright, turning on her abruptly as they walked along the edge of the mill-leat.

"Told them what?" said Meggotta, astonished. "Told who?"

"All of them! You told them about me, about last night!"

"I didn't tell anyone anything," she protested indignantly.

"You did, you must have. They know! I can tell by the way they look at me. Master Carrell knows, and your Alice. . . . They all know you found me bawling like a baby. . . ."

"I never told anyone anything," Meggotta persisted, injured. "Why should I?"

"You did! You did! How else would they have known? Girls always tell!" accused Richard, wild to compound his gross offence and make an end of this, while a small, sane voice within him was impeaching him roundly and rightly of base ingratitude.

"I didn't! I don't lie. And you're unkind!" protested Meggotta, between tears and rage.

"Then why do you stay with me? Why don't you go away and let me alone? I could find my way round perfectly well alone."

She looked hurt and lost, and could find no telling reply; the large grey eyes dwelt upon his obdurate face rather in bewilderment than appeal, and her lip quivered. But she did not go away. And when he swung abruptly on his heel and strode away round the mill as rapidly as he could, she came after him, breaking into a run when he gained too great a lead. By then her own proper pride was in arms. Richard turned furiously.

"Don't follow me! I'm going a long way, I'm going miles. I don't want you."

"You're stupid!" she flared. "I know it here and you don't. You could get lost."

"I shan't get lost. And I don't want a girl with me. Girls are no use, they can't climb, or run, or do anything properly. You couldn't even keep up with me."

The large grey eyes flashed rather splendidly, and the rounded chin jutted.

"You're not so grand as you think, Richard de Clare. You're all boasts. I can do anything *you* can do!"

"Don't be foolish, of course you can't."

"Very well, then, try me! If you dare! If you're so sure of yourself!

I don't claim I can do things better, but I'll match *you,* whatever you do."

Richard drew in his horns a little at being thus confronted. He was not yet sure that she might not turn girl after all, and tell accusing tales of him at home; for no matter how far the earl and countess might be disposed to indulge him at this stage, Master Carrell would not let his offences pass unchecked. So he changed his mind, and turned back stiffly with Meggotta, and let her complete her tour of the manor, though she approached the eagerly awaited task now with no pleasure, and without venturing to take his hand again. But when the day passed, and only unreproaching kindness surrounded him, he concluded that this girl, at any rate, was no tell-tale, whatever other drawbacks there might be about her. And in his perverse mood that was invitation enough to take her at her word, and punish her for daring to challenge his male dominance. If she insisted on following and matching him, wherever he went, she should very soon repent it.

He did not even know, by that time, why he was so hostile to her, for Burgh was beginning to show its charms, and a part of him longed to succumb to the temptation to subside into the place freely offered him here, and abandon his sore clinging to what was gone. He was caught in his own obstinacy, and did not know how to turn back.

They went again to the mill, and he deliberately crossed the race by the single rough plank the workmen used, and Meggotta, who sensibly had never seen any reason to venture it before, followed him, white-faced but unhesitating. He climbed the timbering inside the dove-cote, almost to the flight-holes in the lantern, and the tallest and most difficult trees, and she stretched her short arms and set her teeth, and copied his footholds, arriving breathless but unrelenting at his shoulder; and when he scurried down with wanton recklessness, she was driven to match his rashness, for fear he should escape her before she could reach the ground.

They rode, and he set himself to ignore every warning he had been given and accept every risk, and still she pursued, trailing but determined. He was all the more dangerous because he did not know the country as she did, but she knew by then that he would not heed any caution from her. He drove his pony at foolish gradients, waded him through streams deeper than he realized, galloped him at speeds that left her smaller mount well behind, but still she pursued him with ominous patience.

They had set out one day without Peter's escort, and with strict orders to keep close to home, but Richard had led her several miles out of bounds without shame. He could not shake her off, and could not any longer bear the effort that both accused and exhausted him.

There was a narrow arm of a mere at his right hand, a deceptive green width of water, shallow and reflecting light. A low bank of grass, paled with frost but now thawed and slippery, offered a jumping-off point on the near side, and the farther was low and waterlogged, the ground rising a few yards beyond. He wheeled his pony abruptly towards the leap, and spurred it into speed. She would not dare follow. She would have to go far round to meet with him, and he would light down and wait for her very civilly, never a word of mockery. And he would have defeated her, this creature who hunted him with her goodness and her gallantry, to his eternal humiliation.

He cleared the width of green water, cantered merrily ahead out of the slight hollow, and looked back to take pleasure in his victory. But Meggotta was in the air, copying his action, clumsy and short because she had no schooling at this skill, but hard on his heels like a good hound, ready to risk her life rather than give in.

The pony picked up its heels and sprang, but short, casting up spray and shying at the sudden chill, and stumbled forward in the spongy landing, throwing his rider clear into the grass. She fell spread like a hurt butterfly, and lay still, momentarily winded.

Richard let out a great shriek of anguish, tumbled headlong out of the saddle in his haste, and ran like a hunted hare to plunge into the turf beside her and snatch the limp little form into his arms. He was babbling through frantic sobs. "Meggotta . . . Meggotta . . . I've killed you! Meggotta, don't die! Don't die! I'm sorry. I'm sorry! I *don't* hate you; I *like* you. . . ."

Meggotta opened her eyes, only briefly closed when she had fallen into deep cushions of turf. She saw a frightened, pleading, guilty face stooping over her, and heard the boy exhorting frenziedly, "Don't die . . . oh, don't die!" She was too innocent to realize the magnitude of her advantage. She sat up in his arms, shaking the mild confusion out of her head.

"Oh, Richard, don't be cross! I did try!" She could not imagine why he was sniffing so, and hugging her; his arms hurt. "I *can't* do everything you can do," she said placatingly, "but I could if you would show me." And still he kneeled and trembled, and held her far too tightly for comfort.

They rode home in the encroaching dusk, mud-stained delinquents both, to be questioned anxiously, and scolded, and restricted for some days to the bounds of the manor, and this time Richard did not transgress. It was no hardship; with two sworn companions to share them, there were plenty of delights even within the gates.

2

March to April, 1231:
Burgh; Bury St. Edmunds;
Westminster.

"My mother," said Richard, dropping into the clean straw of the kennels, beside Meggotta, "is going to be married again. I knew she would. I knew she'd have to, whether she wanted to or not. But I think she does want to."

He sounded quite serene about it. Meggotta had realized long ago that he was far more worldly-wise than she, having been closer about the court, where the gossip of the world circulated freely, and little pitchers with long ears knew most of what was going on. All the same, though it was not his mother's fault if she must conform, and he had always known it, only a month or so ago he would have kept this knowledge to himself, and brooded over it with great bitterness. In three months Meggotta had learned a great deal about Richard. Hurts went deadly deep with him, and he had loved his father as vehemently as she loved hers.

"How do you know?" she asked, and let him take the hound-puppy from her to caress and play with. He had one couple of his own for training already, and was to choose another couple from this litter, but the one she had been nursing would not be his choice. It was the weakest, a bitch-puppy brought forth last and belatedly, useless, probably, for hunting. Such unfortunates, turned fortunate, fell into the hands of Meggotta, and survived as pets, nuisances about the manor but indulged for her sake. She had a leaning towards all that was feeble, piteous, and in need of protection.

"I heard mother talking to Alice. You know, there was a courier in from London yesterday. When they're ready, they'll tell us, because we shall all be going to the wedding. I didn't listen in hiding," he said, with slightly defensive dignity. "I was coming along the screen passage, and I couldn't help hearing."

"Mother" was the Countess Margaret. So far had he come in little more than three months. When he had to allude to Isabella, countess of Gloucester, he said almost ceremoniously "my mother."

Meggotta thought of marriages, those wonderful, distant things that happened to grown-ups, in circumstances of great splendour and rejoicing. She was dazzled. It must be splendid to be the centre of such a celebration.

"And we're to go?" she said, charmed but doubtful. "Both of us, not just you?" She had never even set eyes on this far-away countess Isabella.

"I wouldn't go anywhere without you," said Richard indignantly. He held the weak but beautiful bitch-puppy against his cheek, very gently, and it kissed and licked him, nibbling a fallen lock of his fair hair and nuzzling his ear.

"And who is it she's to marry?" asked Meggotta. Ever since the day they had made their peace, she had yielded him the leadership, glad and fulfilled to watch him expanding in this liberty of Burgh like a flower in the sun. He could run faster than she, ride more daringly, leap higher; he was less afraid of hazards, and had more skills with hawks and hounds. But never, never would he go anywhere without her. When he said it, there was no need to question further. She knew it to be truth.

"It's the king's brother, the earl of Cornwall. His name's Richard, like mine."

He was not immoderately impressed by the alliance. An earl of Gloucester and Hertford, a Clare, was as good as a Plantagenet earl of Cornwall any day, king's brother or not. Meggotta came of a new and climbing family, and had felt its ambitious drive. There was no doubt in her mind that her father by native right was the equal of any man living, but she had also an intuitive understanding of those differences that severed him from his fellow-earls and worked all against him.

"That's a great match," she said. And for no reason that she acknowledged, but moved by a great and valorous desire to speak for her own, she said, "My grandfather was king of Scots, they called him William the Lion. My mother is his eldest daughter."

"I know!" said Richard, and leaned and laid the puppy, squirming, back in her round, tender arms, as though giving her a kingdom.

"And the king of Scots now is my uncle Alexander."

"Yes . . ."

"And King Alexander's queen is our King Henry's sister Joan. Did you know they were married the same day as my mother and father? It was at York, a double wedding. And now your mother is to marry King Henry's brother." The tangle of relationships was too much for her, it made her head go round. She drew back with relief into the narrower circle of Burgh. "But now my parents are yours, too." Her own contented words suddenly started a thought that caused her to open her eyes wide with consternation and dread. "But if you're to get another father, a new one, and the king's brother, will that change everything? They won't take you away, will they?"

Her stricken dismay brought the boy rustling impetuously on his knees through the straw, to fold his arms possessively round child and puppy and all. "No, don't be afraid, Meggotta! I won't go away. Nobody will take me away. The king put me in your father's care. Who can possibly upset the king's arrangements? Nobody'd dare!"

"Only the king," she agreed, still short of reassurance. "He might change his mind and give you to his brother."

"He won't, why should he? He's given me as ward to his greatest officer, the one he trusts most. There isn't another in the kingdom he values as he does your father. Don't be afraid, I shan't leave you, nobody will want to separate us."

"I couldn't bear it," said Meggotta, in the low voice of her most solemn moments, "if you went away."

"I couldn't bear it, either." He had never until that moment contemplated the possibility, to discover whether or not it daunted him. He stared the idea in the face for the first time, and was as stricken as she. But then he shook off the shadow, for it would not happen, it was a foolish thought. "No, no, no, don't think of it, it's silly. The king wants me here, and my own father wanted it, too. Give the little thing back to her dam, and let's go down to the mill. I tell you, everything's all right, I shall stay here, it's where everybody wants me to be. And most of all, it's where I want to be."

Meggotta laid the small, wriggling body into the straw with its brothers and sisters and the mildly complaining bitch, who instantly licked away the touch of humankind, and nuzzled the stray to her nipple.

"Are you sure? About the others?" She did not doubt his word spoken for himself.

"Yes, I'm sure! There's a reason! A reason that makes it quite certain." He was out of the shadow, all sunlight and confidence as he was meant to be. He caught her by the hand and hauled her to her feet, and stooped to brush away the debris of straw from the knees of his dark-blue hose. "I know something I thought you knew and weren't going to share with me."

"If I knew anything, of course I'd share it with you! And if you know a secret, you ought to tell me!"

"I will," promised Richard, and his eyes shone bluer than the midday sky over Burgh, on one of those capricious March days when bleak East Anglia relents, and confers a vision of summer before even spring has begun. "I will, but not yet, not here. You'll see why! After we've been to Westminster for this wedding, and nobody has threatened us, and you're quite happy, then I'll tell you, and you'll know it's true."

They travelled to Westminster in the second week of March, in the same benign weather, chill but sunlit, and blessedly free of the steely winds from the North Sea. The lowland countryside smiled and brooded in new ploughing and freshly sown furrow, and the meadow stretches were brilliant in young green, for there had been plentiful early rains, and soft weather after the frosts receded. There would be good pasture and easy lambing. It was a wedding landscape, young, lush, and eager, and they went without haste.

The earl of Kent was already in London with the court, and had had his palace in Westminster opened up and made ready for his lady and her household. The great house lay beside the Thames, close to the king's beloved island enclosure of collegiate church and palace and gardens, where the monks had recently begun the work of rebuilding, enlarging, and glorifying their abbey. Not much more than the foundation stone and the first courses of the walls of the Lady Chapel had risen as yet. Building was slow and expensive, and the monks of Westminster were chronically short of money.

Margaret took her cavalcade south in good time, for so cumbersome a company must move slowly. Moreover, she wished to stay overnight within the liberty of St. Edmund's abbey at Bury, which was dear to her as a staging-post on many such journeys. For herself she provided a good saddle-horse, in addition to the horse-litter to which she could resort in bad weather, or when tired of riding. Chaplain and steward rode beside her. Alice enjoyed a litter, into which the children could come whenever they wished. But all that way they rode, for the pace was not pressed, and their ponies were fit. Whether it was Richard who drove and Meggotta who followed loyally, or the two of them who matched paces the whole way without flagging, all day long they were seen and heard in shrill pleasure and brilliant colours, like birds fluttering along the borders of the cavalcade, drunk with the nectar of premature spring.

"Ah, the creatures!" murmured Alice, watching them very contentedly. "To think it should all turn out to suit so well, and the two of them never sad together, and never happy apart. The good God's done well by us all!"

Margaret also watched them, with even closer and more thoughtful attention, if she said nothing. The boy was handsome, well grown, well mannered, open, affectionate, and kind by nature; and gallant, too, never complaining if he got the worst of it at martial play among the other boys, even those older than he, and, better still, never grudging it if he was honestly bested, even by a groom's son. He was proud and sensitive, and desired ardently to excel, but he would bear his chagrin stoically when he was outdone, and give praise where it was due. Things could not have shaped better. At Bury, hearing Mass in the abbey church, Margaret said a special prayer of thanks and happiness for her daughter's rising star.

Prior Heribert was an old friend, and the lodgings appointed for the countess's company in the dwellings of the liberty were comfortable and quiet, the same she had used before when travelling this road. The children, excited and curious about everything, went willingly and virtuously with her to church, and in the closed gardens afterwards, in a cold but clear twilight, they encountered the abbot himself, tall and austere and gentle. He had a somewhat formidable reputation in the town, being a stickler for the rights of his abbey, and in constant conflict with the guild merchant, but he could unbend with children, even tease them, in courteous ways that made the teasing a shared play between them.

"And is your name really Meggotta?" he asked, opening his old eyes wide in wonder at so outlandish a name, so that Meggotta forgot her awe, and laughed aloud. She had a very high, gay laugh that brought flashing smiles, like echoes, to every face around her.

"No, of course not! My baptismal name is Margaret, after my mother, but Meggotta is my father's special pet-name for me. He made me so many different ones, and Meggotta was the one we liked best. So I am always Meggotta."

"And to me, also?" said the abbot, appealing.

"If you please, Father Abbot!" she said, suddenly shy and subsiding into a whisper.

"I shall pray for you by that name, daughter dear."

"For Richard, too," said Meggotta anxiously, and felt for her comrade's hand. "I could not be blessed unless Richard was blessed, too."

"Richard and Meggotta," said the abbot gravely, "shall be mentioned together always in my prayers." The abbot was old, irascible, uncompromising in doctrine and faith, an impenetrable shield against the assaults of laymen and money-makers into the affairs of his town, his country, and his church; he had but few vulnerable spots, but those two linked hands, so certain of each other in the sight of all the world, moved him deeply.

He looked at the Countess Margaret, who stood withdrawn in

guarded silence behind the children, and her eyes met his and did not turn aside. She was smiling very slightly, the imperious mouth ruefully curved, and she looked at him with that outwardly serene face and those deep, experienced, penetrating eyes, and said not a word. He knew her, though for the most part at second hand, through his prior, who knew her very well, and valued her highly. All the love she had to spare from a husband far older than herself, all that was left, she poured out upon these two small creatures about whose shoulders her shepherding hands hovered protectively. He respected her, and accepted her preoccupations as valid and selfless. Only one of these innocents was her child, but both were cherished as her own. He could not wish the orphan a better destiny.

"It was beautiful there," cried Richard, reining his pony close to the drawn-back curtains of Margaret's litter, and leaning in with his fair hair flying. "I liked it there. Can we stay there again on the way home?"

"Perhaps not this time. We shall be staying some weeks in London, until my lord goes to the Welsh march, to make sure all's secure there. But some day, yes, surely we'll go back to Bury, when we're passing this way. Or if ever we need sanctuary," said Margaret serenely, smiling for pleasure at the beauty of a windless morning, and the blue expanse of a sky unmarred from east to west, even by a cloud no bigger than a man's hand.

In St. Edward's church, in the abbey of St. Peter, built by Edward the Confessor, in the king's royal island of Westminster, Isabella Marshal, widow of Gilbert, earl of Gloucester, was married with great pomp and ceremony to Richard, earl of Cornwall, the king's younger brother. King Henry, who had an eye for decorative ritual, as for all things artistic, presided in person over the arrangements, and saw to it that everything, from his own resplendent robes and the bride's white and gold to the music at the wedding banquet, did credit to a great state occasion and a most discerning taste.

Meggotta and Richard stood in the long, narrow, lofty nave of the church with the countess of Kent among the honoured guests and watched bride and groom, glitteringly attired, sweep slowly towards the round-headed archway in the great rood-screen, and after them in procession the king and his greatest officials and magnates, such an overwhelming array as neither child had ever dreamed of.

Meggotta stared with passionate concentration at Richard's mother, who had let her son go from her so lightly, and was taking another husband so soon. She had had little choice, of course; Richard had said that ladies of rank and property who lost their lords had probably only one recourse if they did not wish to be married off again to someone else, and that was to take the veil and wed themselves to Christ. And even that, he said, grown cynical at second hand, was a marriage that could be annulled if king and magnates decided compulsion was necessary.

But this lady did not look at all unhappy, Meggotta saw. She was slender and fair, like her son, with a lofty white forehead beneath high-dressed hair bound with a gold coronal. She walked slowly, weighted with a great burden of beautiful gold and white brocaded stuffs, tight sleeves dropping long points over long hands, one clasping a prayer-book, the other laid ceremoniously upon her bridegroom's hand. Her head was high; her eyes were brilliant and her cheeks flushed. The small, unchanging smile that just curved her lips was triumphant. Meggotta did not think her half as beautiful as Richard. From time to time she stole a glance at him, still a little fearful that this otherwise joyful occasion might, for all his apparent resignation, recoil into resentment and grief for him. But he was staring with great, devouring eyes, as she was, drinking in the sounds, and the colours, and the splendours, gratified rather than distressed by his mother's triumph.

And the earl of Cornwall, who was in crimson and gold, appeared just as satisfied with his bargain. He was twenty-two years old, several years younger than his bride, a handsome, confident, energetic young man, taller and sturdier than his royal brother, his colouring a darker, richer brown. He swept by, leading his new wife by the hand, and the edge of his long, brocaded mantle brushed Meggotta's toes, and sent a gust of perfumed air spinning up into her face. Next came King Henry alone, very splendid in royal scarlets and purples, and crowned, but only with a thin jewelled coronet. She had hoped to see the crown of England, but he wore that, it seemed, only on very great occasions of state, of more than domestic significance. And after him came all the great magnates of England, except those who were abroad on the king's business, like the earl of Chester, and the Earl Marshal, the bride's brother, who were keeping the king's castles and provinces in France for him. A pity that Richard's uncle William Marshal should have to be absent from his own sister's wedding, Meggotta would have liked to see him. But his wife, the king's youngest sister, was prominent among the court ladies—Eleanor, countess of Pembroke, sixteen years old.

"My aunt Eleanor!" Richard whispered in Meggotta's ear, and he squeezed her hand tightly. "You know how old she was when she married my uncle? Nine years!" Meggotta frowned and hushed him with a motion of finger on lip, for his voice, even in a whisper, was clear and carrying. So a princess had been wed at an age barely in advance of theirs! And some, she had been told, had been given in marriage even earlier, almost in their cradles.

The Countess Eleanor was a tall, vigorous girl with a challenging face, broad of brow and firm of chin, with a wealth of bright brown hair caught up within a gold circlet. She looked certain of her own royalty and mistress of her destiny, and she glanced about her, as she passed, by no means awed by the occasion or concentrating upon it, but eyeing all this assembly of the great ones of England with cool, critical looks, and thinking her own thoughts about them. When her eye fell upon the two children, watching huge-eyed, a brief and almost impish smile flickered over her lips, as though in salutation to her own receding childhood, no less than in friendly acknowledgement of theirs. Then she was past, the skirts of her blue gown swirling.

Meggotta looked beyond, and dug a rounded elbow into Richard's side. "Father!" she whispered.

The earl of Kent passed with only one brief glance at them, and a private flash of smiling eyes. In this royal company he showed as noble as any, very sumptuous in his dress and groomed like a prince, the justiciar of England, the greatest officer in the land. Meggotta thought him the handsomest man of all the company. She was immeasurably proud of him, and warmly aware that Richard felt his heart swell in exultation just as hers did. Everything that was hers belonged equally to Richard, even her adored father.

The tail of the bridal procession passed, and the guests lining the nave fell in behind, and followed through the great archway in the rood-screen, into the choir and up to the high altar, where the bishops waited. And there Isabella Marshal, late Isabella of Clare, countess of Gloucester, plighted her troth to the king's brother, and became countess of Cornwall.

"Don't forget," whispered Meggotta, under cover of the triumphal music, "you promised you'd tell me your secret after this wedding is over."

"Not here," protested Richard, whispering into her ear in haste, "not now! But I will, at the right moment!"

None the less, he held out against her for two weeks more. It was not difficult to avoid answering, there was so much to be done here, so much to be seen. There was, above all, his mother to visit; for at last she sent for her son, and graciously invited Meggotta with him, and was sweetness itself to both as she fed them sticky honeyed fruits. And there was the earl of Cornwall, that elder Richard, now stepfather to her Richard, tolerant and kind and now curiously younger than in his wedding finery, but not therefore less to be revered. He, like his new wife, received these two children as if they had been both alike his kin. It was all very reassuring. No one had made any move to separate them.

Meggotta said so to Richard, when they were home from this visit and alone in the room they had for study and play in Hubert's palace, overlooking the garden he had made there, with trees and bushes and paved paths, like a royal enclosure. It was raining slightly, or they would have been out there, and busy with something more active than toys. April came in with showers and sudden capricious cold. But they had a fire, and glass in the upper half of the tall window, glass in rough-jewel colours of red and blue and green. Very few people were so wealthy and so influential as to have glass, and it sprayed brilliance across the small room, scattering gems over walls and floor. Every fitful sunbeam cast largesse before the children.

"They treated us just as if we had equal rights in them," said Meggotta, gratified. They were sitting together on a fur rug before the fire, over a pair of jointed wooden knights they manipulated on strings in combat; but the strings lay loose now, and the knights were both prostrate, like wounded men, or dead.

"But that's it!" cried Richard triumphantly. He leaned to her across the fallen champions, glowing with knowledge. "Haven't you understood? Did nobody tell you anything, really? It's all arranged! I said I'd tell you. . . ."

Meggotta reared erect from the rug, fronting him with her wide, daunting kitten-face. "Yes, you did say so. You promised!"

"I know, but I wanted it to be after my mother was settled in her new marriage, and you could see for yourself that nobody threatened us. And nobody does! He doesn't want me, he only wants my mother. Don't you see, she'll have more children now, his children, he wants no others. You and I are outside his plans. Plans have been made for us already."

She did not see; she was a little dismayed by these complications that were outside her clear, simple world. She looked at him with silent appeal, and said nothing.

"The king sent me to live with you," explained Richard, grown desperately grave because she looked at him so gravely, "because it's all arranged that you and I shall *marry*, when we're grown up. The bargain was made between your father and my father before my father died, and the king was the go-between, and sanctioned the agreement." Her known, cherished face dimpled and quivered before his eyes, close to tears, close to laughter. No, she had not understood anything until now. She was both shattered and transported. "We shall be married!" he said, reaching out to hug her, over the fallen warriors who lay in sad straits between. "Everyone agreed to it, the king, your father, my father. It's pledged and sworn. We shall be together always!"

"You're sure?" she said fearfully.

"Of course I'm sure. I shouldn't have been sent to live in your father's household, else."

That was good sense, for who is so likely to administer an orphan's estates honestly and effectively as he who stands to reap the harvest of his labours, if not in his own person, for his daughter? Meggotta saw a sunlit future opening before her, a wedding procession as splendid as that of the earl and countess of Cornwall, with Richard by her side still, a perpetual summer, a sky without clouds.

"Then you won't have to go away from me, not even when you come into your earldom and get seisin of all your lands?"

"Of course not! You'll be coming with me. Wherever I go, you'll come with me, unless it's to war somewhere, and then you'll keep all my castles for me, and take care of my lands while I'm away. Did they really not tell you? They will, you'll see! Mother will tell you, when she thinks it's the proper time. Perhaps she thinks you too young yet to think about such things, or care. . . ."

"I never thought about them before," owned Meggotta, staring entranced into a future so well planned for her. "But I do care! I care so much. Now that I know, I'm sure I could never marry anyone else. And now it's all perfect, and I shall never have to. If you knew, why did you never tell me before?"

"I didn't want to, at first," admitted Richard with winning candour. "I didn't know whether I was going to like you, or whether I should want to get out of the bargain later, when I was old enough. And then when you said nothing about it, I wasn't sure what I ought to do. If you knew already, as I did, and weren't going to say anything, I thought it might be because you were waiting to see if *you* liked *me*. And when you still said nothing, I was afraid you might have decided that you *didn't*, and were going to wait and try to get out of the agreement, just as I'd thought I might want to do. And if you really hadn't been told, then I thought I ought not to speak until mother felt it right to tell you." He heaved a huge sigh of dismay at the complexity of his own motives, and amazement at such needless folly, now that everything was clear between them, and they were of one mind.

"And when were you sure," asked Meggotta, plunging straight to the heart of the matter, "that you didn't want to get out of being married to me?"

"Oh, very, very soon! But what does it matter now?" he said simply. *"Everybody*'s agreed, now, and it makes everything perfect for us. You *don't* want to get out of it, do you?" It was a belated qualm, and not a very serious one, but it would be well to dispose of it at once.

"No, never!" she said indignantly. "How can you ask such a thing!"

"Then that's settled. Look, the sun's coming out. It won't be too wet in the stable-yard. Let's leave these stupid things, and get Arnald to set up a target and string my bow for us. It won't be dusk for more than an hour yet."

It was shortly after dusk of that same day when a courier rode in fresh from the coast, bearing despatches from Brittany. The news they brought was such as to send the king's chamberlains and stewards hurrying to summon the justiciar and the chancellor, the earl of Cornwall, and such of the king's inner council as were still within call, to immediate and urgent conference with his Grace.

Death had not yet finished with the allied families of Marshal and Clare. The same infection which had carried off the earl of Gloucester in October had returned to summon his brother-in-law in April. William, Earl Marshal of England and earl of Pembroke, was dead in Brittany, and the earl of Chester had taken command of the king's provinces in his stead.

"So the Marshal's gone," said Margaret, and shook her head over the sudden departure from the world of a lusty man in his prime, who had hardly suffered a day's illness in his life until the fated final one laid an icy finger on him. Hubert had come back to her shortly before midnight with the word. Her candle was burning low, and the bedchamber filled with shadows, growing ever taller as the flame sank. "And childless!"

"It means his next brother inherits, and his Grace is none too happy about that." A prolific strain, the Marshals; the old man had left five sons and five daughters behind him, but this eldest of his sons had no chick or child to follow him. The second brother had lived in France for years, keeping his Norman estates by doing homage for them to the French crown, a process by no means illegal or dishonourable, but hardly likely to endear him to the king of England, or, for that matter, to the king's justiciar.

"His Grace has been known to find means of blocking such claimants before," said Margaret, "when their roots were all in France."

"Hard to justify interference in this case. The man's done nothing to cast doubts on his loyalty beforehand, he'll have to prove himself by his acts. I see no possibility of refusing him seisin. Nobody can deny his plain right as heir."

"Neither had that young man last year committed any offence to condemn him," she said thoughtfully, "the one who laid claim to the earldom of Leicester through his English grandmother. What was his name? You remember!"

"De Montfort," said Hubert.

"That's the man. He had a reasonable claim, too, but the king rejected it, all the same, and left the earldom where he'd already bestowed it for safe-keeping, with Ranulf of Chester."

"That was harking back two generations. This is a plain case of a man's death, and a legal heir waiting to step into his shoes. No, no question but he'll get his office and his earldom, but it won't help his Grace to sleep any sounder, until the incomer's proved himself."

"Another Richard," said Margaret, and the mention of the name and the blood-relationship turned her thoughts to the boy. "Will this come hard to our Richard—his uncle's death?"

"He knows him scarcely better than he knows this new one who'll be taking his place, and I doubt if he's set eyes on him in his life. No, never fret for the child, it's like a death in a story. He knows they're kin, but it means nothing. We'll tell him in the morning, though, and not leave him to learn it from any other. And then," said Hubert, stirring the still-glowing ashes of the fire with the toe of his boot, "there's the matter of the wardships William held. Those won't wait till his brother gets seisin of his estates, and it would be folly to hand them on to him with the property, even if they could. If he must get

Pembroke, an unknown and untried man, no need to hand him over Brecon and Builth and Radnor as well."

"The de Breos children?"

There were three of them, unmarried and in wardship, the little daughters of the lord of Abergavenny, William de Breos, who had been dead for a year; and since their mother was one more of the Marshal sisters, they and their inheritance had naturally been handed over to the Earl Marshal, their senior uncle, as guardian. Now all those wide lands, all those castles along the Welsh border, fell vacant for another to win and administer. With Richard de Clare's Glamorgan already in his hands, Hubert could be master of the Welsh marches from the south to the borders of Gwynedd, the northern principality where his chief enemy held sway and was a constant threat. The prince of Gwynedd was an opponent to be respected, but in the end no man is invulnerable. Even Gwynedd itself might finally fall to English arms.

To King Henry's great glory and aggrandizement, and also to Hubert's. Margaret recognized both motives, and found fault with neither. A loyal servant had also a right to watch his own interests where, as here, they matched those of his master.

"They have another new uncle," she said, putting her finger instantly on the danger to such plans, "and one very close to the king's ear."

"And as quick as we to see his advantage," agreed Hubert with a grim smile. "The earl of Cornwall has already whispered into the king's ear."

"And got his way?" she asked sharply.

"As a temporary measure, yes. His Grace has placed the de Breos wardship in his hands."

"So he was there before you! And 'temporary'? I wonder! He is not a man to let go easily of what he's set his heart on."

"Neither am I. And it's true that his Grace handed over the charge without giving thought to it, he was more concerned just then with the Marshal inheritance, and with confirming the earl of Chester in his French command quickly, before some mischief follows there. But this is not the last word, I'll see to that. Give me that central marsh and

I'll cut Wales in two, and pen Llewelyn into the mountains of Snowdon, with no way south."

"He's shown no disposition to go to war, as yet," said Margaret. "You'll do well to let him lie until he does, though I grant you the clash must come soon or late."

"I am not looking for war, either, but if it arises, I must have my defences as sound as may be, and be ready to turn defence into attack." The candle was flickering, and his shadow had grown so tall and large as to cover half the ceiling. "And I need the de Breos lands for that. And give me but two or three weeks, and I'll have them," promised Hubert grimly, "however firm a grip the earl of Cornwall may think he has on them."

There was one small problem left behind by the death of the Earl Marshal of which Hubert had said no word, but King Henry lay sleepless for a while considering it warily. Now that the complex questions of wardship and inheritance had been faced, there was time to recollect that the Lady Eleanor, countess of Pembroke, was now a widow, which was as much as to say that she was back in the marriage-market, and likely to command a very high price indeed, and stir up some hot debate and a considerable quantity of bad blood among rival contestants. She had just seen for herself how little time young, wealthy widows were allowed for mourning.

She was the youngest of his sisters, and the most self-willed and resolute. At nine years old, it had been easy enough to deal with her, the glitter and fun of being the centre of attraction, the bride in a royal wedding, had been enough to keep her pleasantly entertained, and he did not know that she had ever had cause or inclination to regret her marriage since, having been indulged and allowed her own way most of the time. What if her husband had been a quarter of a century her senior, when she had never seen much of him, since he was always occupied somewhere else, as now in dying. Henry could not help wondering if the marriage had ever been consummated. Eleanor was a strong, vigorous girl, but she had never become pregnant, and indeed, during the last few years, since she had been mature enough to be approached, William had usually been preoccupied with trouble in Wales, or with his viceregal duties in Brittany. It was not a question the king was ever likely to ask his sister; she would certainly have something pointed and stinging to say in return.

But what he now had to deal with was Eleanor at sixteen, experienced, audacious, and incalculable. He had broken the news to her as delicately as he could, though hardly expecting that there had been any very passionate attachment between them; and she had wept, briefly, hotly, more from astonishment and shock than grief, for whether she had cared for him or not, William had been her status and her guarantee, and this was a sudden and savage sword-cut, severing her life in two. And then she had recovered her customary aloof composure, and withdrawn very decorously, but very thoughtfully, and Cecily de Sanford, her demure and saintly confidante and governess, had embraced and led her away. Henry, though devout, was a little distrustful of devout women, especially unmarried ones.

The best thing he could do for himself was to get Eleanor's future agreed as quickly as possible, or he would have no peace from ambitious candidates on the one hand and irreconcilable die-hards on the other, protesting that her person ought to be used to forge profitable royal alliances abroad for the crown of England. There was the young earl of Arundel, for instance, only a year or so older than the girl, and very suitable, but some officer or baron was certain to object, with a dozen voluble reasons to deploy.

Ah, well, leave it till tomorrow! He was very tired.

The Countess Eleanor, quite dry-eyed now, the first shock over, was also lying awake, and Cecily, though silent in the other bed, was not asleep, either. Death is a very final and brutal separation, even of the most casual friends. She was sorry about William, in a way, and sorry in quite another way about herself. But she was beginning to grasp that there can be remedies. If you have no orthodox castles, siege-engines and weapons, you must look for other means of defence and attack, and have faith that such do exist.

I will not be measured and prodded and put up for sale like a horse, thought Eleanor firmly. I will not be handed over to some alien princeling I have never seen, either in his dotage or just out of his cradle, to bolster up my brother with an imaginary prop that will fold and let him fall if ever he dares to lean on it. I cannot think of one suitable lord of my own years who does not sicken me. It's time I let it be known that my person belongs to me, to bestow where I please and never until I please. Yes, I'll do it! I've made up my mind.

Now, she thought, before she slept, and slept deeply, wait, dear brother, until tomorrow. For all I know, you may be just as relieved as I shall.

She came to him shortly after he had breakfasted, while he was sitting glumly but determinedly alone, making up his mind about the difficult and delicate planning of his audiences for the day. She was darkly gowned, her hair hidden under a black gauze veil. She had Cecily de Sanford, thirty years old, and her shadow for five of those years, close at her shoulder.

"I have thought," said Eleanor, and her voice was low and calm, and yet sounded less like grief than like distant trumpets marshalling to battle, "and I have prayed, and I see my way clear. Dear brother, I desire never to be a burden or an anxiety to you. I have lost my lord, and I am moved to absolve all others and turn myself to another lord, who need confer no dower lands, and asks no dowry. Cecily and I have determined to take vows of perpetual chastity, outside the cloister— for I would not forsake such duties as are mine here in the world—and wed ourselves to Christ. Cecily has long intended this step herself, and now I join myself with her in the desire. We have sent for her spiritual adviser, Father Edmund Rich, of Abingdon. In a few days he will be here to witness our vows."

3

May to October, 1231:
St. James de Beuvron;
the Welsh borders.

*J*n the event, Hubert did not have to do more than align himself with circumstances in order to get possession of the de Breos lands, nor was there any need for him to choose the time to provoke, on his own terms, a resumption of hostilities with the volatile tribesmen of Wales. Before the end of April they had made the decision for him. For years the Earl Marshal had been their implacable and formidable enemy, it needed no more than the news of his distant death, and they rose joyfully in arms to raid the territories he had held in trust. And though this natural exuberance was certainly not directed by the prince of Gwynedd, it was reason enough to send King Henry scurrying after total remedies, anticipating, with some intelligence, that that notable personage would not be long a spectator.

The middle lands of the march were vital, and he was by no means sure as yet of his young brother's capabilities in the field, or his strategic gifts. By the second week of May he had made up his mind. He took back his temporary gift of the de Breos wardship from the earl of Cornwall, and bestowed it instead upon his justiciar. That done, and Hubert's privilege and responsibility thereby almost doubled, the king sent out royal writs to call the feudal muster to him at Gloucester at the end of June.

Without waiting for that time, the king moved his court westward to Hereford in May, and thence travelled on to Worcester, where his envoys were to meet those of Llewelyn, and indeed did so, with every sign of mutual tolerance and goodwill, and arranged a further meeting to take place at Shrewsbury on the third of June. The prince had not so far lifted a finger to disturb the king's peace or his own, and showed no inclination to do so. Mutual forbearance suited him well enough.

That did not mean that all was peace along the border; the local Welsh were raiders born. Hubert began his round of his castles in the north, intent on seeing that all the garrisons were secure against the anarchy loosed by the Earl Marshal's death. He arrived at Montgomery on the last day of May. The castle on its great rock was safe enough from Welsh raids, but the little town huddled beneath its shadow enjoyed no such immunity. The marks of fire scarred its outlying houses, and towards the river the farms had suffered losses in cattle and grain.

"For the past three weeks," said the castellan, "we've had no peace from them. The river's low, and no barrier, and whether this is planned by the prince or merely the local Welshry kicking up their heels without orders, we bleed just the same. I've lost no men of the garrison, but the townsfolk complain, and true enough, we should be their protection. But these devils creep across in the night, make a rapid strike, and are back in their own hills before we can get down to them. Once or twice we've reached them and beat them off in time, but you know the hazards, my lord. The castle's safe enough, and can't be passed. But the town is sore, with good reason."

Both town and castle were dear to Hubert, being his own foundation, and he had always chafed at the sporadic raids to which his people were subjected. He listened to the tale of their recent losses, and was angry.

"It seems they've caught the contagion from the south, and think they can do what they please unchecked, now the Marshal's gone. If we do not set a curb to this quickly, the whole border will be in peril."

"Three days ago, my lord, we put a strong party across the river, and cleared some miles into the hills. I know it's custom to observe the border, but it puts us at a disadvantage, since they pay no heed to it. I thought in this pass I was justified."

"You were justified. Do so again as you find it necessary. Only the strong arm will tame them. And if you take prisoners—"

"My lord," said the castellan, "from that sally we hold six prisoners here. I was about to ask you, what's your will with them?"

"Taken in arms?" asked Hubert, frowning over the implications.

"Yes, and well armed. No local tribesmen, by their gear. They may have been among those who sacked the farm near the ford, and killed the goodman. But we've no means of knowing; they'll say nothing. What shall we do with them? No one has spoken or moved for them yet."

Hubert gnawed his lip, and thought of the dead farmer and his pillaged farm, of the affront to his own head, and of the dangerous situation smouldering here like a suppressed heath-fire, ready to burst into sudden devastating flame. A certain level of harassment and annoyance was accepted and acceptable along so volatile a border, and restraint could be profitable until the depredations went too far. But here there seemed no room left for lenience. If the Welsh were growing so insolent, it was time to make an example. It was a decision he could not delegate to any other, and he was in haste to set off south to Radnor, the next point on his inspection and, in view of these conditions, perilously advanced into Wales.

"Execute them," he said at last, heavily but inflexibly. "Set up the heads, and let others take warning."

It was not questioned, rather it was received with approval. Montgomery would applaud the decision, they had wounds still smarting from these or other Welsh. And having given the order, Hubert stayed to see it carried out. He rode south towards Radnor in the late afternoon, sobered and saddened by the work but sure of its justification. He had not maintained his king on his throne, nor survived his own arduous military past, without much resolute killing, but it gave him no pleasure.

He was at Hay-on-Wye when the courier from the north, dusty and tired on a lathered horse, overtook him, and reeled into his presence in the great hall with shattering news.

"My lord, Montgomery town is burned to the ground, church and all. The castle is left an island among the dead. My lord, Prince Llewelyn . . . those men beheaded at your order . . . My lord, they were his, he swears a price for them! He's on his way south with fire and sword and all his muster. . . ."

The prince of Gwynedd made no delay in his acts, but struck like lightning. Within two days he should have had his envoys ready at Shrewsbury, to deal peace with the king's ambassadors. Instead, he had taken fire for the summary deaths of his men, and loosed his whole power in total war, burned Montgomery, and swept south with fire and sword into Marshal territory, with half Glamorgan rising joyfully to meet him. Instead of parley for continuing peace, it was war with Wales.

The host met in haste to march against the threat, but haste in England was by no means the same as haste in Wales, where a man simply clambered onto his pony and rode, shouldering his bow, hoisting his brand at hip, taking no thought for what he should eat or drink. It was well into July before King Henry got his unwieldy assembly into motion from Gloucester towards the west.

In the second week of June, in the hot summer of France, a young man rode alone into the bailey of the castle of St. James de Beuvron, King Henry's outpost thrusting a few miles beyond the borders of Brittany into Normandy, and asked with a candid and confident voice if the earl of Chester would be pleased to receive him.

He was plainly French by his dress, his harness, the manner of his speech, no Breton, and he would hardly have got past the gate without diplomatic warranty at any previous time; but by then there were envoys negotiating for truce, and assured of success, if after much haggling. It suited both sides to conserve their strength and manpower. The French had made their cast, amassing a large army at Vincennes and marching it ponderously towards the Breton border, but Count Peter and the earl of Chester had made some effective raids against the supply columns in the rear, and burned most of the siege-engines and a fair part of the commissariat, and if there was to be this kind of stalemate, it might as well be so ordered as to conserve rather than squander good material. Provided the French could secure Count

Peter's agreement to stay strictly within his own Breton borders and let France alone, they were willing to make a lengthy truce. So was Earl Ranulf, having lost nothing so far, and seeing no immediate prospect of substantial gain for his king. To hold what he had, at the least cost possible, made good sense. So it was no longer so foolhardy an act to ride solitary into this hornets' nest and simply ask for audience of its commander, though it could still cause the guard to look this cool young man over with more than passing interest, all the more because he seemed to take it for granted that his request was reasonable, and would be welcomed without question.

"Is your business to do with the peace-parleying?" asked the captain of the watch. "The earl is engaged with the pope's envoy; nothing has been said of any other messenger expected."

"No," said the young man placidly, "I am a petitioner to the earl of Chester on my own account, and my business is with him alone. I entreat him to receive me, and will wait his convenience."

But his manner of entreating had the same large directness, courteously employing words he trusted his peer to understand as they were meant. He could not have been more than twenty-one or twenty-two, but he approached the veteran earl, the noblest of the English aristocracy and old enough to be his grandfather, as man to man, assured of mutual understanding.

"What name shall we send in to the earl?" asked the captain, accepting the assurance, for whoever he might be, this was no ordinary youth. He wore his nobility as he wore his skin, sunlit and supple and weatherbeaten into gold, and he came unarmed but for the sword proper to his status, and even bareheaded, his thick, close cap of brown hair clasping a large, thoughtful scalp, like that of a Roman emperor. He looked earnest, trusting, and secure, and very disarming.

"My name is Simon de Montfort," he said, and lighted from his horse and looped the bridle over his wrist, confident of entry.

They passed him within, with a guard to announce him and hand him on to a chamberlain, who presently brought name and undisclosed errand into the room where Earl Ranulf sat talking with the trusted go-between of both France and England.

"De Montfort!" said the earl, recognizing the name, as those without had not, having no cause to have heard it ever before, though their sons were to hear it thereafter. "Well, well!" he said, and smiled, between wonder, doubt, and appreciation. "Have you leisure? Shall I hear this petitioner?"

"As you think fit, my lord," said the bishop of Winchester. "Shall I withdraw?"

"By no means. An impartial witness may be of the greatest value to both of us, who knows? I could not wish for one better balanced than you. If you have no objection, do remain." And to his chamberlain he said heartily, "Bring in the youngster. Let us see what we have here."

The petitioner came, striding largely, for he was long in the leg, though not overtall, and walked as God had made him, generously. The room he entered was dark after the Norman sunlight of the baileys, and caused him to check and take stock, looking about him with one sweeping glance to find the focus of his hopes. He had never seen his host until this moment, but he knew him by unmistakable signs, having his age in mind, and the reputation that ringed him like a halo.

"My lord of Chester," he said confidently to the shorter and less outwardly impressive of the two men he confronted, "I am in your debt for this grace. I have never before enjoyed the opportunity of speaking with you as man to man."

"If that's a privilege," said Ranulf goodhumouredly, "you have it now, and I have the like. You are welcome, you have the freedom of this castle. I would offer you refreshment, but I think you have somewhat to say that should first be said, or you would not have sought me out. Speak freely. You may, there is none here with us but Messire Peter des Roches, bishop of Winchester, who is benign, after the church's fashion, to us both."

The young man was not at that time curious about the bishop of Winchester, or even interested in him. He made a courteous if perfunctory obeisance towards the tall, withdrawn, coldly assessing figure in the great chair, and turned all his attention upon the earl.

"My lord, you hold, if not the earldom of Leicester, the custody of those lands that belong to it, and that were left without male heir at the death of Earl Robert. I do believe, also, that you must know how that inheritance fell between two heiresses, and one of them was my grandmother Amicia. The other half has been granted fairly to my grandmother's younger sister, who brought it to the earl of Winchester. But the half due to my family was kept in the king's hands, and rests now with you, my lord. I cry you my claim to what you hold that is mine. And I pray you give me more leisure to enlarge on that claim, that you may be satisfied."

"You've gone a fair way towards making it clear already," said the earl, leaning back in his chair to survey his visitor with sharp attention, and a startled but appreciative spark in his ancient eyes. Just so should a man approach his peer, though perhaps the boy was a thought too intense and earnest about it, and a little plaguing might do no harm, and test his balance, as tackling this confrontation at all must have tested his audacity. Effrontery, the bishop might have called it. Ranulf could feel the chill from that lofty presence. "Say we grant," he said deliberately, "for the sake of argument, that this inheritance should, by your reckoning, have come to your father, yet I do not think you are his eldest son."

"That is true," said the young man readily. "The claim belongs by right to my brother Amaury, but he is content to remain in France and be lord of his lands here, and he has ceded his claim to me, and if I speed, he will take all the legal steps to release to me the earldom of Leicester."

"And you," said the earl, twinkling, "would take up your roots and turn Englishman for the sake of a parcel of land, would you? And never look over your shoulder?" The chill from the bishop's erect presence appreciably sharpened. He had had a long and profitable career in England himself, tutor to the child-prince Henry once, and justiciar, until King John specifically bestowed that office upon Hubert de Burgh; but he was no Englishman, and never would be. Poitevin born, noble, ambitious and energetic, the friend of pope and emperor, and returning with the lustre of an effective Crusade upon him, he found his fortunes wherever they beckoned, and was at home nowhere but in his superb and formidable mind. Winchester had not seen its bishop for four years, but he was on his way back to it now covered with glory, and already busy about great affairs on his way, securing this truce with France. But English? No, no more than this burning boy.

"If I give my homage and receive my seisin," said Simon firmly, "there I make my life and do my work, and do it as well as I may."

"That I believe. But as I think, you have already raised this claim last year with the king, and he rejected it."

"So he did," said the boy, and smiled suddenly, as though the sparks in Ranulf's eyes had found mirrors in his, "upon one ground only, and that hardly a legal one. He replied that he could not entertain my claim because he had already given the Leicester lands to you."

"So only I can now release them," concluded the earl, and laughed aloud with pleasure at having his gentle thrust so gently parried, with courtesy and point. "But have you thought, young man, that there is only one person to whom I can give them, and that is back to his Grace, who bestowed them? And even if I should do so, what guarantee have you that he would then favour your claim?"

"None but your lordship's reputation for justice and generosity," said the boy, suddenly grave again, "which is known to all men, even those who have never seen your face. If you speak for me, I shall speed."

And would he have come there into this alien castle if he had not known the quality of Ranulf de Blundeville? Yes, perhaps he would; he alone among landless young men would have shunned recruiting a party to his grievance, and gone straight as an arrow to the baron who held what he considered his, and expected him to meet the approach as honestly as it was made. The earl had not liked a young man so much in many years.

They studied each other, and were charmed and satisfied. Simon saw a powerful, thickset old man of only moderate stature and workaday, campaigning habit, with blunt features and grizzled hair and short beard, careless of his dignity because it needed no care from him, and never in his life had he paused to consider it, and never in life debased it. There was nothing physical about him to mark him out as the prince of English barons, only the authority that spoke in every movement, and the largeness of mind that made him approachable even to the humblest. They said the people of his palatinate of Chester enjoyed a formulated protection as full and effective as the terms of the Charters.

Ranulf saw a young fellow of a build very like his own, barely above

the middle height, wide-shouldered and long in the flank, very springy
and at ease in his body, with a noble head reared erect on a powerful,
columnar neck. The young, sun-gilded face, shaven clean, gleamed
with jutting, polished bones. His eyes were deep-set and yet large and
full in the lids, loftily browed, and their colouring, under dark lashes,
a deep and luminous grey. Confronting one he judged to be wronging
him, but not of malice, and potentially his friend, they shone wide and
large, letting the opponent into a mind as direct as his own. His youth
was disarming, and his beauty very moving. Ranulf had no sons to
succeed him. Now and again, beholding other men's sons, he ached for
the joy that had been denied him.

"Come!" he said, stirring out of his stillness. "Let's examine further
into this matter without haste. You shall not go without dining and
resting under my roof. And tomorrow I'll tell you how my judgement
stands."

He was well aware, then and in hall that evening, over the music and
the wine, of the bishop's aloof disapproval, never voiced, for des Roches
was the pattern of sophisticated courtesy. It amused him a little, while
he acknowledged Winchester's shrewdness and worldly wisdom. Of
those commodities he had his own supplies, which did not always
march with other men's. The boy was all he seemed, and possibly very
much more. Even when they had made him a little drunk, his utter-
ances were large, forthright, and intelligent. He kept his firm stride and
his even balance, and sat out the evening to the end without disgrace.
Ranulf knew then what he was about to do. He had an opportunity not
given to many, as there were not many capable of offering it, and not
many equipped to accept it. What came of it hereafter was not for him
to question.

"And now," he said, after they had breakfasted next morning, "I am
content to let you take your leave." The disconcertingly direct eyes
continued to regard him in confiding silence, not taking this as simple
dismissal. The boy could see deep enough into a mind so like his own.
"Go and put in order whatever affairs you have at home," said the earl,
"and make your farewells. As soon as this truce is sealed, I propose to
go back to England and make due report to my king. Be back here by
the tenth day, and ready to go with me."

King Henry and the justiciar had got their unwieldy army as far as Hereford by the twenty-second of July, and were considering where best to employ it. What mattered most was to secure the border itself, and mop up the losses beyond as soon as the Welsh attack drew off to pause for breath, as it always did. The English relied on their castles to hold back the tide; the Welsh preferred to move fast and fluidly, by-pass such strongholds as seemed likely to pin them down in long sieges, take all the territory more easily available, and all the booty, and when necessary recoil into their safer fastnesses in the mountains, and let the plundered land go again. They were like flood-water, which circles by all the valleys and cuts off the islands of high ground, and recedes by the same routes when the storm is over.

The army was encamped just outside the city, to the west, in the open meadows north of the Wye on the road to Hay, but the king held council within the town, in the bishop's palace. It was Hubert's contention that they should move west by way of Hay, and thence to the old site of Castle Matilda at Painscastle, and rebuild the fortifications there as an advanced base, not only for temporary use now but as a permanent link in the chain of castles along the border.

They were engaged over details, having moved the vanguard forward, ahead of the main army, when Earl Ranulf de Blundeville's squire rode into the palace yard to announce the imminent arrival of his lord, fresh from Normandy with a three-year truce in his saddle-bags. The earl was not an hour behind his herald. He came clattering briskly into the courtyard with only two attendants at his heels. The full muster of his knight-service from Chester was already present with the royal army, and whatever baggage he needed was following with his arms at a more leisurely pace. One of the young men attending him was unknown to the watch, but passed unquestioned. Ranulf's guarantee was enough.

He came into the king's presence, and the council of war broke up willingly to hear his report and make him welcome. The old man emerged from travel spruce and unstained, though as plain as ever, and made his reverence briefly.

"Your Grace will already have had my despatches. We have truce in France for three years, from the twenty-fourth of June. It will hold; it suits all parties. Count Peter has undertaken not to set foot in the realm of France, and with that France is content. I have left St. James de Beuvron well garrisoned, and there is no need to doubt they will be left in peace. I think your Grace may be well satisfied."

"Indeed!" said King Henry with a heartfelt sigh. "And grateful to the papal interest, and the agent who did the work for us. And have you had good travelling? The passage was calm?" He remembered his own last sea-crossing with distaste.

"Tolerable enough," said Ranulf, to whom a rough sea and a calm were all one, for he had unshakable balance and a constitution of iron. "And we made good speed from Southampton, as you see, to be with your Grace here on the border. I'll gladly render you all the news I can, and answer whatever you may wish to question, at your leisure. But there's one matter on which I beg you'll hear me now, to our general gain, as I hope and believe."

He turned and took by the hand the unknown young man who had followed him into the hall and who had remained quietly waiting in the background all this time. Drawn forward into the light, he was seen to be a very personable young man indeed, too well equipped and armed to be any plain squire from the Chester retinue. He had his sponsor's build, though with the lithe elasticity of youth, and a marked echo of his sponsor's patrician assurance. There may even have been one here and there among the magnates present who wondered for a moment if Ranulf de Blundeville had not brought home the stray fruit of some early seed of his own, sown twenty years or so ago in St. James de Beuvron.

"My lord king," said Ranulf, "I present to you one who desires to be your man, and I recommend him to you as a man you may be glad to call yours. Here is Messire Simon de Montfort, the grandson of that Lady Amicia who was sister to Earl Robert of Leicester, and his joint heiress when he died childless. I beg you to receive him as your man for the lands due to his father through the Lady Amicia, for he has a better right to them than I have. And since I now hold them from your Grace, I surrender again to you all that you gave me. Your Grace need not scruple to receive Messire de Montfort as your man, with my goodwill, and to your own credit and gain."

When he had ended this speech, which he did cheerfully and simply, there was a blank and stupefied silence in the hall. More than one of those present doubted if he had heard aright, or, if he had, whether the old man's mind was not failing at last. More than one resented that such a pattern of the baronage should so casually strip himself of an earldom fairly given him, to bring into reproach other men's quest of further earldoms, at whatever price. Hubert looked on with a mind troubled and curiously sad, willing to feel contempt, and feeling, instead, envy. How many men can afford so huge a generosity? None but those blessed from birth, both with outward and inward gifts of fortune. This grizzled, great man was his most formidable enemy, yet at every turn he was tempted to worship him.

"My lord king," said Simon, feeling the silence weigh upon him, and the gnarled old hand urge him forward, "I pray you pardon so sudden an appearance before you, and let me come as your petitioner, as I found grace and generosity when I came petitioner to my lord of Chester. And of Leicester, too, for so I do acknowledge him, by your decree. I have no right here but in his commendation, and in that I rest. There can no other so speak for me." His voice was very low, but clear, and quivered a little before he ended. Even his grand composure was shaken.

He stood face to face with King Henry now, and Ranulf's hand relinquished him brusquely, and left him solitary there. They looked at each other, wide-eyed. They were almost of an age, somewhat less than two years between them, and something they had in common, the large longings of youth, great designs, an insatiable thirst for perfection, though in divided aims. And whatever might be said of Henry, he could be moved by gestures of nobility, and grant generously where the asking was generous; and these two were already agreed.

If I had seen this young de Montfort before, he thought, last year when he petitioned me, I might have answered differently then. But how much better now, when even the old man is well disposed.

He had, after all, lost two earls within the year; one like this gained might do much to restore the balance.

"Messire de Montfort," he said, and held out a gracious hand to be saluted, "you are welcome. Whoever comes with the commendation of the earl of Chester must be welcome to us. We receive the petition made on your behalf, and grant the request of our well-beloved and faithful Ranulf. And we accept gladly another vassal, to be as faithful and as well beloved. The earl's warranty is enough for us."

"My lord king," said Simon, dropping to his knee with the lightness of a boy, and shining like one, "I am glad to the heart of your grace to me, and I swear that by me you shall never be the loser!" He kissed the long, sensitive hand that rested on his broad brown one. He came from the sunlit plains south of Paris to this northern land, as yet so strange to him, but peopled by one man, at least, large enough to satisfy his demands; and he saw before him a fair, erect, graceful person very well fitted to be loved and served as a king. As yet he had not seen the left eyelid droop. "I will be your man," he said ardently, "while I live."

It was not yet the time for his formal homage, but from this moment he had as good as paid it. When he rose from his knee, he was pledged to become an Englishman, and Henry's man, lifelong.

"We've interrupted your Grace's council of war," said Ranulf, both feet still on this English earth. "May we now, both of us, sit under instruction, and hear what you have planned for the morrow?"

That was an unhappy council for Hubert, and at a time when he could well have done with harmony. In any circumstances the earl of Chester spoke his mind without fear or favour, and could disrupt a previously settled plan with a spare mouthful of words. His views, never extreme, were highly individual, and based firmly on his status as what amounted to a prince on his own lands, his writ all but royal. Such a man could look upon a great Welsh neighbour, and see him not as un-English and potentially the enemy but as an independent peer with rights and privileges as sacred as were his own. Hubert was bitterly aware that Ranulf had far more in common with Llewelyn of Gwynedd than he had or ever would have with Hubert de Burgh, earl of Kent, and thought far more of him. Ranulf and Llewelyn were old friends— no colder word would do—and the border in the north was ideally peaceful by consent of both. But the king saw with other eyes, and so did his justiciar.

"It was unwisely done," said Ranulf bluntly, when he heard how the prisoners of Montgomery had been done to death, "and very ill done, and no wonder to me that Llewelyn struck back as hard as he did. By your own account, he had not raised hand until then. He does not reckon his men expendable."

"I may have acted in too much haste, and without being fully informed," conceded Hubert stiffly but honestly, "but whether the prince's hand was in it or not, Montgomery had had provocation enough. Ill done or not, it is done. Is that to justify the burning of my township, church and all, and all the outrages that have followed? We have a war on our hands; there's little point in arguing now whether we should be fighting it at all."

They were most of them on his side, they would have lopped Welsh heads as readily as he, and yet they were not displeased to have this charge of disastrous folly in reserve against him. The argument flew this way and that, and the young stranger, earl of Leicester now by courtesy, looked silently from face to face, busy learning the ways and thoughts of his new peers, as intelligent children learn a language on which their future depends.

"The firing of the church at Montgomery," said the king petulantly, "left us no choice but to use religious sanctions, and call our knight-service to arms afterwards. What other course could we have taken?"

"Sent with all speed to the prince to open parleys for a truce. Nothing between would have done, I grant you, and if his blood was up for his dead men's sake," owned Ranulf freely, "he might not have listened. Yet again, he might. I do not believe he had war in mind until he was stung. There should have been a conference at Shrewsbury, I understand, only a few days after the business at Montgomery. The timing was enough to give him grounds for action. He must have felt it a glove in his face."

Others, perhaps, had entertained the same suspicion, but forborne from uttering it. Ranulf never forbore when he had a truth in his mouth. Simon's grey eyes observed in silence, and behind the comely face a very critical mind measured and made judgements.

"But challenges cannot well be taken back," conceded Ranulf. "We are setting forth from Hereford in July, not Montgomery in May. We move west, then, that's understood."

They set out fully the plans that had been made, and Ranulf frowned at the mention of rebuilding Matilda's Castle in lasting stone.

"Painscastle is Welsh," he said uncompromisingly. "This is one of the sorest spots you could choose to flay, and has been ever since de Breos encroached, forty years ago. Plant a royal castle there, and you put your hand into a hornets'-nest. Llewelyn counts it his, and I reckon his claim justified, and if he chooses to advance it, I shall support him. I can do no other."

He was not likely to get much backing for such a view, and so they gave him to understand from all sides, but Ranulf was not a man to be swayed by any fear of standing alone.

"I am with you for the purpose of defending English ground," he said imperturbably, "and will fight with goodwill on any ground, but as I would not let any man plant a castle unauthorized on my land, so I'll have no hand in doing the like injury to another man. Plans can be made and modified, and Llewelyn may have plans of his own, more to my taste than building. Let's move west, and see what comes." And that was as much as they could hope for from him, and they were satisfied to conclude the discussion on that provisional note.

"And what news do you bring us of the bishop of Winchester?" the king asked as the meeting closed. "We were fortunate to have him there in France, with the pope's blessing, to busy himself about our truce."

"After the pact was sealed," said Ranulf, "Bishop Peter set off into Italy, to visit Archbishop Grant. I hear the archbishop has fallen ill during this visit to Rome, and is too weak to travel."

Hubert had stiffened at the very mention of the bishop of Winchester. He was well aware that the Poitevin had been instrumental in securing the truce with France, and for some weeks had been wondering uneasily what his next move would be. Only too well he remembered the superb cleric, long, aristocratic and disdainful of face and body and mind, who had been his predecessor in office and tutor to the child king, years ago. Pride of birth and blood divided Hubert from his two most perilous enemies, one secular and here present, and one clerical and, thank God, yet distant. One honest opponent who spoke out what was in his mind, and dealt fair, one subtle, private, and devious, who contained every thought until it could be used as an arrow, or a dagger in the back. If des Roches was bound into Italy to condole with Richard Grant on his sick-bed, praise God for the respite!

"But after that," concluded Earl Ranulf cheerfully, "he's bound for England, back to his see. After four years, he feels some longing to be home. I doubt if he'll be more than a month behind us at Southampton."

News of the castle-building operations at Painscastle very soon reached the ears of Prince Llewelyn, and provoked the expected reaction. Briskly he stated his legal claim to the land on which they encroached, and his absolute opposition to the present activities there. The earl of Chester as forthrightly reaffirmed his support of the Welsh claim, and withdrew his whole company from the host and departed for Chester.

"If you hold with me," he said to his young French protégé, "then come away with me."

"No, my lord," said Simon firmly, "I cannot go from here as long as the king is at war. I have paid my homage, I have no force here to commit to him but these hands, and for them I can answer without fear."

"And when this is over?" questioned Ranulf goodhumouredly. "For soon it will be, I vouch for that. What will be your first resort then?"

"I have an earldom to learn, I'm impatient to begin the study. I mean to visit every manor, every castle, every holding that is mine, and show myself there to be questioned. If I do not yet know them, neither do they know me, we have a shared need."

"Good!" said the earl contentedly. "I see you need no guidance from me. Go into every hovel, boy. Above all, learn the tongue they speak within their own wattle walls, and not first for your own protection, either. Never let any interpreter, however skilled and well intentioned, come between your ear and their grievances. Fair dealing is the first thing and the last your English will ask of you, and everything in between. Fair dealing, and no lies."

Simon looked up, smiling, into the old, bronzed mask with the shrewd bright eyes. "I shall remember all the instruction given me, both by word and act."

"And take what you agree with, and throw the rest away. I know!"

"And your generosity to me I trust to repay upon others, who may some day ask as much of me."

"What have I given you," snorted the old man, "that was not yours already? Go your own gait, and you'll do very well."

Thus those two, the old and the young, likes and opposites, parted and went their own ways.

Ranulf proved all too accurate a prophet for Hubert's peace of mind. At the beginning of August, Peter des Roches landed in England and made his way to Winchester, and thence, at his leisure, to join the king at Hereford. He brought the news that Archbishop Grant was dead in Italy, and buried in the church of the Franciscans at San Gemini. All through August and into September the justiciar sweated and fretted at Painscastle, while des Roches had the king's ear about the camp, or back at Hereford, and made good use of his time. The grand cleric's nephew had been back in England for a year, in some secondary post in the exchequer. Another Peter, this one, Peter des Rivaulx, a very able clerk and tax-calculator, a priest like his uncle, but of another quality. This was a man gifted with figures and words, dry, unscrupulous, voracious, but without the presence to make him dangerous of himself. But with the directing hand of des Roches manipulating him, what might he not do? Already he was being advanced to higher office, nearer to the king's person.

About the terraced plains of Painscastle, burgeoning with stone fruit between their containing hills, Hubert agonized and doubted, but sent back to his distant household only current, reassuring messages.

Des Roches had all the graces needed to dazzle an impressionable young man. It was some small comfort that another almost as impressive and of very different nature had reached King Henry at much the same time. The new earl of Pembroke, Richard, Earl Marshal, had received his seisin in August, and brought a new face and a new mind to the king's council. Strange that a man who had lived a great part of his life in France should at once be seen as an Englishman of Englishmen, aligned with those older magnates who stood heart and soul by the Charters, and should look with aloof distaste upon the array of Poitevin officials increasingly preferred in the king's administration.

It was an inexpressible relief when Prince Llewelyn let it be known, by indirect channels, in October, that he was ready to consider making truce. Hubert urged acceptance of the offer, and was thankful when the king embraced it no less gratefully. They shared the same reason for being glad of truce in the west. Each of them had a grimmer battle on his hands at home in England.

4

Christmas, 1231, to August, 1232:
Winchester; Westminster; Burgh
and Bromholm; Shrewsbury.

"**I** know something you don't know!" shrilled Meg-
gotta, hurtling in at the door of the armoury and flinging herself upon
Richard with embracing arms, jolting the dagger he was holding clear
of the revolving whetstone, and causing him to drop it out of his jarred
hand with an oath he should not have known. He shook her off furiously; they had arrived at terms of candid criticism well worthy of
husband and wife.

"Don't do that! I could have cut myself." He reached and picked
up the fallen poniard, a pretty toy specially made to his measure. The
armourer's boy, who had been turning the stone for him, sat back and
let it run down, whirring like bees in summer, until its momentum died.
"All right, then, what is it you know?"

"We're going to Winchester for Christmas, all of us. Mother and
father are guests of the bishop for Christmas Day, and the king and
court will all be there, too. And somebody else, who sends word he
wants to make himself known to *you.*" She ran a finger delicately along
the flat edge of the dagger, and frowned at a speck of darkness in the
bright. "You've got a nick there, you'll have to smooth it out."

"It was your fault," said Richard promptly, but without any serious
indignation. "You startled me."

"That's the other edge. I saw how it fell. Let me do it!" She knew
how; she was adept at many of his skills, though weaker in the wrist,

and slightly less accurate in judgement.

"No, let it be! Who is this who wants to know me? I don't believe it, I think you're teasing me."

"No, I wouldn't, not about this. Mother told me. It's your uncle from France, the new Earl Marshal, who came over in August. He's called Richard, too. Mother says he seems a good person, who cares about his kin," she told him, grown grave.

"About me?" He knew he had uncles in plenty, the oldest of them dead in France, one about to inherit, and three more in reserve, but he was barely acquainted with any one of them, and knew this Uncle Richard from France not at all.

"You must be the only nephew he has," said Meggotta. "Why shouldn't he care about you? He isn't married, so he hasn't any sons of his own. We shall see him in Winchester. Richard, will he care about me, too, do you think?"

"He'd better," said Richard belligerently, "if he wants to be friends with me."

They set out on the long journey to the south in good time to take their leisure along the way, and the month of December proved moist and mild, for all its short days and dark nights. There was no hard frost, to make riding unpleasant and dangerous; their party was small, and wherever they halted the children were made much of. If there was a shadow on them at all, it was the gravity of Hubert's face, and the anxious frown he wore when he thought himself unobserved; but he was a grave man at all times, and if they felt the chill of his preoccupation, it passed from them easily when he smiled.

And Christmas at Winchester was wonderful, the town so fair and so new to them, and the countryside in the south so benign, warmer by far than the bleak plains of Norfolk, and even the sea-winds that reached so far inland were warm winds from the south. They were lodged in the bishop's own palace, where the king himself was accommodated. The Earl Marshal had his apartments in the grace-houses of the abbey, not far away.

Margaret took them to visit him there in the afternoon of Christmas

Eve. The room into which they were brought was firelit and warm, and decked with green fir boughs that filled the air with a heady, aromatic scent. The man who came in to welcome them looked formidably tall, lean, and grave to Meggotta, until she had time to observe him more closely, and recognize with joy those things about him that endeared him to her in an instant. His forty years had veiled at first his faithful likeness to her Richard. Weathered and slightly lined he might be, and with a few greying strands in his hair, but the fair, opaque, glowing ivory skin was there beneath the fading summer tan, the blue, clear eyes were the same, the clean-shaven lips were both vulnerable and durable, sensitive to wounds and absolute against offence. And this older Richard looked down at her Richard and saw the same likeness, and saluted it with so warm and sudden a smile that Meggotta took him to her heart from that moment.

"Madam," said the Earl Marshal, "I have to thank you not only for this visit but for all you have done and are doing for this child." He kissed the cheek his young kinsman dutifully raised to him, and held him by the shoulders in long, sinewy hands to view him properly. "No need to ask if he is well settled and happy with you, it shines out of him."

"He is very well able to speak for himself," said Margaret, smiling, "and has plenty to say for himself, too. If you find him mute at first, he'll make up for it later, I've no doubt."

"And this is Meggotta!" He kissed her, too. His gown smelled of the fir needles and the warmth of the fire, and his kiss was firm and light. He studied her as attentively and appreciatively as he had studied Richard; she was sure then that he knew she was his nephew's promised wife, and every confirmation of her status gave her deep pleasure. "Your cheek's cold," he said, and laid his warm palm gently against it. "Come to the fire and sit down with me, and tell me all about yourselves. And, madam, take this chair, and the footstool, and let me know you better, since we're almost kin."

He brought wine for Margaret, and hot honeyed water with a little wine in it for Meggotta. Over Richard, she thought, he hesitated, and then considerately gave him a greater measure of wine, but not too much. A quiet, thoughtful man who respected the dignity of children.

There were sweetmeats for them, and a set of ivory draughts to occupy them if the company of grown-ups palled. But it did not. With the fire's warmth, and the encouragement of the wine within, they thawed into loquacity, and began to talk without stint, asking whatever they wanted to know. And with patience and good humour he answered everything.

"Yes, it is true I've lived in France, and I fear much neglected my kin here, and you may well reproach me. If I'd known how promising a nephew I had, I should have sought you out sooner. But I had our family lands in Normandy to care for, when my brother succeeded here in England."

"And isn't it hard," asked Richard, "to come here now so suddenly, and be English?"

"Ah, no! I've always been English, Richard. I was never in doubt. Why else should it be only the younger brother who keeps the lands abroad? And since I came home," said the earl, his voice rueful, "I've learned how very English I am. I find too many here, and in too high feather, who have come out of France, and have no such roots here as I have. I don't altogether like what I see of them. I came to take up duties, as well as privileges, they have privilege without ties." He was aware that he had left the boy behind, though perhaps not very far, for the blue, bright eyes reasoned rather than wondered. "Now my next brother keeps those lands in Normandy, your Uncle Gilbert. My heir, if I never marry."

"And I have still two more uncles, haven't I? Father told me I have five uncles, but I know my Uncle William is gone. And I know some of my aunts—Aunt Eva de Breos, and Aunt Maud. . . ."

"Poor Richard!" said the earl, laughing. "So beset with kinsfolk, and most of them distant as the moon! Never try counting us, we have been a most prolific race. And, you know, now that I see you, you are truly Marshal as well as Clare. Look in a mirror, and see if you are not my very image. Yes, you have still two more uncles, my brothers Walter and Anselm. But if ever you need any one of us, the Countess Margaret here will let me know of it, and I shall be with you as soon as I can, to do whatever may be needful." He spoke to Richard, but his eyes were on Margaret, and hers on him. Here, certainly, was one who shared her disquiet with the way things were shaping in the king's administration, and might prove a formidable ally hereafter.

By then she was certain that they would need allies, that they had a battle to fight; but as yet she had never for a moment acknowledged that they might lose it. Hubert had said very little about whatever qualms he felt, but she knew him so well that no words were needed. His anxiety was centred all upon the Poitevin interlopers, but hers was fixed inexorably upon King Henry, the shifting, unstable, resentful adolescent, never to grow up, without whose perilous whims all the Poitevin officials in Christendom would have been powerless to shake Hubert's ascendancy.

The earl saluted both the children, at parting, with the kiss of kinship, and sent them home with the promise of further visits. All the way back to the palace Richard chattered like a jay of his new and splendid acquaintance, of all the things they would do together while they were all gathered for this feast, and of the secret gifts the earl had hidden away for them, not to be revealed until the morning.

"For me, too?" said Meggotta, astonished and delighted. "But I'm not his niece, he's never seen or heard of me before."

"Oh, yes, he has. He knows all about us, and you will be his niece, so it's just the same." He noted his own indiscretion, too late, and looked up quickly and guiltily at Margaret, who was gazing straight before her with raised brows and a small, startled smile, but did not look greatly put out. "I told her, mother! You're not cross, are you? I knew all the time, before I came with father to Burgh. I wanted to be sure she felt as glad as I did."

"And did she?" asked Margaret softly, not glancing down.

"Oh, *yes!* But of course, you know! Mother, when were you going to tell her—about me? That I'm to be her husband?"

"On her tenth birthday," said Margaret. "That's early enough to be thinking of marrying. But it seems you're before me, and I've nothing left to tell."

Throughout that Christmas feast the bishop was punctilious in giving the earl of Kent his due place as the foremost official of the realm, seating him on the king's right hand at table, and deferring to him at all times. The entire household did almost excessive honour to the justiciar; no scruple of his dignity was ever infringed. Margaret was accorded the respect due to royalty; the bishop even went out of his way to exchange a few words graciously with the children, when he met them walking with her in the close, but he did so in suave French, in which they were a little unready, for though they heard it spoken for the more formal and grown-up part of their social life, their play and their dealings with their contemporaries about the manor were all in English, which came far more smoothly to them, and needed no thought.

The caution and slowness of their responses was not due all to this want of practice, but the bishop's raised brows and clear condescension indicated that that was how he saw it. Richard, stiffening, went so far as to address him in English, most respectfully, and copied his face of condescending resignation when he was not understood. Margaret scolded him for it afterwards, but he was not abashed.

"I don't like him. If he speaks only French—and Latin, of course, that he must!—why should he not be humble about it, instead of so proud? At least we do know some French, but he has no English at all, and yet he has a bishopric here in England. How can he deal with his flock when he doesn't understand a word they say?"

Richard had learned the native tongue from his nurse, in infancy, and used it all his life. Meggotta spoke the vernacular of Norfolk, and had been fascinated by the curious and pleasing variations they found in a shared language.

"*I* shall be able to hear the cases my people bring to me without any clerks to translate them for me," said Richard firmly, "when I come into my earldom. And Meggotta will talk their own language to her maids, too, and we shall get on all the better for it."

In the king's chamber a charcoal brazier burned clear and smokeless like a great red eye, from its low level casting three shadows high along the tapestried wall. The tallest reached the rafters, and, broken at the shoulders, darkened half the beamed roof, a hovering thunder-cloud over Henry's head, as Bishop Peter paced to and fro, long-stepping and soft-footed as a cat. The third shadow stood a little aside, attentive and still.

"I will not conceal from your Grace," said the bishop, "that I find little but disquiet in your affairs. I have been shocked at the disarray of your administration and the incompetence of your finances, and what you tell me of your own state of mind is the only consoling circumstance in this whole sorry picture. If you have seen for yourself, unaided, how much is wrong, and how it behoves you to make yourself responsible for setting it right, then clearly you are on the way to fulfilling your own ideal of kingship. But you will need the counsel, and above all the skills, of loyal officers." The implication that these were now wanting did not escape the king, and was by no means unwelcome to him. He sat listening with soothed pleasure, having feasted and been fêted lavishly at this imposing personage's expense, and finding his host's sophisticated presence and refined tastes exceedingly gratifying. Strange that he had hardly any memories of des Roches as his childhood tutor; but no doubt the bishop, as well as his pupil, had been changed and enlarged by the years, and by his travels overseas.

That started the old grievance over France. "The war we undertook in Normandy," the king said fretfully, "was surely just, those possessions which were ours could have been and ought to have been recovered. And though we are grateful for your efforts in negotiating truce, considering the circumstances, things ought to have gone differently there. Our officers have been lukewarm and unready, and no ardour of our own could have sufficed against that burden."

"The best of kings," agreed the bishop, "cannot rule alone. But he must be the head and source of rule, and not allow power to be dissipated among too many and too self-seeking subordinates. Power should stem from you, through as few chief officers as may be, and those few most carefully chosen, and your hand, through the first of them, should be always on the rein. It is all very well to talk of the council of your peers, but they speak with too many voices, and too loudly, and drown out your own voice, which should give the supreme word. And have you always been as wise as you should in enlarging the circle of your peers?"

The looming shadow halted for a moment behind the king's chair.

The long, chiselled, arrogant face, ivory and silver, glowed above the king's head in the ruby light from the brazier.

"I have been much indebted to the man," said Henry sharply, not pretending to misunderstand the allusion. "Or I believed I was so," he added, weakening. "But now . . . it may be his ability is failing, he grows old. Certainly I have not been happy over his management of the campaign in France, or this last summer's wretched showing in Wales. How am I the better off for all that time and labour? And the expense has crippled me. I spend and spend, and for no return. He has lost his grasp, and I am the one who pays for it."

"In more senses than one," said the bishop drily. "He has not, it seems, lost his grasp on any part of the huge honour he has built up, not one castle or manor slips between his fingers. Your Grace may be the poorer for these recent fiascos, but is he? From all that I see, his grasp runs from Montgomery to Gwent, and spreads a hand over manors in almost every county. I see no failing there." He stressed, but very lightly, the word "failing." Whatever his faults, King Henry was very quick in mind, and needed no spurring. He surprised even the bishop by being the first to speak out clearly.

"Are you suggesting, my lord, that my justiciar has been all this while so assiduous in service not for my sake but for the feathering of his own nest?"

"I do not suggest. I point out facts which you yourself have come to recognize. That while you lose, he gains. That your treasury is beggared by unprofitable wars, while he grows wealthy. Facts which justify you in examining even the most damning possibilities. I do not presume to make up your mind for you. You are the king, you will do that for yourself. I am saying you need loyal and able servants. In particular a man who can draw together all the mishandled threads of your administration, and fill your coffers as they should be filled. Make an end of the old ways. Reorganize wholly, make sense of this chaos. You can do it, and you have the man beside you best fitted to be your right hand in the work."

The third shadow, standing apart from them, watchful and quiescent, made no sound. Peter des Rivaulx did not glitter or tower like his uncle, though he had a quietly formidable presence of his own; a grey man, not faded grey but steely and bright, and for all his modest height built more like a seasoned soldier than a cleric.

"I have been more than content with my treasurer, since you recommended him to me," agreed Henry warmly. "He has done much to repair my fortunes."

"He could do more, but only if you give him the necessary powers. To be truly effective for you, one man must have charge of the entire financial management of your realm, in the shires, the household, and the exchequer. But you will never succeed in creating such a government while the earl of Kent holds his present office. Nor can I see how such a government can possibly accommodate him in any other."

He spoke confidently and mildly, being certain that he was saying only what the king wanted to hear, what he had longed to have said for years, while he chafed under tutelage and felt himself cheated and undervalued. He sat now in considering silence, savouring these daring ideas, half eager, half afraid.

"He has done nothing to make it publicly desirable that I should displace him. Yet I see that he could never be fitted into such a new design. He is too old and set in his ways. It is politic to get rid of officers who have outlived their usefulness, even though they may be clear of actual offence. But it will not be easy to unseat one so well established. As for the earldom," said the king defensively, and somewhat preening himself on his forethought, "it was more a recognition of the lady's status than meant for his aggrandizement. And I took care to limit it to his children by her. His son cannot inherit. There is only a girl to hand on the title, and she is a king's granddaughter. But to justify removing him . . . in the public eye . . ."

"Clear of actual offence, you said," murmured the bishop, drawing nearer to the king's shoulder. "I tell you openly, your Grace, that I am not so certain of the man's integrity. He has used his office for his own advancement, almost certainly. And there are other matters that trouble me nearly. Your Grace knows of this outbreak of violence against the Italian clerks who hold benefices in this country, by irrefutable right, under papal appointment. It began in the north, but in the last month it has spread to many other parts, and is growing. These agitators are well organized, and go about in arms, raiding the barns of these clerics, and selling the grain or giving it away to the peasants. The matter has been discussed in council."

"I know of it," said Henry. "Some are even saying it has sympathizers at court, both clerks and barons. Many people hold that these benefices should be given to English priests, instead of to Italians who never come near them, but only draw the rents and profits. Some lords who hold the right to appoint the clergy in their local churches have had foreign priests imposed upon them against their will, which is at least unwise. But I don't on that account excuse any law-breaking, let alone violence to persons. I have authorized action against the raiders wherever they appear, I can hardly do more."

"Your Grace has acted as would be expected of a loyal son of the church. But I have been enquiring on my own account into the crimes of these people, and have got hold of one of their manifestos. They have their own seal, two swords, with the inscription *'Ecce duo gladii hic.'* They have the temerity to issue warning to the bishops not to interfere with their work, and to command those monastic communities and others who hold the lands of the Italian clerics at farm to withhold their rents. The same source that provided me with this document provided also the information that when their thieving raids are challenged, they produce royal letters patent authorizing their deeds, and forbidding any interference."

"Forged," said the king. The company of objectors to the dominance of Italian absentee churchmen was known to be led by men literate, respected, even noble among their peers in the shires. They could easily provide such writs, and had shown that they were sufficiently daring. And yet . . .

"Perhaps forged," said the bishop softly. "As I heard, they are very well presented and very convincing. And how many men could so make use of the royal seal?" He drew back a little, and let the seed sink deep into very receptive soil; and after a moment he said, "It would be well to send all that is known about these disturbances to Pope Gregory, with copies of these manifestos and letters patent. Let him see for himself how we labour here with unfaithful servants."

There was silence for a long time, while the king gazed before him into the crimson eye of the brazier, and saw a way opening before him into a wider freedom of kingship than he had yet glimpsed. Never until then had he realized the violence of his own impatience with the old men left over from his father's time, who had cramped and hampered him, and reined him in for so long from all large action. The bishop, too, was elderly, but his mind was young, and he desired no official status for himself, only to counsel and aid; and he came with the glory of a wider world about him, loosing perilous light into this insular air of England. He advocated what could only be pleasing to the Holy Father, and enlist his support for Henry's steps towards maturity, the first and longest and most heroic of which would be ridding himself of the earl of Kent.

The king heaved a deep, anticipatory breath, but very cautiously. "It will not be easy to do," he said.

"It will not," said the bishop. "That should not daunt you. There are not many who love the man. And there is no haste."

That was a quiet spring and early summer at Burgh, innocent of the stresses that racked men and divided allies in Westminster. Over the modest uplands of Norfolk, and the seaward dunes and pools flat and glossy under the immense pale sky, Richard and Meggotta rode together, with grooms easy and watchful in attendance, and flew their new hawks at heron and wildfowl, and rewound their creances as taught by Earl Richard the Marshal, the giver of both birds, Richard's peregrine and Meggotta's little merlin. They did almost no damage among the birds, being novices as yet, but they revelled in the chase, and the beauty of these half-savage creatures that gripped with such smooth ferocity on their gloved fists, and glared with round yellow eyes from which everything human, qualities they found without question in their ponies and dogs, was excised. They wandered the low heathlands on foot, and stripped serenely and swam together in the pale, still pools, salt from the invading tides of winter and early spring. They rode to the seashore, and waded barefoot along the tide, hunting for shells and the strange sea-life left behind in rock pools, to be reclaimed by the next tide or to die forsaken. They were supremely happy, and approaching ten years old.

From time to time the Earl Marshal sent letters, enquiring after the health and well-being of his nephew, whom he had not forgotten and would not forget, but he did not visit. The Countess Margaret told them that his earldom of Pembroke was so far from this manor of Burgh that from end to end of the kingdom a man could hardly go farther, so it was no wonder that he could not come. His business was divided between Pembroke and Westminster, where he must wait on the king, as their father also must, and in duty and loyalty there was no cure for it. They had been used to this kind of separation from infancy, and were resigned, however they might wish it changed.

Meantime, they lived in a world without shadows, as long as they were together.

At the king's June council the bishop of Winchester, in the most reasonable terms, but strongly, voiced his view that a drastic change was necessary in the whole cumbersome method of administration, which separated household, chancery, and exchequer, and in his opinion rendered the effective collection of revenue and control of fiscal affairs impossible. The reforms he had in mind, he agreed, had been begun already, but in such piecemeal fashion and so slowly that the changes only further confused a process already confused and confusing, and did more harm than good. Better to cut through the tangle in one slash, concentrate the royal administration in the hands of one man, and make it his task to produce reason and order between the shires and the offices of state. To do that he would have to be given far wider powers than now existed, but in the hands of the right man such powers would be wholly beneficial. There was no doubt in any man's mind where to look for the right man; he sat, taciturn and alert, not far from his uncle's place. He had already, during this same month of June, been enlarged by two royal charters, the first giving him for life the financial direction of the king's household, the second conferring upon him, also for life, custody of the king's small seal. He was the coming man, though his coming had been so inconspicuous up to this point that few had noticed how rapidly it progressed.

Hubert received the proposition, as did some others, with doubt and distrust. That there was room for some simplification in the affairs of the realm he granted, and up to a point what was suggested was sensible, but it went too far. If one man was to control a money structure embracing household, chancery, exchequer, and the shires, it would make him the most powerful officer in the kingdom, and subjugate to him the great state offices of justiciar, chancellor, and treasurer, an unheard-of reversal. The argument lasted long, and at times grew heated. The bishop of Winchester never became overheated. He kept his fires for the king's private presence, and used his tongue in council with the authoritative calm of a pope. And his pontifical force was such that those who opposed him, for all his quiet delivery and fastidious selection of words, felt themselves overshadowed by the threat of excommunication.

Hubert, gnawing his nails in his own house by the riverside, late in the evening, was astonished to receive as a visitor none other than Peter des Rivaulx. The treasurer of the royal household came with soft steps and a conciliatory smile, a solid, seemingly ordinary man of disarming appearance and mild, reasonable voice.

"My lord of Kent," he said confidingly, "I come to you on behalf of myself and certain others, who earnestly desire to be in agreement with you, for the sake of England. We have put forward ideas on which you look with doubt, but in which we believe. You hold views which we consider could be moderated without damage to yourself or any, and with benefit to this realm. We do not believe that an accommodation between us is impossible, and we do firmly believe it to be desirable. We are prepared to go some way to meet you. After all, we are all concerned first and foremost with the common weal, are we not?"

"I trust so," said Hubert impenetrably.

"But trust is imperfect on both sides," said des Rivaulx, and permitted himself a chill smile. "That is the danger. But how if we should all of us compound, in a binding oath, a guarantee that preserves the rights and offices of us all, so that none of us need fear his position will be undermined? Once free of that fear, surely we can all work together for the good of the country, and where opinions differ we can and must hammer out together a compromise that at least appeases all, if it cannot fully satisfy. Better, surely, to be colleagues and friends rather than adversaries. Enmity is waste of power, and England has need of all the power that is in us all."

It did occur to Hubert for a moment that this was a Poitevin speaking so feelingly of England, and that so wooing a sound had never been heard from him before. But that, he saw, was almost irrelevant at this pass. It was not concern for England that moved the man, but deep and real concern for his own career and prospects, and if he had come to the conclusion that his enemy must be conciliated, it was worth while considering what he was offering. That he was exceedingly able at organization there was no doubt, and he could indeed be useful, provided his ambition was curbed to its present bounds. He even loved his work; so much of him, at any rate, was genuine. Perhaps he was seriously afraid that if he encountered the justiciar head-on, he might lose what he had already won. Unquestionably there might be fear on both sides.

"What is it," he asked, "that you are proposing?"

"That we, the chief officers of the realm, justiciar, chancellor, treasurer, and we of the household, shall all go together to some holy place, and there take the mutual oath to preserve in office for life every man of our number, in possession of all the charters, privileges, and grants which he holds now, under penalty of excommunication if we break our vows. Can I hold out any more drastic warranty? Once that is done, what can we do but work together loyally? No man need fear his neighbour, for no man dare conspire against his neighbour. If any among us had ill designs, they would be for ever frustrated. Is this fair?"

"On the face of it, very fair. But all pointless without one more adherent. Have you broached this to the king? Unless he takes part, it is an empty show."

This time the smile was less chill, and even the steely eyes under the large forehead conjured from somewhere within a visible spark. "The king broached it to us," said Peter des Rivaulx. "If you agree, it's he who will direct where we shall go, and he will go with us, and swear to keep faithfully his every pledge to us from aforetime, under penalty like us. His Grace wants all his ministers bound to him and to duty without thought of gain or dread of loss, and holds out this way of ensuring it. Could any man do more? And can you, then, do less?"

"This far," said Hubert drily, "I have only your word for what is in his Grace's mind."

"You show me how great is the need for this mutual pledge!" sighed des Rivaulx. "Very well! You shall hear it from the king's own lips tomorrow, if you come to his private council with the rest of us. And the wording of the oaths can and shall be drawn up beforehand, let every man satisfy himself that he is not being tricked. Well?"

This could not be false. No one would dare take the king's name in vain. He must indeed have originated this extraordinary scheme himself, or at the least embraced it when it was suggested to him. The prompting might well have come from Peter des Roches, but if so, that in itself was an encouragement, for it meant that the bishop was still very wary of tackling his enemy in the open, and preferred an accommodation for his own protection. Better gain half his ends than none, and doubtless in the future he would again try to advance his influence by some other way. It would always be necessary to watch him and be prepared for anything, but to be free of this immediate anxiety, which had grown, in the last few weeks, into a cold shell of compression about his heart, would be immense relief. The next move he could meet when it came. And as for the distinct possibility that this proposed oath might sort very badly with the king's coronation promises to maintain all the royal rights and privileges free from encroachment—well, the wording could take care of that. If Henry had not recognized the difficulty for himself, why bring it to his notice? The compact began to look very desirable, and its proffer at this juncture almost miraculous.

"Whatever his Grace desires," he said at length, "is my desire also. I am at his service in this, as in all things. I will be there."

The earl's letter, received at Burgh late in June, set the entire manor by the ears, and caused such a commotion of preparation and excitement that Meggotta was moved to ask, all too percipiently, "But why is father's coming home this time so much more wonderful than usual? It's always splendid when he comes, what's different now?"

"Why, that the king and his closest ministers are coming too, of course," said Alice. "It isn't every day we get a royal visit."

"But that isn't what I meant," said Meggotta, unsatisfied, and went to ask her mother the same question. For Margaret, who had been grave and preoccupied for many weeks, kind as ever but with her mind on some distant and haunting concern of her own, was suddenly ablaze with an almost girlish exuberance of joy.

"Never trouble to ask why people are happy," said Margaret, challenged. "Ask only why they grieve. Everything I do here is for one man, and he is not the king, and well you know it, madam! And if I am light-hearted, you may be sure it's because his heart is light. Now run away from under my feet, and take Richard with you wherever you choose. My lord won't be home until the day after tomorrow, you still have time to play."

So play they did, with added zest because of the surge of joy they felt all about them. It was highest summer, with Norfolk in its rare angelic mood, veiled in an excess of light from so much sky and so near sea, and the flatness of the meadows and meres all green and silver radiance.

"Mother isn't troubled anymore," said Meggotta, ankle-deep in the rim of a lagoon inland from Bromholm, the water amber and warm against her white skin. "I wonder why she was before. All this year, until now."

"Why wonder?" said Richard. "Just be glad. The king's coming to do honour to them both, and they're glad, so we should be glad, too." He straightened up from dabbling among the reeds, to stare at her in sudden wonder and doubt. "Why did you say she isn't troubled anymore? You never said she was, until now. I didn't see anything wrong. What did you mean?"

"I don't know," said Meggotta, gazing back at him with the grey of her eyes bright silver in the noonday light, and her brows arched in eloquent bewilderment. "I didn't notice, either, not until she changed so. Now that I see her so happy, I know how troubled she's been, that's all."

Therefore there were no troubles left, nothing but excitement and joy. She stooped, and hurled bright water at him from her palm, and ran with slender fans of water at her heels when he bent to heave a double handful of spray in return. They rode home damp and content, with the groom Peter drowsy a yard behind.

Two days later, on the last day of June, the king's company rode into Burgh. King Henry had with him his justiciar, the host here, his treasurer, Walter Mauclerc, bishop of Carlisle, his chancellor, Ralph Neville, bishop of Chichester, Peter des Rivaulx, treasurer of the household and keeper of the king's privy seal, Geoffrey de Craucombe, steward of the household, and his deputy steward, together with a couple of clerks and necessary grooms and body-servants-in-attendance.

Never had Henry been so gracious, as though a load had been lifted from his mind no less than from Hubert's. He saluted Margaret with a brotherly kiss, made much of the children, and was appreciative of everything done to make him welcome and do him honour. At table he praised the wine, the meat, and the music, and presided benignly over the festivities until a late hour. Richard and Meggotta had long since been chased away to their beds by tutor and nurse when King Henry at last declared his intent to withdraw, and made clear his plans for the morrow.

"In the morning," he said, "we will ride to the priory of Bromholm. And I desire, madam, that you will ride with us, for the enterprise we have in mind concerns you jointly with my lord Hubert, and it's fitting you should be present. There can be no holier place than the home of the blessed rood of Bromholm, and there and on that sacred relic we will make our vows."

And on that he left the hall, and was shown to his own chamber, and his officers dispersed to their various lodgings, and at last Hubert and Margaret were alone and private. She walked into his arms without words, and clung to him in silence for a long moment, her cheek against his cheek.

"No need to fret any longer," he said softly into her ear. "I know! This has been a hard year, for you and for me. Harder for you. Better to be on the battlefield than wait at home for news. It's over now, if he but fulfills what he's promised."

"And if he keeps it," said Margaret doubtfully.

"How can he break it? How dare he break it, once sworn? Never fear, there could no oath so bind him as one sworn on the rood of Bromholm.

He has a special reverence for it. If he comes this way at all, he never misses worshipping there."

Margaret was not sure how much faith she herself put in that celebrated relic, brought from Constantinople by the guardian of the relics in the imperial chapel of the Latin kingdom, when that kingdom was overthrown at the battle of Adrianople, and all the trophies of Christian piety were put in peril. The little double-armed cross of wood he had sold to the monks of Bromholm he swore was made from a fragment of Christ's cross, and whether his story was true or not, the fame of their acquisition had brought pilgrims streaming to Bromholm ever since, and made the little Cluniac house wealthy and renowned. What mattered was that Henry believed, and of that there was no doubt. Margaret put away the last of her reservations. It was true, he held the rood in extreme veneration, he could not violate its sacredness by breaking the oaths made upon it. But it was like trying to believe that the veering wind could be bound.

"I shall be happier," she said, half laughing at her own reluctance to accept the peace for which she longed, "tomorrow when he has actually laid his hand upon the feretory and pledged himself before God, but happier still the next day, when his words are down in black and white for all to see, and we have copies of them as witness."

"Love, you are always too hard on him. He is my king, and I am his servant, and if I cannot take his word, and he mine, whom shall we trust? We have lived a harsh half-year; now believe, as I do, that the remaining half will be safe and fair."

"I will believe it," she said, and linked her hands suddenly behind his greying head, and drew him down to her with passion. He was aging before her eyes, for all his vigour, and there was no way she could give him of her years to supplement his own. He put up one hand and gently brushed off the net that held the coils of her hair, and the heavy dark surged down over her shoulders, and lay warm and quivering against his face.

"Come to bed, love," said Hubert into her ear. "I've starved for you all these weeks. These three nights, at least, let me love you with a quiet mind."

The next morning, after Mass, they rode the ten miles to Bromholm, through stretches of forest and out to the open dunes and the level sandy shores of the North Sea. The day was dry and fine, but with a sky faintly veiled, and when they came over the sand ridges into sight of the sea, the waters looked silvery bright but ominous, flecked with brief tongues of white in a ground wind. The sun showed through the veil, but could not tear it; all day the light filtered as through fine gauze, and the meres were metal mirrors, faintly tarnished.

Close beside the sea the priory of Bromholm clustered about the new church built from the offerings of pilgrims, near the rim of the low cliffs. The monks held a privileged position in the king's regard, and saw to it that their ascendancy should be maintained by instant and gratifying service. There was a room made ready for the king's rest and refreshment, and a repast for all his company. Only the clerks attended as witnesses when Henry and the chief officers of his realm went into the church and approached the altar.

After the veiled light without, it was dim and cool within. On the high altar the reliquary of the rood glowed with semi-precious stones, a casket opened to reveal the little, rough cross. Margaret watched narrowly, as the king drew near, hushed and reverent, and with clear eyes and devout face laid his hand upon the casket, touched the precious sliver, and, clasping his Bible, uttered his vow in a firm, deliberate voice.

"I make oath here upon the Gospels, and bind myself and my heirs, that I and they will faithfully, without fraud or guile, and of our free will, observe all the charters which I have granted to the Lady Margaret of Scotland, countess of Kent, and all the grants, gifts, and reaffirmations contained in them. I vow that neither I nor my heirs after me will in any way violate them. For the better binding of my faith, I make God my surety. And should I or my heirs contravene this oath, of free will or malice or at any man's prompting, I submit myself and my heirs to the Holy Father's judgement, renouncing all benefits of privilege, to be by him compelled to the observance of the aforesaid charters, on pain of excommunication, not to be lifted until the said countess has received full satisfaction.

"And the same vow I make in favour of Geoffrey de Craucombe, Walter, bishop of Carlisle, Ralph, bishop of Chichester, Peter des Rivaulx, and my justiciar, Hubert de Burgh, as I have here made in the interest of the Countess Margaret, his wife."

His voice was level and serene from beginning to end, without so much as a tremor. Hubert knows him better than I, thought Margaret. I have been unfair to him all this while. And she prayed his pardon and God's in her heart. She stood at the king's right hand, on the side where the eyelid did not droop.

"Now, my lords," said the king with humility, stepping back from the feretory, "make your vows as I have made mine, and keep them as faithfully as I intend to keep mine."

Hubert was the first to follow him. She saw with a pang at her heart that the joints of the hand he laid upon the casket were a little swollen and awry, and the grey in his thick brown hair had spread almost from temples to crown. An old man's hand, an old man's head. She wanted peace for him, and here at last was the promise of peace, lifetime security in his office and in all his winnings.

"Here I make oath by my king's order, that if ever my king of his free will, or at any man's prompting, should seek to invalidate those charters, grants, gifts, and reaffirmations he has made to me, Hubert de Burgh, to Margaret, my wife, to Ralph, bishop of Chichester, Peter des Rivaulx, Walter, bishop of Carlisle, and Geoffrey de Craucombe, then I, Hubert de Burgh, will take all possible steps to impede that purpose, and preserve the aforesaid charters inviolate."

So they all swore, one after another, the officers of the kingdom and the officers of the household; in the place chosen by the king, on the relic the king most revered, they pledged themselves to maintain the whole collective of the royal administration, and find a peaceful means of resolving all future differences among them, for the good of the realm.

After that there was a solemn Mass, and King Henry remained apart afterwards in the church, in solitary prayer and vigil. They rode home only in the middle evening, when the sun was declining gently inland, and the sea behind them was sewn all over with little reflected stars of gold, shifting and changing too rapidly for the eye to follow. The veiled sky that had hung motionless and mysterious all day suddenly melted between them and the sunset, as if the heat of that molten gold had burned it through. There was already a pale, risen moon on the other side, hazy and withdrawn, without a face. Hubert drew in beside Margaret as they rode at a gentle pace, as if riders and horses were weary and languid from the stresses of the day. She reached a hand to him briefly, and found his hand. Old it might be, but it gripped with power, as he loved with passion. No one saw the clasp, it was loosed at once. They had said all there was to be said.

When they reached Burgh, the high table was decked and waiting for them, and the children were already fed and in their beds, somewhat resentful, as Master Carrell admitted, at being expected to sleep while their parents were still away and themselves in ignorance of what business kept them. Nevertheless, they were both fast asleep. Margaret went to look at Richard, and hung in sudden devoted attention over his slack, half-naked ease and flushed, smiling comeliness. His lips were parted and moist; there was an infinitely fine dew upon his forehead, under the tumbled flaxen hair. Her heart contracted and wrenched over him, as if he had truly been her own. She did not wake him. She kissed his pillow beside one slender, upflung hand, and let him sleep.

Hubert leaned over Meggotta. Her eyelids trembled at his detected nearness, tried to rise and awaken her, and failed. He saw her so seldom, was free to talk with her even more rarely, loved her to excess. She lay naked under a light cover in the night of the first of July, and she had shaken down the linen to her waist, and lay on her back, both arms thrown up to her pillow to let the cool night air embrace her every way. Her face was neither a child's face nor a woman's but caught between, and now, exalted in sleep, seemed to him an angel's face, pure, assured and beyond wounds, and yet the creamy body, fining now from its infant plumpness, had the immaculate, delicate beginnings of breasts; he saw them lift and soften from the bone, the nipples close and private as thought or dream. The curved, confiding hands had ceased to be a baby's pudgy hands, were growing long and fine. She had a narrow waist; the bones of her face were congealing into beauty. He had a budding woman between his leaning arms.

He kissed her forehead, and even that ivory wall was sensitive to his caress. Her eyes opened instantly and widely, she looked up and drowned him in deep pools of iris-grey, and smiled marvellously, and all in silence.

"Margaret, daughter, Madge, Meg, Margery-pearl, Meggotta. . . . Go to sleep again, my heart! We're here, we're home, all's well! Tomorrow I'll love you even more than I do today, and today I love you with all my might."

"What kept you so long?" she said, only half awake. "Why couldn't we come with you? I love you, too."

"I know! We had business with the king. About our future, and yours."

"And is everything as you wanted it?"

"Everything, my love! Go back to sleep. Everything is as we wanted it, and mother is saying good-night to Richard this moment. Tomorrow you shall command me whatever you wish."

Her eyes were already closing again. She slept before he rose from her bedside.

The next day, without ceremony but with every care, the clerks engrossed on parchment the oaths that had been made at Bromholm, set down in their original wording for the future to read. And, that done, King Henry's entourage set out at leisure for Walsingham and Castle Acre, the king's usual round of holy places in these parts, leaving the earl of Kent to follow and overtake them at Castle Acre, after a brief but blissful holiday among his own family. The day was capricious and petulant when they departed, a scud of fine rain bedewing their waiting horses. It cleared and blossomed into fullest summer when they were out of sight. Meggotta queened it that day, loosed from the constraint of royalty and ceremony, clutching Richard by the hand. Playing ponderously but devotedly with his own child and his borrowed child, for two summer days the old man regained his youth.

At the end of July, King Henry announced his intent of setting out to Shrewsbury, to prepare the ground for the further negotiations with the Welsh that must follow the present truce, and try to turn it into a more stable peace. The truce held good until November, but it was a prudent move to meet the envoys of the prince of Gwynedd well ahead of that time, make mutual reparations for such small infringements as were so far complained of on both sides, and agree upon arrangements for a winter conference, for which Shrewsbury was the most convenient base. It seemed hardly necessary for the king to go in person, but if that was his wish, his ministers shrugged, and went with him dutifully.

Important letters followed them to Shrewsbury by the eighth of August. In his private chamber in the abbey guest-house Henry read them, and heaved a great, satisfied sigh, and then, smiling like a cat stalking prey, sent for his closest advisers, omitting only the earl of Kent.

The refectory of the abbey was given over wholly to the king's use, and there he held court and heard petitioners. He had with him all his chief officers, both of the household and the realm, but many of the magnates were in their own honours and about their own business. There were those among them, like Ranulf of Chester, whom Henry preferred not to have as witnesses on this occasion. The first step was the most difficult. But now that the moment came, he found himself not daunted but exalted, tasting his freedom before the collar was loosed. He had a phalanx at his back, no need to be afraid.

He swept into the refectory and the assembly of his officers and peers, with the pope's opened scroll in his hands, and his face fixed and blazing white. Hubert did not at first observe anything unusual in the brilliant pallor, and the ominous, levelled line of brows that slashed it across like a sword. The relief of not having to be always on guard was like new warmth in the sunlight, but there were still bound to be moods and tantrums to deal with.

"My lords," said the king in a high, fevered voice, as sharp as the brightness of his face, "I claim your attention for an item of business we hardly looked for at this time."

His entry had been enough to draw all eyes to him. He made for the great chair that was placed for his public audiences; the fan of his familiars opened about him on either side, and they were suddenly seen to be, almost without exception, the familiars of Peter des Rivaulx, who stood withdrawn behind the chair, austere and impenetrable as ever. Robert Passelew on the right, Brian de Lisle on the left, clerks and administrators of the wardrobe. The bishop of Winchester was not present in the hall. He knew precisely when to be present, and when absent.

"We have received," proclaimed the king loudly, "letters from the Holy Father, sent from Spoleto in June. Pope Gregory writes of his grief and outrage at the offences done here in this realm to his Italian priests, by those miscreants hiding under the mask of the criminal who calls himself William Wither. Papal envoys have been insulted, papal letters treated with disrespect, the goods of the Holy Father's appointed priests seized and sold, and insolent manifestos issued commanding their tenants to withhold their rents. We have all known of this vile movement, which, thank God, is now in retreat before better counsels. But we have not known the identity of those to blame. The Holy Father writes that he has the manifestos of the culprits before him, and knows who they are, and he orders that if found they shall be excommunicated and sent to him for absolution. He has already promised, and repeats that promise, that in future the rights of patrons whose livings are now held by Italian priests shall be respected, and he bids us all remember that we are one fold, and one shepherd."

"But the Holy Father," cried King Henry, "does not name all those offenders in high places who could be named. For we have been pursuing this iniquitous business on our own account, and have discovered strange alliances. The royal seal has been misused, or very cunningly copied, in this cause, for the robbers have shown apparent royal letters approving their actions, which we most certainly never approved. We have been enquiring privately as to who has authorized a use of our seal and sanction never authorized by us. What we have uncovered is hard to credit, but we cannot blink the truth away."

He levelled the parchment scroll as suddenly and viciously as once he had lunged with a sword. "My lord of Kent, you . . . *you* are here arraigned of a most particular and heinous treason. *You* have covered the acts of these criminals against church and state. I charge you with it! I denounce you!"

For a long, mute moment Hubert could neither believe nor even understand the bolt hurled at him. He stood stricken dumb and helpless, tried to speak, and found neither wind nor words. The king rode over the abrupt, deadly silence, his voice rising towards hysteria.

"Nor is that all! Now that my eyes are opened upon this one crime, I see how my trust has been betrayed and misused by you many years. Those lukewarm actions of yours in Normandy and in Wales, which I bore with as the honest failings of an aging man, I see now as much more, as treason after treason to my interests. And if abroad, why not also at home? How many years have you, my lord, done what you would with my treasury? And how is it that though my coffers are empty, yours are always well filled? I have been blind and trusting too long, but now I will have an accounting from you, and look well into all your actions, for I trust none of them. And I bid any here who may have private knowledge of your misdealings to come forward and make their charges without fear, for you shall have no freedom to meddle with them or prevent. We will protect any who can aid us by bringing truth to light."

Yes, that he would! He was prompting malice, appealing to envy for his support, and making his great bid for freedom here, far away from London, where it might have been more dangerous to launch such an attack. Hubert stood alone, suddenly aware of the space that had opened about him, and of the assault of so many eyes, few or none of them friendly. He stood erect but a little shrunken with grief and bewilderment, while his world burst like a soap bubble, and fell in dull drops about him. If this had happened some weeks ago, before Bromholm, he might have been able to fight it, might even have seen it coming, and been able to prevent, or at least to look for allies. Now he was utterly undone, unarmed, already mortally wounded. And now he knew the purpose of the oath of Bromholm, and knew that he had been gullible enough to connive at his own ruin.

"My lord king," he said at last, finding from some enfeebled remnant of spirit within him a voice thick and clumsy with pain, "either those who have already laid information with you are lying, or they are in error. I am as true a man to you as any in this land, and have done nothing to affront my duty or my conscience. Of how the raiding bands in the north managed their forgeries I know no more than you. I never thought to hear such accusations from your lips. Your Grace should know me better; I have laboured for you long enough, and not to your loss, as there are surely some here will testify."

He looked round at them heavily, for the silence and stillness they kept was like a leaden burden upon his heart. But no voice answered him. Those who might well have taken his part were still too dumbfounded to have anything to say; some were perhaps even in genuine doubt as to where truth lay. But the rest, as still and hushed as these, had already begun to let their dawning triumph and gratification show in their eyes. He had known that he was not liked, had never understood how to make himself liked; but he had never until now realized how many of them hated him.

"Examine me," he said, rousing himself with an effort, "on whatever points you will, but let me know exactly what you charge against me, and it shall be answered. I have nothing to hide, and nothing to repent."

Nothing, except that he had rushed so eagerly into the trap they had laid for him! And perhaps also that he had gone so far as to love this ungrateful prince from a child, and borne with his vagaries patiently, never attributing to them the envenomed malice he saw now in the pale, bright, vengeful face. He had loved, and Henry had hated. For how many years now? Ever since he grew a man?

No mystery now about Bromholm. Henry had known all along that he was swearing away certain rights that belonged not merely to him but to his successors, a part of the monarchy of England. Lightly he had sacrificed them, just to catch a credulous old man who believed oaths were for keeping, well aware all the time that he could slide out of his promise very easily by pleading the very fact of its infringement of his coronation oath, and be absolved by papal dispensation on that ground. Small matter to him which came first, the breaking or the absolution. But Hubert himself had also sinned. The only reproach he felt now was that he, too, had gone unworthily into the church at

Bromholm, knowing the king ought not to be whittling away the crown rights, and saying no word to warn a rash, well-meaning young man whom he believed to be acting in innocence.

We are two! he thought, and groaned. But now I shall pay the price for both, and he will go free.

"You shall indeed be examined on all these matters," said the king venomously, "but not here, and not now. You stand impeached already on some five grave charges, and there are still many enquiries to make. This day you will deliver over the charge of all those royal castles you hold into the hands of Stephen Segrave here. I will not leave them in the care of a suspect traitor one day more. You hear me, my lord?"

"I am, as I have always been, at your Grace's disposal," said Hubert wearily. "If that's your will, it shall be done." Segrave, who had worked with him amicably for years, and now to take his stand beside des Rivaulx, and gather in the gains of his colleague's disgrace!

"Now leave our presence. We do not wish to see you in attendance upon us again unless we send for you. But remain here, and hold yourself at our disposal, to answer whatever we shall put to you. Make no attempt to leave unless I give you permission. You will be watched."

"At your Grace's pleasure," said Hubert in a bitter whisper, for pleasure, he saw, it was to watch him trying to assemble about him the wreckage of his world, like a man in rags trying to cover his nakedness. He made an old man's stiff, unwieldy bow, and turned and went out slowly from the refectory, through the silent, staring ranks that parted to let him pass. He walked erect but carefully, as though his feet felt their way by touch, as though he were blind.

5

August to September, 1232:
Burgh; Bury St. Edmunds; London.

A dusty young knight in Hubert's livery, on a lathered
horse, galloped into the bailey at Burgh on the last day of August, left
his steaming mount for the tardy grooms to see to, and went striding
into the solar, to fall at Margaret's feet, and blurt out, half weeping,
"Madam, pardon! Pardon the bringer of bad news. I wish to God it
had fallen to another! My lord the earl . . ."

She was on her feet instantly, quick to terror on his behalf. "What
is it? Oh, God, not dead? What has happened to him?" She gripped
the young man's hand to raise him, staring wild-eyed into his face.

"No, not that! No, my lord lives. But short of death, this is disaster
enough, the worst." He shook with stiffness and exhaustion, having
ridden hard and far. She thrust him gently into the window embrasure,
and sat beside him.

"Tell me quickly. Let me know the worst."

Stumbling a little, his tongue thick with weariness, he told her of the
blow that had fallen at Shrewsbury.

"Dear Christ!" she said, very still and quiet. "False, false as hell, the
most twisted man that ever was born! He came in here brotherly, barely
a month ago, he kissed me at the door! Judas, foul, false Judas!"

"And then, madam, only a few days after that first attack, the king
gave his office of justiciar to Stephen Segrave, and ordered him to
proceed against my lord on the charges laid. He has issued a proclama-

tion—I wonder it has not been cried here yet—inviting any who have grudges—God knows he won't word it so baldly, but that's the meat of it!—to come forward with further charges, and forbidding any man, even his son, to befriend my lord the earl, on pain of excommunication. I wish I might give you a better hope, but surely the king means to go to extremes. He's demanded a full accounting of all my lord's dealings at the treasury, back into King John's day. And when my lord said, truly, that he had a charter of quittance from John remitting any such accounting, des Rivaulx said that John's death invalidated his charter. They are all in it! All! But the bishop of Winchester has planned the whole outrage—that I swear—and pulls the cords that make them all strut."

"I doubt not," said Margaret. But it was the king's face she saw, wherever she turned her eyes, meek and gracious and devout before the altar at Bromholm, lying and blaspheming in the sweet voice of an angel.

"At Kempton we heard that the king had drawn up an order of banishment, bidding my lord leave the kingdom, and we believed then that the charges would be dropped, to prevent such great scandal and contention as there's bound to be. My lord the earl foresaw that he would be forced to leave England, and so he took the Cross. At least the Crusade would have left him a purpose. But now even that way is closed to him. They never sent the order of banishment, after all. Not that the king will have repented his cruelty, I think rather he changed his mind about letting his victim go free, even abroad. He intends to bring him to trial, and do his worst to him. There was no chance to send word to you earlier, my lady, he was watched and prevented from writing. But at Kempton I slipped away by night and got clear."

"You did well, and I am grateful, Robert. But in God's name," she said, clutching her cheeks hard between cold palms, "was there no one to speak for him? Not one? Will they, dare they, let one of their own number go down like this for a vicious child's whim? Can they not see that any one of them could be the next, if he gets his way unhindered now?"

"Madam, they see only too well, the most of them, that if they lift their voices they could be the next to fall. Only the greatest, the unassailable, dare stand up and call a halt. And I have hopes they can and will at least see to it that there is a trial, and not a private slaughter. My lord has been given a day to appear in the case, the fourteenth of next month, and leave to withdraw to the priory of Merton to prepare his defence. Even that, I think, he owes to some of his fellow-earls. The graver sort, who were not at Shrewsbury, and got the word only late, are gathering now in London, Chester and some like him, who will not bend the law even for the king. But oh, my lady, I dread King Henry's spite! I never knew he had so much hate in him. It is not even honest hate, he works himself into a passion deliberately, in his own defence, for when he cools he's afraid of what he does. But all the while there are those behind him who are not afraid, but cold and able, and ready to kill. Oh, madam, I pray you with all my heart, take thought now for yourself, for no one who's loyal to my lord the earl is safe now, not even you."

Margaret sat erect, pressing her hands so hard against her cheeks that her face was drawn and distorted into a long mask, in which her eyes burned red, like hot coals at the heart of a sullen fire.

"Not for myself only," she said, and was quiet a long time. "Robert," she said then, "can you also get back to my lord?"

"If he's at Merton, yes, surely. The monks will be gentler keepers than Segrave's men. But don't write anything. Teach me your messages, and I'll carry them the safest way, in my head."

"And if he's at Merton, he's in sanctuary, at least until his day comes." She drew down her hands, and rose. "Robert, my friend, you need rest and sleep and food, as much as I need thought. There are things I can still do for my husband, but not, I think, here. Go and get your rest, and we'll talk again."

She said no word to any of the household except Alice and the steward, who had grown old in her husband's service, and was a Norfolk man himself, and to be trusted. Master Carrell was a quiet, conscientious man, but not Hubert's man, and she could not be sure of him. True, it was only a matter of days, perhaps hours, before the sheriff would have the king's proclamation cried everywhere, and then all this teeming manor would know how its master was fallen, ruined, threatened with possible death. But no need for them to know also where the countess was gone with her children. What they did not know they could not be made to tell. She knew she was dealing with only brief delays, but every hour gained might be the hour that turned the scale between freedom, with a field of possible action, however restricted, and helpless captivity. King Henry might have molested her before this had he wished, but as soon as he had leisure to remember that she was royal, and had a king for brother, and was a fighter born, he would certainly take steps to render her harmless. Margaret had no intention of being harmless to him; she wished him harm with all her heart, and as long as she kept out of his hands, she could and would do her best to fight him. But she never doubted it would be a grim struggle.

"Find the children," she told Alice, "and say no word to anyone else. I will tell them, when the time comes, all that has happened. And put together their things for a journey, and yours, too. But our packs must be light, we take no extra horses."

Alice went about the packing with her mind in turmoil, tears not far from her eyes and angry curses barely shut within her teeth, but her hands were deft and quick as ever; and when she went to call in Meggotta and Richard from the mews, they found nothing strange in her voice or manner.

"Why?" Richard demanded, displeased, for he was busy with his falcon, and reluctant to be disturbed. "What does mother want us for?"

"She wants you to come and eat now, for we're going on a little journey, my lady, and I, and the pair of you, and perhaps a groom or so to look after us. And you're not to pester your mother with questions or go running and telling anyone else what we're planning, because it's a secret. She'll tell you all about it when she's ready, and till then you be quiet and good, and help her without asking why."

That was different. They could leave even the falcons for an unexpected journey with Margaret. "Are we going to join father?" Meggotta asked eagerly, lighting on the secret that would best please her.

"No, my love," said Alice, shaken but valiant, "not just yet."

By the time they had made ready, with as little stir as possible, Robert Curtal was awake, and waiting for his orders. Margaret drew him aside.

"Are you fit to ride again, Robert? We need not drive you hard this time, we can't, for we shall have the children with us. But you are already in the secret, and I would rather not enlarge the circle. The less my household knows, the better for them."

"Fit and ready," said the young man eagerly. "What do you mean to do, madam? Whatever you may ask of me I'll undertake gladly."

"I am going to take the children into sanctuary at Bury St. Edmunds. Within the liberty there no one can touch us, and the prior is a good friend. My brother of Scotland surely has some influence, and the pope himself cannot close his ears, though I may have trouble getting a messenger through to him. We are not yet finished! We can make Wymondham by tonight, and sleep at the priory there. One more day, and we should be safe in Bury. And then, Robert, you shall go back to Merton, and tell my lord where you've bestowed us. And say, among many other things I'll teach you, that if by any means he can break out and join us there, he should surely do so. If he has scruples that his duty is to wait submissively for judgement, persuade him out of it at all costs. To wait for King Henry's justice is to throw his life away, for there will be no justice."

All through that journey Meggotta and Richard listened and watched and kept silence, as though life had been going its normal sunlit way, while everything about them conspired to invade their peace of mind with tremors of uncertainty and dismay and change. The very fact of this flight, which at first they had accepted with unquestioning pleasure, was soon seen to be ominous, like all unexplained and sudden things. Their mother's dark preoccupation and drawn brows, Alice's angry devotion, relieving its tensions in alternating crossness and fierce affection, their single escort and servantless provision, all these they observed, and long before reaching Bury had begun to decipher. They grew very silent and very grave, and drew close alongside Margaret like a guard, but they asked nothing; only now and again they exchanged glances, and either confirmed the other's mute judgement. In those fifty miles they grew up by some years, but they did it in selfless, disciplined silence, and it escaped the notice of those already grown up, who thought them merely tired by the journey, and wanting their beds.

It was dark when they rode into the enclave of the abbey at Bury, and the porters sent hastily for Prior Heribert, and to make ready the apartments Margaret usually occupied on her progresses. Gates closed between them and the outer world, and Margaret drew breath deeply, and loosed it in a great sigh. Lay brothers came to lead the horses away to the stable-yard, and light the countess to her rooms. And still Richard and Meggotta said never a word, but obeyed and followed submissively, like bidden children.

They were in safety, in the remembered wood-panelled room, dim-lit and welcoming. Alice went off determinedly to unpack bedding and prepare food, and Margaret lay back in a high-backed chair and closed her eyes, and briefly gave thanks for a small, significant mercy. Neither she nor Meggotta could be used to harm him further, or batter him into confession of sins never committed. For a moment she let her mind sink into an emptiness beyond consciousness. It was the strangeness of the silence that roused her again, nothing moving, no one speaking, but an awareness of eyes and intelligences fixed wholly upon her.

She opened her eyes, and they were standing one on either side of her, close, but not so close that there was any dependence in their nearness. Nor did they lower their gaze or abate the intensity of their scrutiny when she looked them in the face.

"Mother," said Meggotta, "what is it that we don't know?"

"We know there's something," said Richard. "We know it must be bad. Why didn't you tell us? We might have been more use to you if we'd known?"

"And why did Prior Heribert so particularly say that he'd had prayers said for you and for father? We know he prays for us, he promised he would," said Meggotta steadily and solemnly. "But this was different. And even before that we knew something terrible must have happened. You hadn't planned to come here. Everything was just as usual, two days ago. It was only after Robert came that you told us to get ready for a journey."

"And Robert says he's leaving very early tomorrow. Why in such haste? Everything in haste. Like running for the high ground when the floods come," said Richard. His lips shook for a moment. "Once, when I asked if we could come to Bury again, you said perhaps, some day— if ever we needed sanctuary."

The fair face, so childish only two days ago when he was busy with childish things, was suddenly seen to be the face of a young man, responsible, concerned, frightened but resolute. Only yesterday it might have cost her a convulsion of protest and pain to see them outgrowing their innocence of evil. Now it warmed and reassured her to know that they had resources of their own, if her forces flagged.

"It was a jest then," she said simply. "It is no jest now. If you want to be my knight, and Meggotta's knight, Richard, now's your time, for indeed we need one to stand by us."

"Then it's true? We are here because we needed sanctuary? Then it must be something very bad," he said, and quivered, bracing himself to bear the weight of certainty, where even imagination had been burden enough.

"Something has happened to father," said Meggotta in a whisper. "Nothing else could trouble you so much."

"Nothing else, unless it threatened you. I meant to tell you as soon as we were in safety here. At least we three are together, and we have Alice to take care of us, and that's an army. But you must make me braver, if I tell you, not weaker. There's to be no lamenting. Are you strong enough to bear it, however bad it may be?"

They gazed back at her steadily, and drew nearer, but said never a word. And she told them, arduously excising from her voice and face the detestation she felt against her enemy. In her it was a force that might yet serve for good, but loosed upon them it would have been a kind of poison. They stood mute and still through it all, whether out of determination to prove their endurance or because they were too appalled for words, unable even to believe in or understand a disaster of such enormity, there was no telling. At the end of it they kept their tranced silence a long moment, and then came shuddering out of it, and breathed again. They did not weep; that might come later, after long communion with the conception of ruin, and in solitude.

"But it's vile!" cried Richard, wrenching at the inconceivable injustice with a passionate detestation that matched Margaret's own. "How could he so demean himself? He *knows* these things are not true! Father is a true man to the king, and everyone in this land knows it. No one will believe such slanders, he cannot make them good, they'll fall to the ground, and the king will be the one to feel shame."

"Plenty of people will believe them," said Margaret grimly, "because plenty of people have envied your father for many years, and will want to believe them. And others who are in no doubt that they are lies will pretend to believe them, and make use of them as if they believed them, and even invent other charges to go with them, out of inveterate hate. No, we must take comfort some other way. There must also be some, a few, who, even if they hate him, hate honestly, and won't say amen to a lie even for their own gain."

"Mother, we must write to my Uncle Richard of Pembroke. He said he would stand our friend. He isn't envious, he doesn't hate father, he's been only a year in England, and has a fair mind. He'll help us."

"So he may!" said Margaret. "That's well thought of. And my brother of Scotland shall know of it, and any others who will listen. We shan't be idle or helpless, here in sanctuary."

"And father's in sanctuary, too, at Merton, so nobody can harm him," said Meggotta stoutly, "not until he comes out to trial." It was a thought of inconceivable horror, that her father could be in such a situation, accused of dreadful things all in a moment, out of a clear sky, like a tall tower felled in an instant by wanton lightning-stroke; but at least for a time he was out of reach of further savagery, and time might change everything again, as the tide changes. "The king may take back what he's said. There are two weeks yet, surely someone will persuade him to a better mind. In his heart he must know it's all false and wicked."

"He does know," agreed Margaret with dry bitterness. "But we must not rely on any change of heart in him. My hope is that your father will be able to slip away from Merton unnoticed and come to us here. I can think of no place that would be as safe for him as this. Robert will carry my message to him, and urge him to join us here. And meantime we can only wait, and pray. And never go outside the liberty; be careful of that."

It was the best comfort and hope she could give them, but it was all too small, they knew it as well as she. Of what use was it to feel safe here themselves, while Hubert was lost to them, and they must agonize night and day over what might be happening to him? For all her courage and anger and defiance, they knew that she was afraid as they were afraid. The king might be mean and contemptible as a man, but he was huge and terrible as the king, with powers limited only very tenuously even by his peers and bishops. If he was bent on persecution, even on killing, it would be hard to prevent.

"But at least," said Margaret firmly, "your father will soon know from Robert that we're safe here, and can't be used against him. Here the king's spite cannot reach."

She knew that for the first time she was lying to them. She herself had not fully realized the final peril until this moment, when she denied it. For God's sake, let this wind veer, and deliver them soon, before they understood the one remaining threat to them. Henry could not send in here by force and hale them out of sanctuary, no. But he could send the sheriff, with his legitimate order, to enter peacefully and claim back, by right of overlordship, a privilege he had formerly granted. As the king had given them Richard, with all the rights pertaining to his wardship and marriage, so the king could take Richard away.

On 14 September the king's council met to hear the charges against the earl of Kent, but the accused did not come. He sent word by a lay brother from Merton that he feared for his legal rights, having no assurance that the law would be properly observed, and that he would not leave sanctuary until he received such assurances from the king. The lay brother confided privately to a clerk he knew at Westminster that the earl had been warned, on good authority, that King Henry meant to have his life, and was well advised not to venture out without better guarantees.

Henry fell into a hysterical rage, sent for the mayor of the city, and ordered him to issue a proclamation to all men fit to bear arms, to assemble and march to Merton, and bring him the earl of Kent, dead or alive. Which gave sufficient colour to Hubert's fears, and appalled some members of council, but guaranteed the king a bloodthirsty mob, willing to do the worst he could wish, as soon as the proclamation had been read sufficiently widely. Hubert in his time had had to deal with dangerous riots among the men of London, and suppressed them with a severity the Londoners still remembered. If he could not make himself loved, he was only too gifted at making himself hated.

It was evening when the business of calling out the mob began, and hundreds had begun to gather, very willingly, with whatever weapons they had, before midnight. Some of the more stable sort heard the proclamation and watched the growing assembly with dismay. Andrew Bukerel said to his neighbour John Travers that there would be murder done if this pack were not called off, and might well be civil war to follow, and the two of them went off in haste to the most influential personage they could think of. The bishop of Winchester was at his house in Westminster, and already in his bed. He came out at the plea of the two merchants, but with some annoyance at being disturbed, and more irritation at finding they spoke no French, and one of his chaplains who understood this barbarian tongue had to be summoned to interpret.

"What would you have?" said the bishop with raised brows, when he heard what they were asking of him. "His Grace the king has issued an order he has every right to issue, authorizing the arrest of a defaulter. I marvel you should ask me to interfere with the course of law."

"My lord," said Travers earnestly, "what comes of this will not be law, but plain murder, if someone does not call off the mob. And not one murder alone, when you let loose such a rabble, for there'll be those will get in their way, whether purposely or by ill luck, and very likely die of it. It wants only a word to start a battle, when men come out by thousands in arms, and untrained and undisciplined. My lord, you could get the king to call off the hunt, if you would."

"I will not lift a finger," said the bishop, very contentedly, "to thwart the will of his Grace where he does only what is within his rights." And he walked back into his house and went back to bed, and slept well.

Shut out in the night, the nonplussed citizens could only listen to the growing din of men mustering and ready for mischief, until one of them recalled that he had heard the earl of Chester was now also in the city, at his town house. They made their way there, but by the time they reached the house, a mob of more than ten thousand men was flowing towards Merton, fed by rivulets of fresh reinforcements along the way. They had about six miles to go, and they set off briskly on their hunt.

At this rate, the earl of Kent had perhaps some two to two and a half hours of life left to him, and some of the monks who might try to restrain the invaders were likely to meet the same fate. The news had already fled hot-foot into Merton. Hubert went heavily to the church, and remained there in prayer before the altar. Certain of death, and so weary that he was almost indifferent, he commended his soul to God, and waited. Life was very dear to him, he had a simple man's natural attachment to it, but he had grown so accustomed to fear and despair that they counted now as known companions.

Ranulf de Blundeville, earl of Chester, had not been at the king's council, because he was not in the best of health. He was sixty-two years old, and had lived a hard, vigorous life, but his years were overtaking him, and he had a cold that rasped his chest and throat. When his chamberlain awakened him, reluctantly, and told him what the two sound citizens below reported, he heard with the fiery exasperation of one of the older generation who sees his successors weakly letting down all standards, and came surging out of his bed, naked and squat and formidable, with an oath that shook the rafters.

"Christ aid!" he said, lunging into his hose and reaching for his shirt. "What are we come to! The boy has run mad!" And he went charging out from his bedchamber swathed in a cloak, his grey hair on end, but halted with due grace and consideration to give thanks to the two merchants who had lost their night's sleep to remedy a gross lapse of law. "Go home and rest, gentlemen," he said, as his groom came reeling, half asleep, to the door with his horse. "You have done all and more than was yours to do, if every man had his share, and now I will do the rest."

Andrew Bukerel and John Travers went away quite satisfied. There are men into whose hands you can let your worries fall with confidence, and they had found one of the best of them.

In the palace of Westminster, King Henry, lying in his bed, fevered with anticipation and excitement and vengeful hope, was startled and shocked to be interrupted in his dreams of triumph by an agitated chamberlain, full of apologies, closely pursued by the apparition of the earl of Chester, gaunt-cheeked and hoarse and blunt, perfunctorily echoing the apology, but demanding his attention. Another old man, only less detestable than the other, not even unlike him in appearance, two square, sturdy, immovable bodies, two lively, vigorous minds, independent to the point of obstinacy. He had never realized before that they were not only as opposed but also as like as mirror images, the supreme aristocrat of his realm and the rawest parvenu.

"My lord king," said Ranulf, "I hear you have sent the hue and cry of London after the earl of Kent, to bring him dead or alive. This you cannot and must not do. It will be shame to you for ever if you do not send and countermand your order, while there's still time."

The king sat up sullenly and angrily, and began to expostulate that he had every right to send by force for a defaulter and felon who failed to keep his day, but the earl rode over him ruthlessly.

"Defaulter he may be, but he has not decamped, and he is not a felon until he is tried and convicted. He asks only for guarantees that he shall be tried according to law, and whosoever he may be, friend or enemy of mine, I say he has a right to make that stipulation, and you have none to make him virtual outlaw on one default, and loose a city mob to hound him. What will the nobility of Europe say of you when they hear it? And especially in France, where you hold lands still, and desire to stand well! What manner of foster-child is this king of England, they'll ask, who turns on his best friends, even those who have preserved and maintained him from a child? The earl of Kent has fledged a cuckoo in his nest—so they'll report of you. If you want to avoid such a reputation, call off your men now; give the man a further respite and the guarantees he asks. But now, at once, or it's too late for you and for him."

Henry writhed, and hated him, but feared him more. "It is too late already," he said, between panic and satisfaction at the thought. "They are on the march long ago. No message can overtake them now."

"Yes, it can, and must. I have the chancellor below, and we have two fast horses and trusty men to ride with your order. Everything is ready, we need only your permission to use your seal in this cause, and countermand the former order. Bid their leaders have them turn back and disperse quietly. The rest can wait. This cannot."

The king would have liked still to equivocate, to wring out time until it should really be too late, but face to face with this peremptory and scornful righteousness, which might well have acted without him had he delayed, he gave way, authorized the errand and the use of his seal, and flung himself back in his bed in feeble rage as the earl went striding out of the bedchamber, with only the most perfunctory of bows by way of farewell, and no conciliatory thanks at all. Small consolation that no third party had been present to see him scolded and humiliated; they would hear about it soon enough, even though he was bound to admit that Ranulf was unlikely ever to tell the story. But, at least, if the old autocrat went safely back to his sick-bed and stayed there, it should be easy to withhold any further concessions. Hubert would have to be given another day for his arraignment, but not one word of reassurance should he have to ease his mind. Let him sweat!

Earl Ranulf saw the two horsemen despatched on their ride, made experienced estimate of times and distances, and rightly judged that they would overtake the marching horde at least a mile or so short of sighting Merton. He went back to his own house and his own bed satisfied that a gross offence had been prevented. He was glad to lie down; the night air made his stiff old bones creak, and scoured his throat raw. And the man waiting for life or death in the priory church was only a year or two short of him in age. Ranulf believed in none of the farrago of charges made against the earl of Kent. He disliked the man, as he always had, but he had never doubted his loyalty and honesty, notwithstanding the acquisitive passion that drove him. The list of supposed enormities was now so long, and such a fantastic medley of practical possibilities, like the misuse of treasury funds, and wild flights of fancy, like the use of magic potions to win ascendancy over the king's mind, that even some less frankly sceptical than Ranulf might well find their capacity for belief growing strained. God send you just and fair deliverance, Hubert! thought the old man before he slept.

At Merton the brothers, alerted to a danger that could hardly fail to menace them as well as their guest, kept careful watch until one of the chancellor's messengers, thoughtful for their peace of mind, rode on to reassure them that the disappointed mob had turned, thwarted and grumbling, in its tracks, and the siege was lifted. They brought the news to Hubert, chilled and weary on his knees before the altar. He sank his head into hands shaky from sudden relief, and asked, "Is this truth? By the king's order? Not of his goodwill, that I know. Who forced his hand?"

"The earl of Chester," said the prior.

"Twice he has given me back my life," said Hubert, after long silence. "And I have thought of him always as my enemy. I would to God some I called my friends had dealt by me as generously. Leave me here awhile yet, let me at least thank God for such an adversary."

News filtered through to Margaret in Bury St. Edmunds of the further delay allowed to her husband, still immured but as yet safe in Merton. But there was other news, which showed that the king felt no relenting, indeed was bent on taking out his spite for one frustration by using all the other weapons available to him. Hubert's son, John, fell into disgrace for merely being a de Burgh, and was stripped of whatever castles he held. There was even talk of proceeding against Hubert's nephew who held high office in Ireland, in case he should seek to take action on his uncle's behalf, though he showed no sign of doing so, and they had never been in close touch at all. One last blow Henry still had left to strike; he stripped from his fallen minister the earldom of Kent, which he himself had created and bestowed on him.

"My title of countess," said Margaret scornfully, "he can have, and welcome. I am still a king's daughter and a king's sister without benefit of any gift of his." And she wrote all these developments to King Alexander, and the earl of Pembroke, and Luke, archbishop of Dublin, who had been Hubert's chaplain once and was still his confessor, and already engaged on his behalf.

There remained the matter of the children. Day by day they went loyally about the business of living, and gave her every help and comfort in their power, subdued, alert, quietly valiant. And day by day she watched them grow closer and kinder, and wondered how many days she had left before King Henry had leisure to turn in her direction, and send someone to tear these two apart. That it would happen sooner or later she knew, and there was nothing she could do to prevent.

No, but perhaps there was something she could do to make the blow ineffective! From the time it came into her mind she thought about it constantly, and watched Meggotta and Richard with even more intensity of pain and fear and hope. Their faces had changed, grown thinner; strong, shapely bones showed through. Their eyes had a deeper gravity and steadfastness, and their lips a sterner set. They no longer embraced each other, or went with clasped hands; they seldom touched each other, yet never went out of reach one from the other. A manner of shyness and wonder had grown between them, as though for either the other's flesh had become too sacred to handle lightly. Even the voices in which they spoke together, though the words were still child-like and innocent, had a conscious quietness and deliberation, as be-tween man and woman. They looked into each other's eyes, attentive and absorbed, as girls stare into their first mirror, and saw themselves there, Meggotta within Richard, Richard within Meggotta. Love had been play, and suddenly, at ten years old, was play no longer.

"There is something I must talk over with you," Margaret said one evening, when the three of them were alone. "I haven't spoken of it before, but now I must, for it concerns you two very nearly, and you should know the whole truth. I know you are brave, I believe you are wise. There shall be no decision made about you over your heads. You shall make it."

They came to her in silence, great-eyed, and stood, waiting.

"You know about the compact made between your two fathers, with the king's approval, that you should marry when you're grown, and how the king sent you to live with us, Richard, because of it."

"Yes," he said, and she saw apprehension in his eyes, and saw his face set grimly to dissemble it.

"Now that the king has turned against my lord, and is doing every-thing he can to hurt and crush him, have you thought—I see you have! —that he might also take you away, out of our charge, and dishonour the compact that was made? He has proved he can break oaths without a tremor, and will gleefully break this bond as soon as it dawns on him what a cruel blow it would be to us all. And this he could do, not honourably, true, but legally. As overlord, he can dispose of such wardships as yours, child, as he pleases. I have been afraid all this time of his sending someone to snatch you away. I fear it still. Richard, it will happen. Meggotta, you must be prepared for it."

Meggotta said, "Then I shall die." Not wildly, not angrily, only with such quiet, considered certainty that Margaret's heart turned in her.

"I won't go," said Richard, setting his teeth. "You are my mother and the earl is my father, and I won't have any other. He can't make me."

"He can make you. Never think you can defy King Henry. You have not your earldom yet, or you might do much. You have seen how even earldoms can be snatched back, and yours could be denied you for ever. He can take you by force, he can give you into the charge of whom he pleases, and if you displease him, he will give you into hateful charge, with full leave to beat or starve or by any means batter you into submission. He can hold you imprisoned as fast as if you lay in a dungeon. But most of all, whatever offence you give him he will avenge upon Meggotta and me, and in particular upon your father. You know him very well by now, you know I speak the truth. No, that is not the way. But what if you knew that the separation would be only for a time, and had an assurance that in the end you would be together again? To wait a few years—you are not grown up yet!—that I'm sure you could bear with a good heart. For each other!"

They said yes to that, almost gladly. The years might be tedious and trying, but, provided they were certain they would end in reunion, they could be borne, even with a good grace.

"Then you could go with the king's officer, when he claims you, Richard, knowing you had a secret that made obedience easy and empty. You could behave yourself wisely and amiably, wherever the king places you, and avoid giving any offence, any excuse for revenge. And Meggotta could wait here with me patiently, knowing she is yours, and you are hers. Even if it takes five years, or six, for all this trouble to pass over, what would you be then? Only sixteen, barely out of childhood. And all the years afterwards would be yours."

"Oh, *yes!*" said Richard, eased and ardent. "*That* we could bear. But how can we make so certain of the ending?"

"Wait, there's more yet. You would have to keep it secret from everyone, never show by word or look that you know more than others know. Until times change, and the king relents again. That's a hard thing to do, and if once you betrayed yourselves, everything would be ruined, and there would be a worse revenge on us all. Can you, dare you, undertake such a great thing?"

They said yes together. Meggotta said, "For Richard I can do more than that. And so can he for me."

"Then if you are sure of each other, and of what you want, though you're not old enough yet to be man and wife as the world goes, it's never too early to invoke the sacrament of the church and the blessing of God. Here in Bury you can be married secretly. If we do that, then you are fast bound to each other, and it will be more than any man can do to separate you. In the end they will have to accept that you *are* man and wife. Are you brave enough to do this, and keep it hidden from everyone until the right time comes?"

Meggotta said, "Yes!" radiantly shining.

Richard said, "Yes!" in a muted shout of joy. "Oh, mother, yes, yes, yes! When can we marry?"

"First I must speak with the lord abbot. We are guests in his house, and debtors to his great goodness. I would not take any grave step in his domain without his knowledge. Whatever cheating tricks are used against us, we shall use none. Let me have until tomorrow, and we'll talk again."

She went to the abbot's lodging that night, after the children had gone to their beds. But first she went into the church, and prayed passionately at the shrine of St. Edmund, king and martyr. For Hubert first, as always he came first with her, that he might find comfort within, who had so little comfort without. Then for her daughter and her son, for long since she had thought of him as her own flesh and blood, that they might outlive malice and anger, and come into safe harbour together. Last, and briefly, for herself, that she might be sustained in order to sustain all those she loved, and felt dependent upon her.

Then she asked audience of the lord abbot. She was admitted to him at once, without question. Thin and frail, visibly older than when he had blessed the children and promised to link them in his prayers, he made her gently welcome, and made no flurry of words while she considered hers.

"My lord abbot," said Margaret, "you know the history of those two young creatures I have with me here. You know they were promised to each other, by the wish of both fathers, some years ago. You know one of those fathers is dead, and the other arraigned and awaiting trial at the king's instigation. Innocent of all offence, I say, guilty as hell, so the king says. Doubtless you have your own view. I do not ask to know it, nor seek to question or combat it. I am concerned with those manifestly innocent, whose lives are caught up in this anguish and anger which is none of their making. Father, you have seen these children, talked with them, looked into their hearts. So you may again, as privately and often as you wish. I would not influence your mind, or theirs."

"Daughter," said the abbot very gently, "I make no question concerning your integrity, which is known to me and to God. Go on!"

"Father, those two have known their destiny some time now. So may others have done, and shrunk from knowing it. Not these! If ever I saw love, I see it in my daughter and her chosen husband. They have grown together, and gone beyond brother and sister into something rare and blessed. They love each other as few who marry ever love. And they are pure as few are ever pure, for they know love without sin, either preferring the other before self. As children they loved, and now, driven out of childhood, they love in a larger measure, and when they come to man and woman, that will be such a love as God must welcome and cherish. And, Father, I am afraid for it; I dread both they and God may be cheated."

She was silent, gathering her harried forces, and he waited, patient, mild, and calm.

"Father, I speak to one versed in man, and long experienced in princes. You know, as I know, that the king may snatch back my son out of my hands, and despoil all that has grown between these two. And deprive me, also, but I am not worth consideration here. That I love the child, that is nothing. That he loves my child, and is loved in return, for that I claim privilege. It is my intent that these two shall be married, now, while no man's goodwill has been withdrawn from them, while the compact uniting them still holds good. But I would not procure this sacrament within your pale unless I have your blessing. If you deny me, I shall take them elsewhere at great risk, and see them united. But I would rather they made their vows here in sanctuary, knowing that you spread your hand over them."

"Child," said the abbot, wrung, "with what end in view? How do you read these troubled omens? What is to become of these innocents?"

"Father," she said, feeling her way scrupulously among many dangers, "as I see it, the king shifts as the wind veers. Many times I have been tempted to hate and curse him, and shall be so tempted again, and yet I see here a child who will be a child to his life's end, and is pitiful as well as blameworthy. As he has changed now, so he will change again, and some day, maybe within the year, he will show a benign face again to my children's union and my lord's faithful service. Then, as I pray, this marriage may be pleasing to all, not least the king, and may bear good fruit to him and to us. But most to these two whom I love more than my life. This is my wager. God is listening as I speak."

"And have you thought, and have they thought," he asked, moved and troubled, "that such a match must be hidden away from all but the witnesses? Perhaps for years? If it became known now, it could mean your husband's death, he being the victim close at hand. Is that a load to lay upon innocent children?"

"It is a counsel of desperation," she owned, shuddering, "but we are desperate who take it. Yes, they know how much may depend upon them. Yes, I believe they are able to bear it. It will be hardest for the boy. Meggotta will be always with me, her they cannot touch. But for Richard, once he is away, what may they not try to trick or threaten out of him! I know what I am asking of him, I will see that he knows it, too. There are deaths all round us, with every word and thought we take our lives in our hands. I am fighting for the future, which belongs to the children."

"And when do you wish this marriage to take place?" asked the abbot, and by the mildness of his voice she knew he had made his decision.

"Soon. Tomorrow. He will not be left with us much longer."

"And whom will you trust to marry them and keep their secret?"

"I had thought I might ask my confessor, who knows even the dark places of my mind, and will know if I am acting from a right motive."

"I also know these things," said the abbot, "and I also am a priest. Why let one more, however willing and worthy, into so perilous a secret?"

On the twenty-first day of September, St. Matthew's day, in the abbey-church of St. Edmund, late in the evening and in complete secrecy, Meggotta de Burgh was married to Richard de Clare. The abbot himself blessed their exchange of rings and received their vows. No one else was present except the Lady Margaret of Scotland, and Alice, Meggotta's nurse.

6

September to November, 1232:
Brentwood; Bury St. Edmunds;
London.

*A*ll the former justiciar's enemies, and they were legion, had foregathered in London to support King Henry's campaign against him. There were new charges every day, beaten out of the bushes like game, charges of treason, embezzlement, witchcraft, of having conveyed to Prince Llewelyn of Gwynedd a stone that rendered him invulnerable, of having interfered in certain of the king's tentative attempts at finding a suitable bride, even of having tried to assassinate him once at Woodstock. The tone of the times came in very clearly to Merton, like a cold east wind that no house, however well built, can quite shut out. And whatever was in doubt, and however many sober people, disgusted by the sheer frenzy of the persecution, were beginning to feel some sympathy for Hubert, there was no question but the king's obsessive hatred grew every day more vindictive.

Hubert was certain he would not get fair trial; his enemies, King Henry chief of them, meant to kill him. On the very day when his daughter took her marriage vows, he did what until then he had refused to do—slipped away out of Merton under cover of darkness, with only Robert Curtal for company, and set out to try to reach Margaret in sanctuary at Bury St. Edmunds.

Until they were well away from London it was necessary to lie up by daylight. The bishop of Norwich, who was a kinsman of the de Burghs, had a house at Brentwood, close to a chapel that had been built at an important road-crossing, in a cleared section of forest, and attracted to itself a new and thriving village. The bishop was not in residence, but his household servants took the fugitives in willingly, and gave them shelter, and during the day kept a sharp watch for any activity that might indicate that the pursuit was bearing in this direction. Before night the escape was being cried abroad on all the roads out of the city, and there were sheriffs' officers everywhere, and Hubert was urged to lie in hiding overnight, at least, until this hue and cry died down.

How the word had leaked out they never knew, but in the night the servants roused Hubert in wild alarm, with a report that the king had sent a company of armed men under his own steward of the household, to hunt the escaped felon, and whether they had information of where to look or not, they were bearing down upon this house with fell intent. There was barely time to dress in frantic haste and get out of the house, none to saddle horses. Hubert reached the chapel successfully, Robert was cut off before he could get to the door, and made for cover in the woods, as the leader of the armed band sighted his quarry, and swung from the house to the chapel with a dozen horsemen streaming after him.

Hubert, in the dim light of the sanctuary lamp on the altar, turned to face his pursuers as they burst in. He had lifted the small cross in one hand, and in the other the casket of the Host, but neither availed him. Geoffrey de Craucombe did not so much as check at sight of the holy things, but plunged across the tiled floor with sword drawn, and struck the casket out of Hubert's hand. The Host was spilled and trampled underfoot, the cross fell clattering on the tiles from a numbed hand, as one of the knights following struck at the old man's forearm with sheathed sword. Three or four laid hands on him, and dragged him out of the desecrated chapel into the night. Robert, crouched among the bushes, could do nothing but follow at a distance, at least to know the end of it, if he could not help. Hubert's attorney, Lawrence of St. Albans, was left behind at the house in Westminster, at least it might be possible to reach him with the news of this outrage.

Traffic being brisk and plentiful on the high-roads that crossed at Brentwood, the village had a thriving smithy. De Craucombe sent ahead to haul the blacksmith out of his bed and get him to fire his forge and clamp irons on the prisoner. The smith came out yawning and ill-humoured at being disturbed, a big, weather-beaten fellow who shrugged at the order and mention of the king's business, and was about to turn to work when he looked again, and more closely, at the forlorn figure of this aging man, dishevelled and bruised and pinned hard by the arms, standing haggard and erect, with closed eyes, resigned to his fate.

"Wait!" said the smith of Brentwood, narrowing his eyes. "Surely I know this man! What are you about, master, wanting chains on him? This is Hubert de Burgh, that held Dover against the French, and went to sea against Eustace the Monk, off Sandwich. I had a brother was in the ship with him. Never ask any man of my family to lift a hand against the earl of Kent. *Is* this he?"

"Your news is well out of date, fellow," said de Craucombe, amused. "This is de Burgh, true enough, felon and fugitive now, whatever he may have been in your brother's long-past day. Get to work now, and hobble him. In the king's name!"

"In the king's name, eh? And where's your order to me? And it had better be to me, for I can read, and know my own name when I see it writ, and I doubt if you know it, writ or spoke. And without you can show me the king's order to me, and no other, I will see you dead and damned before I'll put fetters on a better man than you."

"Fellow," bellowed de Craucombe, spurring a yard or so towards him, "do you know who I am?"

The smith stood straddle-legged, solid as a tree, and casually swung a hammer the length of his own long shanks in a hand that turned it into a toy. "No more than you know who I am, and care as little. I don't like your custom, and I ask you to leave my land." And to Hubert, whose eyes were wide open long before this, and lost in wonder and grace, like a child's, "Pardon, my lord, that I can do no more for you."

"Friend," said Hubert, dazed, "there is no man living who could do more for me than you have just done."

For want of chains, and being in too much haste to linger, for the king was waiting for their news, they made use of their sword-belts to pinion his arms, and lashed his feet together ignominiously under a horse's belly, and so set out with him back to London. A miserable ride, shaken, and without the use of his hands, but the smith's face and words went with him like a brazier in the chill of the night, all the way to the Tower. And all the way Robert Curtal, having retrieved a horse from the bishop's stable, followed faithfully, and, when the gates had closed on his master, went to tell the story to the remains of his London household.

De Craucombe sought out the king at Westminster, and reported to him that his enemy was safely installed in a cell in the Tower. And Henry, who had been pacing his rooms in a fever for two hours, sighed his pleasure, and went contentedly to bed.

He was less content next morning, when his privacy was invaded by Bishop Roger Niger, of London, in an exalted fury, and threatening excommunication. A whirlwind of a little, stout man, bursting with righteous energy, and demanding amends for a gross breach of sanctuary, for violence done not only to a sacred place and the holiest of vessels but also to a human creature's rights under heaven. The prisoner snatched out of sanctuary at Brentwood must be restored to the chapel there, and granted the statutory forty days' grace before food and water were withdrawn from him. On pain of excommunication, whether the offender were royal or not.

Against bishops in arms about canon law there is little to be done. Fulminate as they might, they could not get Hubert out of his hands, they could only cause an irritating delay in the inevitable. Against the grain though it might be, Henry could grant them that, and without even loss of face, for it was easy to exclaim indignantly that he had known nothing of the breach of sanctuary, that all that had been reported to him was the capture of the fugitive, and his safe delivery to the Tower. Bishop Roger was unlikely to interrogate de Craucombe against his king. Never, never would King Henry, that most Christian monarch, have countenanced sacrilege. He lied, but he had the scared child's gift of believing his own exculpatory lies.

Hubert's tragi-comedy resumed accordingly. By now he hardly understood what was done with him; the one thing that remained with him as comfort more palpable than all his prayers was the face and voice of the smith of Brentwood, defiantly declaring an unfashionable faith.

Somewhere below the ranks of his peers and rivals there was a stratum of solid citizens who remembered his services, and held no grudges against him.

They took him, without explanation, from his cell in the Tower, and mounted him again, pinioned as before, and rode with him. He did not realize, until they drew near Brentwood, what was in the wind. The sheriff of Hertford, waiting with enough armed force for an insurrection, told him of his rights, and the orders limiting them. They shut him within the chapel with food enough for the day, and so left him, deploying guards everywhere about the place, to keep watch in case he attempted flight. Forty days was Our Lord wandering lonely in the wilderness before His Passion, thought Hubert. Forty days I have now to make my soul's accounting before I am brought out to mine.

What could be done for him his confessor, his attorney, and the servants of his household did, but it was little, and daily constricted by new deprivations. Archbishop Luke moved to the house at Brentwood with some of Hubert's attendants, to provide him with his food and with spiritual comfort, and for the first few days Luke was allowed in to him briefly. Lawrence of St. Albans went from magnate to magnate, arguing for due process of law, with every safeguard. But the king's spite could not let anything alone. If the sheriff had wished to soften the rigours of the siege, he never had opportunity. He had orders to seize the prisoner at once, if he ever set foot outside the chapel, and take him back to the Tower. Within days he was being hectored to exercise yet greater care, and make sure that nothing was conveyed within to Hubert without being examined first by his guards. Two days later came orders forbidding anyone to speak word to the prisoner, and denying access to everyone but the sheriff's men; even Archbishop Luke was shut out. Hubert's private seal was to be taken from him and crushed before his eyes. No longer could his servants take his food to him; he was to be issued only with a single halfpenny loaf of bread and one measure of beer each day. At last even his psalter was taken from him, to deprive him of the comfort of reading in it.

Up to this point Henry had been so passionately concentrated on his persecution of the man himself that he had spared no thought for the possibility of attack through others; but now that there was this enforced inaction for forty days, he bethought him of Margaret. He knew where she was, and knew he could not touch her there; but if no move was made against her, she might think herself immune, and venture out of sanctuary. He would have the sheriff of Norfolk alerted to the possibility, and warn him to do nothing to alarm her prematurely, if she showed signs of returning to one of the manors still left to her. There was also, he remembered, one piece of highly valuable property he had not so far taken back from his fallen minister.

Archbishop Luke, forbidden entry to the chapel, went daily as far as the door, and there prayed aloud, to be heard within. It was about the eighteenth of October when by chance he overheard, while approaching, an exchange between the sheriff and his sentries that sent him back to the house in haste, to look for Robert Curtal.

"There is some threat afoot against the Lady Margaret. I heard 'the sheriff' mentioned; that can only be of Norfolk. 'Both to the Tower' was said."

"They cannot," said Robert at once. "Not even the king would risk breaking sanctuary so soon; he has had one fright already."

"And laid one siege here, and can do as much round the liberty of Bury. We should send and warn her not to set foot outside."

"I will go," said Robert, and rode the same hour. He was by half a day ahead of the king's courier, despatched to Bury on two errands, to order the sheriff to arrest the Lady Margaret and take her to the Tower if she ventured over the abbey threshold, and to take out of her care and bring back to London Richard de Clare, heir to the earldoms of Gloucester and Hertford.

Geoffrey de Craucombe entered the enclave of Bury St. Edmunds decorously and peaceably, with only one attendant, and asked audience of the Lady Margaret of Scotland. He did not make the mistake of asking for the countess of Kent, she would have reminded him coolly of his error if he had. He had been her guest with the king at Burgh on the pilgrimage to Bromholm, had drawn his own benefits from that meeting, and still enjoyed them by harassing those to whom he had then sworn allegiance. With all her heart she despised him, but he was armed with power over her, and she could not deny him entrance.

He was arrogant but uneasy. "Madam, I am sent by the king to relieve you of a charge. His Grace requires that you surrender to him the wardship of the boy Richard de Clare, and all rights in him and in his lands."

With a calm face and even voice she required him to show her his written authority, as if he had been some errand-boy from the lower reaches of the court. And when she viewed it, she took her time, and read every word, while he chafed and reddened, but could find no foothold for resentment. "You will understand, sir, that I do not hand over my responsibilities lightly, especially those towards a child. The boy has been happy with my household. I trust you'll treat him with consideration if he does not take kindly to another change. No doubt his Grace will have that in mind when he disposes of him to a new guardian."

"It is the king's intent," said de Craucombe emphatically, "that this wardship shall remain in his own hands."

"By proxy, however, I imagine. The king hardly has time or temperament to care in person for a boy of ten. I let him go, if that gives you or his Grace any pleasure," said Margaret, taking fire suddenly, "very reluctantly. The children I have reared have my love, I part from them with pain. Tell his Grace so! He should be glad to know his ward has been loved. I will send for Richard." She looked at Alice, who stood sentinel by the door, her gaunt, handsome face unreadable. They had rehearsed it many times, since the night of the marriage. All of them understood what was necessary. "I think the children are playing ball in the abbot's garden," said Margaret. "Will you ask them to come?"

Both of them. Meggotta had been promised she should not be cheated of this farewell. Alice curtseyed, and went out to warn them yet again, and hold them both in her arms a moment, but briefly, because any longer and there would surely be tears. She hugged them, and said bracingly, "Now you have to act your parts well, and remember you're fooling them all. You have the whip hand; you've only to be patient."

They came in separately, something they had learned of their own cunning, Richard first, Meggotta behind, half withdrawn in Alice's skirts. Richard halted in the doorway, and looked from Margaret to the intruder, his face pale and fixed as an ivory carving, wary and sharp-chiselled. "You wanted me, mother?" Dutiful and deliberate.

"Richard, this is Geoffrey de Craucombe, steward of the king's household. He is sent to fetch you away. King Henry wants you to return to Westminster and join him there, you will be in his wardship from this day, no longer in mine." It was well to let the slight bitterness show through, there would be no satisfaction for the king unless he was assured of dismay for her. "We are all in the king's hand, child," she said, and held him in her eyes, forbidding any tremor now, enveloping him in the secret glow of their conspiracy.

"Must I go?" said Richard, sounding indignant rather than dismayed. "What, today, at once? I'm not ready. Most of my things are still at Burgh, I shall need them. And I'm not going anywhere until I've had my dinner." He jutted a mutinous lip, and looked de Craucombe over with dubious eyes; it would not do to be too self-possessed, or too ready to quit a household in which he had clearly been very much at home. "It will all be strange again," he said fretfully. "Why can't I stay here with you?"

"Because we owe allegiance, and must do what the king orders. What we must do must be done with a good grace, Richard. And it would be well," she said briskly to de Craucombe, "to go as far as Burgh, while you're here in these parts, and see to it that all Richard's belongings either go with him or can be quickly sent after him. Both Master Carrell and Richard's own groom are still there, you will find it a help to yourself if you take them with you. And then he could also have his hawk, the peregrine his uncle of Pembroke gave him." She watched the steward's face, in hope of some flicker of recognition at the name, which might tell them whether the king had considered handing over the boy to the Earl Marshal, but the solid features remained impassive, and indeed de Craucombe probably knew no more of the king's intentions than she did. If the Earl Marshal had taken too strong a stand in defence of Hubert's cause, he might well be in disfavour with Henry himself. The boy would have to take his chance. He knew it, and was prepared for it.

"We ride as soon as you can be ready," said the steward shortly. "His Grace is in haste. Put together such belongings as he has here, and the rest must follow. You could, madam, if you wish, go to Burgh yourself and see them despatched."

"I thank you," said Margaret very drily, "but without better guarantees of my safety than his Grace has so far offered, I am not likely to consider a move from Bury."

He shrugged at that, and pursued the matter no further. But he would not wait to eat at Margaret's table, nor let Richard stay to take leave of the abbot; she judged they were not going far at this stage, the only haste was to get possession of the boy. The moment was hard upon them, and Meggotta had not said a word. She stood close beside her mother, large eyes earnestly studying the king's messenger, and looked only rarely and briefly at Richard, for to look at him now was such pain that it was better to think only of the future, when all this would be over, and the pledges they had given in secret could be declared before the world. The one thing she must not do was to weep, or show by word or look her love, her misery, or her comfort, the final certainty that sustained her through this hour.

Mercifully it did not last long. "Say your farewells," ordered de Craucombe, not unkindly, when Richard's small possessions were packed, and the horses at the door. Richard went to Margaret's arms, and lifted his face for her kiss. She felt his lips shaken by a brief spasm of anguish, but that was all; he had learned his part well.

"God go with you, Richard. Be obedient and dutiful to those to whom the king gives authority over you, and you will do very well."

"Yes, madam," he said meekly. "Please make my farewell to the lord abbot for me, and say my thanks to him, since I may not."

"I will, Richard, be sure. Kiss Meggotta, too. She will be thinking of you, as I shall, and praying for you."

He approached her with wide eyes and pallid face, took both her cold hands, and kissed her. Since their marriage he had done so every night, when they went to their beds, but then there had still been a morrow, and now there was none, only a blank until that far-distant future when the stability of the world would be restored, and the clouds lifted from the house of de Burgh. Dearly as they both believed in that time, and triumphantly though they rested in the knowledge of their union, made before God and not to be unmade by man, yet when their lips touched it was like a small splendour and a small death. Nothing had ever been like it before, or ever would be again. Yet it looked to the intruder like nothing more than the easy parting kiss of two ten-year-olds who had been brother and sister for a while, but could just as well live apart.

"God be with you, Richard," said Meggotta. "Be happy, and think of us sometimes." And still it sounded the voice of a child, placid and cheerful.

"And with you, too, Meggotta." God, at any rate, knew their secret, and it was safe with him. "I shall always put you in my prayers." She had his ring on a chain round her neck, inside her dress, where it could not be seen. He had hers sewn into the collar of his tunic.

"Come," said de Craucombe, "we must be moving."

They went down into the courtyard to watch him go, but did not follow to the gate. They had agreed on that long since. He looked back once, and waved, and then no more. When the riders were out of sight behind the jut of the gatehouse, Meggotta turned without a word, and led the way back into her mother's room. On the stairs she stumbled and went slowly, being blind, and in the doorway she had to feel for the step, and reach a hand to help her along the wall to the window. When her mother touched her arm, her whole body quaked, and she put up her hands to stem the shattering flood of her silent tears.

"Ah, now you may!" said Margaret, and opened her arms. "Now I'll weep with you. Now we have both of us to wait, and pray, and work for our husbands. Never doubt that we shall win them back, my lamb, my love, in spite of King Henry and all the world."

Archbishop Luke came to ask audience of the king some days before the period of grace ended, and dared to protest at the savagery of Hubert's treatment, begging for a more charitable approach, which should allow of an honourable solution. The king had three choices to offer. If Hubert desired an accommodation that would make trial superfluous, he could leave England for ever, submit to perpetual confinement, or publicly confess himself a traitor. These sorry proffers Luke was obliged to take back to his friend, for he could get no better. He was allowed to come to the door of the chapel to deliver the king's word.

"Tell his Grace," said Hubert from within, after no pause for thought, since thought was unnecessary, "that I refuse all three. I cannot stand before my peers and declare myself a traitor, since I am none. I will not submit to perpetual imprisonment, since I have committed no offence to deserve it. And not for any cause will I forswear England. Since I have taken the Cross, I will freely offer to go abroad for such time as I may usefully join the Crusade, but I will never agree to leave my country for life."

"So I was sure you would say," agreed Luke heavily, "and so I would have said on your behalf." And he took back the answer to King Henry, who was not displeased with it, for trial and condemnation were still what he had in mind. So it was a matter of licking his lips and containing his impatience only a few more days, when all food and drink could be withheld, and the prisoner starved out if he did not come out of his own volition.

In his castle of Wallingford, Earl Ranulf of Chester was dying. Nobody knew it better than he. He was neither glad nor sorry; it was simply the current business he had to deal with, and he approached it without fear or deference, as he did every task that fell in his way. In all his life he had never repined and seldom repented. It angered him that he felt his powers weakened just when he needed his strength most, to rise to the greatest of all adventures. There was also unfinished business here close about him, chafing his firm and lofty mind. He saw standards being lowered, principles being compromised, the understood relationship between monarchy and nobility, the whole system of hierarchies, complete with its honourable acceptance of duty in advance of privilege, shaken and endangered, and here was he, tied to his bed, unable to rise and go out into the night to recall kings to reason and peers to decency.

Concerning his own honour of Chester he was at peace. He had no heirs of his body, but his nephew and heir, John the Scot, knew and shared his uncle's mind. John would take good care of Chester, and maintain all its liberties, the envy of other men's tenants. His other earldom, of Lincoln, he had ceded to his sister a few days ago, knowing that she intended to hand it on to her daughter's husband, John de Lacy. Lincoln would do well in his hands. And the third earldom he had held for a time, Leicester. That was in other hands now, those of the young Frenchman who had come with his claim, honestly and confidently, knowing his own worth, believing in Ranulf's, asking for the surrender of an earldom as trustingly as a son of the house might ask for his portion. He had set out, with energy and devotion, once acknowledged, to get to know every manor in his honour, to learn how to be English and take pride in it, and he had shown a gift for it. He was young yet, decently reticent in council, though by no means deprecating or timorous. Surely Leicester would be in good hands there.

The young earl, it so happened, was on his way south to Westminster, obedient to the king's order to all his magnates to attend for the business of the former justiciar's trial. At Oxford he heard with grief the news that his patron and friend was on his death-bed at Wallingford. Immediately he set out for the castle, and begged admittance to the old man's bedside. The felled oak lay massive and worn, hawk's beak jutting, gaunt cheeks fallen and grey, but at Simon's almost silent approach he stirred and wakened.

"What, is it you?" said Ranulf, opening eyes still shrewd and keen. "I was thinking of you only a while since. Glad I am to see you. Bound for London?" His voice rasped in a sore chest, he drew breath short and hard, and gathered his powers between words, but what he had to say he would say, whatever doctors permitted or forbade. The voice, however, did not carry far. Simon went on his knees beside the bed, to be the nearer. "My lord, I grieve to see you thus. If I'd known, I should have come before."

"Wherefore?" growled the old man. "You have work of your own to do. You owe me nothing."

"Who spoke of debts?" said the young man as briskly. "I should have come for my own sake. I must not say my own pleasure, when I find you on your back. For the good of my soul, perhaps."

"Your soul got on very well without me for twenty-two years, and must soon get on without me again."

"No, never that. I have had a year and more between, and you will remain with me henceforward." He did not pretend it would be in the flesh. "May I render account for an inheritance, as it might be to a father? The honour of Leicester is in good heart, I begin to know my own people. And I have learned some English—as you see!"

"And speak it like a Frenchman," said Ranulf, grinning.

"That will mend. They give me credit even for trying. But as to this business in London," he said doubtfully, "I wish it could be in hands like yours, and no part of it left to me. I know nothing of the man's dealings before I came to England, these charges hark back many years. Who knows what is truth when half the witnesses are dead? It troubles my mind."

"Good!" said Ranulf. "Then go with a good heart, and listen, and speak as you find. Any right-minded man should be troubled at having another's life or death, ruin or freedom, on his conscience. If he feels it no burden, he should not be allowed any part in it. I wish there were more as troubled as you. And I tell you, boy, I'm right glad I brought you back with me to leaven the bread of my peers, for sometimes I find them sad dough, these days. Go and bear my part in this ill business, for I'm past reaching London again."

"But your part might not be my part," said Simon.

"True, true, I ask your lordship's pardon!" Ranulf laughed, and the convulsion caused dry leaves to rustle eerily in his chest. "I should have worded more carefully. Go and shoulder your own load, then, as I'm shucking off mine. Go your own gait, as I know you will. It may not be mine. For all I know you may yet undo and make over again everything I've lived with and believed in, but you'll do it with conviction and generosity and courage. And wisdom? Who knows, you may get a little of that, too, with time. To life's end most of us go feeling our way." He had talked too much, he ended coughing hurtfully and labouring for breath, sweat on his forehead. "I have received my Saviour," he said then, in a dry whisper. "I can go when I will. God bless you, boy! Kiss me, and be off about your own business. Now that I've made up my mind, I grow sick of this waiting."

Simon bent his head, and kissed him as a kinsman should. "Go with

God, my lord." He rose and left the bed. Before he reached London
that same evening he was overtaken by the news that the earl of
Chester was dead.

The same word reached Hubert, in the chapel at Brentwood, which
from a refuge had become a prison. He heard the news passed between
his guards, and spent an hour in devout prayer for so faithful an enemy
and friend. Not until he was lost was he fully known. The forty days
of grace were all but over. I will wait, he thought, until it draws to a
close, not now because I am afraid to leave this place but because I need
every moment to prepare myself for what follows. And now there is no
Ranulf to declare absolutely for law and reason. Unless the rest of my
peers stand between me and extremes, the king will have his will, and
I shall also be on my way out of this world.

Early in November, a day or two ahead of the end of his
respite, he walked out steadily from the chapel, stood blinking in the
unaccustomed light of a dim, chilly morning, and addressed the sheriff,
who had scarcely left the scene these latter days, and closed in now like
a hawk on a heron.

"Sir, I surrender myself to you, to answer whatever his Grace the
king may charge against me."

For all his submission and quietness, they loaded him with chains
before they took him away to the Tower. He had been living on Lenten
rations and less for almost a month, he was lean, haggard, and shabby,
though he had done his best to make a good appearance on issuing
forth. Hair and beard had grown long, and showed ash-grey where
before they had been only salted with silver. The flesh he had lost so
changed his appearance that they were almost startled at seeing him
again in daylight. His face was resigned and calm, only a pace short of
despair, but still short of it. He looked like a battered pilgrim in pagan
captivity, close to his goal but uncertain of ever reaching it. Some felt
compunction on beholding him. King Henry did not yet have to behold
him, and felt no compunction. There was, in any case, only one way
he could justify what he had done already, and that was to insist

implacably upon the truth of the crimes alleged against his old servant, and press the penalties to the limit.

"It has come to light," whispered Peter des Rivaulx into the king's ear, "that the man has a coffer of treasure deposited at the New Temple. Your Grace might do well to take possession of it, for certainly your own coffers must have been plundered to fill it."

"He is said to be very rich," agreed the king, brightening eagerly, "and you are surely right, these gains may well be ill-gotten. Send to the brothers of the Temple, order them to give up what they hold for de Burgh."

He had underestimated the integrity of the Templars. The master agreed that he held a coffer deposited with him for safe-keeping by the earl of Kent some considerable time ago, but flatly refused to hand it over to anyone but its owner, who had entrusted it to him, without that owner's authority. Des Rivaulx was reduced to visiting the Tower in person, and interviewing Hubert in his captivity. The treasurer was conciliatory, persuasive, almost sympathetic.

"Your trial opens in three days' time, at Cornhill, in the great hall of the house. His Grace's mind is open towards you. Every move upon your part to avoid further ill feeling may well bear good fruit. If you are accommodating in small matters . . ."

Such small matters, thought Hubert, as handing over my keys, and sending word to the Temple to let the king take what he pleases of mine. What a reputation this man gives his king! He can be bought for a few pieces of jewellery and plate! And who can tell? It may even be true. He loves such things, especially if they are exquisitely made, he might be disarmed and distracted, even if he has no intention of being bought. And of what use is wealth to me now?

"His Grace has authorized you to make promises?" he said, bitingly direct.

"No," said des Rivaulx complacently, "that he cannot do, this is matter for your peers. He can promise nothing on their behalf. But you can hardly lose by showing submission and duty to his Grace."

He gains, I neither gain nor lose, thought Hubert wearily. But if he refused, Henry would be so much the more vindictive.

"I will give you my keys," he said, "and written authority for the master to surrender the box to you. For proof the keys must suffice. I no longer have a seal."

The king, in high content, had the coffer brought to him intact, took everything in it for his own, and had an inventory of the pieces made, the items of jewellery, the pieces of silver and gilt plate. It amounted to a considerable value, but nothing to be compared with the rumours that went spinning round concerning it. Nor had Hubert, for all his acquisitions in lands, ever been a very rich man.

His attorney was allowed in to talk with him, and brought no very hopeful report of feeling among the council and those at court, but did suggest that certain of the earls had combined to produce a means of warding off the worst threat of violence and scandal. They could not prevent his arraignment, but they had argued their way to a form of agreement that the king, though he might not like it, would not dare to rule out of court. Whether out of qualms about the way the prisoner had been treated, or out of concern that the nobility should not be brought utterly into disrepute, they meant to stand between Hubert and the worst of the king's hatred. Perhaps even the surrender of his valuables might have played some part in inducing Henry, however reluctantly, to allow such a compromise.

"The Earl Marshal has been the chief mover," said Lawrence of St. Albans, "but his lordship of Cornwall has backed him steadily, and the king treads warily where his brother is concerned. There are others who have joined with them for the good name of the baronage and for their own protection in the future. It grieves me that I've been able to do no better for you, but if you are willing to take this course, this is what you should do." And he outlined a procedure, drear enough and still very far from justice or right, but delivered from the shadow of death.

So it came about that at the great council of his peers, held in the hall of the Cornhill house, on the tenth of November, when the farrago of charges against him had been read, and he was challenged to plead, Hubert made his reply in a low, drained voice, but in a silence so deep that every word was heard clearly: "My lord king, my lords peers, I make no defence. I will not plead, I do not submit to judgement. Here am I, the king's man, and in the king's hands I place myself, life and all, and to the king's will I submit, and to that only. Your Grace, do with me what pleases you."

The king left the floor to his magnates, who had plenty to say, much of it vindictive and bitter, some measured and restrained. The earls who had already fought out this field in private let every man have his say before they spoke. To Hubert it was tedious, sad, and tiring. But it ended at last.

"Since submission is complete," said the Earl Marshal, "the prisoner stands not convicted but surrendered, and if it is thought the state can be served only by his losing his liberty, then some of us, servants of the state and his peers, are willing to stand as guarantors that he shall be no danger to the state, and shall himself be maintained in close retirement. We will provide his guards from the knights of our own followings."

"In the matter of all royal offices," said the king, "these he cannot regain. All royal castles, wardships, escheats, he sacrifices."

"It is understood. But his private lands ought to be restored to him. He has not been convicted and is not a condemned felon."

The king said yes to that, because it was part of the bargain; not gladly, but not too sadly, either, even with a glint in his eye. He was by no means finished yet with Hubert and his lands.

"Then, your Grace, with your consent, the Earl Warenne, the earl of Cornwall, the earl of Lincoln, and myself will take charge of the prisoner and convey him to close imprisonment in the castle of Devizes, and provide his guards there, and they shall have sole control, without right of interference by any other person. A proper declaration can be drawn up to define the terms."

The terms were indeed defined later, in a long and wordy apologia which the king published to justify all that he had done. The contention thus arduously resolved was reflected in the whole tone of the document. Lawrence of St. Albans, who had power of attorney from Hubert to administer his remaining lands while he was a prisoner, memorized and recited to his principal the whole of it, when he was allowed a business visit.

" '. . . that his body should remain in the castle of Devizes in the custody of the earls of Cornwall, Pembroke, Warenne, and Lincoln, until he take the habit of the Templars, which now he cannot do, being married, or until he shall be liberated by the common council of the king and the barons, his keepers, and the magnates of the land. Should one of the said keepers die, those remaining shall appoint another in his place.

" 'Also the said Hubert, while prisoner, if he holds any lands unjustly, may surrender them if he so wills, even though they may be in the custody of the said keepers. And should he get out of prison in any way contrary to these provisions, then judgement shall be pronounced against him, and he shall be deemed outlaw, and all those lands left to him by the king's Grace shall be forfeit, and pass to the lords of the fees. The king declares that he will do to him no other grace or severity than the above.' "

"He is leaving himself loopholes," said Hubert, too drained to care overmuch, "through which he can draw out by degrees all that remains to me and mine. Those lands he gives me leave to surrender of my own will he means to get, whether I will or no. He is also inviting all who still have a grudge to come forward and declare that certain lands of mine belong by right to them. Well, I foresaw it when he gave way so graciously."

"But hear the proviso attached to this document: 'Grant is hereby made to the above keepers that the king shall be bound by the above provisions. And should he hereafter order anything to the violation of them, it is his will that the said keepers shall neither do nor permit to be done anything against them, and their resistance shall not be to their damage.' Cornwall and Pembroke, I think, drew this up between them. Read it how you will, they have got him to acknowledge that those four earls stand between you and the king's hatred, and whether you see them as your jailers or your protectors is but a play with words. I wish they could have done more for you."

"They have kept me man alive," said Hubert.

In his favourite small parlour at Westminster, King Henry sat over his wine after supper, and turned upon his long fingers a jewelled chain that flashed sparks from its set stones in the firelight. It had come from Hubert's coffer, and its workmanship pleased the king's sensitive taste. On the whole, he was content with his arrangements. He might have had to concede more to silence his brother, for one; after all, they had not always seen eye to eye, and the earl of Cornwall had a strong will, and an annoying ability, in most disputes, to keep his temper, which the king regarded as an unfair tactic. If he was not totally rid of his enemy now, at least Hubert was out of the way, and could remain there lifelong, which was much the same as being dead, so far as his ability to meddle in the king's affairs was concerned. This valuable and beautiful thing he dandled was worth a gesture in return.

"I am still of the opinion," said Peter des Roches, regal and upright in the chair opposite, "that your Grace should have stood firm for death. These bickering bargains do not become the crown. You might have rid the world of this upstart and felon, I do not believe your magnates would have made much resistance. A clean break would have saved much contention hereafter."

"There'll be no contention," said Henry blithely. "And we still have freedom to move against him, while he has none to lift a finger against us. Beware of alarming the peers of England, they are quick to see omens of their own fall. As for his lands, there will be claimants coming forward, and we may justly make a fine to repay the losses of those Italian incumbents who have suffered from his acts. And by the by, I think we should soon be sending an appeal to the Holy Father for absolution from our vows at Bromholm. I have let it slip, with all this business. Will you frame it for me?"

"There'll be no difficulty there," said the bishop disdainfully. "Your coronation oath is and always was in such dire conflict with this tying up of offices in life-tenures, there can be no question the oath of Bromholm was invalid. I will draw up the application, if you wish."

"And I have something else to confide to you, another charge arising out of this great case. A valuable one. I have asked de Craucombe to bring him here this evening."

The steward of the household came prompt to his hour, leading a young boy beside him, one hand on the slender, straight shoulder.

"Your Grace, here is Richard de Clare. He has been looked after here in your household since he came from Bury. You sent for him here tonight."

"So I did, Geoffrey. Come here, Richard, let me look at you." The king sat forward benignly, eyeing the slight but finely made form, the fair, curling hair, the sky-blue eyes wide and alert, the mouth and chin braced and challenging, but sensitive to every injury. They had something in common, pride easily pricked, feelings easily vulnerable; he felt he could manipulate a creature so open to wounds, and perhaps so susceptible to courting. He held out a hand, smiling, and the young thing slipped a hand under it, as to the manner born, as God knew he was, with his ancestry, and kissed it with the barest cool touch, and stood back, great-eyed, to look at him more attentively.

"You are taller than I had expected," said Henry benevolently. "Almost a man, and only ten years old still. Richard, I have thought it right to take you back into my own charge, seeing you have such a great inheritance coming to you. You are potentially a magnate of England, most precious to us."

Richard had been some days in the court circle, and lonely and neglected until Master Carrell came from Burgh to restore him a part of his world. Like himself, Master Carrell had been long enough at Burgh to move to its rhythm and feel it to be home, and his coming had clenched Richard's unhappy mind upon what was left behind, but not, please God, lost. The shock and strangeness of his abduction receded; he knew who and what he was. Best, he thought, at this stage, to say nothing at all but the timid and dutiful responses expected from him. He was only too well aware of that erect, chilly, perceptive figure in the other great chair, and of the eyes that studied him, of so light a colour that but for the shadowy sockets they would have seemed colourless, like clear glass.

"I am placing you," said the king pleasantly, "in the guardianship of the lord bishop of Winchester here. You will be in his household now, but always close to our person. And you will be obedient to him, will you not, Richard, and do whatever he orders for your instruction and your good?"

Richard said, "Yes, your Grace," submissively, though his heart shrank a little, and he shut his mind from remembering the Countess Margaret, and the family warmth of Burgh in the happy days.

"The royal escheaters will administer your estates from now on, and see that they are efficiently run."

"Yes, your Grace!" said the muted voice, wilfully childish.

"My lord, he's yours. It's late now, and you will have time to consider your dispositions for him tomorrow. Do you wish to say anything to him now?"

"Come here, boy!" said the bishop in French. He still despised English, and withheld himself so fastidiously to work his wonders through others, from the island of his own privacy, that he had no need of it. And when Richard had advanced obediently to stand before him, the light, critical eyes in the austere face looked him over from head to foot at leisure, and slowly back again to his face, with no reassuring effect. Richard bore it with impenetrable patience. He is remembering, he thought, that I was impudent to him at Winchester.

"Now that you are placed in my hands, Richard, it will be well if you forget these two years you have spent in the former justiciar's household. Look upon it as an error which has been corrected. You are to begin fitting yourself for your place among the magnates, and expunge from your mind the insidious influence of traitors and felons. It was not your fault that you were exposed to such influences, but dire contagion can attack even the innocent. I require that you will be schooled by me, now, and the schooling for such a one as you, born to greatness, must be hard, as your responsibilities will some day be immense. Do you understand what I am saying?"

"Yes, my lord!"

"You shall have new tutors. There must be a clean break. You have much to learn, all that becomes an earl. French you must master. It is not fitting that you should address me in the vernacular. You should be proficient in all clerkly skills, learn something of philosophy, of the arts, of all the graces a nobleman needs, and all the skills in arms, in venery, in falconry and the chase."

"Yes, my lord!"

"Are you ready to work hard at all this? To make yourself the most accomplished horseman of your years, to excel your peers in handling sword and lance, to become wise in books and in the craft of managing lands, ready to take your place among the king's magnates?"

"Yes, my lord!"

"Very well! Tomorrow I'll send for you. Go to your bed now, and remember the undertaking you have given me."

A disdainful hand fleetingly blessed him. A beautiful hand, long and elegant and strong, and exquisitely ringed. Richard backed from the presence, bowed low to the king, and marched out of the room with Geoffrey de Craucombe at his heels. For a moment he seethed with rage and detestation; the next he was chilled to the heart with foreboding. He had to remind himself at every step that he was Gloucester and Hertford and Clare, and unless he brought about his own fall by some desperate folly, no one, in the end, could take these honours from him. His Meggotta was countess of all these lands, and some day would again be countess of Kent, to make their joint lands the greatest in England. By which time the lord bishop of Winchester, this overbearing Peter des Roches, would be disgraced and exiled, a mere memory in this land.

Long after he had gone to his bed he lay awake, clutching the pillow to his face to stifle tears, as once in Burgh, surely longer ago than a mere two years. Yes, he vowed into the smothering softness, I will learn all that he said, and more, and better and faster than he thinks possible. Yes, I will make myself master of horse, and hound, and sword, and book, I will outdo all the rest at all manly exercises, and at studies, too. I won't rest until I excel. But not for him! For Meggotta! To make her proud of me, when we win back to each other at last, and stand up man and wife before them all!

7

March to November, 1233:
Bury St. Edmunds; Gloucester;
London; Devizes.

In the cold, hard spring of the following year, in March, when the easterly winds pared flesh from bone across the flats of East Anglia, and the high tides crept up the rivers and overflowed dune and meadow, the sheriff of Norfolk—Peter des Rivaulx's appointee, like all his colleagues, and subservient at all points to the new order that ruled England—came to the liberty of Bury St. Edmunds, and asked audience of the Lady Margaret of Scotland. The asking was not quite an order, but clearly the prompting came from the king, and it was impolitic to let pass any opportunity of knowing the king's mind. Hubert was in Devizes, prisoner never convicted and never judicially condemned, and she knew, from Archbishop Luke and from Lawrence of St. Albans, how the knights of the four guardian earls, whatever the official records said, stood stoutly between Hubert and any further onslaught. His retirement was close and probably tedious. Certainly he was deprived of all he most prized: family, work, freedom, even, so the world might say, honour. Yet he lived, after a limited fashion, at peace. He had what was needful for life, he had guards who talked with him as with another human creature, he had a measure of protective kindness. On those terms, Margaret could still wait.

But Henry's vindictiveness had not yet given up, all the more because it was beginning to be deprecated, criticized, even condemned in some quarters. The only way he could give any semblance of validity to what had already been done was by continuing along the same path with increased fury. If he could not now get at Hubert's person, he must find ways of getting at his remaining possessions. In December he had distrained eight knights' fees in the county of Salop, and given them to William de Cantilupe, handed over other lands in Lincolnshire to the abbot of Croxton, and on the seventh of February bestowed the manor of Banstead on the Templars in payment of Hubert's outstanding debt to the order; he had begun to invade even the hereditary de Burgh lands that he himself had restored at the judgement, by taking possession of seven manors, including Burgh itself, on the pretext that they were due as reparations to the wronged Italian clerics. Even in his triumph, king at last in despotic fashion, with an efficient exchequer making him rich, Henry was digging the pit into which he must at last fall. Every landowner who sees another dispossessed is visited by the dreadful vision of his own dispossession.

Yet Margaret owned to herself that she was still afraid of him. He had dangerous gifts, not of his own deserving. He was graceful and charming as a cat, he could turn and strike like a cat, sheathe his claws at will like a cat, and, like a cat, he had an inborn genius for falling on his feet. Hubert was an old, knowledgeable hound, set in his ways, uningratiating, calculable. It was an unfair duel.

"Let him in, Alice," said Margaret. "Let's hear what the sheriff of Norfolk has to say for his masters."

He was a man she had seen before, in some minor office, but she did not know him well; an uneasy soul at this moment, perhaps less happy in his masters' service than they realized.

"Madam," he said, "I am ordered by the king to bring you his Grace's word that you are at liberty to move from Bury without restriction, if you please, to any of your lord's manors which is still in his hold. His Grace does not wish to confine your movements in any way, if you care to take up residence elsewhere you will not be molested."

"The king is very gracious," said Margaret, with raised brows and a smile the sheriff did not altogether like. "And what is the price of this concession?"

"Madam, you wrong his Grace! There has been no word said of

bargaining. His Grace entertains no ill feeling against you, and intends no action against you."

But he was not comfortable in her presence, especially as his errand was but half done, and the other half came harder after what had already been said. The woman was of so commanding a presence, and even the young daughter at her side, now beginning to grow out of childhood into grace and slenderness, had the same disconcerting directness of gaze, and something of the same worn brightness about her, as of long or deep experience of suffering, mastered and transmuted into an enduring calm.

"His Grace has not yet exhausted the possibilities of action, however," said Margaret drily, "since not long ago he took even Burgh from us. On the whole, I think I prefer to stay where I am. What guarantee have I that his present mood would endure?"

The sheriff began of necessity to be voluble, since what he had to say could hardly be said bluntly, after such a welcome. But he got round to it at last. "You could help your own cause greatly, madam, if you would cease these activities of yours which justify his Grace in considering you also as an enemy. It has come to light that you are writing to various powers, letters complaining of his Grace's justice, and enlisting sympathy for your husband's cause. I speak in your own interest. It would be better not to exert yourself in this fashion. You malign the king, which is as much as touching on treason, and hardly likely to dispose his mind to leniency towards you and yours. You would be well advised to forbear."

"Indeed! Has his Grace, then, been taking measures to intercept my private letters? If not, how does he know what is in them?"

"Madam, you are determined to be unjust to him! You must know, by your own messengers, whether your letters have reached their destinations."

"Some, the most distant," she said deliberately, "have so far to travel that as yet I have not received my envoys back again. It is a long way to Rome, my lord, and the Holy Father is known to be cautious where accusations are made, and to take great pains to enquire on his own account what is truth. I did not expect early results from my letters to him. I take it that his Grace is more likely, by this time, to have had representations from my brother, the king of Scots, who is not so far away. I hope he is considering them carefully. There will certainly be others. Say so to his Grace, when you inform him that I am perfectly comfortable, and feel myself among friends, here, where I am."

There was nothing he could do, after that, but accept her scepticism, and bow himself out, though he doubted if he would report this conversation too precisely to his master.

Meggotta stood mute and still until the last echo of his footfalls was lost below, and his horse's hooves rang on the cobbles. Then she stirred, and stood listening still, in a hope to which she had already learned she must not open her heart too easily. It was a woman's voice, not a child's, that said softly, "He is trying to buy our silence. He is already frightened!"

"He is easily frightened," said Margaret grimly, "and then even more vindictive. In a panic he will do anything, hit out everywhere blindly, with any weapon that comes to hand. He has to be much more afraid before he turns coward and surrenders."

"But he will!" said Meggotta, with burning certainty.

The king had gone a-Maying, to spend Whitsuntide at Gloucester, much of the time in tents, for the weather was warm, sunny, and placid, an ideal spring. For all his new freedom, Henry was not quite such a happy man as he had expected to be; there were small anxieties nagging at his mind like summer flies, the intransigence of Margaret of Scotland, the first formal protests from King Alexander on her behalf, and also some mutterings among the nobility of England, who seemed to have awakened to the consciousness that the onslaught upon one earl could forebode similar dangers to others, even a disruptive attack upon the whole system of hierarchies within which they functioned.

"It is the Earl Marshal who is at the bottom of this reserve concerning your Grace's personal rule," said the bishop of Winchester, among the flowering orchards of the vale of Evesham, after the festival. "The man is uncertain in his loyalty and has an unfortunately wide following.

This man is your peril. He has great lands and many castles in Leinster, and never forget, de Burgh's nephew, tried and trusted or not, is a power in Ireland, and may yet be dangerous to you for his uncle's sake. How if those two should come together?"

"I have thought of it," said Henry truthfully, but without great concern. He was young, and the spring was a season for blossom and freshet and bird-song, not for glowering over dangers to his monarchy. The fruit-trees sprouted everywhere a celestial, balmy snow, and the fields of these border regions were green and moist and murmurous with lambs. He resented having to think of less pleasant things.

"And I do not trust these knights at Devizes," said Peter des Roches. "They mean well, but I fear they are lax and easy. They think all peril from de Burgh is past, and none to take his part now, but they have not looked carefully at this alliance the Earl Marshal has built up among the baronage."

"There are always malcontents breathing fire somewhere," said Henry impatiently. "I never knew a time when they were all dutiful and reconciled, but as long as they mutter aloud, and are not too many in one nest, they do very little damage. I think you exaggerate the danger, my lord."

"Your Grace is too easy. The Earl Marshal absents himself from court, and perilous men like Gilbert Basset and Richard Siward gather about him, men of considerable power and substance, and all critical of your Grace's new regime. It crowds them too close, functioning as well as it does. They lose somewhat of their freedom and licence, and grudge you the fruit. But this goes beyond personal resentment into something more sinister. Basset has been heard to declare openly that de Burgh is unjustly held, and worse, to vow that he must and shall be set free. And there are more of these recalcitrant barons and knights joining an alliance that borders on treason. Yes, treason! You would do well to be prepared for nothing less, however they hold their hand thus far. Your Grace has gone to some exertion," said the bishop emphatically, "to rid yourself of the heavy hand of de Burgh. You may well take thought to prevent having to do all again."

"I do not see," said Henry, between alarm and irritation, "what more I could have done to make the fellow secure. He is in Devizes with four earls between him and the world. What can he do?"

"He is in Devizes with four earls between your justice and him! He will never cease to be a vexation to you as long as he breathes. There are those with more freedom of action than he enjoys who will gladly make use of him. If you loose your hold of him now, you have also loosed your hold on all your gains. Never think he has lost his importance, though it manifests itself through others. You are not safe while he lives, and turbulent souls like Basset dream of setting him free."

At that stage the king, whose mind was on a pleasant assembly he was planning at his manor of Feckenham, paid only limited attention to these warnings. But he did store away the bishop's insinuations at the back of his mind, to rise like frightful dreams whenever a morsel of ill news reached him. It was at Feckenham that he received further disquieting accounts of the private assemblies in the west country, and the signs of discontent boiling up even in other quarters against Peter des Rivaulx's all-too-efficient administration. There was talk of "aliens" and of "the rule of council" allegedly shrugged off in favour of rule from the wardrobe. At Feckenham, Henry was scared into issuing extraordinary orders for the keeping of the peace, involving restrictions on free movement, on hospitality, on trade, all framed to allow rigorous enquiry into the activities of all persons in motion about England.

"Your Grace will have to take some definite action in the matter of this alliance in the west," said des Rivaulx firmly. "The Earl Marshal and his fellows are recruiting support in the name of the Charters, and having some success. And have you considered that they are holding their gatherings in Wiltshire for the most part? Basset has a manor at Compton, all too close to Devizes, and Basset has said publicly that de Burgh ought to be freed. It is no long step from the word to the act, and their meetings in those parts already have the air of a conspiracy."

"And I have said before," des Roches added severely, "that your Grace cannot rely on the present system of guard in Devizes castle. Your magnates may be in good faith—excepting, I fear, the Earl Marshal—but they are not there in person, and it's clear that their men take their duties too lightly. Carelessness and neglect may prove as damaging as treason. I wish your Grace would place the matter of the prisoner and his security in my hands. I have urged you to do so, I urge it yet again."

The king gnawed his knuckles and wavered. "I cannot displace the present guard. I am bound by the agreement." He had been bound by many agreements in his time, but none of them had proved any obstacle to his actions in the end; his brother, however, was a more formidable barrier. "But I can at least send an officer to the castle to see how things are being conducted there. That I'll do at once, and if there is any ground for complaint—"

"Your Grace might also do well to call the Earl Marshal and his allies to the great council, and keep them at your side. Since they complain that the council is being robbed of its privileges, they can scarcely make further complaint when called to attend it, and it would be better to have them under our eye, where they can do no harm, or none undetected."

"Yes, that shall also be done. See to it! A date late in June, and in the meantime we'll see how matters shape at Devizes."

The great council was called, therefore, for the twenty-fourth of June, and Henry sent three chosen knights of his own to Devizes, with orders to the guardian knights to let them in to the prisoner, and to allow a strict inspection of their precautions. He flew into a towering rage when they returned to report that they had been refused access. The king, said the earl of Cornwall's representative flatly, had vowed not to interfere in any way with their regime, and instructed the guards to prevent if he attempted interference. The declarations had been published with the judgement, and were irrevocable. He had no rights within, nor had any of his envoys, and they would not be let in.

Henry forgot both his bond and his caution, and sent a detachment of troops hot-foot to Devizes, to lay siege to the castle, let no one out or in, and admit provisions only for each day as it came. The allowance even for this was withdrawn, the knights within were forced to bear the charges themselves. He expected an early capitulation, but the four guardians and their garrison settled down grimly to maintain their position.

"Let them bide!" said the king vengefully. "They'll tire of emptying their own purses. We can wait!" But he could not wait in inaction, his anger and spite required a victim of some kind. "Send," he said, "to the sheriff of Wiltshire, and order him to seize this manor of Compton, where Basset and his fellows do their scheming. If they plan to deliver de Burgh, it shall not be done from there."

It was an expropriation without any ground in law, and a miscalculation of disastrous proportions on the king's part. It alienated many barons who certainly had no connection with the Earl Marshal's faction, and it did away with any chance that the members of that faction would place themselves within Henry's reach by attending the great council which should have taken place on 24 June. They sent word, one for all and all for one, that they refused attendance unless and until the king dismissed his present officials and advisers, and amended his arbitrary rule.

Suddenly the specious edifice of his freedom was threatening to fall to pieces round him. At Devizes the siege went on without progress, and the stubborn guardians continued stoically to resist all pressure. And in the west a faction had turned abruptly into an army, if not yet in arms.

"What do you advise?" demanded the king fretfully.

"It is customary to summon defaulters three times," said des Rivaulx, "and it would be well to observe the form now. If they surrender and make their peace, well and good. If not . . . Your Grace had thought of summoning the knight service for an expedition to Ireland, I believe."

"So I had," agreed the king impatiently, "but I have reliable reports that there's no need for it. This Richard de Burgh is loyal, and knows very well his interest lies in continuing loyal. He's showing all the more zealous because of this relationship. We need not trouble about him."

"That is true. But if your Grace summons the knight-service to Gloucester upon that pretext, at about the time the third summons to council is rejected, you will have your army very well placed in the west for another use."

"Good! Excellent!" said Henry, enlightened. "That is what we'll do."

The third summons to council appointed the first day of August, at

Westminster. A few waverers from the west obeyed it and came to make their peace, but very few. The rest of the faction gathered for yet another defiant council of their own at Gilbert Basset's other manor of Wycombe. When he had the list of those attending in his hands, the king sent out orders to the sheriffs concerned to seize all lands belonging to them, and issued at the same time the order to the knight-service of England to gather at Gloucester at the end of August, to mount an expedition to Ireland.

At Hereford he announced suddenly that he was satisfied of the safety and good order of Ireland, and swept his startled army into siege against the Earl Marshal's castle of Usk. Henry's military ambitions met with their usual reverse; after two days outside the castle it was clear even to his hopeful eye that he had no chance whatever of taking it. It was well provisioned and well garrisoned, and strong enough to tie his army down for weeks that he could not afford. He changed his tactics with his usual agility, and sent in a pacific embassy to the garrison. Where many things might be at stake, the one that must at all costs be saved was Henry's face.

He had, he said through his messenger, considered the earl's complaints and grievances, and he desired above all things to have the consent and goodwill of his baronage. If, therefore, the earl would compound with his king in a generous compromise, and make a formal surrender of Usk into the king's hand, and allow its occupation, the king would restore the castle to him within fifteen days, and gave his promise to look into all the magnates' grievances without prejudice, and study how to give them satisfaction.

Earl Richard accepted without hesitation. He had no wish whatever to fight against his king; he wanted a land ruled constitutionally according to the Charters that had become England's second Bible, the great offices of state working efficiently but subject to examination, criticism, and reform, every man maintained within the sphere of his own rights. He marched his men out of Usk and admitted the royal garrison, himself retiring voluntarily to other of his lands, to await the keeping of Henry's promises. On the eighth of September the king graciously declared himself satisfied of the earl's good faith, and sent him a friendly summons to council at Westminster.

Isabella, countess of Cornwall, was startled when one of her ladies brought in word to her, in her rooms in the earl's London palace, that her son, Richard de Clare, was asking for her in the hall, and seemed to be in a state of suppressed agitation. She had him brought in to her at once, and, after one look at his face, dismissed all her company and opened her arms to him.

"Mother"—Richard breathed on her heart, strangely torn for his distant mother in Bury St. Edmunds, whom he had thought closer kin than this one, and now found himself confusing with her—"mother, if they send after me, say you wanted me, say you sent a man for me, don't let them know I came of my own will. Don't let the bishop know! I'm afraid of him! He's so cold, he freezes my blood."

"Child," she soothed serenely, holding him close, "you're safe here with me. I'll go back with you myself. Don't be afraid! The bishop knows who I am, and who my lord is. He was not home when you came out?" The bishop's house was not so far away, the boy could run the distance in five minutes. He was still breathing short and hard when she took him in her arms.

"No! But my tutor is his man, I'm watched. He was asleep after dining. If you say you sent for me, all will be well. Mother, I had to come! Uncle Richard is in danger!"

The fair, smooth, mildly pretty face was not so empty and frivolous, after all. "Trust me! And tell me what you mean. Never doubt I love my brother, whatever men may say of him where you are."

"Mother, I overheard something I was not meant to hear. In that house I listen. They think I am quite cowed—I hope they do! My uncle is to come to Westminster, to council—is that true? But I heard des Rivaulx say to his uncle, after they had supped, and thought themselves alone—they speak French always, but I know more than they think! —he said, 'There are three brothers yet of the same getting.' And the bishop said, 'Let us be rid first of Richard the earl. Without him they are headless.' And then I had to run, because the steward came, and I heard no more. Oh, mother, what shall we do?"

"Sweet son," said Isabella, rocking him gently in her arms, "we shall make our own dispositions, as others may have made theirs. You are my own darling, never think otherwise, however I may be severed from you. And now I know how you are hemmed in, I will be one way out as often as I may, and I have weapons, too. You and I, child, will take good care of Uncle Richard. His Grace will not be rid of my brother if I know it! Wait here, now! I go to make ready." She held him off from her and smiled, leaned, and kissed him. "Wait! I'll come back."

She came, having despatched her messengers by two ways, in case the Earl Marshal should vary his route to Westminster. Richard rose to meet her with courage renewed.

"Mother, are you sure? He will be safe? He gave me my peregrine. And he gave Meggotta the little merlin."

"Yes," said Isabella gently, almost sadly, seeing the intensity and secrecy of his face when he spoke of the girl, "yes, don't be afraid, my men will find him, whichever way he rides. Uncle Richard is never going to put his head into the lion's mouth here in London. And now, my heart, I shall provide us such an escort back to your household that nobody in his right mind shall question it, not even the bishop."

Somewhere on his way to Westminster, Richard, Earl Marshal, was intercepted by the messengers of his sister, the countess of Cornwall, bringing him warning that King Henry, or at any rate the king's officers, had designs against his life or liberty should he ever come to the great council, as he intended. He took the warning, and turned back into his own west country.

From that point it was war. The king repudiated his vassal; the Earl Marshal took back his oath of fealty. This was no longer a rebellion, it was war between two sovereign lords. The earl's lands, such as lay within the king's reach, were disseised. The earl, for his part, took back Usk into his own hands briskly and easily, and leaving his accessible castles well manned and invulnerable, swept westward into South Wales, and like a hurricane, hurled all before him.

Hubert, in his enforced retirement, heard the rumours from the outside world distantly but clearly, and they had a most ominous ring. Closely confined as he was, with only one small courtyard in which to take air and exercise, he lived within the circle of decent men, under the order of the earl of Cornwall's trusted knight, who felt no animosity against him, but was simply doing the work he was appointed to do, and saw no reason why his men should not talk to their prisoner as man to man, and treat him with the common respect proper among human-kind. Thus he knew from them of the siege of Usk, and the abortive summons to council, and how war had flamed across the marcher regions of South Wales, and was soon drawing in Llewelyn of Gwynedd as a formidable ally for the Earl Marshal. They did not know, and could not tell him, why the earl had turned back and resorted to arms, but the smell of treachery was rank. Hubert was well aware that Devizes itself was also under siege, and devoutly grateful to his guards for the stout stand they had made on his behalf ever since the middle of June. But he did not believe it could continue much longer. Henry thwarted was Henry vicious and vengeful, and it was no secret that Peter des Roches was close at his elbow, prompting him to extremes.

Archbishop Luke, permitted a rare visit to his spiritual son in captiv-ity, had warned him plainly that the bishop intended, by one means or another, to get the custody of his enemy into his own hands. Easy to guess what was to follow the achievement. To announce the death in seclusion of an ageing man, past sixty and worn out with stress and grief and imprisonment, would occasion no surprise and little enquiry. The body duly returned to Margaret need bear no marks and betray no secrets.

"Hear my confession now," said Hubert, "and shrive me, for I doubt if they'll let you in to me again."

"I bid you remember," said Luke faithfully, "that despair is also a mortal sin."

"Then I confess to it, and repent it, shrive me also for that offence, and pray for me, that I may be delivered from it. I find my flesh is weak indeed," said Hubert grimly, "when I look upon my own death, not in battle, not in the course of nature, but by the malice and ingratitude of men."

Useless to protest that he had no right to his fears, for Luke knew that he had every right. Sooner or later some minor irregularity would enable the king to claim that the terms of Hubert's imprisonment had been broken, and the agreement was void, and then he would send his men in by force to take charge, and within the walls they could do whatever he commanded.

It was the earl of Cornwall who inadvertently provided the occasion. He was uneasy about the state of affairs in embattled Devizes, and withdrew his senior knight in order to get a firsthand report from him, without immediately supplying a substitute. That was enough for Henry. He proclaimed that the agreed terms were not being observed, and gave orders to his constable of Devizes to take over custody of the prisoner, remove him from his relatively pleasant quarters to a stone cell, and put him in chains, hand and foot. The knights who remained on guard over him were faced with a demand apparently legal, and resistance would have been treason, and easily swept aside by main force. Reluctantly they stood back and surrendered their charge to his fate. In cold and darkness, heavily fettered, Hubert waited for the death of which he was now certain. It had been clear within his sight for many months, now it was close as a lover and gazing steadily into his eyes, every feature clear and known, even in the darkness of his cell.

In the night he awoke from a shallow sleep to the glimmer of a candle, flickering in a draught from the open door, and started up, to see two men standing over him. He braced his feet and sprang back against the stone wall, at least to die erect, but one of the intruders hissed softly at him and put finger to lip, aghast at the rattle of the chains.

"My lord, quiet!" came in an urgent whisper. "Don't move, or we'll be heard!" And the other, without a word, softly shut the door behind them, and, setting the candle down in a crevice of the stone floor, stripped the two rough blankets from the bench that served as a bed.

Hubert knew them then; they were two of the young men who had served among his guards under the four knights, his keepers. Never had they shown him either discourtesy or violence, but rather a degree of wary sympathy.

"William. . . . What is this? What do you intend?" he asked on an almost soundless breath. "I thought my murderers were come. . . ."

"And we dread they're on their way," said William de Millers as softly. "But, please God, too late! With his help we'll get you out of here now, while we can, before they send us away and give you over to their own men."

Hubert's heart beat up into his throat like a desperate bird, netted and wild to break free. And he believed them! This was credible, even though they were taking their own lives in their hands.

"I cannot walk but in a child's stride, I'm hobbled. And if I could, I am louder than church bells. Only a smith could loose me from these. William . . . Thomas . . . think better! I may well be your death." His agitated whisper had grown into an echoing hiss. The young man laid a warning hand over his mouth.

"We'll carry you. No other way."

"Hold still, my lord," said Thomas Chamberlain, on his knees muffling Hubert's leg-chains with one of the blankets, securing the ends of the twisted mass through the links. "Now your hands. . . ." He was a big, burly young squire, powerfully muscled, a head taller than Hubert, and his burden, but for the weight of the irons, was worn away to little more than half his proper bulk. With Hubert's linked arms drawn over his head, and his own hands clamped fast on the manacled wrists, he raised his load on his back with a grunt of effort, stood braced to balance it, and was ready to move. William de Millers quenched the candle and opened the door a crack to listen. They knew their way here better than those who were being brought in to displace them.

Twice on that slow journey through the dim passages of the castle they halted and froze, drawn back into dark corners while feet trod echoingly along stone floors somewhere not far away. But they reached the narrow postern for which they were bound without incident. De Millers had the key, and locked the door carefully again after them. The night was not as dark as they would have wished, but they made what haste they could, and kept to the shadowed places under eaves as they wound their way towards the edge of the town.

"We have horses at my uncle's farm, if we can reach it," whispered William, "and there we can get these chains off you. But it's half a mile yet."

"Set me down, friend," urged Hubert, as Thomas halted to draw breath. "You cannot endure this longer. Take a rest, at least."

The young man, for all his strength, was labouring heavily, and glad to ease his aching back. "We'd best take cover in the church," William suggested, "and I'll run ahead and try to bring the horses here."

Between them they helped Hubert into the dim, cold nave of the parish church, but before William could slip away again into the night, they heard, with sinking hearts, the clatter of hooves distant behind them, towards the castle, and the blare of a horn.

"They're after us," whispered Thomas, rigid, listening to the fluctuations of the sound, as buildings loomed between and then fell away again. The hoof-beats seemed to be passing by at a little distance, certainly not along the back streets they had followed. "They haven't hit our trail. If they move farther off, we may get safe out of here yet."

But the blast of the horn, repeated and repeated, had blocked every way within minutes, for half the town was up and leaning out to see what this alarm could mean, and word of the escape and the hunt was being tossed from door to door, and all the busybodies of Devizes were clambering into their clothes to join the chase. In the darkness of the church, where the single red eye of a small lamp glowed on the altar, Hubert looked at his rescuers, and they at him, steadily and with little hope.

"Young men," said Hubert, "I doubt if these townsfolk know you well by sight. Take your chance and slip out into the streets with them, two more can be lost among all those I hear howling. Make your escape now, while you can. What you tried to do for me was noble, and I thank you, but now you can do no more. It would ease me if you were clear away. One of us is enough to go back into prison. Go and reach those horses of yours, and make good use of them."

As one man they shook their heads. "No!" said William. "We set our hands to it, and we'll either finish it or pay for it. We'll not leave you. If we can break out, we will. If not, we're at least in sanctuary here."

"I have had some sour experience of sanctuary," said Hubert. "I urge you to go and leave me here. What use is it to throw your lives after mine?"

"Very little," agreed Thomas, "but that I should prize it even less if I abandoned you now. But indeed I think we have none of us much chance of breaking out of this snare."

He was a true prophet. All night long there were hunters in the streets, or gossips even if the hunters moved away, and there was never a moment when they might have got their crippled charge away into fresh cover unseen. It was a marvel that it took so long for someone to hit on the idea of looking in the church. Daylight was already brightening the dark interior, and it was almost time for the first Mass, when a woman peered in and saw them, and let out a screech of triumph that brought others running.

"Stand close now," said Hubert, drawing them to the altar, "and lay hand all three upon the cross." But he knew all too well that history had wheeled about in a circle, as though he were condemned to live, over and over for his whole lifetime remaining, the horrible months between Brentwood and Devizes. They would not have to look for a smith, this time; that had been his own need. But for that, and the disaster he had brought upon these two generous and gallant young men, this adventure looked sickeningly like the former. "Pardon, gentlemen," he said with weary bitterness, "that I have done this to you."

The door of the church was hurled wide, and half-armed men came bursting in with swords drawn. Their only hesitation was to blink their way into clear vision after the brightness outside. Half a dozen rushed at the three men clinging to the altar cross, three or four more bounded after them, to bring down the quarry heavily on the tiled floor, and send the cross clattering and bounding into a corner. The lamp was flung down and broken. The prisoners were dragged out by hair, arms, feet, whatever came handiest, William bleeding from a sword-cut across his cheek, Thomas half stunned by his fall. Hubert, since his feet were too closely manacled to allow him to walk except with an infant's tiny steps, was dragged along the road towards the castle on his back. All three, soiled, battered, and bruised, were flung into separate cells below ground, and the constable, satisfied with his performance and thankful that he had not more unwelcome news to send to the king, despatched a messenger to the court at Oxford to report the whole occurrence, with emphasis on its successful close. King Henry saw no more wrong with the arrest than did the constable, and was even gratified at having the opportunity to condemn Hubert to even more stringent punishment. Back came the order that he was now to be chained constantly to three pairs of iron rings fitted in his vault, and apart from supplying him with the food necessary to life, no man was to go near him, certainly none who had known him under the former rule, and none, even of his new guards, was to speak to him. Though he breathed and lived, at least as yet, from this day Hubert was to be as a dead man out of mind.

In the course of King Henry's life, history was more than usually given to repeating itself, since he seldom learned from his mistakes. It was as great a shock to him as on the former occasion when he was suddenly confronted, some ten days after the escape and recapture, by a very angry cleric, eyes flashing and voice thunderous, denouncing the blasphemous breach of sanctuary at Devizes, and demanding that it should be atoned for at once. Robert Bingham, bishop of Salisbury, had not wasted the days between. He had gone first to the constable and his men on guard at the castle, and made the same demands upon them. When they replied, from their point of view reasonably enough, that they would rather see Hubert hanged than hang themselves, and refused to restore the fugitives to their violated sanctuary, the bishop excommunicated them on the spot, and set off to follow the court, which by then was back in London. And before bearding the king, he had secured the support of Bishop Roger Niger, of London, and several others, to strengthen his hand.

Sulkily Henry gave in. This time he was not even able to pretend that he had been ignorant of the breach of sanctuary, since it had been reported to him in full and was known to have given him great satisfaction. It galled him sadly to have to send orders to Devizes to replace the three offenders in the parish church and allow them their forty days of grace, but he consoled himself by issuing even more strict orders that the sheriff of Wiltshire should surround and guard the place day and night until they had used up their respite and could be starved out.

They were brought out of their underground cells on the nineteenth of October, St. Luke's day, and put back into the church almost as roughly as they had been snatched out of it, but at least detached from their manacles, since those were bolted to the stonework. All of them bore the broken wounds of irons round wrist and ankle, and certain bruises from blows and harsh handling, for the garrison had been terrified of penalties when they lost them, and had exacted payment accordingly. At least the young men were in fine physical condition, with only this brief ordeal to damage them, but Hubert was worn and frail and broken by long excesses of hope, despair, and ill usage, his spirit brought into a limbo of resignation by the injustice and ingratitude of his disgrace. His bleeding wrists and ankles would not heal, his skin seemed so thin and tender that a touch brought out black bruises. Also, it was mid-October, and the king's obedience to clerical censure did not run to warm clothing or blankets, or any means of heating, and the food was minimal. By one means or another, the king meant to exact the full penalty this time.

Nevertheless, there were things about that penance in the church of St. John that Hubert remembered afterwards as warming drops of the grace of God. First, the two young men, of irrepressible spirit and ever more obstinate kindness, in very good conceit with themselves because they had stood by a fellow-creature to their own hurt, and never repented it. It gave them a kind of elation in their misfortune, which reflected back upon Hubert in strange comfort, for he was the unwitting instrument of their content. And then there was the parish priest, who came and went perhaps more often than he need have done, made them welcome in all the services, and, if he did not bless them, was himself a kind of blessing.

"Well, I'm learning many things," said Thomas sturdily, "not least how to live from day to day, and be glad to have even forty of them in hand. Forty days is enough to change the world."

"And I," said Hubert, "to be most grateful for human goodness where I find it. More—and more often, I doubt—than I deserve." But he did not say that he hoped for a changed world, for his world, these last years, had changed only for the worse. He wished he need not have involved these two stalwart souls in his ruin, but at least they were young, and after his death might escape into better favour, and better promise. He no longer had heart to regret his own losses; his greatness was gone beyond recovery, for even if honour and title were restored to him now, they would taste only of ashes.

The days passed, one like another, with all their difficulties, limitations, and laboured courtesies. Learning to live day and night within the pale of a holy church is a leavening art, requiring great consideration between man and man, and a great and apologetic reverence towards the sheltering roof. They were making great strides towards mastering it by the last days of October.

The nightly quiet that closed down with darkness usually passed unbroken. Their sentries dared not sleep, but at least preferred to make themselves as comfortable as they could, leaving but one or two to stand absolute guard. So it came as a shocking change when the midnight was suddenly split by a horn-call from the east, followed by the receding clatter of hooves and clashing of weapons. The three prisoners started up from light and uneasy sleep to listen, and heard the guards from the west door rushing to pursue the sound, some afoot, two officers mounted. Somewhere there in the streets to the east there was the continued clamour of struggle and flight, swords clanging and a horse bellowing indignation.

"In God's name," said Thomas, "what are they at now? Has someone risked his own head to try and reach us? Or are they tired of waiting for us to come out, and bent on fetching us a second time?"

The west door was suddenly flung wide, and armour gleamed in the faint red glow from the altar, outlining a big man in light mail, with two or three others looming at his shoulders.

"Would you break sanctuary yet again?" said Hubert, advancing clear of his companions.

"God forbid!" said a deep, hearty voice. "We are not come to haul you out of your refuge, my lord, only reverently to bid you come forth with us, all three, if you want your freedom. Ride now, question after! We have horses for all, here at the door, and by the time my lads have led the sheriff's men twice round the streets of Devizes, and got clean out again, we can be some miles west of here."

"Dear God, is this true?" asked Hubert, trembling. "I cannot see you well, but I should know your voice, surely. You would not torture me with hope only to hurl me back into hell, would you?"

"No, faith, it's not hell we're bound for, but Severnside. If you want my name, it's Gilbert Basset of Compton, and Richard Siward is outside with the horses. Before noon tomorrow, if you stir quickly now, we can be at the ferry at Aust, and tomorrow night you shall sleep, free men the three of you, and welcome, in the Earl Marshal's castle of Chepstow."

8

November, 1233, to May, 1234:

Westminster; Bury;

Woodstock; Gloucester.

*K*ing Henry might rage as he would, deal out penalties and reproaches left and right, turn his sheriff of Wiltshire loose on the possessions of every man who could be implicated, declare rescued and rescuers alike outlaw—which in fact he had only very dubious right to do, they never having been convicted at law—and seize every manor they had left within his reach, but nothing provided him consolation for this humiliating defeat. De Burgh was clean gone, safe over the Severn in Chepstow, the two daring squires gone with him, and doubtless thumbing their noses from the ramparts at all the power of England.

Nor were things going well with the king in other ways. The war he had provoked was proving disastrous to his prestige. The Earl Marshal had rapidly possessed himself of most of South Wales, while Llewelyn of Gwynedd had joined forces with him and swept irresistibly south to burn Brecon, and roam the middle march at will. Henry's reputation as a soldier had never even begun to establish itself, now it was a byword and a laughing-stock. And worse, there were increasingly influential voices beginning to be raised, questioning the wisdom and legality of his present rule. The bishops were the worst, which was all the more scandalous, since a bishop, the most travelled and distinguished of his kind, was the key-stone upon which the arch of that rule reposed. Even in the summer, one notable Dominican brother, of an eminence to discourage all reprisals, had declared openly that peace was impossible while the bishop of Winchester retained his supreme power. Other voices were taking up the same theme, cleric and lay magnates uniting with unusual warmth. And after a long interregnum, at last a new archbishop of Canterbury had been chosen in succession to Grant, and he was none other than that Edmund Rich of Abingdon who had been treasurer of Salisbury, and spiritual adviser to Cecily de Sanford, the Countess Eleanor's confidante, the man who had led both of those strong-minded women to take vows of chastity and wed themselves to Christ. And this Edmund Rich was known to be the close friend and associate of that same imperious Dominican who had attacked the influence of Peter des Roches.

Worst of all, Henry had received a strongly worded letter from Pope Gregory, written at Agnani on the seventeenth of October, deprecating the harsh treatment of Hubert de Burgh, and urging more compassionate usage. The Holy Father appeared to have forgotten those offences Henry had urged against Hubert, wrongs done to the Italian clerics nominated to English offices. Was it possible that he did not believe in Hubert's guilt? Somewhere in this coil was also the influence of Alexander of Scotland, indignant for his sister and her husband.

Henry felt himself enwound in numberless gossamer threads, glutinous and horrifying, that coiled about him like a spider's web, every strand fragile as breath, but the entire lacy membrane unbreakable and deadly.

A miserable Christmas he spent at Gloucester, and the company of the bishop of Winchester no longer gave him the exhilaration and courage he had once derived from it. All very well for Peter des Roches, his interests reached across Europe, across Christendom, he could as well exercise his talents in Jerusalem as in London, in Rome as in Normandy. Kings have no such freedom.

It was well to bear in mind, also, that this Peter des Roches had in his household and wardship the most valuable of all the heirs at present under age in England. Henry had seen the boy de Clare about the court several times, a handsome boy and, they said, advanced at his books, as well as very promising in arms. He had already been taken away from one undesirable guardian, better keep an eye even upon this present one. The child was doubly an earl. There are not many such matches.

Christmas had its lustre again for Meggotta. The harsh December shone like spring, the withering wind she bore as gladly as kisses. Alice sang about her work, and Margaret sat eased and smiling and languid to death after so long a time of tension and suspense. For Hubert was away across the Severn, in Chepstow, a free man, among friends who had gone to great pains and risk for him, and brought him off safely at last into an impregnable fortress, where he could rest and be healed. A strange thought, that in the beginning he had had nothing in common with the Earl Marshal except distrust and anxiety concerning the Poitevin grasp upon government; their followings had been as separate and irreconcilable as oil and water, no contact ever offered or accepted. Time and circumstance, without help from them upon either part, had drawn their two causes together, and made them allies even while the one was out of fealty and at war, and the other a disgraced prisoner cast aside by an ungrateful king.

"Father has an army on his side now," Meggotta told the immense pale-grey eastern sky over her, and the flakes of snow that melted on her lips, "and a party at his back, and no enemy can touch him. Now he need never put himself in the king's power until this war ends, as they say it must end, for all the earls and all the bishops—except one! —say that it cannot be resolved except by reconciliation, and the king must give ground, as the king has been at fault. And when they make peace, they will stand by my father, and see to it that peace is made also for him. This is only the beginning, I know, but it has begun! It has begun!"

She had thanked God devoutly and constantly, at every festival-service since the news came. She had prayed rapturously for Richard, Earl Marshal, for Gilbert Basset, the firebrand of Compton, for Richard Siward, his ally, for the two young squires who had risked their own lives and liberty, for all the garrison of Chepstow, where the household did honour to her father still as justiciar and earl of Kent. And for Richard, most passionately of all for Richard, as much a prisoner in that terrible bishop's household as her father had been in Devizes. Never had she ceased to think of him, and embrace him in the secret places of her heart. Now it seemed to her that the day of her second marriage had drawn nearer, she felt its promise like warmth all about her, and walked immune through the frost. For the thaw was surely beginning. Her father's escape was more than a mere escape; it was the first warning crackle of shattering ice. Meggotta's heart sang louder than the heartfelt singing of the brothers, and her eyes shone brighter than the festival-lamps about St. Edmund's shrine.

"Daughter," said the abbot, meeting her as she crossed the cloister, "you are like a lighted candle in a dark place, a joy to see."

In the last year he had grown frailer and greyer, and went lamely with the twinges of age, and the eleven-year-old girl, slight and springy as a willow sapling, came up to his shrunken shoulder. She looked more than her age, and wiser. He did not repent of what he had done for her and her bridegroom. She was becoming translucent and radiant, like fine stained glass, delicately coloured. Immurement here within his walls had paled her to pearly refinement. In a little while she would be beautiful, very beautiful.

I must make some record, he thought, of what was done here with my blessing, in case it may be needed if I am gone. But not yet. We have no proof yet what is to happen, which way this matter of England is to go. To write down any word until the time is ripe would be to endanger many innocent souls. Wait awhile yet, and keep the secret within the original circle. It's safer so.

It was nearing the middle of February then, and everyone knew that the king's armies were helpless along the Welsh march, that from north to south the Earl Marshal and Prince Llewelyn did as they pleased; even Shrewsbury had fallen, outpost of England now ravaged and abandoned disdainfully in a scarred and plundered countryside. The king's fortunes were low indeed, and certainly there was no way of amending them in arms. He had but one advantage: that the Earl Marshal had never sought this war, and wanted nothing more than to end it with honour and reconciliation, though never by surrender. After the sacking of Shrewsbury, so rumour said, King Henry had run frantic with rage, and vowed he would never receive the Earl Marshal until he came as a surrendered traitor with a rope round his neck, in total submission. But when his temper cooled, he himself knew, and there were now many saner voices ready to tell him, that he had no choice, that he would have to make concessions and abate his demands if he wanted to end a war he could not win.

At the great council held at Westminster on the fourth of February, when Archbishop Edmund Rich had received the royal confirmation of his election, there had been some high words spoken, and the whole concourse of bishops had supported their new head in insisting on the necessity of reuniting the nobility of England. If that could be done only by a drastic reappraisal of the king's policies, and above all his relationships with his ministers, then he must face the fact, and set about a grand reassessment and a return to the Charters. And the king had swallowed his chagrin meekly, and accepted the archbishop's guidance, promising serious thought on the matter, and pleading for time for meditation and prayer. That was the last news that had found its way to Bury.

Meggotta walked back towards the house in the close, where she had lived now for the better part of two years. There was always a bustle in and out of the gatehouse, and she did not at first pay too much attention to the group that was just riding in, until she noticed how the grooms ran in haste to receive them and tend their horses, and was dazzled by the richness and brilliance of their dress and harness. Four were clearly magnates, and the number of their attendants made clear that they were of very high rank. At her own doorway Meggotta halted to study them, curious about such imposing visitors.

The austere, clerkly gentleman in black she did not know, nor the florid, well-fleshed man with the square-trimmed beard, the kind of beard men cultivate to disguise an irresolute and unsatisfactory chin. She had never until now seen Peter des Rivaulx or Stephen Segrave, and their coming meant nothing to her. But the third, tall and princely, she recognized at once. It would not be easy to forget the handsome, aquiline face of Peter des Roches, bishop of Winchester. And the fourth of the party . . . Meggotta stared, incredulous, slow to realize that the four of them had turned in her direction, and were advancing towards the doorway where she stood.

She turned and darted into the house and up the staircase to Margaret's room.

"Mother, mother . . . quickly! The king is here! He has the bishop of Winchester with him. I think they're coming here!"

Margaret sprang up from the table where she had been writing one more letter to her brother in Scotland, and Alice came running from the next room, where there was a window that overlooked the court. "It's true, my lady, there are four of them, making for our door. But who, that I can't see clearly. . . ."

"It *is* the king," said Meggotta, eyeing her mother's face between apprehension and hope.

"What can he want with me? And Winchester in his company?" Margaret drew her dark brows together. "Have they thought of some new devilry? No, he'd never come himself, he has others he can use for that. Or is he come courting, in defence of his own face? Has it gone so far already?" She stood listening, and the light tread of feet and the approaching murmur of voices came clearly up the stairs. "I'll go down myself to meet him. Bring wine, Alice! I doubt if he'll stay long." Face to face with her, if he had indeed brought himself to face her at all, he would be very tender of his dignity, while seeming to be tender of hers. But he would not wish to have this first encounter prolonged. Later, perhaps, when he had made the necessary adjustments, and exercised his usual faculty of forgetting what he wished to forget, he might enjoy being gracious and patronizing to this royal woman he might have married. But not today!

She was standing framed in the doorway when Segrave hastened his step to go ahead of his lord as herald.

"Madam, the king is travelling in these parts, and comes to assure himself of your welfare. If the visit is not inconvenient to you . . ."

"His Grace does my cramped domain great honour," said Margaret, and made her dignified obeisance at Henry's feet. "Will it please you come in, my lord?" She retained the hand he had extended to her in greeting, and led him in and up the staircase, and brought him ceremoniously to the great chair, herself withdrawing to the chair beside the table, where her half-written letter to Alexander stared him in the face. His retinue followed him in, filling the room with the overwhelming aura of power, for these were the inmost circle of government, here startlingly compressed into this small chamber where she had chosen to confine herself for nearly two years, rather than trust in any mercy from them.

"Madam, I rejoice at seeing you in good health," said Henry. "And this is your daughter?" Meggotta came timidly, bringing his wine, and made her reverence with downcast eyes. "How she is grown!" He was not aware, in fact, of ever having noticed the girl before; she was no more than a name, a pawn in an old agreement, now fortunately dissolved.

"Madam, we have been grieved at seeing you confine yourself so closely here, when, as you'll recall, we have already made it clear some time ago that you are at liberty to take up residence in any of your remaining manors. You are our kinswoman, your condition touches us nearly, we mean to ensure that you shall have proper maintenance for your estate."

"We have been hospitably entertained here in Bury," said Margaret mildly, "and have no complaints about our welcome. We could not have wished for kinder hosts."

"That may well be, but still we have decided to transfer to you eight of your husband's former manors, to maintain you as is fitting. You may move to any one of them whenever you please." He named them, almost self-righteously; they included Newton and Sotherton in her beloved East Anglia, and above all, and kept till last, Burgh itself. She hated him most of all for that deprivation, and despised him most of all for this gracious restoration, for which he even seemed to expect thanks. He gave Burgh back to de Burgh, and considered he should be praised for it!

"Your Grace is most considerate," said Margaret, her voice placid ice, most treacherous of all to the foot, inviting to humiliating falls.

"Title reverts to you at once. I have already had the charters drawn up, they shall be delivered to you."

"At your Grace's convenience. There is no haste, I have almost turned recluse here. And how comes it that your Grace is travelling in this part of the world, and at this season? Our easterly winds are not kind to travellers."

"I have undertaken a pilgrimage through the shrines of this country-side," said Henry. "I and my ministers have been too much beset with England's business," he went on, with proper compassion for his own overburdened shoulders. "We have great need of a quiet interlude, to take counsel with the saints."

"I have been glad of their protection, also," she said with bitter significance; this very conference took place within the shielding shadow of St. Edmund, who had given her asylum from this man's venom. Whoever forgave him, and for whatever offences, Margaret did not forgive. "Is it your Grace's intention to sleep overnight here in Bury? Where do you go from here?"

"No, we shall lie at Wymondham tonight, it is an easy stage from here. We are on our way to Bromholm, which is particularly dear to us."

"Ah, to Bromholm!" echoed Margaret softly. "If we had received today's favours earlier, we should have been happy to offer you the hospitality of Burgh. Your Grace will recall how convenient it is to Bromholm."

The king maintained an impervious front, relieved, if anything, that she obviously had no intention of asking him anything concerning Hubert. "Afterwards we shall go on to Walsingham, Castle Acre, Ramsey, perhaps Peterborough. And if we are to reach Wymondham priory by daylight, we should be setting out at once." He rose, and his silent companions accepted the signal and rose with him. "Madam, I entreat you will approach us if you have any needs that we can supply. I do not forget what is due to Margaret of Scotland."

No, she thought, you did not forget what is due to me when you issued orders that if I set foot out of this liberty, I should be seized and taken to join Hubert in the Tower. Or do you think that never came to my ears?

"Your Grace's visit, however brief, has greatly consoled and encouraged me," she said at parting, and went down with them to the court to watch them mount and ride, Meggotta silent at her shoulder. All the brilliant colours and glittering harness cantered away out of the gates.

"And that was no lie," said Margaret, when they had vanished, "for he has told me more than he supposes, and all of it good. Eight manors that he took from my lord to give to the Italians in compensation, and now he snatches them back and restores them to me! A little grain to lure the chickens before he wrings their necks? So it might have been, but I think not! No, he is making his surrender by inches, giving graciously what he knows he'll be forced to give ungraciously if he waits longer. At all costs he'll keep his face, but the costs will be paid by someone else. And not by us! Not this time!"

"No, not by us," said Meggotta. "He is taking the bishop and his nephew to Bromholm." She had understood more than Margaret had expected, or perhaps intended.

"Yes, again Bromholm. And we know, do we not, why he takes his officers of state to witness his devotions at the rood of Bromholm: to lull their fears and give himself the cover of sanctity, while he lays his plans to discard them."

Henry and his sacrificial lambs pursued their pilgrimage round the holy places of eastern England, and returned by the end of the month to London, to take counsel with the archbishop and work out some sort of formula for general peace. At the council of the ninth of April, which fell a week after Archbishop Edmund's consecration, Henry renewed his promise to reform his administration and dismiss his present councillors and ministers, and the archbishop in return promised to take charge of the peace negotiations. Firstly with Llewelyn, since he was accessible; Earl Richard, it seemed, was less so, for in February, finding all his possessions in England and Wales safe enough, he had set sail for Ireland, where some of his castles had been unlawfully seized. The first approaches for peace pursued him there, and until he had come to fair terms in Ireland, it would be impossible to concentrate his mind upon terms of peace in England. By late March letters were being exchanged even with Hubert and the garrison of Chepstow, for clearly any permanent peace entailed the proper restoration of the earl of Kent. None of those allies would make a separate peace. Llewelyn in Wales firmly refused any settlement until fair terms were also extended to his friends.

A further meeting of the great council was to take place in May at Gloucester, and if negotiations continued favourably, it seemed possible that Hubert and his fellow-outlaws would receive safe-conducts to come and meet King Henry there in a grand reconciliation. True, Henry never let go very generously of lands, wealth, or honours, and there were still a great many details to be settled, such as whether the earldom of Kent should be restored, or regarded as never having been lawfully stripped from him, whether he should be granted the status of a royal councillor again, and many other matters; but that he should be received again into all the liberties of an English magnate, cleared of disgrace, was now taken for granted. The general peace demanded it.

The king was almost reconciled to his about-face by the time he arrived at Woodstock on his way to Gloucester for the council. On the whole, he was content with his own performance. It was his intention that des Rivaulx and his fellows should be allowed to slip out of office and out of the public eye without scandal. He had contrived to increase the distance between himself and those he had to jettison, and to achieve a growing coolness in the air between them, by such subtle degrees that a process almost as sudden as a thunderstorm had been made to appear gradual and logical. At Woodstock he instructed Peter des Rivaulx to prepare a full accounting of all his receipts, within the royal household and elsewhere, and reminded the bishop of Winchester benignly that the three-year truce he had so helpfully arranged with France was now drawing to a close, and it might be well if he made ready to travel to that country should his offices be required in renewing it. Then he went on to reply with cautious encouragement to the latest form of terms suggested by Hubert and the Chepstow garrison. Things were going as well as he could hope, in the circumstances. He could always extricate himself from any residual blame by turning on his associates.

It was at Woodstock, only a day later, that a courier from Ireland, long delayed by troubles ashore and gales at sea, reached him. The messenger was a knight in the service of the justiciar of Ireland, Maurice Fitzgerald. His news, nearly four weeks old, came like a thunderbolt, throwing all the plans for peace into confusion.

"My lord king, the Earl Marshal, Richard, earl of Pembroke, is dead!"

"Dead?" echoed the king in a voice hollow and small, and sat struggling with a turmoil of emotions swinging between perverse but horrified triumph and appalled dismay. Grief came a little later, whether for himself, or the Earl Marshal, or the plight of England, or the whole inexorable destiny of man, which cuts off the great at their height, there was no telling. Those who were present had little doubt that the shock was genuine and deep. Young men in positions of power do not like to be reminded that the young and powerful can also be cut off in an instant, without pity. "How can he be dead? We have had no word of any fighting, surely before now they should have been talking truce. In God's name, what has happened over there?"

"Sir, it was indeed truce they should have been talking, but it fell out very ill. Your Grace's officers there made use of the Knights Templars to send word to the earl to meet them on the Curragh, on the first day of April, to arrange a truce. And what happened I cannot say of my own knowledge, for I was not there, but as I am bidden to tell it, it was thus. Both sides came with some force, but your Grace's men had much the superiority in numbers. They say that the earl demanded the restoration of such of his castles as he had not yet recovered, before he would discuss truce, but Fitzgerald refused this, saying that no such restoration was due merely for the purposes of truce, but could only arise in the terms of final peace. Then the earl refused to deal further unless his condition was granted, and would have withdrawn, and I do not know how it began, but he was surrounded, and it ended in a bitter fight, and the earl was badly wounded and made prisoner. There are some say he himself never laid hand to sword, but was set upon by several at once, without warning."

"But how could it happen?" The king wrung at the unbelievable disaster with plying fingers and contorted face. "They knew that we had opened negotiations here with the prince of Gwynedd, that we were in quest of peace. How could they so mismanage affairs as to let this thing turn bad? And this was the beginning of April? Why have we not had word before?"

"Sir, it was not thought at first that he would die of it. He did rally, but then his wound rankled, and things went very ill, and on the sixteenth day he died. I put out twice from Ireland, and twice we were driven back, the winds ran so high. I have made all the haste I could."

"You shall go back," said the king, quivering, "with better haste. I want Fitzgerald here in person, I want to hear his story, and take counsel with him over Ireland. Get back there and bid him come to Gloucester, where we are bound, with all the speed he can make, for this may have ended a war in Ireland, but it will surely prolong one here if we do not act quickly. God knows what ugly things may be said concerning this piece of work!"

He shut himself up with his thoughts until they were clearer, unwilling to face Archbishop Edmund with the news until he must. Llewelyn would recoil from making peace until all his friends were protected, and might well require a strict accounting concerning the Earl Marshal's death. All the earl's allies, the Basset clan and their fellows, would be enraged, and perhaps refuse to come to terms, for there would surely be strong suspicions of treachery. Siward was still in arms in the south, ranging much as he pleased. Everything was again falling to pieces, unless he could hold things together still. He needed the archbishop. He could not worm his way out of this alone. And, most strangely of all, he was suddenly seized with a genuine passion of grief for a fine, stubborn, difficult man who had troubled his peace, but in whom he could find nothing mean or evil, someone who might have been a tower of strength to him if they could have come to terms now. Briefly and privately, King Henry wept for his enemy.

The rumours began, and were ugly enough; that he had expected. He did what he could to allay any doubts of his own good faith in pursuit of peace by issuing safe-conducts for Hubert, Gilbert Basset, Siward, and all the rest, to come to Gloucester and be received with gestures of reconciliation. There was also the vexatious matter of the succession to the earldom of Pembroke. Gilbert Marshal had been close in his brother's confidence. Henry had carried the war quite justifiably into Ireland, if only the ending had not been so foul, and that he had not intended. He toyed with the notion of withholding from the heir seisin of certain of his Irish properties, but in the end gave up the idea, and acknowledged Gilbert as earl of all his brother's lands. Such a gesture was needed, he could not afford to neglect anything that would calm the fears and remove the suspicions of his opponents.

One more thing he could do that might be recorded to him as merit. He sent safe-conducts to Bury St. Edmunds for Margaret and her daughter, to come to Gloucester for the great reunion. His own difficulties now were different ones, which did not stem from de Burgh, and his feeling towards the old man had changed; it was as though he looked at a harmless stranger, irrelevant in present circumstances. He wondered at his own previous fury against this diminished figure. He even came within viewing distance of being ashamed, but never closer than that.

Henry had a special affection for Gloucester, where he had been crowned as a threatened and innocent child. He loved the abbey of St. Peter and its great church, the beauty of the cloister and the spacious guest-house, given over entirely to his use whenever he cared to stay there. At Greyfriars, Blackfriars, and St. Oswald's priory there were ample lodgings for all who came. He would ensure a lodging for the de Burgh family close to himself. Gradually he was learning to consider trifles, and study how to others they might not look trifling.

He had worked hard and selflessly on this occasion. It was unfair, it was cruel, that in the assembly of the great council he should suddenly find himself confronted, before all those judging eyes and critical minds, by Edmund of Abingdon, erect and stark, that austere, kindly man unaccountably hardened into stone, and holding out before him a handful of leaves of vellum. By their closed and unapproachable faces, several of his bishops already knew whatever it was he knew, and the king did not. Henry shrank, dismayed. He had never seen Edmund Rich thus distanced, like a judge looking down upon some felon in his court. The kind eyes were all accusation and pain.

"My lord king," said the archbishop heavily, "I hold here in my hand certain letters and charters sent under the royal seal, to the justiciar and the barons of Ireland. I have been much troubled in mind over this tragedy, and have questioned wherever I might. Does your Grace know the content of these letters?"

"I never sent any," said Henry from a dry throat, in a voice barely audible beyond the first rank of those peers close about him, "but to urge the fair defence of our cause, there as elsewhere. We were at war, I had, as my enemy had, the rights and privileges of war. I give you my word I did not exceed them."

"Yet, my lord king, these letters and authorizations that I hold, which you may read at will, urge the justiciar and the barons of Ireland to take measures, at all costs, to ensure the Earl Marshal's death. They give the widest authority, no matter what the means. And they promise a fair distribution of the Earl Marshal's lands in Ireland to those who comply with the order. Here, your Grace, I deliver you these instruments, that you may confirm for yourself the purport and the seal. Is it yours?"

He held it in his hands, and he knew it. It was his. The royal seal cried out against him, struck him silent for long moments while he laboured for breath and words, for the defence of his soul and his honour. For one moment he felt his multiple dishonour, achieved by a hundred minor stratagems in a hundred minor arguments, all unworthy, but not, as this would have been, eternal damnation. He knew he was innocent, but could not feel that he was, having so leaned and manipulated in other matters.

"My lord archbishop," he said, articulating with effort and pain, "I swear before God I never sent any such orders, nor knew that they went out from any office of mine. I did not connive at the Earl Marshal's death. I did not desire it of any man of mine."

"Yet your Grace does not dispute the seal?"

He could not dispute the seal, it stared him in the eye.

"I own," he said brokenly, like a child rehearsing a lesson learned very hard, "I have not been as scrupulous as I should with the management of my seal. I have let it be used. . . . I have trusted, and have not read. . . . I had officers whose word I accepted as to what they did with my name!" He reared up abruptly, taller than his proper stature, as though a hand from above had seized and stretched him aloft. His face was pale and translucent as ice, and his eyes burned in it like reflected light upon glass. He was looking round almost blindly for those who had had the use of his trust, fool as he had been, and most of all for Peter des Rivaulx.

"Villains! Traitors! Serpents! What have you done to me? How dared you misuse my trust so vilely, and make me unwitting partner in your wickedness?" He was trembling violently, in a rage all the more frantic because he knew he was himself to blame.

Des Rivaulx, always close about his master for his own reasons, had come to this council quite unaware of any threatening exposure, and had never before seen the king's rage at its height turned against any but Hubert. He stood dumbstruck, as Hubert had stood when the lightning flashed out as suddenly at him, two years earlier. He saw the king's hand drop to the dagger at his hip, and drew hastily, stumblingly, back out of reach, but the archbishop laid a restraining hand on Henry's wrist.

"My lord king, this is matter for law, and not for your own hands. You yourself have much to answer for, to God if not to man, if you have let your seal be set to articles you have not even read."

"I acknowledge it! I am at fault! But murderer and betrayer I am not, as God sees me. And matter for law it is indeed, and law they shall have, every man who has part in this treacherous slaying. But law is slow-moving, and am I to endure the presence of false, foul servants about me while its mills grind? No! You yourself have urged that I should cleanse my house, I lay claim to your support now that I am driven to do it thus drastically. I will have the poisoned flesh cut out now, I will not see the faces of my betrayers again but at the bar of justice." He had himself in hand now, white and incandescent with passion as he was. He whirled upon his justiciar, whose ruddy face had turned to the grey of stale dough. "You, Segrave, you I name! What is there goes on in my administration that you do not know? Hand in glove with those who have misled and perverted me, caused me to turn on some who were honest servants, and outlaw some who were true men to me! You are dismissed my service, you are my justiciar no longer. And you, Passelew, I do not hold you guiltless, you have been in the closest confidence of these two. You shall not be officer of mine a day longer."

Segrave, falteringly, made an attempt to speak in his own justification, but the king silenced him with a cry of rage, and turned upon Peter des Rivaulx.

"And you, sir, what can be said of you, whom I most trusted, upon the lord bishop's recommendation? You, in whom I found great gifts, and relied on you as my right hand. You have duped me, made use of me to your own tune, and now at last gone near to dishonouring me in my own eyes. That ever I should so have delegated what I ought to have kept in my sovereign hands, and at your instance taken to myself more than my sovereign due, and gone far to estrange my own people! I have been at fault, and the blame for that I'll bear, but I will not bear the guilt of your murder. You are no longer in my service; I dismiss you with ignominy. And I will have a strict accounting from you of all those moneys you have handled, of every distraint and fine and levy you have inflicted. Hold yourselves at our disposition, all three, for you shall not escape the probings of law. And quit your offices here and now, and get out of my sight. Murderers!"

Des Rivaulx, pallid and stiff, said in a strangled voice, "Your Grace, in justice hear us! We have done nothing that was not done for your gain and in your interest. . . ."

"My interest!" raged the king. "To kill so basely one of the greatest magnates of my realm? And to drag my honour in the dust, and make foul use of my seal? Not another word! Justice shall hear you, in due time. Now I want only honest men about me, not stained by treachery to the earl or treason to me. Out! I sicken at the sight of you!"

They shrank from him and gave back, creeping away out of the hall in a shocked silence. When they were gone, men stirred slowly and stiffly, as though out of a dream, and turned to follow the king's fixed and frowning gaze. The bishop of Winchester stood tall and erect and cold, staring back steadily at his pupil, who had broken away so abruptly from under his hand. His nostrils quivered briefly, but his chiselled countenance gave no other sign.

"My lord bishop," said Henry with soft-voiced deliberation, "it seems to us that the business we are about here can hardly be giving you any great pleasure. If you would prefer to retire to your see of Winchester, we will hold you excused. Nor need you trouble yourself to attend further on us until we recall you."

"I am, as always, at your Grace's disposal," said Peter des Roches icily. He was too intelligent not to recognize that his reign was over, not for a while but for ever; it was not in Henry to readmit to his favour one who had dominated him, though some day he might take back the discredited but efficient clerks who had also offended. It was not in des Roches to clutch at honours slipping away from him, or enter into protest or appeal. This was an ending. He swept the king a deep bow, and strode out of the hall to prepare for his departure. He had reached the doorway when the king called after him clearly, "One moment! You have one of our wards in your charge, Richard de Clare. He is present here in Gloucester with you?"

"He is, your Grace."

"You will leave him here, I relieve you of the charge. In a day or two his uncle, the new Earl Marshal, will be here, it's fitting the boy should be here to meet him. We will consider our future dispositions for his welfare. You need not be inconvenienced further."

The bishop made him another silent bow, and went away with no more words to any man in Gloucester but his own servants. Within the hour he had left the town.

Nothing could have ensured the triumph of the Earl Marshal's cause so decisively as his untimely death. Against the onus of that killing there was nothing to be done but make every concession, strain every effort, to bring about a general reconciliation, and do away the hideous suspicion that the king himself had connived at the murder. Henry surrendered himself to the guidance of Archbishop Edmund as totally as he had formerly surrendered himself to Peter des Roches. It was impossible to be too conciliatory to all those of the Earl Marshal's party, or to pursue with too severe threats those who had misused the royal seal to bring about his death. All details and difficulties that might otherwise have delayed the return of the exiles were swept clean away, seen to be of no account beside the overwhelming need to reunify

England. In self-defence King Henry worked desperately hard to make the reunion ceremonious and successful.

The dissident lords from Ireland had arrived. And in Wales, Prince Llewelyn had signified that he was satisfied of the king's good faith towards all, and was willing to proceed with talks for a permanent peace. The entire court had gathered in Gloucester to provide a gracious reception when the archbishop himself conducted the exiles from South Wales, no longer outlaw, into the great hall on the twenty-third of May, to be received by a glittering company, and the king in splendour.

9

May, 1234: Gloucester.

It seemed to Meggotta that this was the happiest and most hopeful day she had ever known. The small pleasures of the childhood time, before she even knew what trouble was, or sorrow, could not be compared with this. Her father was free, soon she would see him again, he would be taken back into grace and favour, be the king's vassal again, be earl of Kent again, regain all the lands of his inheritance or purchase, hear his outlawry formally rescinded. And then the joy of seeing his rescuers restored to all their lands and honours, and the two young men who had risked their lives for him accepted back freely into their own country as peers among their peers.

She knew the main terms of the peace very well; Lawrence of St. Albans had visited Margaret and talked over everything with her, though there were still tiresome details to be worked out. The restoration of the hereditary lands, for instance, was complete and unconditional, but the acquired lands were to be restored to a fixed value, and the amount was not yet agreed. Meggotta did not understand or care about such minor matters. Two things were important: her father was free, vindicated and re-established in his lands and titles, all reproaches against him withdrawn. And Richard had been taken out of the hands of the bishop of Winchester, and was present in Gloucester, and there she could see and speak to him, even if they must still keep their secret for a while. Soon even that might be unnecessary. Surely now the king would give him back to them, and everything would be as it had been before.

According to Lawrence of St. Albans, Hubert was renouncing all claims to the office of justiciar, but he would again be a member of the king's council. Nor was he to hold any royal castles. Better so, said Margaret, holding anything from the king was a life's risk. Meggotta in her happiness had almost forgiven the king, but Margaret never would.

"We two shall have to be very loving and kind and careful of your father," she said to her daughter, as they were dressing for the reunion, in their apartment in the guest-houses of the priory of St. Oswald. "He has been through so much that he needs to be quiet with us, and rest."

"Oh, yes," said Meggotta ardently, smoothing her blue tunic with its gold embroideries over her creamy gown. Everything she had on was new and charmingly mature, in the mirror she looked like a miniature image of a great lady, a delicate toy with a startling human face, withdrawn and wise. A child's face with a woman's eyes, Alice said. Her hair was in two long, thick braids, down to her waist, and threaded with seed pearls.

"He will look older, you know, Meggotta. It's been two years, hard years for him."

"Yes, but this will be joy to him, as it is to us. He is restored, he has his freedom, his honour, his lands, his title, he comes back to us justified. Everything now will be healing for him."

"I pray God so!" said Margaret.

"And I'm older, too, he will have me to discover. I've grown, I'm changed. Will he like me?" she asked, straightening the thin gold coronal that bound her hair.

Margaret looked at her and was comforted. It is a very vulnerable joy that looks about on all sides for comfort, but at least she found it. The girl was quickening into beauty as a tree buds with unbelievably delicate green leaves in spring. A birch tree or a poplar, something slender and silvery, with a bark as clear as the immense grey eyes.

"He will love you as always he loved you, but more. Come, you and I have to do him honour." She had taken great pains with her own regal splendour; there would not be many about this queenless court to come near her, and none to match her. It was right that the king should see what pride she took in the tired old man she knew she was going out to welcome home. She had tried to warn Meggotta. What do the young know of two years in terror and in chains, with life itself hanging always by a thread?

They entered together into the great guest-hall, festively hung with tapestries and green branches, and brilliant with the shimmering panoply of nobility. King Henry was already seated, ready to receive his guests, and he rose to greet her and, briefly and distractedly, to compliment Meggotta. Margaret forgave him his absence of mind, this occasion would not be easy for him. If he knew it, and was sweating over it, that was some credit to him. And by reason of the complaisance of his greeting, some among the company came courting her, spoke warmly of Hubert, noticed Meggotta with thoughtful approval. Some, perhaps, had sons to marry? The restoration of the earldom of Kent made Meggotta a most desirable match. Margaret smiled, and let them gaze.

The archbishop made his entry at the further doors, with his returned exiles: Gilbert Basset, solid, sturdy, and self-confident as ever, with three loyal brothers at his back, a private army; Richard Siward, fresh from his southern possessions, where he did much as he liked, and had little to fear; one or two others, less known. And these parted their ranks to let one man through. He was the centre of their phalanx, as though they grouped to guard him, and when they opened to give him precedence, it was because they reverenced him, and had brought him to where he could stand forward in his due place with safety.

He had never been of tall stature, but now appeared tall, being lean to emaciation. He went haltingly on both feet, pacing as though expecting pain at each step, and took his time about advancing into the room. One winter in Wales had not tempered his dungeon pallor, and the bones of his face stood stark under the skin. The richness and sombreness of his dress only served to show up, by contrast, the decay of the meagre body within, the stiffness of his movements, the aging of his face. His hair and beard were carefully trimmed and curled, but they were white, not the ivory whiteness that sometimes crowns men of fair colouring in old age, not the silver whiteness that threads itself into dark hair like strands of jewellery, but dead, lustreless white, as though every hair had grown too weary to retain colour or life. And his eyes, which had been restless and shrewd and quick with ideas, had become impenetrably patient and resigned, though in them, at least, life and feeling remained. He looked about him at the assembly of his peers, and trod slowly and heavily down the long room to the king's chair, his companions following silently at his heels.

Meggotta held her breath and clasped her hands tightly, and did not cry out, but the contortion of shock and pain was like an iron hand grasping and crushing her heart. She had thought herself prepared for hurtful changes, but there could be no preparation for this. He was an old, old man, tired and broken to a heart-rending, submissive gentleness, noble still, dignified still, but as a pilgrim or a recluse may have his nobility and his dignity. Never again the great general, the defender of besieged Dover, the sea-fighter of Sandwich; never again the superb man of affairs, the first lord of the land. Well he might renounce all claims to his old office, he could not, and would not have wished to, hold it again. This was a man whose public life was over.

"My lord king," said the archbishop, advancing beside his charge, "here I bring to you the lord Hubert de Burgh, the lord Gilbert Basset, the lord Richard Siward, and all these men of their following, who are come in goodwill seeking reconciliation with your Grace, and readmittance into your favour and renewal of their fealty. I beg you receive them with the same goodwill, to the great gain of your realm."

King Henry was gazing with dismayed fascination at his own handiwork. Margaret doubted if he felt any real relenting, but he was not beyond feeling some shame, it seemed, for when Hubert, with grim patience, essayed to kneel before his sovereign, she saw a flush rise like a tidal wave out of the king's golden collar, and he reached both hands to take the returned exile under the forearms, and prevent the painful effort. She judged that he was instantly pleased with his own magnanimity, and followed it up as a child follows a pulled toy; for certainly he was unexpectedly gracious in word and gesture thereafter.

"My lord Hubert, you are welcome. We have also desired this agreement, and rejoice in it." He did not go to the length of asking that a seat be placed for the man he had half crippled, but at least he cut mercifully short the public part of the day's business, so that Hubert might not founder in full view of the whole court. The outlaws, by this act no longer outlaw, though a formal edict would be necessary to make their return hold fast in law, all paid their homage and received gracious approval. So did the new Earl Marshal, Gilbert, the third brother, already earl by courtesy in advance of his official seisin. He was not as impressive as Earl Richard, for whom Meggotta had shed tears in private, and of whom she thought very often. This next brother was shorter, darker in colouring, a pleasant enough person, but diminished by comparison.

Archbishop Edmund Rich was happy to have this public reconciliation over, and to withdraw the parties to the negotiations into the king's private rooms, with their law-men and their confessors, and all those who had word to say in the hard bargaining still to be completed. If any demands remained unsatisfied, any claims unmet, somehow the rival interests would be reconciled; none of them would have been here but on the clear understanding that they were already agreed upon all vital points, and were prepared to compromise upon what was left. He saw to it that the earl of Kent was seated, and well able to continue discussion, and had Lawrence of St. Albans at his side throughout. The corpse-pallor was misleading; there was more durability in that misused body than either his devotees or his enemies suspected.

Left behind in the hall, and knowing few people in this assembly, Meggotta kept close to her mother's side. There were plenty of people willing to woo Margaret of Scotland now. She was again countess of Kent, and who knew what influence she might have in the future, if her lord ever returned to office? Meggotta moved at her side, responding only very distractedly to whatever was said to her, for her thoughts were all on her father. She longed for the time when this formal business would be finished, and he could come home to them in quietness, hold her in his wasted arms, feel her round, valiant arms about him, her cheek against his cheek again, and know that after so much sorrow he was back with his own, loved and valued beyond measure. What else could possibly matter?

The bright tide of movement among the ladies in the hall parted momentarily in two smooth waves, and at some distance from her, before the ranks closed again between, she saw Richard. She stood spell-bound, letting Margaret move away from her unheeded.

He was the same, yet not the same. He had come, as she might have guessed if she had given it proper thought, with the countess of Cornwall. She had almost forgotten that he had a mother other than her own, but here was this fair, smooth, courtly lady in white and gold and faint blue, very becoming to her flaxen hair and cornflower eyes, lightly guiding her son before her with a hand on his shoulder. Richard marched ahead, head reared and eyes ranging to left and right, searching eagerly for someone. He had grown several inches since last Meggotta had seen him, in one of those bursts of bodily energy young things experience, and had lost the softness of his boyish flesh, and acquired a great deal of mannish bone, brow, and cheek-bones, and firm, jutting jaw. He moved like a young stag, long-stepping and lissom, and his eyes, wide and alert in his search, were the heavenly blue she remembered, like the midsummer sky. He had set out boldly on the way to his manhood.

His fair head, craning to left and right, turned towards her, and he had found what he sought.

He halted in mid-stride, and froze at gaze, like a wild thing in the forest. His head reared yet a little higher, his eyes flared a little wider, and blazed into a blueness too bright to be borne. She did not know what he was seeing, she had not realized that she was as changed as he, as strange and yet as faithfully the same. Joy pierced them both like a burning arrow, turning their bones molten; but that was for an instant only. She must not go to him, not thus, openly and straight in unmistakable claim to possession; he must not come to her. They both knew it.

Then the ranks closed and swirled in a dozen bright colours between them, and he walked on with his mother, and she hurried to overtake hers.

He came to her shoulder among the throng of young people in the great hall, when the king's festive supper was almost done and the musicians were already playing. Those children of the nobility old enough to wait on their elders at table had been busy with flagon and finger-bowl and napkin, proud to be in attendance on such an occasion, and now that there was no more work for them they might sit and listen to the music, or dance to it in the cleared space below the tables. Meggotta stood drawn back into the folds of a curtain near the screens, watching her mother and father at the high table, side by side at last, and close to the king. Her turn had not yet come. So long and ceremonious a day, not one moment of it could yet be spared to let father and daughter embrace and kiss. And how weary he must be, and how desperately in need of rest.

She felt the presence at her shoulder, the soft, steady breath on her cheek. "Meggotta!" said Richard in her ear.

"Richard!" she said in a whisper, and did not turn her head, but reached a hand behind her for him to take.

"Get your cloak, and come out to the south doorway now. Some of the guests are going to Vespers at the abbey church. We'll be among them, and lost on the way. No one will be noticing or counting."

"They may look for me," she said, her eyes still fixed upon her father.

"No, they'll not escape yet, no one can leave until the king retires. Tell Alice I shall be taking care of you. We shall be back here long before they're free to go home with you."

His lips brushed her hair as if by chance, and he was gone. He knew she would do whatever he asked of her. She let him vanish among the throng, and then flew like a bird to take her cloak and do his bidding. The May evening was still bright, the sun not yet low, and it was warm enough to go cloakless, but the subdued blue was unobtrusive and anonymous over her festival finery, and there were enough royal guests, old and young alike, crossing the close to swallow her up unnoticed. There was no need to look for Richard, he was soon beside her, silently guiding her to a slower and slower pace as they drew into the shadow of the abbey church, so that at last they were at the end of the procession, and it was easy to catch her by the hand and draw her aside quickly, through the narrow doorway in the north aisle, and into the south walk of the cloister. In the twilight within the church, after the clear evening light without, they vanished like silent shadows, unnoticed.

Under the vaulting of the cloister walk Richard drew her into one of the carrels of the scriptorium, and on the stone bench within they crouched, clinging together and listening, as though afraid of pursuit, until he shook himself almost angrily, and sat up straight and proud, still with his arms about her, and kissed her fiercely on the lips.

She held him off fearfully, but held him tightly for all that.

"I may kiss you," he said firmly. "You are my wife."

"Oh, hush, Richard! Yes, yes, surely . . . but we mustn't say it aloud yet. Not yet! We might spoil everything."

"If the king is restoring father all his rights, except royal office and the constableship of royal castles, then surely he means to restore me. It was a proper bargain, he had no right to interfere with it."

"He had, Richard. Oh, not any kind of right except legally, but that he had. Mother explained it. We can wait and be patient a little longer, surely, to make everything certain. Even when you come back to us, we mustn't let anyone know that we're married. It could make the king angry again, just because we acted without his knowledge. Let him think that everything is just as he arranged it, and if we must still keep silence, and have a second marriage, what harm is there in that?"

"None!" he said with a great sigh, and drew her closer against his shoulder. "I would marry you every day, to make it always a festival, and have people look at you and worship you. Oh, Meggotta, when I saw you in the hall among all those people, this afternoon, I was almost afraid. You've grown so beautiful. I was afraid you might be changed."

"I don't change!" said Meggotta indignantly. "I shall never change towards you, you know that. I didn't think that of you, although you've grown so tall and mannish. If you loved me when I was fat and childish and wanted my own way, why shouldn't you love me now, when I'm growing much slimmer, and take better care of my dresses, and have learned to be kinder? Only a few more days, Richard. You know there are so many documents for the clerks to draw up, it may take the king a few days to get to us."

"I know you're right," owned Richard. "But if I can't see you and talk to you, how shall I bear it? I'll ask my mother to come and visit your mother, and that will be something, but then we shall have to be simply two people who were brother and sister for a time. I want more than that. I want to be able to talk with you properly, and say I love you, and call you my wife as often as I like. Will you come here tomorrow? And every evening, until we can really be together again at home? At this same hour, when they're at Vespers? And to this same carrel?"

"It may not be easy," she said doubtfully.

"Yes, for you it will, easier than for me. You can tell your mother the truth, I can't do that. She'll help you, not stand in your way. And it can only be for a very few days."

They were both so sure of that!

"Yes," she said, "yes, I'll come. Whatever happens, I'll come!"

They had been apart so long that it seemed they should have had endless things to say to each other, and yet this first meeting passed, after that promise, almost in silence. To be together, each feeling the warmth and touch of the other, was enough bliss; they needed nothing more. They could barely hear the chanting within the church. It was like starting out of a dream of absolute peace when Richard stirred and straightened, listening, and said, "It's ending. We'll slip out by the west walk and mingle with them as they leave."

But some of the devout, it seemed, had chosen to leave by way of the cloisters after the service. Out through the door from the north aisle came two ladies, prayer-books in hand, and paused to breathe the evening air appreciatively, for there were roses already in early flower in the cloister garth, and at this hour their distilled fragrance hung on the light breeze, an intoxicating sweetness. One of the women was plumply built and somewhere in her thirties, with a devout, humourless face and folded hands, self-consciously nunnish in her dress. The other was a tall, handsome, brown-haired girl of about nineteen, with large, confident dark eyes and a proud, erect carriage, very richly dressed, one who would know her own mind and fight for her own way. At sight of them Richard drew Meggotta back into the darkest corner of the carrel, a finger at his lips.

"The king's sister," he whispered, "the Countess Eleanor. Hush, let them pass by."

The two ladies passed by, indeed, oblivious of the children sitting still as stone in their corner, withdrawn from the light. But they were in no hurry to depart. The evening was fair and warm, and halfway along the south walk the girl halted to admire the roses, stooping to smell one in full flower that leaned close, and adjusting a briar that had encroached through the embrasure where she stood. Watching her decisive profile against the sky, Meggotta thought that she had the face the king should have had, resolute and clear, with eyes that did not hood their looks. She might be impulsive, stubborn, and hot-tempered, but she would not be mean, or fearful, or hesitant.

In through the doorway at the end of the east walk came a young man, who by chance turned right and chose to circle the garth by the north walk, moving briskly, as though he had business either in the church or, more probably, out beyond the west range, where the abbot's dwelling lay. He was halfway along the northern side when the roses also drew his eyes, and he glanced up and gazed at them as he walked, and, lifting his glance a shade higher, was suddenly confronted by the apparition of the tall girl opposite across the garth, framed in the stone pillars of the embrasure and the green briars and glowing buds of the roses.

He halted, not as she had halted but abruptly, as if a cross-bow bolt had stopped him dead in mid-stride. He turned fully into the embrasure facing her, and stood and gazed. He was not a very tall man, perhaps only an inch or so taller than the girl; he was built like a beautiful machine for exercise and sword-play, for horsemanship and the handling of the lance—long in the shanks, short, compact, and neat in the body, with wide shoulders, and every joint and muscle in very smooth command. A close cap of brown hair moulded a fine Roman head. He was shaven clean, there was nothing to disguise the lines of cheek and chin, and they were impetuous, generous, and young, surely no more than twenty-five. The eyes that had fixed upon the Countess Eleanor, and clung in astonished pleasure, were large, well set, and of a pure, deep grey.

It seemed an age that the brown eyes and the grey linked and held fast, gazing rapt and helpless through the roses, though it was less than a minute in reality. She was the first to lower her eyes, frowning, but she raised them again quickly to observe how he flushed hotly at the reproof, and hastily turned to continue his passage of the garth. She had gone no more than a dozen yards when she asked her companion, with no pretence of indifference, "Who was that young man? I don't think I have seen him about the court."

"Madam, you have not frequented the court so much recently," said Cecily de Sanford, with the meekness that added sting to rebuke. "If this had not been so important an assembly, his Grace would not have required us to attend. I believe that is the young man de Montfort, the earl of Leicester, the French claimant the earl of Chester brought over with him a few years ago."

"Indeed!" said Eleanor thoughtfully. "Ranulf must have thought a great deal of that young man. I never saw him before."

"But, madam, I would remind you that you have a vocation above other women, and should not be concerned with enquiries about young men. God witnesses all!"

"If he witnesses the passage of Messire de Montfort," said Eleanor, unabashed, "he cannot but take pleasure in it. If he had not wished me to rejoice in beauty, Cecily, he would not have given me sight. I think it no compliment to him to misprize his gift."

They had reached the end of the south walk by then, and were turning into the east. And there Eleanor stopped and looked back, and in the west walk the young man de Montfort had reached the doorway by which he would pass out into the evening, and he, too, had halted and turned to look back. The brown eyes and the grey met again, and clung, not wishing to part. Then he was gone, whisking out at the door of the west walk with a lunge that spoke of effort and regret; and Eleanor gathered her gown in her hands, and set off for her own lodging in the abbey guest-house at such a pace that Cecily de Sanford had much ado to keep up with her.

In the last carrel of the south walk Meggotta drew breath like a sleeper waking, and looked into Richard's eyes, dark blue in the onset of dusk, and dazzled and enlightened like her own. They leaned together in their secret place, and kissed in prolonged, mute passion, heedless of all precautions, as though they kissed by proxy for those two elders of theirs who had not so much as exchanged a word, much less an embrace.

When they stole out into the mellow dusk, all the worshippers were gone from Vespers, and they were alone, but they walked back towards the guest-hall hand in hand, invulnerable, like creatures in a dream.

When the king at last rose to withdraw from the hall, he beckoned Hubert to go with him.

"My lord of Kent, I must detain you yet a few more minutes. There is one small thing still to be settled between us, one which is purely between us two, and needs no documentation. Will you walk with me as far as the church?"

It was twilight by then, but there was still an afterglow. In a little while the brothers would be assembling for Compline, but when the king and his silent companion reached the church, it was deserted. Dim light gleamed from the high altar. Henry took Hubert by the hand, and started almost guiltily at the dry, light boniness he held.

"The articles drawn between us this day, my lord, have omitted all mention of one matter, but I wish to have it understood and agreed as between us two. There is no need for anything more." He drew the earl with him to the steps of the altar, and mounted them. He laid the hand he held upon the cross, and with his own hand kept it there. "I desire you to make solemn oath here, upon the altar, that you will never again claim or seek to regain any rights in Richard de Clare."

It was a name from a former life to Hubert; he had almost forgotten that he had ever had the boy in his charge, or dreamed of seeing him united with Meggotta, the two of them established in the greatest earldom of the realm, uniting the honours of Clare, Gloucester, Hertford, and Kent. Such ambitions were over. He recalled the child himself, gallant and frightened and piteous on that journey to Burgh, and felt one deep pang of affection and regret, but that was all. Thank God they had been together only a matter of two years; no, even less, and as young children. Young children forget easily, and take comfort easily, and these two had been separated now for as long a time as they had ever been together. Thank God it was no worse! If he was slow to respond to the king's order, it was not from any thought of resistance, but rather because it cost him a slow and weary effort to remember how important these matters had once been to him, and to understand how important they still might be to Henry. But the king chafed, suspecting protest.

"I have taken the boy into my own custody, my own escheaters administer his lands, and I wish it to remain so. No matter in whose household I place him, Richard is my ward, and all rights in his affairs are vested in me, and only in me. You shall not have my favour, my lord, unless you swear this oath, never to meddle in any matters concerning him."

"Your Grace mistakes me," said Hubert simply. "I am ready to make you the quit-claim you want, there is no need to labour it." He spread his gnarled fingers under the king's hand, and strung the necessary words slowly. "I swear by the holy altar that I will never again claim or seek to win back any rights in Richard de Clare, or interfere in any way in any affair of his. Those rights I had in him are here surrendered. I call God to be my witness."

"See you keep it," said the devout prince who had not only sworn but planned the oath of Bromholm. He was cautiously satisfied. He drew away his hand with a wary sigh.

"I am not accustomed to break my oaths," said Hubert. "I shall not break this one."

Henry, having got his way with less trouble than he had anticipated, went out of his way to be gracious all the way back to the guest-house, where Margaret and Meggotta were waiting to claim the old, tired man at last, and lead him away to his own apartments in the priory.

They asked him nothing that night; he was worn out with the stresses of the day, and at the end of the day there was the disintegration of relief that all the worst was over. They saw him at his weakest, for he had no force left to maintain a front for them, but sat collapsed and tremulous, almost too exhausted to speak. Meggotta shuddered at sight of the scars of irons on his wrists, blue-black, engrained in his flesh for life, the wrists themselves so lean and misshapen from the damp and cold of stone cells. The healed wounds would thin and fade, but never completely, the wrists would flesh out again, but the finger-ends would never again be straight, or so deft as before. The same marks he bore round his ankles, fretted more deeply, as the shackles had been heavier. When she looked at him, she had no thought of anything but his need and her desperate desire to fill it, to pour out on him every lavish gift of love until he was himself again. She sat beside him, her arm round his neck, and even then holding him with such careful gentleness, for once, for a short time, he had also worn a collar of iron, and she feared even the slight weight of her arm upon the scar. She talked to him of nothings, of her new clothes, of how they had visited Burgh and begun to make it ready for him, of anything that would ride painlessly over the pain of this joyful day. And he held her close, and smiled a faint, grey smile, and stroked her, and called her by her many love-names that always ended with Meggotta.

But they did not ask him anything. When at last his new charter was agreed in detail, and delivered, then Margaret would go over it word by word and clause by clause. The wonder was that Hubert had had the force and fire still in him to argue points as they arose, to reject suggestions, even to refuse a formula the king had pressed upon him. All he needed was time, and rest, and peace of mind, and he would be Hubert de Burgh again, white hair or no.

When Meggotta had gone to her bed, in the room she shared with Alice, Hubert and Margaret still sat for a while, and it was then that she asked him, expecting nothing of great moment. "What was it he wanted of you at the last minute, tonight? Meggotta had been waiting and longing for you so patiently, he might have left a few things for tomorrow."

"Ah, that!" said Hubert heavily. "I meant to tell you. A pity, but no worse than I expected, and it was little more than acknowledging what's been fact for nearly two years. He wanted my oath not to try to recover the custody of Richard de Clare, or meddle with his marriage."

Margaret was pouring wine for him as he spoke. Her hand shook, and the wine spilled over on to the table like blood. For a moment she was motionless, staring down at it in silence; then with composure she mopped up the drops, and wiped the rim of the cup. Her hand as she surrendered it to him was steady enough to guide and steady his while he drank.

"And you have sworn?"

"Why not? A pity, but that was over long ago, no hope of taking up again where you lost him, my heart. We must begin from here, where we stand. The king will never let go of the boy a second time, to me or to any. He means to keep him for himself. Blessedly, they're both children yet. Meggotta won't want for suitors, now she'll be bringing them the earldom of Kent again. And she so lovely, too," he said with pride.

"Yes," said Margaret gently, "she will grow up beautiful. There were some noticing her today."

Her heart felt cold and heavy in her breast, but he must not know it. She loved him, and here he came back to her a wreck of a man, broken, aged, marked by fetters, having lived through many months of daily fear for his life. How could she possibly lay yet another burden on him? Of course he had given his oath when it was asked of him, he knew of no reason why he should withhold it. He did not know that those two children had made their own pledges, given their love once for all, and sealed it with the act of marriage. He had no notion that separating them now would be a death. And he must never have any suspicion. Whatever followed, he could not be made guilty of what had been done and concealed without his knowledge.

"I'm sorry, though," he said, sighing. "You had grown fond of Richard, I know. I saw less of him, of course, but I liked him well."

"Yes," she said, "I was fond of him. But I've been without him a long while now."

Time, she thought, time is the only weapon we have now. Time and patience and courage, and the fact that they are still young, and no one yet has begun to talk of betrothals. But whatever happens, no part of the responsibility for what I have done must ever be cast up against him. He has made his oath in good faith, not knowing he was undoing us all.

"I wish I need not have made you sad," said Hubert ruefully.

"On the day when I recover you, however hardly, how can I be sad?" She leaned and took the cup from him, and set it down on the table. She went on her knees, and took his head between her hands, and kissed him. "Come to bed, my lord, my love! I have been without you too long, I want you in my arms."

"This wreck that I am now?" he said bitterly. "I am old, and useless to you, my heart!"

"Better the wreckage of Hubert de Burgh than King Henry in his youth and flower. And you are no wreck, but only in need of laying up and fitting afresh, and you have time yet for many another voyage, and you have me for crew. Come!" she said, lifting him by the hands. "Come and sleep!"

She admitted no servant to him that night, let no one but herself touch the worn body that moved her to rage and grieving love with its marks of captivity and humiliation. Nor did she quench all the lights, but left one small lamp burning, for fear he should start awake into the darkness of dungeons out of some ill dream. But when he had lain in her arms a little while, the exhausted stiffness ebbed out of him; she felt it pass as though he had bled and was eased, and then he sank far beyond the common levels of sleep, into a great deep where surely no dreams could follow him. All night she held him on her heart, while she lay thinking what was to come, and what could now be done to alleviate it. And towards daylight, when she was sure he would not wake, she slipped softly away from beside him, and went to Meggotta's bed.

Meggotta opened her eyes to see her mother's face leaning over her in the first pearly light before dawn. In the other bed, at the far corner of the room, Alice was snoring.

"What is it? Not father? Is all well with him?"

"All's well, he's asleep, deep asleep. I must talk to you, Meggotta, before he wakes, before you speak with him again. Put on a gown, and come out to the other room."

Meggotta had grown used to unexplained demands that were good sense if not questioned, and abrupt alarms that had taught her more than mere endurance. She slid out of bed and drew on her gown, and followed her mother into the room where the ashes of yesterday's fire still showed a single small red gleam among the grey. Margaret closed the door softly after them, and drew breath upon the hard thing she had to do.

"Meggotta, God knows I grieve to have to ask of you still more patience and courage, but now at least I know how much you have within you, and for a good cause I dare ask it of you, to the last drop. There is something I learned from your father only after you were asleep. It's a hard thing upon you and Richard." She pressed her weary cheeks with chilly palms, and told it almost in a breath, as it had been told to her. "He has had no word from us all this time of what we have done, it was too dangerous ever to be told. He did not know you loved each other as you do, he did not know you are man and wife. He thought you just two children who played together for a time, two years ago. So he was doing you no wrong. How could he guess?"

"Oh, no!" said Meggotta in a whisper. "He couldn't know! How could I possibly think to blame him? But now, surely now, we shall have to tell him. . . ." She caught herself up there, biting into her lower lip, and wrestled with all the impossibilities she saw before her. "No! No, we mustn't ever let him know. We can't! Because then, either he would be forced to confess it all, and say openly that he took his oath in good faith, but now finds he is forsworn against his will, or else he would keep our secret, and be guilty and forsworn indeed! He could not bear that. And he has suffered such cruel injustice already, and is so weary! The king would hound him to his death this time!"

"Child, I must say it, there is now no safe way. For a while we may have a respite yet, and there may be hope of another change, seeing we are contending with a man so changeable. But if we speak out now —"

"No, we must not. No matter though we took the whole blame upon us, you know it would be visited upon him. I will not let my father be persecuted any more, if I can prevent. No, we have to go on keeping our secret, as we have kept it up to now. You must tell Alice as much. I will tell Richard. We have not lost everything," said Meggotta stoutly, "only a few more years of waiting to face. In the end, whatever they do, we are man and wife."

"Girl," said Margaret, with tears starting in her eyes, "surely to God you were bred royal! I thought I should have to tell you all that you are telling me. Are you never afraid for yourself?"

"Yes," said Meggotta, "but not enough to turn me back. I hoped we should be going home to Burgh with both father and Richard, and everything would be safe and agreed, as it was before. But even if that had happened, we could not have told the truth yet about our marriage, we should still have had to wait until we were a few years older. If we could do that together, we can do it apart." But her voice shook a little as she said it, and she swung her head and spilled the long dark hair about her to hide her face.

"Listen to me," said Margaret with careful gentleness. "You are both barely twelve years old. In two years, or three, men may begin to talk of marriage plans for you both, but I think not until then. We have so much grace. And in that time things may change yet again. We have seen how quickly change can come, so it may once more. Never forget, we are dealing with a changeable man, one who extricates himself from his inconvenient oaths as lightly as he extorts them from others and demands they be kept. Just now he is bent on keeping Richard in his own hands, but there'll be no love and no living together there, no taking a son into his heart, this is only a matter of an earldom or two. In a year, or a year and a half, who knows? The truce with France may break down, the Welsh may break out again, the king may make a marriage of his own and forget everything else. A time may come when we can readily approach him on your behalf and Richard's. Better, a time may come when he is hot after some other pursuit, and loses interest in Richard, and is glad to hand him back freely where he is wanted. A time may come when your father is whole and vigorous and needed, and the king may be anxious to placate him by gifts for the sake of his support. All these are possible. I say we should wait and hope and watch events, and take our opportunities when they come."

"So I think, too," said Meggotta. "But if none of these things happens? If the king makes proposals for Richard's marriage? Or someone bids for mine?"

"Then we shall do what we always knew we might have to do in the end. We shall come out into the open, and tell what we know, what we are, and what we have done, and fight for it to the death. But *we,* who did it, not your father, who will have taken and kept his oath in innocence."

"Oh, *yes!*" said Meggotta, lifting her head to uncover the face she had briefly hidden. The first sun-rays above the horizon found the red glints in her hair. "Yes, that is right, that is what we must do."

"And while we wait, we shall come and go between Burgh and Westminster. Remember, my lord is still a councillor, and you are old enough now to travel with us. You may see Richard and talk with him as any young men and women may meet at court. If he remains in London, we have a palace there, too. It will not be all loneliness."

In the bedchamber the old man stirred, drew breath long and deep, and was torn by a fit of coughing. Meggotta drew her gown about her, and turned her head aside. "May I go to my father? He may look for one of us, or be lost. And you should speak with Alice, while there's time."

In the first of the carrels along the south walk of the great cloister, at the hour of Vespers on the twenty-fourth evening of May, Richard and Meggotta sat clenched together in the darkest corner of the stone bench, almost silent, altogether still, flank warm against flank and head leaned to head, in one entire and prolonged caress. It was he who had wept, not she, briefly and passionately, in a terrible anger for which he had no adequate means of expression. His energies and frustrations cried out for expenditure in action, and here there was no possible room for action, only for resolute and disciplined inaction, which to him was a kind of death. He did not know any other way but in arms of attacking his enemies. The weapons of silent patience and endurance were heavier to him than denunciation and pain would have been. But he loved not only Meggotta but also the earl of Kent, who had been kind and fatherly to him in his saddest hours, and he was capable of great devotion to what he loved, even against his nature.

"You will come?" he said anxiously.

"You know I will, whenever I can. Whenever father comes to the council. But how do I know you'll be there? Now that the king has given you into the keeping of your uncle Gilbert . . . Oh, why could he not leave you with your mother, if we were not to have you?"

"I think," said Richard dubiously, "my mother may be hoping for a new son, early next year. I'm not sure, but I think so. And the king is jealous of his brother in any case, and doesn't want him to have me in his care. But I don't think Uncle Gilbert is very interested, either. If I can get him to leave me in his London house, I will. Then I shall be there nearly all the year, only perhaps for the festivals, if the king sends for me. Then I shall always be able to see you, when you come."

It sounded better than they had dared to hope, but there were all manner of dangers in the way. They clung so close that they forgot to kiss, because from head to foot they were one anguished and ecstatic kiss.

"And you'll come again tomorrow? And every day until you go home to Burgh? Oh, Meggotta, tell father with what affection I think of him. At least I can send him that message."

"I will, surely. And I'll come, every evening. It will be two or three days yet. He isn't fit to ride so far."

They forgot to move away before the end of Vespers. They saw, yet hardly saw at all, the young man Simon de Montfort, earl of Leicester, enter by the door of the east walk, and pace very slowly along the opposite side of the garth, dawdling at every embrasure to look hopefully across the gardens; but it seemed that the Countess Eleanor, the as-yet-unknown lady of the rose-briars, had chosen to leave by another door, in defence of her vows. Simon reached the west door disappointed, and, after some minutes of waiting, withdrew crestfallen. They had not marked his coming, and hardly noticed his going. Only as he vanished, very slowly and reluctantly, Meggotta suddenly said, astonished, "That is the same man, he was here yesterday."

Then they remembered. "He is looking for her," said Richard, wrung by his own frustrations to feel for another's. "But she has taken vows," he said, awed. "He can't know! If only he knew he has no hope."

They had been silent again several minutes when the Countess Eleanor came out by the narrow door close to their refuge, and walked, very slowly, by the end very slowly indeed, along the south walk, and thence with reluctant feet and ever-turning head along the east walk to the farther door. She played with the roses as she went, but she did not see them, she was watching rather the opposite side of the garth. Perhaps it had taken her some minutes to rid herself of Cecily de Sanford, for tonight she was alone, and those few minutes had cost her what she had come to seek, for the young man was too early, or she too late. They both went thence unsatisfied.

"Richard," said Meggotta in a whisper, "she, too—"

"Yes! And she doesn't know he came."

"Oh, Richard, if they mean it—if they truly mean it—they will have to be so lion-hearted!"

Richard sat staring into a future perilous, uncertain, and bleak, and if his jaw was set defiantly, his eyes were immense with anxiety. He drew her more jealously and closely into his arm. "So shall we!" he said.

10

January to February, 1236:

Westminster; Bury St. Edmunds.

KKing Henry arose on his wedding day, in his palace of Westminster, as content and excited as a child waking on one of the high church festivals. It was mid-January, and the morning was frosty but brilliant; the sky had a pure, wintry blue, and after several days on the edge of frost and without any rain, the roads were sound and dry. There could not have been a better setting for a noble procession.

He was twenty-nine years old, and it was high time for him to think of marriage and heirs, and constantly all his successive advisers had urged upon him the duty of considering the future. So he had done, at irregular intervals during the past ten years, with varying degrees of lukewarmness, but something had always happened to break off negotiations. Once at least he had fallen in love, but not disastrously, for when it was urged that the marriage he had in mind was impossibly unsuitable, he had let himself be counselled, and made a philosophical recovery. Once, quite recently, he had come very near to marrying the daughter of the countess of Ponthieu, but there had been some delay because the lady was related to him within the prohibited degrees, and fortunately a much more glittering match had offered in time. And today he was to be married to Eleanor, daughter of the count of Provence, and sister of the new queen of France.

Henry was relying on the match to stand him in good stead in all his disputes and relationships with the French court; King Louis, no doubt, had precisely the same considerations in mind on his own part. It would be a contest of wills and intellects that would determine who drew the greater benefit from the union. But on this marriage morning Henry was not thinking of political gains. To do him justice, that infuriating quality in him that kept him a child all his life at least conferred on him the virtues of a child. Ceremony charmed him, his imagination was open and optimistic, he had no doubts at all that his life with his bride would be happy, and mutual love could be taken for granted. When not frightened and vindictive, he approached life with an exasperating innocence.

The bride, they had assured him in advance, was already known at home as "La Belle," and when seen, she had justified her reputation. She was indeed as lovely and lively a child as could be found in the kingdom, and he had had no difficulty at all in falling in love with her at first sight, and was to remain infatuated lifelong. She was in her thirteenth year, and all the daughters of noble families of the same age had been assembled to attend her.

In the exhilaration of happiness and excitement Henry was at his best and most devout. He had even spent several hours, the previous night, in meditation and prayer, going over in his mind the events of the past year, and reflecting on the present state of his kingdom, which on the whole gave him good reason to thank God.

Not that everything was settled and easy yet. Such an upheaval as England had gone through in those disturbed years before the Earl Marshal's death inevitably gave rise to further reappraisals, exposing every article of government to close examination, in the hope of working out a better order, one less subject to similar storms in the future. Once such a re-examination began, it went on probing deeper and deeper into details. There would be violent differences of opinion before a new constitution was evolved, but the great thing was that now everyone came to the task with sincerity and goodwill, and quarrels would not drive them away into factions, but only make them louder and more assertive in the proper place for differences to be aired, the great council. Magnates, bishops, and judges had all one end in view, the establishment of a better and juster rule, consented to and kept by all. And when this royal marriage was over, and the new queen crowned, the entire great council was to meet at Merton to get its teeth into the supreme task.

He knew, as he always knew after the event, that he had been a fool to be influenced by the bishop of Winchester's interpretation of the royal plenitude of power, and he had been glad to escape back into the safer, less heady world of the Charters of Liberties, guided by Archbishop Edmund. For a long time he had, indeed, nursed a bitter and growing resentment against Peter des Roches, and had even gone so far as to write a warning letter to the Emperor Frederick, on the occasion of his sister Isabella's marriage to that potentate, pointing out how insidiously des Roches had led him into unwise and evil courses and alienated him from his subjects. The bishop was in Italy, and, as before, in the confidence of both pope and emperor, and Henry's denunciation, according to report, had bitterly wounded him. But now the king found it difficult to recapture his furious indignation. They said the bishop would like to come back to Winchester, and surely now it could be allowed. He need not be readmitted to the king's council, nor to any political influence. This was a time for general reconciliation, for a new beginning.

And those others, Passelew, Segrave, even des Rivaulx—their offences had been rank, and for a time he had pursued and harried them from pillar to post, inviting all who alleged injustices against them to come forward with their accusations, proclaiming their villainies the length and breadth of England. But for the restraining hand of the archbishop and his colleagues he might even have impeached them for their lives. But now, in cooler humour, he could see very well that they could be useful and efficient servants, properly controlled, and might well be readmitted to public service in some capacity—with care, of course, and never again in possession of power.

Yes, this was to be a new dawn. Let the past be shut away; let general forgiveness prevail. It seemed that affairs in England were shaping most favourably for a regime nicely balanced between that wild experiment in absolute monarchy and the too rigid and cramping adherence to rule by council and charter. And the queen had brought over with her a most beguiling company of her Provençal kin, and her mother's relatives from the house of Savoy. Her uncle, the bishop-elect of Valence, in particular, had impressed and attracted Henry's ready affection. Such a man would provide wisdom without timidity, and daring without rashness.

All in all, King Henry arose in the best of humours on his wedding day. London and Westminster were full to bursting, every possible lodging as far afield as the Tower filled and overfilled; all the nobility of the land had gathered to do honour to the marriage, or to attend the council, or both. Every baron who had a claim to some minor office either at wedding or coronation had seen to it that his demand for his rights was put in in good time. A week of feasting and shows awaited the city.

The earl of Kent and his countess attended among the highest in the land that day. Hubert was one of the king's sworn royal council, the inner circle of government, and even without his former establishment, shorn of the royal castles he had once held, his honour remained one of the greatest in eastern England. He was much restored in body for the past year's rest and privacy, but the white hair and the scarred wrists were unfading mementoes, and even in council he was now subdued, gentle, and silent. They said he had forsworn arms for ever. Certainly he sought no office. If he felt that he must speak out in council on some debatable point, he would do so clearly and without fear, but in a manner measured and calm, as if he had also forsworn anger, even when other voices were raised and other tempers high. Among the magnates attending the king on this occasion he was magnificent, but like a gentle ghost within the splendid garments. It was well known that though the king was markedly, even suspiciously, correct and courteous to him, he could never like him. The fading blue scars under the furred sleeve, the twisted finger-joints that had to handle documents so slowly and carefully, were tactless reminders. Des Rivaulx, though he had had to take shelter for a time in Winchester, had never been shackled or imprisoned, or hunted through the night by a London mob; he could reappear looking much the same as of old, and cause the king no discomfort. But the prints were on the earl of Kent for all to see. Walking beside his tall and handsome countess, he looked like her father, and a sire who had made an ageing marriage at that.

Richard de Clare was a page of honour among his young contemporaries, grouped to the left of the great arch of the rood-screen. Among all the glitter and colour round him he was merely one insignificant youngster, and no one, this day, was going to be noticing his movements or limiting his freedom. He had certain small duties to perform, like his companions, but provided he carried out those promptly, he could do what he liked with the rest of his time. His only anxiety was that Meggotta might be less at liberty than he. He had seen her briefly at Mass the previous day, and he knew that she and her parents would remain in the city until after the council at Merton. That would be six or seven days at least, and everyone would be busy about the festivities, with no attention to spare for errant pages, or, he hoped, stray damosels.

Until yesterday he had not seen her for four months, an age of waiting. She was thirteen years old, the new queen's age, and chosen as one of the girls to attend her. And here they came, in the bride's procession. He craned his neck to look for her among the gold and white ranks. He did not even see the small, glittering figure of the bride, stiff with gold, a beautiful southern doll, her dark hair wound into a coronal sewn with pearls, her white ivory prayer-book dangling a gold marker half a yard long. In the second rank behind her there was one who far outshone her for Richard. Having found her, he never looked away from her again. She did not at first see him. She moved with measured, careful steps, her eyes fixed ahead upon her duty; and such eyes, wide and clear as crystal within their dark fringes, under a brow like a smooth, sheer cliff of ivory, for her hair was drawn high and piled on her head within a band of silver. Some of her companions were fair, some dark brown or black; only she had this thick, curling, live hair that seemed darkest brown until light, whether of sun or lamp, lit upon it, and then glittered with points and sparkles of crimson. Long, resolute, dreaming lips she had, curled in virginal passion and locked tight upon a secret. Only four months, and she had grown so formidable in beauty, who had been beautiful even before.

Then she saw him. She had not been looking for him, she had been devoutly rapt in contemplation of the mystery of marriage, remembering her own. She met his eyes by chance, and the crimson that coruscated in her hair flashed into her eyes, welling up out of the pure grey.

She glowed into such brightness, he marvelled that all that regal company did not see, and forget everything else. But they did not. They
were gazing at the stiff golden doll with the pretty, confident face, and
at the king, who now drew in to meet her, and took her by the hand.

Throughout that marriage ceremony, Richard went through every
response in his own heart, with passion and rapture, and knew that
Meggotta in her place was replying as ardently. When they took their
places in the royal procession afterwards, and paced out of the abbey-
church into the winter sunlight, they were twice married, more irrevo-
cably husband and wife even than these two they attended.

Others besides Richard had observed among the girl attendants one who was graceful and promising beyond her years. The young
earl of Arundel, twenty-two years old and unmarried, asked the old earl
of Derby, beside him in the retinue, "Who is that child with the great
eyes, and the red in her hair?" The light from the windows had just
caught the coils and started the hidden fires.

"That?" said William Ferrers, peering. "That's de Burgh's girl, the
heiress of Kent. Like her mother, the Scots blood shows."

"De Burgh," said Arundel thoughtfully. "And not yet spoken for?"

There were others, also, viewing the assembly of marriageable girls,
and selecting what best pleased them. A dowager of the Bohun family,
seeking a wife for a favourite grandson, a collateral of the Chaworths,
with a son to set up in life, a Hastings, a Warenne. This was a most
convenient occasion for considering the possibilities, and weighing the
respective fortunes.

Two of those who were thus planning the future of their growing
sons and nephews took the opportunity to speak with Hubert on the
subject, the day after the new queen's coronation, which was another
glittering, lengthy, and exhausting occasion. In the privacy of their
bedchamber at the end of the day he mentioned the conversations to
Margaret.

"The baronage is beginning to notice," he said, "that our Meggotta
is growing up, and growing up very attractive. I suppose it will soon be
time to consider her future. It seems there are others doing us the

honour of considering it for us." He sounded proud and indulgent, but not enthusiastic; even a little jealous and possessive, perhaps, of his darling.

Margaret was sitting at her toilet, mirror in hand, and watched her own face become wary and veiled, receiving a confidence she had feared now for many months. She had even tried to keep the girl cloistered, aside from the necessary appearances in London, and even then to enclose her within a small circle of acquaintances, which did not exclude her escape into Richard's brief company. No one knew better than she how beautiful her child had become. She had dreaded the first approach, now it was here. Tentative, probably, sounding out the father's response, but ready to move on if the father proved complaisant. These things were never done in haste.

"Someone has made a proposal to you?" she asked, her voice carefully level and calm.

"The Earl Warenne opened in favour of his son. We have good relations with the whole family, it's true, and his lands march well with ours."

"His son is an infant," said Margaret disparagingly. "The difference of age is too great. Remember, I was all but betrothed to a man twelve years or more my junior, it matters more than you may suppose. I should not like Meggotta to be placed in the same situation. Besides, she's only thirteen, let her be young a little longer."

"Very gladly," agreed Hubert heartily. "I hate to think of letting her go at all, but it would not be fair to leave her unprovided. I want to see my girl set up happily and in her rightful place in the realm before I quit this world, not to leave her in some stranger's hands. For I doubt if they'd leave her in yours, my love, with the earldom of Kent in the bargain with her."

And that also was true, and must be taken into consideration. Into what a tangle, thought Margaret, staring into her own eyes, have I brought us all! And yet I do not know what else I could have done to try to save them, when things were at their worst. If only we can hold on a little longer. Now the king has a bride of his own, he may soften enough to be approached with confession—provided I can keep Hubert clear of all reproach.

"And have there been others? No wonder, I suppose, in her finery she dazzles even me. And the earldom of Kent, as you say, is a very valuable property."

"Young Hugh d'Aubeny spoke up for himself. A presentable young man, and Arundel will be parted among his sisters, and the earldom will lapse, if he does not marry and get heirs."

"He is some years too old," said Margaret. "I'd rather see Meggotta with a husband of her own years."

"So would I, and we both know with whom. But that's over, my heart! He'll never let me have art or part in Richard again." He said it with absolute certainty, and in her heart she knew he was justified. "But Arundel is only twenty-two, and ten years on that side is not amiss. Well, let it rest there for a while. I am no more anxious to part with my girl than you are, be sure I'm not going to hurry her away to the first comer. I fancy the earl of Hereford was looking thoughtfully at her, too, among the queen's attendants. She did shine so!" said Hubert fondly.

He rose and crossed the room to stand behind his wife, his hands resting on her shoulders. In the mirror their eyes met and held fast. "And should you balk at ten years, my heart's love, who have not balked at five and twenty? And never once wavered when the going was deadly hard? I never told you this, Margaret—it started too deep a hurt for me, I could not bear to speak of it—but at Merton, when the whole coil began, when they told me he was banishing me from England for life, and I took the Cross as the only worth-while thing left to me, then I also took the first step to have our marriage annulled. If I could never see you again, I wanted you free. Young and splendid and royal as you are, you might still have had a life, if I had none. Thank God he changed his mind and never sent the order of banishment, preferring to keep me within his grasp or slay me. Whatever happened to me after that was better than tearing out my heart. So it never went further, and I still have you. Undeserved, I doubt, but mine!"

She was shivering under his hands. "Oh, God!" she said in a whisper. "You could not! What manner of life would that have been to me? Or to Meggotta? I never thought I should thank Henry for anything, but I do thank him for preventing such a violation. Without you I should have died!" And she reached up both hands and drew his head down to her, turning to fold her arms round him and lift her face for his kiss. And while they were locked thus in an ageing embrace that shook them both with its unexpected passion, she thought, deep within her, as an inescapable extension of her own words, Without Richard, Meggotta would die!

On the eve of the earl of Kent's departure from London for Burgh, Meggotta and Richard met in their chosen secret place, the dark cloister of the abbey-church, under the monks' dormitory. It was not only dark but also cold, but they did not mind that. The overhanging roof of the *dortoir*, long and shadowy, loomed over them like a protecting hand. They could enter and leave either by the great cloister or through the narrow archway to the prior's lodging and its court, whence they could make their escape through the stables. There were so many ways out of there that they felt quite safe in their silent retreat. The great cloister was too apt to be sheltering other creatures desirous of privacy.

"It's fine," said Richard in a whisper, "that it's winter. So dark, no one sees us. A man would have to walk up and shine a lantern in our faces to know us. And no one comes here."

It was true; no one did, except, and rarely at this hour, one of the brothers bent on some urgent errand; and if any such observed them, two slender, linked forms huddled on a bench under the eaves, he averted his eyes and refrained from seeing. For even monastic brotherhoods are composed of human creatures, some among whom have left behind them in the world remembered loves; some, even, still bleed.

"Richard, are you sure? Was it certainly of you they were talking?"

"Yes," said Richard, "no question. 'The disposal of Hertford and Gloucester is a royal matter,' said my Uncle Gilbert. And the king's clerk said, 'The time seems to be ripe, we should be considering the possibilities. His Grace has ambitions for the boy in France.' Then I had to run, because somebody opened the door. But I know what I heard. I know what they were discussing. I am to be disposed of as a valuable property, to buy some foreign princess, some connection of his

Grace. That mother of his, in her second marriage to the count of La Marche, is breeding sons and daughters like mice. I am wanted to provide a stay for one of these French kinswomen. I'll die first, Meggotta! I want nobody but you!"

"Nothing has happened yet," she said, clutching at hope that slipped all too easily through her fingers.

"But it's beginning. If they're talking of it, it's because the king has made up his mind that it's time. The only help is that they may fall out about it, and go on arguing for a long time what's best to be done. I need not notice until someone speaks of it openly to me. But then I must speak out and tell the truth. What else can we do?"

"In the end," said Meggotta sturdily, "whatever they say or do, they can't separate us. Let them be as angry as they will, they'll have to acknowledge us as man and wife. A marriage once made can't be broken."

"I don't know! Meggotta, I'm afraid of what they can do. I think it can be broken, even if we refuse to connive at it. We're still under age, both of us, they can do things in our names, even against our will. Oh, I know father would not do anything to hurt us, but I'm afraid the king could override him—and afraid of what he might do to him, too, even though he knows nothing of what we did. I think it isn't even very hard to get a marriage annulled, when it hasn't gone beyond the ceremony. I asked my confessor once about marriage—oh, no, not betraying anything about you and me, only asking as one might out of curiosity, especially at my age. People begin to look at us—have you noticed?—as though we were goods they were thinking of buying, or would have liked to buy if they could afford them. I'm sure he didn't find it strange that I had a lot of questions to ask him, and I made sure they were not all about marriage. He likes to be questioned, if he's sure I'm in earnest, he thinks it shows I'm taking my future as earl of Gloucester seriously. He said . . . he said that even after the vows have been made, and the blessing of the church given, the sacrament is not complete until husband and wife have lain together and loved."

He felt her tremble in his arms, and he himself was shaking, not all with cold. The very utterance of the words was piercing and startling, like ice or fire.

"And then it is a full marriage? And can't be broken?"

"He said that then the union sanctioned by the church rites has been consummated, and man and wife are one flesh. Then how can they be separated?"

She was silent for a while, and very still; the trembling had ceased. She turned and wound her arms about his slender, springy body within the warmth of his cloak. With her cheek against his she said in a whisper, and very gravely, "Richard, this is a very hard thing we have to do, sooner or later, to stand and fight for our right to each other. It will be danger and pain. Are you quite sure that you don't want to come to terms with the world now, and make the best of what's left? I shall never blame you, or cease to wish you well, if you do. No, don't answer me in anger; it isn't that I doubt you. But you must pause and think now, and so must I, before we go any further together."

Her voice was so solemn that he bit back the indignant outcry which had risen to his throat, and sat silent and fearful for a long moment.

"Answer me truly, do you mean that *you* want to give in, and let me go?"

"You must give me your answer first, then I will tell you truly."

"Then no, and no, and no!" he said passionately. "We go on together and we fight. I will never give you up, unless you yourself ask it. Whatever happens, you're mine, and I'll never let go of you. And now you speak!"

"I say the same," whispered Meggotta. "Without you, nothing else would have any worth or any lustre."

"Then we go on keeping our secret as long as we may, and hoping for an occasion when we can tell it openly without fear. And if that never comes, then when we must we shall tell it and fight for our rights just the same, whatever they try to do to us."

"Richard, there's one thing more we can do in our own cause. You have just told me we have a remedy. There is a way to make ourselves one, so that not even the king can tear us apart."

He did not at first understand. When he did, he began to shake like a creature in fever, not with cold or fear, but with the sudden onset of blinding, terrifying joy at what was seen to be within his reach. Never for a moment did he doubt that she meant it with all her heart, and desired it as he did, wholly reverently, with the same awe and gratitude with which they had knelt before the abbot in St. Edmund's Church at Bury. They were so nearly one already that there was little need of words between them. All he said was, "How?" And then, "We should tell your mother. I think she would say yes."

"I will tell her, but afterwards. This must be your act and mine, no one else's."

"And tonight! It must be tonight, you leave for Burgh tomorrow."

"Can you slip in and out of the earl's house without being seen?" The Earl Marshal had a house across the palace court, near the entrance to the canonry. By the bridge over the Long Ditch it would be only a short passage to the earl of Kent's house.

"I have done, sometimes. I know ways. Uncle Gilbert doesn't keep a close watch on me, or set anyone else to do it for him. He's easy, he doesn't much care what I do, I've never caused him any trouble. And I sleep alone."

"Then come as soon as you can after nine, to the wicket gate in the alley behind our house. You remember it? I'll leave it open for you. The little stairway from the garden door leads up to my room, and I shall hear you if you whistle from the garden, and I'll come down and let you in. I'll go early to bed, no one will disturb us."

He had not forgotten the layout of Hubert's palace, which had once been his own London home. "Yes, yes, I'll come! Oh, Meggotta, are you sure? I would not for anything in the world bring harm on you."

"What harm? You are my husband, and I am your wife. With all my heart I want this—I want *you!*"

He kissed her rapturously, eager and anxious, in terror and bliss. "Oh, Meggotta, what if I'm clumsy, and hurt you? I know what to do, but I may not be very good at it . . . the first time. . . ."

"You can't hurt me. You love me, and wish me nothing but good, how can you hurt me? And I love you, and we shall learn together. You'll see that everything will be perfect. I'll help you, I'll love you as well as any woman could. And then we shall be married indeed, and no one will be able to part us."

They slipped away out of the dark cloister somewhat too late to pass for devout worshippers emerging from Vespers, having forgotten the time in their dream. But those left at home would not know where they had been or what they had been doing in the chill of the January evening. They went together only as far as the bridge; then he knew that she had only a few minutes of safe walking to be home. If she had indeed been to Vespers, there would have been enough of the pious going that way to ensure her safety, though even so it had cost her some persuasion, and Margaret's backing, to be allowed to go to church alone.

Richard turned back from the bridge, and in at the west gateway, under the high tower, into the king's island city. From within the gate, the palace court swept away on his left hand to the river Thames, flanking the massed buildings of the palace. He turned into its long, narrow ride, treading wintry, tufted turf. Sometimes magnates who were guests here exercised their horses on this stretch. On his right a towered gateway opened into the precincts of the palace. Somewhere to his left was his own present abode, though he could not think of it as home. He dawdled, in spite of the cold of the January night, unwilling to go in and face lights and eyes. No one had any right to intrude upon his exalted solitude at this moment, on this night. He veered rather towards the palace gateway.

Then he saw, by the light of torches that burned unseen in sconces fixed under the archway, that two shadows were walking ahead of him towards the same gate. They had been so silent, and the darkness without was so uniformly deep and still, that he had not realized they were there in front of him. These might well be church-goers returning, if they were also of such rank as to be living within the king's own house; but if so, though this was a reasonable way home, they had been very dilatory in making use of it. They were going very slowly now, and somewhat strangely, some yards of empty night between them, and yet some private tension linking them together. As soon as the torch-light from under the gate fell full upon them, the woman caught up her skirts in hands cumbered with a prayer-book, and hastened her step, sweeping ahead through the gate, as though she discarded her escort, and then unaccountably lingering within to draw her cloak closer about her, so that he might overtake her where the light again dimmed. And the profile, as it surged forward into light, was the youthful, impetuous, passionate face of Eleanor, King Henry's youngest and most spirited sister.

The man who followed, not deigning to hurry when she hurried, or not caring to embarrass her by doing so, was equally unmistakable given the light that fell upon him as he passed. Simon de Montfort, earl of Leicester, strode with imperturbable tread into the precincts of the palace, and overtook the Lady Eleanor with composure and respect, but the brief glimpse of his face as he passed was illuminating indeed. So bright, so intent, so crystalline in resolution, the deep eyes fixed only upon the girl. He saw nothing else. Nothing else existed.

Richard suffered a great lunge forward in his assault upon manhood. He did not understand what happened within him, the hot spring of compassion and fellowship, the triumphant surge of pity, for this was a lover who had not yet achieved his fulfilment, as he, Richard, had. The woman fled him, strong but desperate and divided. She fled him, and then she lingered.

Suddenly aware of profanation, Richard averted his eyes, and hurried away.

At the great door of the palace Eleanor said, without turning her head, "This is useless! You must not follow and harry me any more. You know as well as I that I am bound."

"The more shame to those who let you take such a vow," said Simon hotly. "At sixteen, and innocent as a babe of what living is, and what it can be. If you think what you did was pleasing to God, you make a terrible mistake. I do not believe he meant you to waste your life— such a plenitude of life!—without husband or children or any real part in the world."

"No one prompted me," she said fairly. "I did it of my own will, and to suit my own purposes. I made use of God, and now I must pay the price for it. I took my vow because I wanted to be free of proffers of marriage from men I despised, and to keep my body still my own."

"Then perhaps it was God who prompted you, after all," said Simon. "It was his way of keeping you for some man you would *not* despise."

"For you, my lord?" she flashed.

"I did not say so. But I think you do not despise me."

"Nor love you, either," said Eleanor firmly.

"Then I must wait and follow and harry you, madam, until you do. For I love you, and I will have no other."

"You are mad," she said helplessly. "I have told you it's useless. I cannot break my vow."

"There can be dispensation for such vows. The Holy Father will absolve you from what was a criminal folly in the first place. He can take no pleasure in such waste of what God made beautiful and gallant and able, meant to live greatly. It is not worthy of you to wither away in celibacy. If I had created such splendour, do you think I would value a barren vow above its proper use? And it is more honourable to own frankly to a sorry mistake, and ask pardon and release, than to go on stubbornly holding fast to it when you *know* it was a mistake."

"It's wicked of you, Simon," she burst out in a bitter undertone, "to wind about like this to get me to break my oath. Do you so lightly discard your own word of honour?"

"*Lightly?* Do you think what I feel is light? Do you think I hold these beliefs lightly? I mean every word! What you are doing is *wrong*. What they did, who let you swear your life away—*that* was wicked and light. Whoever was your spiritual father should have used every persuasion to prevent you from such base ingratitude to God who made you wonderful."

She drew her cloak half over her face with a smothered moan of protest. "I will not listen to you! I am committed! And I bid you, order you, leave me and stop this pursuit. I will not see you again."

Simon stood silent for a moment, frowning fiercely but not attempting to touch her. Then he said grimly, "Very well! On one condition I will go, and if I go, that will be the end. If you can tell me, on your faith and truth, that you are utterly indifferent to me, that you have no love for me now and never will have, that my going will add to your happiness, then you will have no more trouble from me. Say it, if you

can, if you dare! And remember, God is listening just as attentively now
as he was then!"

She tried. She stiffened her back and reared her head, and began
defiantly, but at the word 'indifferent' her throat closed, and she could
not utter another sound. She drew breath deep, and gave a muted wail
of anger and perplexity, and, catching up her long skirt, sprang up the
steps and ran from him into the doorway; but even so she heard him
say, in a startled gasp, "Eleanor!" It was not a long word to express so
much, but it began in consternation, and ended in triumph.

Richard slipped through the narrow door into the walled
garden, and softly closed the wicket behind him. The cold of the night
was edging into frost, stars snapped overhead like sparks from a fire, in
a vault black as ebony. The fire in heaven and the fire in his bowels kept
a matched rhythm, lifting him out of himself into a heroic growth. He
could do wonders. He had forgotten how to be afraid, even of the
wonder he had never tried before, the mystery that made marriage
complete and unassailable. He thought of Meggotta, and there was
nothing he could not do for her. He thought of the lovers he had left
both chained and severed in the archway of the king's gate, and was
so sorry for them that his heart seemed likely to burst. He sent up a
soft, true whistle towards the window which he knew belonged to
Meggotta's chamber, and felt his way along the path to the small rear
door. It opened before him as he touched, and Meggotta's hand
reached for his hand, and drew him within.

In the darkness she seemed stranger, older, more mysterious than
when he saw her in the light. She leaned and kissed his cheek; she could
see better than he, having waited for him here in this night and silence.
Her breath warmed his lips, she whispered, "Come!" and drew him
very tenderly and solicitously, all blind as he was, up the staircase and
into her own room. There was the glimmer and warmth of a dying fire
in the hearth, but no other light. And yet suddenly there was Meggotta
all white and radiant and slender before him, like an altar candle,
spilling from her shoulders the gown that had covered her. His heart
rose into his throat, choking what might otherwise have been a shout

of triumphant joy, and his body began to do strange and marvellous things that troubled and hurt and exalted him to the limit of what he could endure, but never beyond.

It was not as he had thought it would be, it was more. He laid trembling hands to strip off tunic and shirt, his cloak already dropped within the doorway; and she was close and gentle and adroit, lending hands to aid his hands, though all four shook, and, meeting, clung long seconds between, and loosed like souls parting from bodies. And the silence and the warmed darkness within the room were a powerful magic, like nothing ever known before.

Naked and candle-pale, taller than she, he reached and embraced her, and her coolness and warmth, and his, melted into one perfect glow of passion. He knew what to do, and his body was roused and famished and crying out to him to do it, and be at peace. How they found their way, linked as they were, into the opened bed he never knew. Somehow it was accomplished, for there was an enfolding warmth that bound them together as once, he remembered, in child-hood, at the very beginning of this incomprehensible and lovely thing that bound them together now. Even the glimmer of the fire vanished, they were engulfed in exquisite darkness under covers that caressed like maternal hands.

And all the while, even at the most extreme translation into woman and man, they spoke to each other ceaselessly in the voices of children, doubtful and wondering and innocent. "Am I heavy? . . . I'm hurting you!" "Oh, no, no, no. I love you. . . . I love . . ." "Is this right? Should I?" They shed tears of laughter and bliss. They lay wreathed together in lovely languor, tired out with pleasure, and revived to something far beyond pleasure.

"Meggotta . . ."

"Richard! I love you!"

"I love you! Are you happy? Have I pleased you?"

"Did you know it would be like this?"

"No, never, never! What could be like this!"

"Nothing ever before, nothing ever. . . ."

Gradually the words stilled in their lips, and their stroking hands, which alone had some drowsy energy left to spend in caresses, lingered and lay easy, still embracing the beloved. They lay entwined, and drifted fathoms deep into dreamless slumber.

Meggotta awoke well before dawn, her concern for Richard goading her out of sleep, for it was vital that he should return undetected to his own bed before light came. She drew herself out of his arms, and propped herself on one elbow to look down at his sleeping face, serene, childlike, and vulnerable. A strand of her hair, falling, brushed his eyelids, fringed with dark gold, and they quivered at the touch, and fluttered as though about to rise, and then were soothed and eased into stillness again. She had to kiss him, brow and throat and breast, light as a butterfly, and then hard and long on the mouth, before he awoke and opened great eyes to stare in wonder, finding himself in this place at once strange and familiar. He reached up and pulled her down to him with a soft, exultant cry, his body quickening into defiant desire. She had budding breasts, firm and round, that seemed to pierce his heart like lances.

"No! Richard, it will soon get light. You must go!"

"I don't want to go!"

"I don't want you to go. . . ."

"This once, this once let me. . . . You're going away!"

"We shall be together again. We shall do this again. . . . Oh, yes, my heart. . . . Yes. . . ."

The second essay was more tender, more solemn, more at ease, and yet more sacramental than the first. He lay on her heart afterwards, his lips exploring her throat and bosom very softly and reverently. And then there was certainly a fading in the darkness, and he rose with infinite reluctance and began to put on his clothes. She slid naked from the bed and knelt to serve him.

"Don't come down! I don't want you to. Go back to bed and keep that place warm for me a little while. Go back to sleep, and I shall be there with you. You're mine now, no one can take you from me."

"Just to the door," she said, pleading. "The garden gate will still be unfastened."

"To the door, then, but no more."

They crept down the stairs hand in hand, and kissed at the foot. He drew back the bolts gingerly, touched her cheek, and was gone. Meggotta shot the bolts into their sockets, and went slowly back up the stairs.

In her room Margaret was standing beside the bed, her fingers touching the warmed space where two had lain. She looked up as her daughter came into the open doorway, and for all the darkness, as yet barely touched by the grey fingers of dawn, she saw the still radiance of the half-glimpsed face, and knew that Meggotta was smiling.

"Yes. We have made ours a marriage no one shall be able to unsay."

"I know!" said Margaret in a whisper, and opened her arms to her daughter, who walked into them with a serenity far beyond the reach of thirteen years, and sat down with her in the warmth of Richard's marriage-bed. "Why did you not tell me?"

"I was going to tell you this morning. This was a thing for us to do, not for any other. We decided it, we did it. No one else bears any responsibility for this."

"I came only to wake you, not to spy on you. Because we should get ready to leave early."

"I know, mother. But be glad for us. Oh, you should be glad! We must tell Alice, and she'll help us, the next time. He will come again, you know, whenever we're here in the city. And father must not know." She felt that violation, but it was inevitable, and she could bear it. He was the one who at all costs must be protected.

"God grant, child," said Margaret gravely, "that you've done the best thing, the guided thing, and can make it good against the world. And that we may not all of us have cause to regret it."

"No," said Meggotta, exalted, "that I never shall, no matter what happens to me. I have held Richard, and loved him, and lain asleep in his arms, and never, never shall I have any regrets."

It chanced, some weeks after this day, that the lord abbot of Bury St. Edmunds, rising at seven in the morning for Prime, got no farther than the doorway of his lodging when he suddenly threw up his arms and fell on his face. He was taken up, with congested countenance and blue lips, to die an hour later without opening his eyes or speaking intelligible word. Though frail in body, he had been in apparent health until that day, considering his years, and had been in no fear of the sudden summons which thus incontinently called him away. Accordingly, he had left no written record of certain private dealings within his competence that concerned the affairs of persons of importance, and were of vital moment to their future fortunes.

11

September to October, 1236:
Westminster; Eagle; Kempton.

Richard had long outgrown the clothes he had worn at ten years old, in Bury St. Edmunds. While he was in the bishop of Winchester's detested household they had still fitted him, and throughout that time he had left Meggotta's ring where it was, sewn into the collar of his favourite tunic, afraid to draw attention to it even by fingering the place, but careful always to keep it where it would be handled only by himself. But by the time he had been released into Earl Gilbert's care and found himself treated like a responsible youth, fit to have his liberty within reason, the tunic had grown decidedly too small for him, and he had unpicked the stitches that held the ring in place in good time, before the steward's wife, who saw to his laundry and kept an eye on his needs, made a clean sweep of all his outgrown garments and recommended to his uncle the making of new.

It was still essential that the ring and all it meant remain hidden. For a time he wore it on a ribbon round his neck, but as the summer came on, and he walked and rode lightly clad and with shirt open, that became too dangerous. Finally Meggotta sewed it into the collar of his cloak for him; for a cloak is serviceable for years, and not soon outgrown. That was in late spring, when council business had brought Hubert to town again, and his womenfolk with him. Nights were shorter then, and Richard had to come later and leave earlier, but there were still some few hours for being together. The night Meggotta did her sewing they did not sleep at all, but lay whispering together all night when the first ecstasy was over, as though they had to be frugal with passion, and yet drain every moment of a more lasting joy. Never before had they had time to caress over again all the "Do you remember?"s their brief past provided, and savour them all with new, unchildish delight. Living always on the edge of disaster and loss sharpened the savour of pleasure, as well as the sting of pain.

It was about this time that Earl Gilbert Marshal married. No doubt his match was also a matter for grave discussion, for the honour of Pembroke included several castles of vital importance, and must be linked with a family well disposed and useful to the crown, as well as suitable in rank and station. The marriage did not take place in London, and Richard was not required to be in attendance, but he opened his eyes wide on hearing that the intended bride was a younger sister of Margaret de Burgh. The sisters were almost strangers, for Margaret and Isabella had been confided to King John's care in their early teens, with a view to those promised royal marriages which had never materialized, while this much younger Marjorie could then have been little more than an infant, and had grown up at home in Scotland. King Alexander was busy pressing his claim to certain lands in the northern counties of England, and no doubt welcomed the alliance with someone so influential as Pembroke; it was tacitly agreed in the bargain between them that Earl Gilbert would back his claims now that they were brothers-in-law.

Richard had a shrewd grasp of these matters of policy, but no great interest in them except as they threatened his own secrets. Gilbert was indifferent but amiable, and for the most part let him alone, and he was relieved to find that the new countess seemed inclined to do the same, being totally absorbed in her husband. She had brought with her a bevy of maids from her own country, one of whom, not many years older than Richard, and of exalted parentage, began to take an inconvenient interest in this boy who was heir to one of the greatest earldoms in England. If he had been a little more conscious of his own attractions of person and fortune, he would have been more wary of her, but he was almost without vanity, though over-provided with sensitive pride, and never noticed the girl at all, which caused her to notice him all the more.

It was mere chance that she should be up very early one morning at the beginning of September, and look out into the garden of the earl's house, withdrawn behind the array of buildings that lined the palace court. She saw Richard walking in a dream under the orchard trees. She could not know that he had only ten minutes previously slipped back into the garden from visiting Meggotta; it seemed to her simply that he had risen early to take the air on a fine morning. But she thought it curious that he should have found his cloak necessary, and even more startling that he should shrug it from his shoulders, gather it in one arm, and lift the right tip of the collar to his lips in an unmistakable and impulsive kiss. She knew she was not deceived, he held the fold of woollen cloth to his cheek a long moment, smiling, before he passed round the corner of the house towards his own rooms, and vanished from her sight.

Nothing would do for her, after that, but she must know why the collar of a cloak should mean so much to him. It never entered her head that he had been abroad all night, and needed the cloak both for warmth and concealment. At a time when she knew he was out at exercise with the younger gentlemen of the court, and would be away for some hours, she slipped into his rooms and looked in the presses that held his clothes. The cloak was easy enough to find. The cloth was too thick to surrender the impression of the ring to her questing fingers, but she did observe that Meggotta's thread, chosen by subdued light, did not quite match the deep blue with which the whole seam was sewn.

Perhaps she had nothing in mind but a very small service to a boy who had taken her fancy, or perhaps there was something more sinister in her act, when she set to work with small scissors to unpick the fine stitches and discover what lay within. Certainly she was murmuring to herself that she could replace the flaw with a perfect match, even as she fingered out the ring from the tiny pocket in which Meggotta had concealed it. A thin, rounded golden ring, one face flattened to take a seal, and a single letter engraved there. And Richard had kissed the place where it was hidden, believing himself alone and unobserved.

She did not replace the ring. Her own probing fingers had not been able to feel it through the close-woven wool, neither would his fingers detect its absence. But she sewed up the slit she had made, most carefully and deftly, and put the cloak back in its place, before she took the ring to her mistress and told her where she had found it.

The Countess Marjorie revolved the ring in her fingers with lowered lids and inscrutable face. Gold varies as to where it is found and how it is worked, apart from any distinctive marks left upon it. Just such a ring, almost indistinguishable, she wore on her own finger. She did not say one word to admit as much. She thanked her maid, expressed neither approval nor disapproval, and sent the girl away unsatisfied.

Earl Gilbert had gone north with the court, a progress into Lincolnshire. Marjorie sent for Master Carrell, who was again installed as Richard's tutor, at the boy's request, willingly granted once the bishop of Winchester had ceded all rights.

"Master Carrell, I think you attended my lord's nephew Richard, when he was ward to the earl of Kent. As I understand it, the boy was pledged in marriage to the earl's daughter, and that contract was broken by the king when he discarded the earl and committed him to prison. Do you think—I ask frankly—there was an affection there, between these children?"

"A very deep affection," said Master Carrell warmly.

"And—I ask it as you have been here with Richard since my lord took him in care—has there been, to your knowledge, any renewal of this alliance?"

"No, to my knowledge, madam, none."

"Forgive my insistence. *Could* there have been such? Either before your reinstatement, while he was in the care of the bishop of Winchester, or since then, while my lord has had him in charge?"

He pondered that carefully. "I believe while the bishop had him any such thing would have been inconceivable. He was most closely watched, on the bishop's orders. Since then, I cannot say. Earl Gilbert has trusted Richard, and I believe that trust is justified. But his freedom has been gratifying. He *could* have misused it. He was at liberty to come and go much as he pleased. That he has been much happier, and respected his uncle's goodness, that I do assert."

"This ring . . ." she said, showing it in her palm. "The boy had it closely concealed, and handled it with passion. This is gold worked in

214 t The Marriage of Meggotta

Scotland. I know it. I wear another—you see?—almost its match, except that it bears my initial in a somewhat different script. But the same letter, *M.* We all had them, made alike, with the lion of Scotland —small, but you may see it clearly—engraved on the reverse of the initial. This ring once belonged to my sister Margaret. The *M* would serve also for her daughter, if . . ." She did not end the thought. "Master Carrell, I know you can be discreet. . . ."

So he could, but the inquisitive page outside the door had quick wits, a garrulous tongue, and no discretion at all, and the girl who had stolen the ring, balked of any satisfaction from the countess, made do with the pleasure of spreading the story elsewhere. Within three days the rumour was stirring, in two or three households, that the earl of Kent had contrived to marry his daughter to the earl of Gloucester, in despite of the king's head.

The Countess Marjorie was not at ease with Richard, now that she possessed this knowledge, and never taxed him with it, but understandably took the most comfortable path by sending a messenger to her husband in Lincolnshire, with all that she knew, and leaving the matter in his hands. By that time several baronial households had got hold of some version of the story, and were spreading it and improving on it. When it reached the king in the north, there were several earls and lords prepared to bring the charges of sacrilege and treason against the earl of Kent.

The courier who brought the king's summons to Hubert at Burgh was armed with no further message, and delivered Henry's bidding cheerfully and respectfully, so that even Margaret, always ready to look for the evil implication in any unexpected embassage from Henry, could find no cause for anything but optimism. The messenger had received his orders at third hand, and even the chamberlain who sent him out to bid the earl into Lincolnshire had not seen the king's suffused face, or heard his voice mount into shrill outrage when he issued the order.

"If the king wants father's advice even when the council is not meeting," said Meggotta eagerly, "it must mean he's warming to him as he used to. Surely they'll come together again, and we shall be able to beg the king for a hearing, and not be refused."

"We may pray for it," said Margaret, wary of hope.

The king was at the preceptory of the Templars at Eagle, near Lincoln. Hubert and his companion, riding by way of Lynn and Sleaford, took two days upon the journey, which was wearisome to an old man, and reached the preceptory on the day after Michaelmas, the last of September. Henry was private in his own apartment when Hubert announced himself as arrived and at his disposal, and the king did not immediately admit him, but requested his attendance in audience in the hall within half an hour.

There were a dozen or more magnates present, those among the baronage who were most in the king's grace at this time, as well his own household clerks and officers, all gathered about the royal chair. Hubert, who came without anxiety if without any very hopeful expectancy, checked as he entered the hall, as though he had run his breast into a wall of spears. It was too chilling a reminder of the black day at Shrewsbury, still unexplained, unjustified, an unhealed wound in his spirit; all those pairs of eyes turned upon him as upon an alien and enemy, in silent, burning accusation. He had no warning at all; he knew of nothing they could hold against him, and he was too old and tired to face another prolonged cycle of time's game with him.

He approached the king, and met the old look in his eyes, angry, affronted, righteously rejecting him, except that now the anger was not so calculated or so deliberately whipped up to frenzy, but bright and open and even composed. Was it possible that he felt he had a genuine grievance this time? Hubert knew of none.

"My lord king, you sent for me. I am here." Why use more words than were needed? Even words cost him effort.

"Yes, I sent for you. My lord of Kent, there is a matter here to which you are required to answer. Certain of your peers have opened a proceeding against you in the royal court. You are charged by Earl Gilbert Marshal, by the earl of Lincoln, and by the earl of Cornwall, and others, that you have sacrilegiously and treasonously married your daughter in secret to Richard de Clare."

Hubert stood dazed and staring, for it was utterly absurd, when this man knew very well that he himself had broken the bargain made concerning that proposed marriage, and snatched away the boy from the place where he was happy. He almost laughed aloud, the charge was so foolish, hardly worth answering. But all the hotly accusing eyes kept their dangerous gravity. This was not simply a new caprice of the king. Cornwall, Lincoln, Gilbert Marshal, all steadier men by far than King Henry, meant their charge to be taken seriously, and meant to drive it home.

"Need I remind you, my lord," said the king sternly, "of the oath you swore on the altar at Gloucester, more than two years since, to claim no rights ever again in Richard de Clare? Do you deny your solemn oath?"

"No, your Grace, why should I deny it? I made my oath, and I have kept it. I have never exchanged word privately with the boy since that day, never meddled in his affairs."

"So you say. Yet the word has leaked out, for all your secrecy, that this clandestine marriage has indeed been celebrated, in violation of your sworn word."

"If rumour says so," said Hubert, "rumour lies. If any of my peers present says so, I will believe in his good faith, certainly, but I tell him he is deceived. I hear for the first time of any such rumour. I hear for the first time of this marriage. And I tell you, it is impossible. Your Grace knows, none so well, that Richard de Clare was taken out of my wife's hands after I was impeached, and from that time I never saw him again but among the young men of your court, in public. For the very affection I had for him, these last two years I have refrained all the more carefully from his company. Since I made my oath at Gloucester, you, my lord Gilbert, know very well that he has been in your hands, and you should know it is folly to suppose he has contracted a marriage without your knowledge."

"In my care," said the Earl Marshal, "he has had a large measure of freedom, to come and go as he pleased, and I will say for him I knew of no misuse he ever made of his freedom. Yet the proofs exist that he has so misused it, and someone older surely procured him to the folly. It is your daughter, my lord, who is involved, why should we look further than you? You always wished for this match, you have gone about to secure it, and Gloucester and Hertford and Clare with it. The boy is my nephew, I had the right to a voice in the disposal of his person and fortune, and I accuse you of defrauding me of that voice."

"While the bishop of Winchester had charge of Richard," said the earl of Cornwall, "it is certain this could not have happened. My stepson, I must say, was *too* strictly watched and guarded, no one could have got to him, to suborn him to such folly. If it happened at all— and it seems certain that it did, unless you have proofs to the contrary —then it happened since the oath you took at Gloucester, and you are forsworn and guilty of sacrilege. My wife and I have undoubted rights in this boy, and I demand that the law take its course with you." Richard of Cornwall had a son of his own now, a year-old half-brother for Richard de Clare, but he would still demand full satisfaction for his rights in his wife's firstborn.

"My lords," said Hubert, "I am taken at a disadvantage, since I hear these charges for the first time, and know nothing of them, and have no counsel, never having supposed I needed any when I came. You are convinced that what you say against me is truth. I know it is not. But if you say you have proofs, produce them. It may be they can be disposed of more simply than you think."

The Earl Marshal was more than willing. "Richard de Clare was in possession of a gold ring, such as might be exchanged in marriage. He kept it stitched into the collar of a cloak, and he has been seen, when he thought himself private, to kiss and caress the place where it was hidden away."

"He is fourteen now," said Hubert with a rueful smile. "Is it so strange if a green boy should think himself in love, and treasure some girl's keepsake? How does that inculpate me and mine?"

"The ring, my lord, came into the hands of my wife, who is the sister of your countess. She has one very like it, also engraved with her initial, *M.* She recognizes the gold and the make of it. She says it must have belonged to her sister, Margaret, your wife. Within, it also bears the lion of Scotland. Is this enough?"

It was enough, certainly, to drive the breath out of Hubert's body, and set him gaping helplessly, groping after some idea that would make sense of this whole farrago, but he could find nothing that did not crumble at a touch. He looked about him, greedy even for some word or look of balanced, sane doubt, but they were all united against him. Only the earl of Leicester, drawn a little back behind the king's chair, gnawed his lip and knotted his lofty brows in a dubious frown, and said never a word.

"All this is utterly strange to me. May I see this ring?"

"It is not here. My countess keeps it for the present, until we get to the bottom of this," said Gilbert. "But need you see it, to say if your lady had such a ring?"

"Yes," said Hubert in a bewildered and despairing whisper, "she had such a ring. For all I knew, she had it still, it was grown too tight for her to wear. But if it was given simply as a keepsake, when the boy was taken from her . . ."

"Then why hide it?"

Hubert turned to appeal to the king, who brooded with vengeful satisfaction over his distress, but left the accusations to others. "Your Grace, has Richard been questioned concerning this matter? Will not his replies clear up whatever is mysterious about it?"

"He has not, not yet. It's well that this scandal should not be spread around until due process of law uncovers the truth. When we return to London, I myself shall speak to him. At present he knows nothing, he is not aware that the ring has been discovered." He added significantly, "It is you, my lord of Kent, and not the boy, who stand arraigned of sacrilege by your peers. It is your solemn oath that is broken, you who are dishonoured, not the boy."

"That I deny," said Hubert, quietly and wearily. "And I ask as my right that I may have a proper day, and time to make my own enquiries, and clear myself of these charges. The oath I made has been kept."

"You may have two weeks," said the king, "before your case is heard by your peers. We shall then be back in London. Until then you will remain in attendance on us, though you need not present yourself unless we send for you."

History repeating itself sometimes produces a somewhat paler copy, yet essentially the predicament is the same. He would be as effectively, though not as brutally, imprisoned as in the dungeons of Devizes or the cells of the Tower.

Earl Simon spoke for the first time, a little hesitantly, though he was not generally given to hesitation. He had had little to do with Hubert, who belonged so clearly to an older generation, his active life almost over when Simon first came to claim his inheritance; but he could not feel that this was the bearing of a man lying in his own defence.

"My lord king, the earl will need free access to his own household, if he is to examine into this matter. We cannot assume his guilt, and his means of preparing his defence should not be hampered."

"No!" said the king decisively. "I will allow no going back to Burgh, to compound some better story with his countess, or meddle with possible witnesses. After the case has been formally opened in London he can have a further day, and communicate with his lady through his man of law, but not until then."

"But if he were escorted—"

"No, Simon! We will not take that risk. Our witness could hardly follow into the bedchamber, where the best conniving is done." He would not soften, but surprisingly he did not turn upon the earl of Leicester with one of those poisoned reproofs of which he was a master. This young man was becoming a close friend, in and out of council; if he had influence, it seemed it might be used responsibly. Hubert was grateful even for this small gesture.

"You may withdraw," said the king.

Hubert made his obeisance with stunned dignity, and went out from the hall utterly confused and ominously resigned, as though already condemned.

The case was formally opened in the king's court of peers on the fourteenth of October. Hubert had Lawrence of St. Albans beside him as counsel, and pleaded innocent in a strong but almost indifferent voice, and Lawrence thereupon immediately asked for a further delay. He had not yet been able to travel to Burgh, and no message had been sent to the countess of Kent, though by now the city of London was buzzing with the news of this fresh trouble that had fallen upon the earl, and if the word had not yet reached Norfolk, it certainly must do so very soon, and probably in some corrupted form. The Countess

Margaret, said Lawrence, ought not to be left to the mercy of wild rumour, and it was also essential that he should have access to her evidence as soon as possible.

The king granted the adjournment, to a day at the end of the month. "We shall then be at Kempton, let the case resume there. That will give time enough to consult the countess."

"It would be gracious," said Earl Simon, close to the king's side, "to allow the countess and her daughter to return with Master Lawrence, to visit the earl. At such a distance their anxiety would be hard to bear. Your Grace will not wish to impose worse suffering on the lady."

Henry jutted a lip, but benignly accepted the suggestion. "Very well, certainly they may come to Kempton."

"The issue of safe-conducts would be a reassurance," said Lawrence, "if the earl's accusers are agreeable."

Richard of Cornwall said yes without hesitation, and the rest made no objection. Safe-conducts were issued the same day for Margaret and Meggotta, valid for the rest of the month. Hubert was led back to his guarded seclusion uncertain whether to be glad or sorry for the concession. His mind remained in such despairing confusion that he both desired and dreaded clarification. There could not be anything in it. The ring he had been shown, the ring he accepted. But why should not Margaret give a small gift in remembrance to the child who was so roughly torn away from her? For that matter, why should not Richard, in a vulnerable moment and believing himself alone, kiss the hidden memento? Even the hiding of it was not inexplicable, considering he had been tossed into the bleak household of the bishop of Winchester, who might well grudge him even this tiny reminder of a happier home. But if it was so, why had he never been told? No, Hubert was too tired, too sick with this unrelenting round of persecution, these blows that felled him afresh just as he began to believe he dared stand upright. He longed to see his two Margarets, but feared what might yet be discovered. Better if they were free of him, once for all, before he destroyed them in his own destruction.

In the king's palace of Westminster, Richard was just as surely a prisoner. He had no idea why he had been suddenly whisked out of his uncle's house and installed here in the king's own apartments, nor why his freedom of movement was so closely and yet so unobtrusively restricted. He could not go out now without an escort, or ride without a groom. Nor was there ever anyone available to tell him the reason, or answer any of his indignant questions. Everyone he managed to get hold of was always subject to the orders of someone else, and knew no more than he did of the reasons for their orders. He knew that fate was holding over him some blow that could not be parried, but neither could he even guess from which quarter it might come. He had been here more than a week, and no one had explained anything to him.

One thing was clear: He could not be here but at the king's wish, and in due time the king would reveal what lay behind his abrupt personal interest in his farmed-out ward, extremely valuable for his possessions but of no importance in himself. Richard raged, and sickened and fretted, cut off even from rumour.

Not until the first day's hearing was over, and nothing made public, did King Henry send for Richard. The king was handicapped by not knowing what there was to come out, but it was expedient that nothing whatever should. If the boy knew anything that could compromise precious plans, it must be at least contained until everything was known and could be manipulated, even if it was impossible to suppress it for ever. His marriage, with every advantage it might involve, belonged to the king, and the king meant to have it. Even if there was some juvenile folly here, some hole-and-corner match brought about by de Burgh, it could very well be annulled unless things had gone even further, which was very doubtful, considering the age of the parties.

Richard came in erect and brittle, very proud, very frightened. Henry was pacing his favourite small parlour, looking engagingly informal but none the less royal and perilous. No crown, no coronal, only the fair hair rather pleasingly dishevelled, and the face smiling and debonair, one would have said barely past adolescence, but for the droop of the eyelid, which was very marked.

The boy took the extended hand on his, and brushed it with lips very cold and stiff with apprehension.

"Richard, I have neglected you. I have such a load of business upon me, there's little time left for those private duties I would prefer to cultivate." The neglect had been total, thus far, but Richard had counted it rather as a credit to him, and was not anxious to have the regimen changed. "Sit down, boy. It's time we talked together."

Richard held his tongue, and let that ride. He did not think the blandishments would last long, but he had better have his wits about him to disentangle such hints as they provided.

"You may not have heard, Richard—I wished you to be spared the anxiety—that some of my magnates are making serious charges against the earl of Kent, who was, of course, your guardian for a time. They say that the earl, who pledged his oath not to make claims upon you after his reinstatement, has since brought about your marriage—yes, no wonder you start, these are the allegations!—your marriage to his daughter." The watchful eyes were very intent and sharp. "Is this true, Richard?"

So it was come, and thus obliquely, through some unaccountable lapse elsewhere, as he supposed, not through him. Richard stiffened his back and licked his lips, and fumbled for his safest way, not yet sure whether this was a peril to be avoided at all costs, or his best opportunity of making his confession and standing fast on his claim. It was easy enough to answer this truthfully, and volunteer nothing more; but curiously he had a very strong conviction of what he was required to say. It might well be pleasing enough to the king to convict the earl of whatever crimes offered, but he would rather, much rather, have this marriage disproved, even if that meant vindicating Hubert.

"No, your Grace," said Richard from a throat dry with tension, "it is not true. I have not so much as spoken with the earl of Kent, or been in his company, since I left Bury St. Edmunds. He has not broken his oath, if it concerned me."

"I am glad to hear it. Then you assure me that this story of a marriage between you and the earl's daughter is an empty rumour?"

The tone this time was emphatic, benevolent but ominous, promising kindly patronage if the right answer was given, threatening worse if it was not. And this could not be answered truthfully without letting loose the whole deluge of recriminations and anger and punishment. Richard hung in agonizing irresolution, and it was the king who drew a wary step back from provoking the landslide. He sat back, relaxing his stern manner, and smiled, and, extending his closed hand towards the boy, opened it to show Meggotta's ring lying in the palm.

"I am told this belongs to you, Richard, and it is being offered as evidence of the supposed match. But I think there may be other explanations for how this came into your possession." He got no answer yet, and wanted none. Richard was staring in dreadful bewilderment at property he did not know he had lost. The king talked on, smoothly and persuasively. "No doubt this is a shock to you, and you are wondering how it came into my hands. Well, never mind that now, there was no ill intent towards you, only a matter of mending a cloak. But the countess of Pembroke has recognized this ring as once belonging to her sister, Margaret of Scotland. I fear some of my magnates have leaped too hastily to the conclusion that your possession of it, and the fact of keeping it hidden, is proof of a secret marriage with the young Margaret de Burgh. Too hastily, I say, but your once having been in the same household with the girl does lend some colour to the idea, on first sight. I can think, however, of other explanations," he said insinuatingly, guiding the boy in the direction he wished him to take, with almost sinister solicitude, and allowing him only limited time for speech, or none, since a mere minor hardly dared interrupt the king. "I see that you do know the ring. It is yours?"

Richard whispered "Yes" from a dry mouth.

"You had it hidden in your cloak, sewn into the collar?"

"Yes."

"Well, you may tell me the truth without fear. Doubtless the countess gave it to you as a memento when you left her in Bury. It's very natural, you had been a son to her for two years then, I know she was sad at losing you," said Henry gently and sympathetically, as though he had had no hand in parting them, but some unexplained act of God had swept the boy south into London. "And as I remember, I committed you next to the care of the bishop of Winchester, who was no friend to the earl and countess of Kent, and might be harsh enough to deprive you of all reminders of your former life. It was a mistake to give so young a boy to so austere a guardian," the king owned winningly. "No wonder you felt it needful to hide your treasure away from him. But you need not do so now. The Lady Margaret's gift belongs where she bestowed it, and may be worn with impunity."

And he held out the ring, slowly dangling it before Richard's eyes, and smilingly demanding the agreement he needed.

Richard stood motionless, his blue eyes wide and defiant and terrified upon Henry's face, and said slowly and clearly as he put out his hand, "The ring is mine. But that is not how I got it. I got it in exchange for my own, in the abbey-church at Bury St. Edmunds, when I married Meggotta de Burgh."

The king's face blazed into white, glittering rage, and his hand was snatched back without surrendering the ring. "Wretched boy, do you dare tell me such a story? Have you not just told me these rumours were false?"

"As they touch the earl of Kent, my lord, false they are. I dare not and will not tell you lies. He had no hand in it, he knew nothing of it, and knows nothing to this day. Your Grace knows well the earl was in Merton priory when I was with the countess in Bury. It was then we were married. Four years ago, in the abbey-church, on the twenty-first day of September. The earl has never violated his oath to you, never by word or deed, I swear it."

Richard was trembling, as much with passionate fervour as with fear. It was done now, he had heaved the load from his shoulders, and the relief was greater than the terror. He stood breathing deeply and watching Henry's face, now congested with blood after its drastic pallor.

"Do you tell me that woman ventured this alone? Drove you, mere children, into this enforced match? Such marriages can be undone. . . ."

"No!" cried Richard, loud in protest. "It was not enforced! We wanted it, we loved and love each other, we consented most gladly. And the countess did no wrong, nothing against your commands as they stood then. We were pledged to each other, with your blessing, nothing had then been changed!"

"Silence, miserable fool! At ten years old, to make your own match? Idiocy! We know who planned and carried out this outrage. Are you even sure it was a valid marriage? I cannot believe she got any devout cleric to join you. Who was this hedge-priest who dared marry you? If, indeed, there ever was a marriage!"

"Sir, this was not done lightly. It was the abbot himself who married us."

Richard saw the rapid processes of thought hurrying through the king's head, by the ripples that passed over his countenance. The instant calculation of years, the cautious relief, the vengeful satisfaction. "There is a new abbot in Bury. The old man died last February. You can hardly hope to cite *him* by way of proof. Who else was present at this marriage, if marriage it was?"

"Only the countess, and Meggotta's nurse, Alice."

"Her nurse! We can hardly question a servant against her mistress," said the king loftily, and with growing satisfaction. "Your evidence shows somewhat thin, I'm afraid. It's as I thought. A ten-year-old boy duped and made use of, it cannot be permitted to stand." He drew the veil of benignity over his face again, but without greatly caring now if it frayed here and there. "You will do well to be guided, boy, we can do far better for you than that."

"My lord, I neither know nor want better." Richard flared, forgetting to be afraid. "I have the only wife I want."

"Folly, child! We shall see! You may come to see sense in time. And hark, boy, you will say no word of all this to any other, or it will do no good to the cause of the earl of Kent, that I promise you! Only to me, when I demand it, will you speak of this affair again, do you hear? You are my ward now, whatever liberties that woman may have taken four years ago. Now go, leave me, and consider on your duty to me. Even at ten you were not too young to know you did wrong. I shall not forget it! Go, go back to your room." He flung away petulantly, but when he looked round again, Richard was still standing as before, with white, set face, waiting immovably to be noticed. "Well? What more do you want? I bade you go."

"May I have my ring?" said Richard, blanched and aghast at his own daring. "Your Grace was about to give it to me. You said I might wear it freely now." His voice shook a little, but his eyes were steady and blue as steel.

"God's wounds!" shrieked the king in sudden furious rage, a child in a tantrum, and flung the ring in the boy's face. "Take it, and get out of my sight!"

Richard stooped and picked up the ring, and gently wiped it. It had slightly cut his lip, there was a smear of blood upon it. Without a word he threaded it upon his finger, and walked out of the room. His legs were shaking under him, and he felt sick, and close to tears, but it was said now, it was out, and he was proud of it, and in the end they would have to accept it, for it was a true marriage, and could not be undone by man. Let King Henry labour by whatever means he would, with persuasions and bribes and threats, with beatings or imprisonment, to force or trick him into withdrawing his claim or denying his story, he would never cease to assert his right, as long as he had voice to utter it, or a heart in his body to feel love.

It was some days before the hearing appointed at Kempton when they finally let Margaret in to visit her husband.

Throughout that journey south from Burgh she had ridden in almost complete silence, all her force gathered to carry the load that fell upon them all. This she alone had done; and still, as she went over the whole history time and again, she could not see how she could have done otherwise, without worse agony and more unbearable loss. Nothing done then could have helped Hubert. For herself she was not concerned, all she felt for threats against Margaret was mailed contempt. But the children—the children could be saved. If we are all fit to be heroes, she thought, they may still be saved, and to a glorious future. We have only to stand together, in the phalanx for which we are fitted, and they cannot break us.

Even so, she was afraid. Not for herself; but fear for another is a more terrible ordeal.

As for Meggotta, she had waited a long time for this, she was prepared; she was her mother's daughter, and she had possessed, and please God would again possess, her husband and lover. She knew what was required of her, she had rehearsed it in her own mind month after month, and she would not give back. Of her, Margaret was sure. Still she was afraid.

When they opened the door of Hubert's secluded room to her, she entered silently, and saw him before he was aware of her. His door was not locked. There was no need, it was very well guarded. He had the semblance of freedom but not the reality. And the room was comfortably furnished; it was not a cell, but the whole chill aura of prison was in it, stone-cold, heavy with threats. Hubert was sitting in a low chair by the table, his hands lax in the lap of his gown, the old, misshapen fingers curled on emptiness. His head was sunk on his breast, the brow under the dead-white hair knotted in pain. The very lids of his eyes were weary, and hung heavy over the sunken eyes. Once he had fought and laboured his way back from despair and utter disillusionment into a respectable form of life, but a man cannot go on for ever repeating efforts that only fail under his feet, and precipitate him back into the abyss from which he climbed.

She went forward into the room and stepped within the field of his vision, disturbing the fringes of his thoughts. He turned his head with an obvious effort, as though he lifted a great weight, and saw her. He did not reach out a hand to her, he said only, "Margaret!"

"My lord!" she said.

"Lawrence has told you all about this madness?" His voice was almost as full as of old, but distant, as if he had withdrawn from hope, and therefore from any concern with what befell him. "I am sorry they have troubled you. To what avail? This will also pass."

She went forward and sank to her knees at his feet, and took both the old, gnarled hands in hers. She would have wept, but found her eyes dry and her throat clear: tears had forsaken her.

"They spoke of a ring," he said. "But that you might well have given to him. An absurdity! There cannot have been such a marriage, and so they'll find in the end."

"Yes," said Margaret strongly, "there was, there is such a marriage. My lord, hear me patiently. It was necessary that I should come. As you know nothing of this matter with which you are charged, so I know everything. Richard and Meggotta are man and wife. *I* made this marriage between them, four years ago, when you were besieged in Merton, and I was in sanctuary at Bury with the children. I told the abbot my mind, and he saw no wrong in joining together those who were already pledged, and who loved each other. He himself married them and gave them his blessing, at St. Edmund's altar, with every proper benediction of the church. Now you must stand by them, as I will. Alice was the only other witness. We have kept it secret all this time, now it must out, and we must all testify to it and maintain their right, their sacred right, against whoever questions it. There was no ban upon me then, he had not taken Richard from me, he had not rescinded his grant. And I carried it out! Now it cannot be invalidated, if we all stand fast."

It seemed that though he had certainly heard all this, spoken as it was slowly and emphatically, he had taken in no more than the half. Groping after understanding, he said faintly, "Are you in earnest? Is this truth? You had them married and I knew nothing of it? Nothing, either then or after? Nothing, all this time?"

"I had no means of reaching you, I could not ask your leave. I did what I believed best."

"Four years ago! Two of them, I know, were lost to us, but afterwards . . . In God's name, why did you never tell me? He asked for my oath, and I gave it!"

"Do you need any more reason why we never told you? What chance had I to speak with you until after that oath was extorted from you? All that day they kept you walled away behind charters and agreements, we never spoke word together privately until night, when you told me what the king had demanded of you. Was I to tell you then that I had already rendered it far too late to forswear interest in Richard's marriage? Until that moment I believed he would be given back to us on the old terms, and all in good time they could marry publicly and gloriously. What matter if it was the second time? And could I confess it then, and tear apart fatally that fragile new peace you were making? No! He would have turned on *you,* not on me. He would have hunted you into the grave."

"You could have told me," he said heavily.

"The result would have been the same, for you would have taken it straight to him. For your honour's sake! You would have said to him, 'What I promised you on oath I find is impossible of performance, Richard de Clare is married already!' "

"Yes," said Hubert, "that is what I should have done. What else could I have done?"

"And you think he would have accepted it tamely? Or loosed his anger upon me? No! He never loved you, any lash was welcome that could be used on you. You kept your life from his malice twice already by a hair's-breadth. This time he would have made sure of his revenge."

"And is it so different now?" he said bitterly.

"It is! Your accusers are others, they have brought it into court, into the open. They are angry at seeing their rights of consultation infringed, but they are not simply men who hate you and want your death. They want the truth! They shall have it, in full, and the truth publicly vindicates you. All we have to be afraid of is being afraid!"

But he was afraid! Not only of imprisonment, fetters, secret death, but of the hate and enmity and anger, of the whole burden of being persecuted and having to endure it, of the total disintegration of the quietness of mind he had somehow recovered in his semi-retirement. Trouble and turmoil themselves were the things he could no longer bear.

He drew his hands away from her hold. "Mere children, ten years old, it may not be so grave a matter. . . . A simple annulment—it would be granted without hesitation. Meggotta is only a child still. No reason why she should not make an honourable marriage, a brilliant marriage, to someone else. The earl of Arundel has been pressing me. . . . The king would be satisfied with an agreement to dissolve this match by consent. . . ."

"No!" said Margaret. "There will be no consent. Your daughter and her husband will fight for their rights, and so shall I."

"Have you forgotten," he demanded in a voice harsh with pain, "that they are both minors? Their voices will be overridden. There is no legal problem. It is only a marriage in form, it has not been consummated. . . ."

"No!" she said again, more peremptorily. "You mistake! Meggotta has gone so far with Richard that annulment on that ground is impossi-

ble. I said they are man and wife! To the full! This past year we have
not been a night in the London house but he has come to her . . . never
until now!"

And he had known nothing! His darling brought her lover home
nightly to her bed in his house, and he, old blind fool, was kept always
in the dark. He clenched his crooked hands in anguish and rage.

"You have done that to them? To make your work binding, you'd
take their childhood from them?"

"Their childhood was long gone," said Margaret gently. "But no,
this was not my doing. It was their own. To make the work binding,
yes, that is what they had in mind. That, and love. They are indissolu-
bly married, and that is what we must abide by, and fight for, all of us."

"I do not believe it!" cried Hubert in sudden desperate fury. "You
are lying to me!"

She sprang up and away from him in bitter offence; never before had
such words passed between them. But when she spoke, her voice was
calm and sad. "When, tell me, when have I ever lied to you?"

"When? Ever since the king turned against me, by your own admission, you have been deceiving me. Why should I trust you now?"

She was silent for a long moment, pierced and shaken by pity—for
Hubert, with his justified complaint against her, for herself, above all
for the two valiant children. He is my lord, she thought, the same I have
loved all these years, and he is old, old, old, and afraid of being hurt
and tossed and buffeted again and again, when all he wants is peace.
But if he will not stand up and fight with us now, we are lost.

"Very well!" she said gently. "I cannot blame you. Discount my
word, then, if you must, but listen to one whom you may question
alone. If they'll let me, I'll send your daughter to you. You may ask her
whatever you need to know. Then believe and do as God shows you
your way."

12

November, 1236, to January, 1237:
Kempton and Westminster.

*H*ubert's case was resumed at Kempton on the day appointed.

Since Margaret's visit he had slept little, and had continually put off requesting a visit from Meggotta, because after he had spoken with her there might be no refuge left to him, no possibility of disbelief, which was his only hope. Lack of sleep had drawn his face into deep, despondent lines, sunk his eyes into his head, made his gait less firm and steady, and his carriage less erect. On his thin wrists the blue-black marks of irons showed up more cruelly than before. The more piteous he appeared, the more King Henry turned from him in revulsion, even in anger, as though his very existence were an accusation. But on this occasion the king was not the only one pressing charges, and he could afford to sit back and preserve an attitude of impartiality, even if it deceived no one.

Hubert had made it clear to Lawrence of St. Albans that what he chiefly needed from this hearing was a further adjournment. It was reasonable that he should ask to question his daughter, and that would certainly not be done in court. He was already sure that not only the women but also Richard would be kept out of court. The last thing the king wanted was to allow the two young creatures any voice in the disposition of their persons, and even to summon them to testify before the magnates would have been as good as an admission that they had a right to such a voice, a concession he could not afford, let alone what they might blurt out. He had made certain that Richard was watched constantly, and could not confide in anyone. This was men's business.

The charges were read formally. The king was leaving the active part here to his own man of law, so far as the offence against himself was concerned. In a calm but toneless voice Hubert asserted his innocence, repeated that he had never heard anything about any marriage until he was accused at Eagle, and went on to recount, briefly, the story Margaret had told him, of the union compounded at Bury, at a time when he himself was at Merton priory, and had no communication whatever with his home and family.

"Do you assert, then, that this marriage did take place, at that time and in those circumstances?" asked the king's lawyer. "And that you had no knowledge of it?"

"That I had no knowledge of it, whether the story is true or not— that I assert. As for the rest I can make no assertion, by the very fact of having no knowledge. Whatever I might say to the question," he said with weary care, "could only be based on hearsay. I cannot reply."

"You made an oath on the altar, did you not, at Gloucester, when you were reconciled with his Grace?"

"I did. And I have kept it."

"How did you understand that oath?"

"I understood that his Grace meant it to be a quit-claim to him of the marriage of Richard de Clare. I also accepted it in that sense. And have so kept it."

"You are aware, are you not, that a breach of that oath would also invalidate the agreement then made concerning the lands returned to you? The two matters were linked."

"No," said Hubert, for once surprised, where even surprise was almost a relief and refreshment, "they were not linked. The formal agreements between us were all settled, apart from some small points to be worked out in detail. When the lord king required my oath, that was in the evening, and a thing apart." And he thought wonderingly, *He never gives up! He has always regretted returning all that he did return. Is he now trying to make use of this matter to filch some of his* losses back again? "But it's of small moment," he said, "seeing I have not broken my oath."

"Your memory is at fault, the two matters were linked, in a charter which was sent to you through the precentor of Hereford. Here it is, inscribed in the chancery roll."

"That may be. I acknowledge the sending of such a draft, but I declined to receive it. We had then no precise agreement."

"Did not the lord king tell you, when he required the oath from you, that you would not be received into his favour unless you swore it?"

"He did. And I complied, and have kept it." He came back stubbornly to that. The king would do everything possible to exploit any offence in order to regain lands, but if no offence could be proved, then his opportunist greed would be balked. All these questions about a possible means of gain, and so few about the marriage itself! What was required was that that should be eased away into the background, so clouded by uncertainty that it should be almost forgotten, recalled only as a sensational and scandalous rumour that proved to have nothing in it.

"The earl asks for a further day," said Lawrence of St. Albans, as the questioning drew to a close, "in order to obtain further information. I request an adjournment, perhaps until after the Christmas feast. Your Grace would not wish to break into the festival, I feel."

They debated their plans and commitments, and the lawyer consulted the king.

"Let it be in London, then, on the octave of St. Hilary. By then all the festivities will be over."

"The earl also requests that he may receive a visit from his daughter, whom so far he has been unable to see."

The king gave him a sharp look at that, and hesitated, but in the end it would have looked too bad to refuse. Better, of course, if the girl could have been kept away from him. If she was of the same mind as the stubborn little wretch of Gloucester, what might she not put into the old man's mind, and to what noble folly might she not stir him? But on reflection it did not seem so great a risk. This was a man so battered and broken, it would take more than a love-sick girl to thrust him into battle.

Meggotta came to him two days before Christmas, in the secluded room in the palace of Westminster to which the king had moved him. She and Margaret were installed in the de Burgh town-house, but the king would not let him go to spend the feast at home with them. Hubert was quite clear, by then, about what the king wanted. He had always a gift for closing his eyes and wishing away whatever truths were unwelcome to him, and he wanted assistance in so distancing this truth that it might vanish in cloud and mist, and be forgotten. He wanted, if he could have had his way in full, to see the marriage disproved and discredited. If that was impossible, he wanted so much doubt cast upon it that the result might be much the same, and his plans, temporarily and rudely disrupted, might be resumed with impunity. They said he had first toyed with the notion of binding to him, by way of Richard's marriage, the most influential branches of his queen's Savoyard or Provençal kin. His ambitions and dreams still leaned passionately towards France, he still had visions of recovered grandeur there. Now it seemed he had also one eye upon his own half-sisters of La Marche, the exuberant fruit of his mother's second marriage to a man far younger, and once intended for her daughter. La Marche could also be very useful to the king's French plans. Mere children in love, even mere children married and blessed by Holy Church, were a minor obstacle.

And then Meggotta came, slipping into Hubert's solitude, strange and tall and beautiful, flushed rosy from the frosts. Within her dark cloak she glowed bright as a star, having walked across the bridge over the Great Ditch, and across the palace court, in the teeth of a biting wind. It was not so long since he had left her at the king's summons, so high in hope, but she came to him another person, a young woman, solemn, still, and kind.

She shrugged the cloak from her head and shoulders and let it fall behind her, and came straight across the room to kiss him. He had been sitting with prayer-book in hand, but not praying, not reading, unless his battered heart still prayed when his mind was tired out and fallen into indifference. She sank to her knees and clasped his hands in hers.

So had Margaret done, and to what end? For a moment he did pray, in good earnest, that Meggotta would unsay all that Margaret had said, undo all that Margaret had done, but he knew she would not. It wanted but one look into her clear eyes, the shining grey of morning just before sunrise, and he knew that she was a wife.

"I wanted to come before, but they wouldn't let me. And you are so thin! And so tired! Because of me!"

"I am not ill used," he said, sighing. "Oh, my child, my pearl, if this is true I have heard of you and Richard, why did you never tell me?"

"So that when it came into the open at last, you, at least, might truly say that you knew nothing, and were innocent of all, and no one could dispute it. We wanted you set quite apart from what we had done, first and last. And so it will be! They will have to acknowledge that you had no part in it, however they threaten and complain. It may be that we were wrong," she said simply, "but that was why we did as we did. Not because we had no trust in you, never, never! I trust you utterly, with my life, my honour, everything."

Yes, she was trusting him now with her love, and it was too much for him to bear.

"Mother has told you everything?" she said.

"But let me hear it from you."

She sat at his feet, her head against his knee, holding his hands in hers, and she told him. How Richard had told her they were destined to marry, and how that had been perfect, seeing they already loved each other, and could not conceive of a life apart. How at Bury, when everything else seemed lost, Margaret had put it to them that they were bound to be separated, and the only way to save their future was to marry at once, for once married they could afford to wait for their happiness. How the abbot had not only approved but taken upon himself the burden of responsibility, and himself married them.

"The lord abbot died, some months ago," said Hubert, shaking his head. "He cannot speak for you, unless he left a record somewhere of what was done."

"I fear he didn't. Mother has sent there to ask, and so, I think, has the king. No one else there knew. If there is nothing written, we've lost our best witness. And he died very suddenly. I know! But that does not alter the truth. Richard and I know it, mother knows it, Alice knows it. We've none of us ever been liars. Is not that enough?"

"The king will never admit Alice as a witness. A servant trusted as she has been, and for so many years, is always suspect as swearing whatever is pleasing to her lady. Is it also true, child dear, that you and Richard have slept many nights together in my house, and unknown to me?"

"Yes," she said at once, glowing, quite without shame. "Ever since the king's marriage, when we began to be afraid because people were talking of us as getting old enough to be affianced. There was only one way of making sure our marriage could not be broken, and so we took that way. We were entitled to it, you see, for we *were* married. And I'm glad, so glad, that we did. It was my only remaining regret that we couldn't tell you, but you see that we couldn't."

"And now?" he asked with difficulty. "They don't let him come to you now?"

"No. He's shut up somewhere here in the palace, no one sees him, except the king's servants. A prisoner like you," she said, and her lip quivered. "But when you've told the king's court the whole truth, they'll have to give him back to me. He is my husband, and I am his wife, for as long as we both live. We can bear this evil time. There will be a better."

She trusted him too much, and knew too little of what the king could do, not only to a man's body but to his courage and self-respect and will. He was the one who had known Henry's venom, and still bore the scars, worse scars than those blue bracelets and anklets where the irons had bitten.

"Mother has tried again and again to get an audience with the king," said Meggotta, "but he refuses. They tell her this is now a legal matter, and must be probed only in the courts, where it belongs, and it would be improper to hear evidence elsewhere. I have tried, too, but he won't see me, either. I tried through Earl Gilbert, but he wouldn't help me. If only I could get to the king, surely he'd believe me, and accept it that we are married."

No, he would never let her in to him, that was certain. If ever he found himself face to face with this clarity and valour, he would have no choice but to believe her, and that was the last thing he wanted.

"I did manage to see the countess of Cornwall," she said sadly, "but she's so taken up with her new son, she doesn't realize how deeply Richard feels, she thinks him still a child who's best off letting his elders order his life for him as they see fit. She was kind to me, and sorry, but she can't help me. And the men, they say only this is men's business, a matter for the king's court and your peers, where it now rests. So, you see, I have only you to speak for me."

That was his fear, and the burden was so heavy he doubted if he could carry it. Where was he now to find the courage to fight, even for this child he adored? And was it so grave a matter as she thought? At fourteen, with a whole world of men before her, and a fortune still as her dowry?

"Meggotta," he pleaded, moistening lips dry with anguish, "is this truly so great a thing to you that you must have it? Are you sure of your own heart? For you're very young yet, and have seen so little of life, to be certain your fancy now will be your fancy in three years' time, or ten. Must it be Richard?"

"Richard or no one," said Meggotta, in so quiet a voice that it chilled his heart. "This is not a fancy. I have loved him since first he came to us, and now I've held him in my arms, and loved him with my body as well as my heart and soul, and I know the worth of what I have, and if I lose it, I've lost everything. This is life or death to me." She stirred and shuddered, and then reached up for his hand, and lifted a face again fierce and resolute. "But I shall not lose it! What mother and I are not allowed to come into court and say, you will say for us. Whatever storms there may be, however angry the king is, we must stand fast, and we can't be defeated. Now we've told you everything, and you will tell them, and they will have to accept it. When the truth is out, they'll see that you can't be blamed. There's nothing to be afraid of, if you stand by me."

Nothing to be afraid of, but hatred and imprisonment and death, and this continual pain if death failed to reach him. After she was gone he sat motionless for a long time, trying to pray, but there was no force in him even to form prayers. She was still an innocent, she believed in justice, she thought that a man who had had no part in the offence could not be hounded for it, but Hubert knew better. She was braced and ready and brave, willing to submit to whatever penalty fell upon her, provided she won her way in the end. No price would be too high to pay for Richard. Or so she thought! She did not know, even now, that nothing would be visited upon her, all upon him. And he was so tired, so crushed by disaster upon disaster, all he wanted was a quiet hermitage, solitude, silence, a little warmth, Margaret. . . .

There was no way of putting off the last day. He had had all the time they were going to grant him, nor did he blame them for being impatient for an end. They wanted a clear decision on a vital issue affecting all their own sons and daughters, claiming the rights they held to be consulted and to have their interests protected in all important marriages. In other days, in another situation, he would have felt as they did. Now he was caught between the millstones, the one soul who had done nothing amiss, stood to gain nothing and lose all, and had no way of escape from a trap others had prepared for him. And somewhere within his shut heart there was a creature slowly bleeding to death for Meggotta.

He had not seen her again. King Henry also wanted an ending, though on his own terms, and had no intention of providing his prisoner with food for his starved soul until he had delivered himself at law. Hubert entered the hall for the last hearing like a man walking in his sleep, still unresolved, unreconciled, having no notion what he was going to do or say. His world was shrunken into a single room, an impenetrable fence of eyes, and a moment of time.

Answering to the matter of his oath was easy. Yes, he had made it, at the king's request, and he had kept it. In that matter his conscience was absolutely clear.

"Yet, as we understand, you do declare now that there was a marriage between these two, concerning whom you vowed to make no claims and take no action?"

"I do not declare," he said, moistening withered lips, "that there was such a marriage. I do declare that my wife and my daughter have told me there was."

"Rehearse once more, if you will, what was told to you by your wife."

He did so, faithfully if briefly.

"Let us be clear. This marriage was celebrated by the abbot of Bury St. Edmunds?"

"So it was told to me."

"The lord abbot at that time is dead, and cannot testify. Nor has he left any record of such a marriage. Nor has any other, even his prior, within the liberty heard or known anything of this matter. You have been so informed? His Grace's examination into this was scrupulous."

"I do not doubt it. Since the marriage was secret, I should not expect any written record, unless or until the abbot had reason to fear the secret should outlive him, and ought to be recorded. And as I hear, his death was sudden and unexpected."

"And perhaps convenient? There were no other witnesses, except your countess, who told you the story, and her daughter's nurse, who certainly would support it. Well!" said the king's lawyer, and sniffed in disbelief. "Perhaps we should hear once again your daughter's account of what happened."

He gave it with care and pain; what she said was sacred.

"You assert, then, that this marriage was not merely made at Bury, but later consummated in London?"

He said, feeling his way with labour and distress, "I assert nothing for my own part. I tell what was told to me, adding nothing and omitting nothing. I assert only what I know of my own knowledge, and of this matter I know nothing of my own knowledge."

There were several of them there who had questions for him, some biting in disbelief, some not unfriendly. He had time between to look about him, through a curious haze of unreality like a ground-mist, dimming faces and yet making their very vagueness ominous. Richard of Cornwall, who had the makings of a balanced man, however insistent on his full baronial rights, was watching him with an expression half blame and half compunction. Gilbert Marshal brooded and frowned, torn two ways, knowing what his nephew wanted, believing the judgement of others knew better for him, but not an ill-disposed man.

The earl of Leicester, too young to have a father's worries or a father's ambitions, stood back silently in this assembly, but followed everything with sombre care, and was not happy. When at last he did speak, it was to say bluntly and forcibly, "We have surely heard enough to come to an agreement on the very matter we're here to fathom. Nobody can be in doubt that the earl of Kent was in close confinement at the time of this alleged marriage, and had no communication with his family. And as far as I remember that day at Gloucester, it is equally true that he was not alone with his countess until after he had sworn the oath your Grace required. He says that he took the oath in good faith, and has kept it, and I see no reason to disbelieve him."

Two or three cried out on him that that was not all the matter, that this alleged marriage was four years old, that for the last two of those the earl of Kent had been restored to his household, and if he did not know what was going on in it, his neglect was as culpable as bad faith.

"He is charged with marrying his daughter to Richard de Clare in violation of his oath," insisted Simon impatiently, "and if he had no hand in the marriage and never broke his oath, how can he be guilty?"

But they had shifted their ground of complaint, and were willing to shift it again. The marriage itself affronted the rights of the entire nobility, and the head of the household must be responsible for the offence. The king let them argue for a while, his face thoughtful and cold; then he leaned to whisper into his lawyer's ear, and quietened the wrangling voices with a lifted hand.

"His Grace reminds us, my lords, that by far the best way of ensuring acquittal would be to show that no offence has been committed. We have heard how few are the living witnesses who claim to have been present at this marriage, and how slender the evidence for it, depending on the accounts of three people, two of them minors in the care of the third, who may not have understood fully the significance of what was done, or, indeed, been capable of knowing whether it was a valid ceremony at all. When first these charges were made against the earl of Kent, he said that if he could not disprove the marriage, he would submit to the judgement of his peers."

It was true, so he had, so sure had he been that there was nothing in this silly rumour but a residue of spite against himself, and that he need only enquire, and the phantasm would vanish.

"Are you of opinion, my lords," asked the king mildly, but watching Hubert closely beneath his drooping eyelid, "that he has so far disproved it?"

They were not, and said so forcefully.

"Well, it could be said he has gone some way towards it," conceded Henry, "and perhaps complete disproof, where events are well past and there is no written record, is more than we could expect. But by this time the earl must have formed views of his own, which we could at least hear, and perhaps accept as coming as near proof as we are likely to get. You may question, Master Roger."

Hubert understood that he was being offered a way out, and, provided he gave the right answers, he would be set at liberty. More, he knew, if not yet the questions and the answers, the end to which they were meant to proceed. To set Richard and Meggotta before this assembly, or admit Margaret's direct evidence, would only prove beyond serious doubt what Henry wanted discredited. But here he had a victim he could threaten, and the threat was just as implicit as the promise.

"My lord of Kent," said the legist sternly, "do you accept as true the story you have heard from your wife and daughter?"

"It is not to the purpose whether I accept it or not," said Hubert, choosing his words with desperate care, "since that would prove nothing. I have no knowledge of any of these things. Whatever I might answer could only be based on hearsay. It is for the court to make up its mind, not for me."

"You prevaricate. Surely only the guilty need do so. We are not asking for a judgement, we want only an opinion. Do you believe your wife, or no? Do you believe there was a marriage? Do you believe it was consummated? Do you consider your daughter to be an honourable wife? Answer, yes or no!"

This was the moment, he knew, when he must stand up and speak out, when he should rear his head and forgo all care for his own fate, and say loudly and clearly, "Yes, I more than believe, I know! There was a marriage, and the lovers are bedded as well as wedded, my daughter is the true and honourable wife of Richard de Clare, and nothing you or I can do now will change that. They are husband and wife in the sight of God and man, and you cannot part them."

That was all he had to say, and the children, whatever the storms that followed, would be vindicated in the end. And he would be flung back into the stony darkness of the king's endless displeasure and malice, which had a thousand ways of making life hell, even if he escaped imprisonment and chains, and the private death that came so easily to old men in prison. He writhed, knotting his hands in his sleeves until his nails bit into his flesh. Twice he parted parched lips to make the great effort, and could not proceed. The words would not be formed, there was no breath in him to drive them forth.

"Come, are these such hard questions? Have I framed them in such a way that you cannot say yes or no to them?"

"I will speak only as to what I know of my own knowledge," he whispered hoarsely.

The king was leaning forward, so far not displeased, eyes wide in warning, willing him to see reason. And by one means or another he would get what he wanted. Annulments were procurable, even where a marriage had been consummated, given a little patience and much influence.

"Let us try another way," said the legist, fiercely smiling. "Can you take your wife's word? Is your daughter to be trusted? And may she not have been deluded in thinking herself legally a wife? Even if there was a ceremony, do you accept absolutely that it was valid and binding?"

"I cannot answer yes or no," gasped Hubert in torment. "I know nothing of the matter."

"You can vouch only for yourself?"

Hubert cried out with infinite bitterness, "In this world, who can do more?"

Slowly King Henry leaned back in his chair, drew a long, soft breath, and smiled. "Well, well!" he said. "We cannot press you further, and I think there is no need. I fear we have tired you already. Place a seat for the earl."

It was done, and the old man sank into an inert heap, his hands open and loose in his lap. So he had said enough, and held back enough. Henry was satisfied, he had got what he wanted, thus publicly, declaration enough to allow king and peers to pretend disbelief, and proceed accordingly, perhaps with some slight sense of guilt, but very little. Though surely every man present here knew in his own mind that Meggotta's marriage had indeed taken place, and was valid in every particular.

"My lord," said the king, gracious and coolly smiling, "I am satisfied of your good faith. Unless any man here has anything further to urge or to object, you are free to go."

No one raised a voice, no one stirred, as Hubert gathered himself within the torn folds of his dignity, and went out heavily and slowly from the court.

It was only his due that Meggotta should be the first person he saw when he entered the courtyard of his own palace. Was there not an earl in the Bible who promised his God a sacrifice of the first creature encountered on his return home, in payment for victory over his enemies? He, also, suffered this horror of seeing his daughter rush to meet him with open arms, loving and glad, not knowing she embraced her death. Only then, when she saw him and cried in a shout of joy, "Father!" and flew like a bird to his heart, did he fully realize what he had done. He had not even the excuse that he had promised her to God; he had sold her to the king in return for his freedom and peace.

He caught her into his arms, so tightly that she was crushed and breathless, but he could not say a word to her; and before he could swallow the suffocating weight in his throat, she had pulled free again and gone running before him into the house, calling for Margaret, and crying that he was home, and freed. He followed her with a leaden heart, through the hall and into the solar, where Margaret had just started up from her chair, and stood with one arm folded about Meggotta.

"It is over? He sets you free?" Fierce hope flamed in her face, too, but only for a moment. He stood mute and still, meeting her eyes with so little hope or life in his that her own brief flame died for want of fuel. She also was very still.

"Yes. He sets me free. Flays me and sets me free." He sank wearily into a chair, and shut his face in his hands with a groan. Meggotta, in distress at seeing him distressed, would have run to fold her arms round him, but Margaret said, "Let him rest, child, he's worn out. You run and fetch some wine for him."

"Oh, yes, gladly!" She whisked out of the room, and ran.

"She will not be glad for long," said Hubert hopelessly from within his sheltering hands. "God forgive me! I have put an end to her gladness."

Meggotta's light footfalls receded and were lost. Margaret closed the door, that she might have some brief warning when her daughter returned.

"What have you done?" she asked, but very gently, for the least note of harshness or reproof would have been like striking down a sick child.

"Told the truth, only the truth, but turned it into lies. Followed the signals the king gave me, pointing me where I could escape out of his net, and what would happen to me if I failed to read the signs aright. Bought my way out cravenly, as he wanted, and given him his excuse to proceed as if this marriage never was, and is not now. Publicly, I cannot take it back now if I would, the word is out ahead of me, and running through the court like spring floods, that I have admitted I hold my wife to be a liar and my daughter a whore."

Margaret stood like a tower, erect and stony. Her voice was still low and composed as she said, "You had better tell me. And be brief. Those words I know you never used. Let me hear the truth without outcry." And when the sorry recital was done, without excuse, in self-detesting pain, she said in a whisper, "How am I to tell Meggotta?"

"There is no need," said Meggotta's voice from the doorway. The closed door had covered completely the light tread of her feet; she had lifted the latch upon the harsh complaint of her father's voice, and frozen into stillness with it still raised and silent in her hand. She released it now and came in, the flagon of wine and the cup carried in one hand. Her face was like a waxen mask, drained of blood.

"I could not choose but hear. I had a right, I am not sorry I listened. You are spared the hard thing, mother."

With slow, soft steps she walked to the table, moving as though her feet knew the way while her eyes were fixed somewhere far beyond the walls of this room. Soundlessly she set down flagon and cup, looked down at her empty hands, and seemed to wonder what they were about with these alien things. She looked at Hubert's bowed shoulders and hidden face, and her eyes were wide and sad.

"It would have been all the same, very likely," she said for grievous comfort. Then in an instant the white mask blazed into bitter red, burning like fire; she pressed her cold hands to her cheeks, and cried out, "You might have spared me my face!" Then as quickly that also passed, and she said grievingly, "His whore. Richard's whore. I wish to God I were, on those terms they might have let me keep him."

There was nothing more. She did not look at him again; she turned and went without haste or hesitation out of the solar, and closed the door behind her.

Hubert raised himself with a rending effort out of his self-loathing and despair, to stumble and cry after her, but Margaret took him by the shoulders, and pressed him back into his chair.

"Let her alone," she said. "Enough has been done to Meggotta. None of it can be undone. At least she had her love. Now let her be!"

"She's no more than fourteen!" he protested, trembling. "Is this possible? Have I done her such mortal injury?" And piteously he asked, clutching Margaret by the arm with a deformed and bony hand, "What are we to do now?"

"Live," said Margaret, with bitter resolution. "As best we may."

As soon as Cecily de Sanford had set out to keep her evening vigil of prayer in King Henry's unfinished Lady Chapel, the earl of Leicester erupted unannounced into the Countess Eleanor's apartments, his normally confident and serene forehead drawn into an anxious scowl.

"It's over, then," said Eleanor, giving him her hand to kiss, "and he got all that he wanted."

"You know how it ended? God pardon us," said Simon, "for I fear we've done a very evil thing."

"I knew how it must end," said Eleanor ruefully. "Marriages are about lands and alliances and status, not about boys and girls in green love from childhood, nor about men and women in ripe love, either, for that matter, as you and I are likely to discover. Lands and status, and getting heirs to continue both! Any two clods," she said angrily, "without a wit between them, can be born to lands and titles, almost any two fools can get children. Neither the boys nor the girls are allowed to quibble over the partners chosen for them, however old and idiot, or callow and silly. Do you wonder I thought better to marry myself to chastity rather than take my chance in the market? It was the one way of stopping all the gaps. Even my brother would not dare argue with that. And now, because I took the easiest way, I have to undo it, if it can be undone, the hardest way."

"Are you repenting," demanded Simon jealously, "the promise you made me? This bad business has not frightened you into surrender, surely."

"No," she said scornfully. "It makes me more determined than ever that nothing so dire shall happen to us. At whatever cost! If I fought my way out of one snare, I can fight my way out of another, and I will. But it also gives us warning of what we're facing. Not only the king, but a horrified archbishop. And I do grieve, Simon, for he is a kind man, and he never prompted me, and he was glad when I said I had chosen the way of chastity of my own will. He recorded my vow himself. God knows how I'm to face him when I unsay it!"

"You'll face him with me beside you, and if there's to be blame, it is mine, and I claim it, and I'll do whatever penance he requires. But I do not believe you and I could so love, if God had not intended it to be. I cannot feel like a sinner, though I'm tempting you to what the old man will call sacrilege."

"But listen to me," she said, reaching up to take his face between her hands and hold him facing her, close and intent. "We must go softly, and make no haste. If I have to outface the church, I mean to have my brother on my side."

"Do you believe that can be done?" he asked doubtfully.

"It can, it must. He has a conscience, if he never acknowledges it. If he feels guilt for so using these children, he'll die rather than admit it, but he'll go gently the next time, and be gracious if he can, for a sop to his soul. I know him! You think you know him, and think better of him than he deserves. But it's true that he has an affection for you, and will do for you more than for most of those about him."

"I have both a duty to and an affection for him," said Simon sombrely. "I should be loath to make unworthy use of either."

"How 'unworthy'?" she flashed indignantly, and knotted her fingers in his thick cap of brown hair. "You tell me what you want of me is not wrong, but right and good, how can it be unworthy to enlist the king in it? If you'll be guided by me, we shall not be deceiving him at all, we shall tell him the simple truth, that we love and wish to marry, and that we look to him to help us."

"Openly, before the world? In the archbishop's despite?"

"Yes, if he dare! *I* dare! Dare *you*?" Her hands held him tightly, her face, roused and challenging, was very close to his. He uttered a strange, small sound compounded of laugh, sigh, and groan, and caught her to his heart, and kissed her long and passionately. It was the first time they had embraced, and it shook them both out of words and breath, so that they clung together in amazed silence, cheek against cheek, even after the kiss was over.

"Simon, Simon!" she whispered into his ear. "Now I'm afraid! Suppose I'd never taken vows? I should have been married off to some Lusignan relative, or some count from Provence, and never known you."

"If God put it into your mind to fence yourself about with this blessed barrier," he said with fiery conviction, "it was surely to keep you safe for me. If I lost you, I would have no other, but I have you here on my heart, and by God, I won't lose you, not unless I lose life with you. Yes, we'll win the king to stand by us, publicly or privately, what does it matter? Yes, I will tread softly and slowly, if that's what it costs.

I'll wait as long as I must, but I'll have you and hold you, against world, and church, and all!"

          In the evening, after he had supped, King Henry retired to his small parlour, and sent for Richard de Clare. He had had his will, he was kindly disposed to all, even those who had stood obstinately in his way. In any case, the boy was pitiable, because helpless. His fate had been sealed in his absence and ignorance, while he chafed and fretted here in closely guarded seclusion. It was doubtful anyone had even visited him to tell him the outcome of the day's hearing. His mother was taken up with her new son, Henry, named for his royal uncle, and Gilbert Marshal had grown used to leaving his nephew in the king's ward, and had a beautiful wife to come home to. Someone should pay a little attention to the boy, especially as his co-operation in important plans, though not essential, would certainly be helpful.

Richard came in with the gait and the carriage of a man, and with a man's conscious pride in his own bearing. He had grown thinner in his royal captivity, and looked taller and more sinewy as a result. His face was as it had been since this struggle began, white, closed and inimical, but his eyes were wild and bright with desperation.

"Your Grace sent for me," said the hypersensitive lips, curling back from the words as though they stung.

"Richard, to our grief we have left you without news until now. This case of yours has given us great trouble, we have wished to do only what is right and just. I must tell you that the result of our inquests leaves us in the gravest doubt whether any such marriage as you have believed in ever took place. Consider the difficulties! The abbot of Bury died some months ago. It has been said that he himself conducted this marriage ceremony, but he cannot now testify yea or nay, he has left no deputy who knows or ever heard anything of it, and no written record to prove that it happened. Of uncommitted witnesses there are none. The servant of the countess of Kent is the only one, and it is not right or proper to question a servant against her mistress," the king said virtuously, but made no mention of the possibility of questioning a servant *for* her mistress. "Even the earl of Kent himself"—Henry sighed with deep sympathy—"does not assert that there ever was a marriage. He testifies to what his lady has told him, but he himself knows nothing of the matter."

"He could not know," said Richard, sick with apprehension, "seeing we kept it from him. But *we* know, Meggotta and I and her mother. Is not that enough?"

"I am sorry, Richard, we have done our best. The earl was questioned closely as to the opinion he had formed from what had been told him. Asked if he believed and accepted the story of the marriage, he refused to make any such declaration. We are satisfied both that he never broke his own oath to us and that his refusal to support the testimony of his countess casts too much doubt upon this supposed marriage for it to be safe to give legal validity to it."

"But he could not!" cried Richard, stunned and disbelieving. "How could he speak so of his wife and his daughter . . . and me? He knows me, he knows none of us would lie! And even if he so failed us—though I cannot credit it!—still he could not *deny* what we have said. If he could not know that it was true, how could he know that it was untrue? What he said should count for nothing. We who *do* know the truth ought to be believed. He should never have been asked the question in such form, it sounds too like a threat. . . ."

Henry's acquired and well-fed complacency melted fast, and the perilous steel showed through. "Take care what words you use to me, boy, and how you accuse my court of mispractice! You are not yet Gloucester, and I may well have scruples about granting seisin to the insubordinate and undutiful. I say the court has discharged the earl of Kent as having no blame, and regards it as unproven and dubious indeed that a valid marriage ever took place."

"Your Grace," said Richard, shaking as much with shock as fear, "if I submit to that judgement, I beg you'll hear me out. There is an easy answer to this matter, if you permit it. If our first marriage was in any way irregular, give us your sanction to be married a second time, publicly." He rushed on despairingly but doggedly, for the elegant royal hand was already lifted to silence him. He flung himself on his knees, and caught it to his lips to evade the order implicit in the gesture. "Once, your Grace approved this match, you were patron to the agreement between our two fathers, and gave us your blessing. Why do you object to it now? Meggotta is my equal, she's my love, and she loves me, she's my wife, and I want no other. Be gracious to us both, don't tear us apart!" Frantic tears burst from his eyes and moistened Henry's hand. The king withdrew it, gently and indulgently enough, and shook the drops from his fingers. He had the whip hand. However long it took to tame this half-trained falcon, he need not even be put to the annoyance of undertaking the taming himself; he could afford to be indulgent. He dropped a tolerant palm to stroke Richard's bowed flaxen head, as he might have stroked a handsome puppy. The boy's tears came painfully, wringing him hard, and dried long before their time, leaving him still with a leaden weight filling his breast.

"Richard, you make it hard for us. We are doing our best for you, in changed times, and you are ungrateful. You underprize yourself and shame your ancestors, to cling so to a childhood folly. It would more become you to pull yourself together and study to fill your proper place in our realm. You will be one of our foremost magnates, a leader in this land. Early mistakes can be forgiven, if you please us hereafter. But do not raise this matter again, if you want our favour. We will not hear you on the subject. Put it out of your head now, once for all. Your marriage is in my hands, as you are my ward, and I will not permit the perpetuation of this sorry error of yours. Understand that, and never speak of it again. Now go back to your room, and think carefully of what I've said."

Richard arose paler than his shirt, made his half-blind obeisance, and withdrew. He knew then, but still could not believe, that it was over. In his own rooms no one else came near him, except the new tutor they had imposed upon him, a scholarly man enough, but a jailer rather than a tutor, as Richard well knew. There was no hope of eluding his vigilance during the day, but at least he did not occupy the same room at night. Richard sat out the rest of the evening in apparent dulled acceptance; but in the night he rose silently and dressed in his darkest and plainest clothes, and made the first of several bids to escape from his prison and reach his wife.

He did well to get safely past two of the watchers set between him and freedom, but the third received him into burly, welcoming arms as he swung his legs over the sill of a high window and dropped into a rear court. There was neither dignity nor gain in struggling, for a second guard was at hand instantly. Richard marched back where they led him in bitter silence, and heard the key turned upon him when they left him. He lay face-down on his bed, his arms laced tightly about his head, as if it might burst with the pressure of grief and anger that bulged his ribs and made his temples heave and thud like drums; and suddenly the great gathering of outrage within him burst in good earnest, in storms of convulsive weeping. The leaden weight about his heart poured out of him in agonies of sobs, emptying him of feeling and consciousness until he foundered in the bitter, unrefreshing sleep of despair.

13

May to November, 1237:

Burgh; Westminster.

Meggotta, after that first desolate cry of love and despair, never again uttered any reproach, never made complaint. Within the hour she had come back to him, dry-eyed and still of face, kissed him, and asked pardon of him who had no courage left to ask hers. But something in her looks forbade that he should ever probe within the closed temple where she had buried her hopes. She was gentle and serviceable, but withdrawn into a silence that set her far distant from them, even when they sat together at table, as though the savour had gone out of a world that could so betray both her and those she loved.

Only once did she venture out while they remained at Westminster, and that was to go with her mother to visit the countess of Pembroke, and even then it was at Margaret's urging. Only there could they hope to get news of Richard, and nothing but news of Richard could ever rekindle the fire that had been extinguished in Meggotta.

It was a strange, sad meeting between sisters who were strangers, heavy with ineffective goodwill on one side, and on the other the lingering burden of a hope crueller than despair. And for all her willing kindness, the Countess Marjorie could not help looking at Meggotta with curiosity and pity. Those same looks Meggotta had already encountered on the way, and they burned like acid. Who was there at court who did not know the story by now? She thought, and it was her only consolation, It may not be so hard for Richard. For a young man to have had a mistress is no reproach to him, rather a feather in his cap. I hope he never tastes this gall.

"The king keeps Richard close," said the countess, shaking her head, "and won't let him come back to us unless he gives his word not to try to see or write to you. And he refuses. He has tried, you know—he tried that same night to escape and come to you, but they were ready for him, and now he's kept almost under lock and key. I have not been let in to him, though I've asked, and keep asking—only Gilbert. If only I'd understood, when the ring was brought to me. . . . I never knew I was doing such harm in telling my husband."

"It's all one," said Margaret heavily. "It would have come out, sooner or later, now the king's bent on making use of Richard for his own purposes. We could not have put it off much longer."

"He will never let him go," said her sister, very gently, and looked with compassion at Meggotta's pale, proud face, which never so much as quivered when his name was spoken. "It's no use . . . no use at all."

No, no use at all. When they took their leave, Meggotta asked, "When they let you see him, will you give him a message from me? Not through your husband, I think he might feel it his duty to tell the king. And it is only that I would rather he took what happiness he can find than refuse it all for what is gone. For he's too much alive to die of losing me, however he may wish it now, and I would want him to live with all his might. And say that I shall always love him."

She walked back beside her mother, over the north bridge, and looked down into the grimy waters of the Long Ditch, and pondered the very little journey between life and death, but was not tempted. The one could not be more death than the other. Why make the exchange? She felt the curious eyes that studied her, pitying and enjoying the young noblewoman who had given away her virginity in the belief she was a wife, and found herself no wife after all. And even then she could think proudly, If they knew everything, they might still envy me, for he was mine, and the first and best of him will always be mine.

None the less, the city where men looked at her like this, however constantly and chivalrously the earl of Arundel might still press his suit for her, was a place in which she could not live.

"Take me home to Burgh," she said, when they reached Hubert's house. "I cannot be in this town ever again."

They were glad to take her back to Norfolk, to the budding spring, and the vast, luminous skies, and the lowlands glimmering with meres, and the keen, cruel winds of her childhood that stung colour into her cheeks again. But she did not come back from the private place into which she had withdrawn. A kind of effortless sweetness made her manner towards her parents seem to promise more than it ever bestowed. She was not idle. She busied herself about the manor with many tasks, but all as though the interests of others drove her to activities which meant nothing at all to her. She rode out often to the sea, and over the low hills inland, where she had played and wandered with Richard; and when the summer came, she walked a great deal, always alone through the meadows and woods, and among the pools left by the tides along the shore.

"It might be well if I encouraged young Hugh d'Aubeny," said Hubert, haggard and sick with watching her and knowing himself helpless. "He is still persisting in his offer for her. Surely she could not fail to warm to him, in time, a fine, loyal young man, and a good match."

"You forget," said Margaret harshly, "she is mated already." And he was shocked and silenced, reminded again of the barrier between them. He had fallen in with the king's wishes and plans, but Margaret had not. Nor would she ever forgive either the king or her husband.

Only once did he steel himself to speak of his betrayal to Meggotta, with terrible humility, and she opened her eyes wide at him, but the silver-grey pools had no sunlight in them, and she kissed him, but her lips were as cool and still as the petals of water-lilies. "Oh, my dear," she said, "it was not you did this to me. Life has done it to us all. I would not want you to grieve."

Once he had taken this first step, he found he could speak of a future. "Girl, dearest, you're young yet, not fifteen till after midsummer, you'll be countess of Kent, you have great possessions. This has only been a sad mistake. You'll come back to court, no one will remember this for more than a year, you'll be beautiful and rich, there'll be suitors eager to win you. There's one now, Hugh d'Aubeny thinks of no one else. Even if we must wait a while, you can still make an honourable marriage, a happy, successful marriage. . . ."

All that, she thought, I have had, in a few years more joy than most are given in a lifetime. Perhaps my lifetime's share. But she did not say it, not to him, she only smiled her white, consoling smile for him, and laid her arm about his neck to comfort him by touch.

It was different with Margaret, when Hubert was away. For he was still a royal councillor, and the summons called him back to Westminster from time to time, when the council met. In the city the affair of Richard de Clare was already half forgotten, and it was rumoured that the king was cautiously reviving his plans for the boy's marriage. The less said about the past, the better.

When the two women were thus left alone, for Meggotta would not leave Burgh, and Margaret would not leave her, they talked together more freely and in another fashion, with more blood in it.

"You have been out of the world long enough," said Margaret. "He's lost, and you have no choice but to accept your loss, and face it, and tread it under your feet. You are a king's granddaughter, and a great king, too, and I know you have his heart in you. Royal women in grief and misfortune still take up the burden of living, and carry it with pride, as I have done. So can you."

"My pride," said Meggotta, "goes by a different way. I have lost my honour and I have lost Richard. Everything that remains I despise."

"All this fair world, at fifteen years?" said Margaret, quietly raging.

"I have seen and possessed the fairest of the world," said Meggotta simply. "Why should I make do with second-best?"

Earl Gilbert Marshal went often to visit his nephew in the king's hold, that summer, troubled in mind at a close confinement that had pared the boy away into a lean, pale, burning solitary, immured from the world because he would not give any parole, but hugged to him the right to every freedom, if only he could break free. They let him exercise in a small court from which escape was impossible, and provided him playmates of his own age and condition, but they dared not let him ride out from the island city over the bridge, even escorted, since he was a notable horseman for his years, and exceedingly venturesome of his life at all martial play. It was no life for a brilliant boy rising fifteen, and matured some years beyond his age.

"For God's sake, child," said Gilbert, exasperated, stamping about the narrow room on an evening in July, "will you not have some pity for me, if not for yourself, and give the king the word he needs to turn you loose? You're like a mewed hawk, I despair of you. Better men than you have had ado with kings, and lost. De Burgh, for one, poor broken veteran! Will you not get it into your stubborn head that you cannot win? Make terms with life, for God's sake, and take what you can get."

"Whatever I can get now," said Richard immovably, "is poor pay for what I had. I have a wife, and I love and want her, and as often as the king comes near me he shall hear the same complaint, and if he kills me for it—but he dare not!—he is no better off, as I am no worse. Tell him so, if you wish. What more can I lose?"

"You talk like a fool," said the earl roughly. "What can you lose? Gloucester itself, if you go too far. Liberty, life, all the good things left in this world. Dare to tell me you've never felt a moment's pleasure since you lost this girl of yours, and I shall not believe you. The very feel of the sun on you, trees in bud, a horse under you—you're not deprived of all these. Be grateful even for the small gifts, and stop this fool's talk."

The momentary contraction of pain in Richard's heart reminded him that sometimes he had thought the same himself, and felt all the more unhappy and disloyal for thinking it. But a live young creature of fifteen could not be despairing every moment of every day, however relentlessly the great grief returned to pierce him after every reluctant breath of joy. Nor was it true that he felt no fear of the king. On occasions when he had spoken a little too recklessly and seen the half-loosed fury flash out at him, he had feared blows and worse, and understood better than before how Hubert could have longed for safety and peace beyond all things.

"Even if I were resigned to being what you call sensible," he said wretchedly, "I am still married—as I know, if you do not—and to give my vows a second time, to another, would be mortal sin. So even if I wished, how can I obey the king? I don't wish, but the barrier is there, and real, whether you believe in it or not."

He remembered Meggotta's message to him, faithfully delivered by the Countess Marjorie on the one visit she had been allowed. The countess was somewhat suspect in the king's eyes as being Margaret's sister, just as in Richard's eyes she was somewhat suspect as being his uncle's wife, and dutiful, and therefore anxious, like her husband, to see this troublesome boy brought, as gently as possible, to see reason. But at least she had told him what Meggotta wished for him, and though he had wept himself to sleep that night for the pity and the loss of it, yet every touch of sun on his face, every glow of exercise, every sight of a bird soaring, confirmed him in knowing that he was indeed, as she had said, too full of life to die for sorrow. He wondered if the countess had also carried his message of love to Meggotta in return, for he had never again had the opportunity of asking her. He doubted it; she had been careful not to promise, and she might well have consulted Gilbert, and allowed him to persuade her that the least said, the best for them all. As well, perhaps, if she never had delivered it. His passionate outcry that he would never love another, never know happiness again in this world, that life and love and joy were over for him—what could that do now for Meggotta but rip open again a healing scar? He hoped healing! Or he wanted to hope for that, though the pain it cost him might indeed kill. No one told him anything about her. The king was well served.

"Listen, fool boy," said Gilbert patiently, "you need not question what state and church seem to have decided on your behalf. You have made a very stout stand for being bound, but in spite of it the court has declared you free. No need for you to have scruples on the score of mortal sin. And never forget that you're not of age, no boy in your situation can hope to take the decisions about his own future, and neither can he prevent them when they're taken by his guardians. Whether you will or no, child, they'll marry you! Even if you refused at the altar, there'd be a way of overcoming the difficulty."

"That I doubt," said Richard grimly. "At least it can be tested." But since his uncle was so set on persuading him into line for marriage, and so sure it could be done with or without his leave, he could not choose but feel some curiosity, as well as apprehension. "What are they saying about me? What is it the king wants? He tells me nothing but that I must be dutiful and submit. The rest seems to be none of my business."

"Oh, you may draw breath a few months yet, they'll take their time over settling your fate. There are some among the earls who have daughters they'd gladly match with you, but his Grace's mind is set on an alliance with his Lusignan kin. There are several of his young half-sisters among the La Marche brood, he'd be glad to forge close ties with Count Hugh to strengthen his hold on Poitou. The earl of Cornwall is less favourably disposed. It will take some time yet to get agreement."

"And they can discuss the disposal of my body like this," blazed Richard, outraged, "while my wife is driven into hiding and I'm held prisoner here? They know, they know—*you* know! you *all* know!—she is my wife and I am her husband. And you all pretend it's legal to close your eyes to the truth. Liars and hypocrites, every one!"

He expected a blow, and might very well have returned it, he was in such a fury, but Earl Gilbert was of equable temperament, and genuinely concerned and perplexed at his nephew's condition, and all he did was take the boy by the shoulders and shake him sharply but not unkindly. "Don't, I advise you, take such a tone with the king, or you may find yourself in a far worse place than this. Don't put him to the test, he has powers you'd best let alone." He released him with a sigh, clapped him resignedly on the back, and turned to go. "You're incorrigible, and if you go too far, I can't protect you. You are the king's ward, not mine. God send you better sense!"

In his bed at night Richard wept, clenched hard about the unrelenting fire that gnawed heart and loins, and burned up anew in the darkness when he was solitary and unseen. But nightly it seemed to him that this anguish receded a little from the extreme of bodily longing, withdrawing into the memory of an innocent grief, until at last, just before he slept, and slept deeply, he was back in the shared bed on his first night at Burgh, and Meggotta's round arms embraced and comforted him.

Meggotta walked barefoot along the shore near Bromholm, the ripples of the incoming tide lapping over her ankles and spraying the skirts of her gown. Here she had walked with Richard, and played with the small creatures cast up in the rock pools, and listened to the gulls crying as they were crying now. After the long fine weather, September came in blustery and uncertain, with windy nights and immense noonday skies. She was aware of beauty without being moved by it, though there was a core of gratitude somewhere deep within her that still felt warmth, and approved the world as a work worthy of God. But a world not for her. She had lost the knack of living in it, since half of her being had been severed and gone astray. Now she could not bear to be anything but alone. More and more she left Burgh, and rode or ran into the wild places she had known from childhood, and stayed away longer and longer while the light lasted and into the dark. Yet she came home composed and sensible, answered mildly, was astonished that they should have been uneasy about her, seeing she knew all this region like her own translucent palm.

"She eats too little to keep a bird alive," Alice fumed with tears. "And see how I've had to take in all her gowns, she's grown so thin."

Alice had wept over her often and long. Meggotta wondered at it and tried to reassure her, but it was as if she were comforting her in an unknown language, unaware she was not being understood.

They brought Hubert's physician to watch her, and then to tend her, but he shook his head forebodingly, and though he said nothing to hasten the breaking of Hubert's overburdened heart, to Margaret, whose heart, however pierced, would not break, he said, "There is nothing wrong with her body but that she has almost discarded it. She has not set out wilfully to die, but unless the one thing she lacks is restored, she will die. She is living without that which for her is necessary to life. It cannot continue long."

It did not continue long. Early in October she came home through rain from the shore, riding at a languid walk, surprised to find cloak and gown soaked through. Alice hurried her to her bed, streaming tears and muttering fury, wrapped her up warmly, and sat by her until she slept. In the night she turned and smiled, embraced a shadow, and slept again more serenely. But in the morning she could not rise, and her forehead was moist and hot, and then dry and hot, in a savage fever. Hubert sat by her bed, clinging to one thin white hand, veined between blue and green, like nothing so much as a snowdrop flower or the petal of a wood anemone, as fragile and as cold. Even fever she accepted with unearthly calm, only the flush and fade of burning and chill signalling the changes in her condition, for her face remained pure and still.

After long days the fever passed, and she opened eyes huge and deep, half her face drowned in their depths, and spoke clearly and gently, grieving that they should have been grieved for her. She smiled at Hubert, and he was cheered out of all measure. But not for long. For though she had put off the fever, it had eaten so much of her substance that she never rose from her bed again. If she had attempted it, she would have fallen at the first step.

It was then no more than a matter of time, and time was in no great haste with Meggotta.

The wrangling magnates of the king's council returned to the subject of Richard de Clare in the middle of October, with renewed confidence, though none of them mentioned a reason. Word had gone round that the daughter of the earl of Kent was lying very ill at Burgh, and unlikely to rise from her bed again. No one said any such word at court, but it was noticeable that they entered briskly and full-voiced into matters that had heretofore been touched on only delicately and imprecisely. No one said openly that it would end an embarrassing situation, be a huge relief to the king's plans, and remove a load from a great many uneasy consciences when Meggotta died.

With the interested parties thus encouraged to hope that difficulties might soon be smoothed out of the way, the discussions this time proceeded to a form of agreement. The earl of Cornwall was not enthusiastic, but he did agree to the compact that was finally made. The king was to have his way, and await the response of the count of La Marche to the overtures already made to him, but a time limit was set for his reply, and failing his interest, another claimant was recognized. The agreement was inscribed in the Patent Rolls on the twenty-sixth of October. King Henry granted to John de Lacy, earl of Lincoln, that if the king could not attract Count Hugh to his support by the marriage of Richard de Clare to the use of one of the count's daughters before Hilary of the following year, 13 January 1238, the aforesaid John de Lacy should be entitled to the said Richard's marriage to the use of his eldest daughter, Maud, for a consideration of five thousand marks, already guaranteed to the king.

Two thousand of this sum was remitted. Three thousand marks was the final value set on Richard, who was the last to be told of it.

"I will not and cannot," he said flatly, when Earl Gilbert did at last acquaint him with the plans made for him. "You know it is impossible. I want neither a Lusignan nor a Lacy, I want my wife, Meggotta. I tell you, if they drag me to church, I shall still refuse. For God's sake, uncle, what else can I do? I am married!"

Gilbert was sick and tired of repeating patiently that the court held a different view on that point. Hilary of the following year was still nearly three months away, and he knew what Richard did not—that the news from Norfolk promised to cut through that particular knot long before January. He even debated within himself whether it would be kinder to give the boy some warning now, or leave him in ignorance. He was unhappy enough as he was, probably the cruellest thing would be to blurt out to him that Meggotta was on her death-bed while he was shut up here and could not even pay her one last visit. If she died, then he could be told, as kindly as it could be done, not, please God, by King Henry in one of his totally insensitive moods! Death is a final separation. However devastating in itself, it solves many problems. Even for Richard, in the end, it might be a relief.

Tentatively and carefully, he tried another way. "If the king should ask the Holy Father for a dispensation, to remove all doubts, have your marriage formally annulled—you have a duty to marry and get heirs to your earldom, for your father's sake and your grandsire's—then you might come to terms with his Grace's plans for you?"

"Can he do that?" demanded Richard, roused and frightened. "Without my consent? I'm not a child, I'm fifteen. Surely he couldn't divorce us without my word? And I'll never give it! Never!"

"Well . . ." said Gilbert, sighing. "Let it rest awhile yet. The count may delay. . . . Who knows what can happen in three months?"

"I know what will not," said Richard inflexibly. "There'll be no change in me, I shall still be saying no, and no, and no, plans or no plans, bride or no bride. The only bride I want is kept from me in Norfolk, but she is my wife, and in the end I mean to have her."

He knew already, none the less, that he was flying a defiant pennant against the wind. And to be defeated but not to surrender is only a very bleak and barren victory.

In mid-November, when the easterly winds were hoisting spray over the dunes of Norfolk, and driving the chilled leaves before them in frightened flocks, like storm-lashed birds, Meggotta died, so privately, so secretly, that neither father nor mother, watching close on either side her bed, knew the moment when she left them. She had lain so still for so long, her breathing had hushed so imperceptibly from hour to hour, her breast lifted so shallowly, sank so gently, that it was impossible to detect where motion ceased at last. Even her body seemed to have sunk into her bed until it barely lifted the covers over her, and her head into the pillows until her face floated like a water-lily flower, half submerged. She left the earth as dew sinks into the grass, or dries on a leaf in the sun, as decorously, as mysteriously. And what thoughts she had through all the last days of her life, if she had any thoughts at all, no one ever knew.

They knew she was dead only when Hubert, persuaded to leave her for the night and rest, stooped to kiss her forehead, and found it cold as sea-foam. Even then, in the face of her admirable and awful reticence, outcry would have been indecent. He looked at Margaret across the bed, and said low and clearly, "My daughter is dead, and I have killed her."

"Well, well!" said the king, when he heard. "Poor child, I am sorry! It has been a sad business throughout." His face was grave and devout, but his left eyelid drooped strongly, and he drew deep breath, like one shedding a burden. "We should soon be hearing something, surely, from the count of La Marche."

"That poor girl in Norfolk is dead," said Simon de Montfort to the Countess Eleanor, in the king's own small parlour, where of late they had been able to meet. His face was unhappy, and his voice angry. "I wish to God we had done that business better. I dread we all have her death on our souls."

"You at least spoke some words for them," said Eleanor. "What more could you have done? Not even you could have moved my brother to relent where de Burgh was concerned. He always hates those who have caused him embarrassment, or those he has injured. You know it as well as I."

But he did not. He had heard her say it, but he had still to learn it on his own skin, and as yet he was the beloved, the bosom friend, who at this stage could do no wrong. And shrewd as he was, he had an innocence still very vulnerable to this manner of immoderate and unstable affection.

"Yet he is being more than generous to us. . . ." He fretted vainly at the puzzle. "I am thinking of the boy . . . Richard. He has maintained throughout that his marriage was real and valid. How will he bear this?"

"I doubt if you need fear for the boy," said Eleanor gently. "He'll suffer, but he'll live. There are compulsions, you know, on young men of your breed. They do not die for love. They are not allowed!"

Earl Gilbert went very heavily to visit his nephew in the palace. It was not an errand he welcomed, but he undertook it to prevent worse. The king, when he had his own way, could be charming and generous, but not, unhappily, compassionate. Childlike, he expected joy everywhere when he was joyful; consternation, grief, and rage would be personal affronts, to be visited with indignation, if not outright vengeance.

It was late afternoon, and Richard was sitting in his apartment, frowning over a book done in fine French script. He put it aside languidly when Gilbert entered. His scholarship was known and respected, perhaps by reason of this unnatural confinement of his, for an active mind must find exercise somewhere, and his field was limited. The blue eyes had withdrawn rather deeply into his skull for a fifteen-year-old, and the lines of his face were too fine and too formed; the look these features could command was the look of a man, mature, wary, withheld from too candid contact. He trusted no one, or no one who had ready access to him. He expected duplicity.

Earl Gilbert sat down opposite him, eye to eye, spread his elbows on the table between them, and told him. Why make many words about what could not be altered? The fewer the better, if they were the right words.

"Richard, we've had news from Norfolk that will come very hard to you, and I'm sad to be the bearer. Meggotta de Burgh is dead."

Richard stared at him for a moment without understanding, and then flinched violently, as though from a stab wound, and thrust a hand forward across the table, sending his book flying to the floor, as though he warded off an enemy as intangible and irresistible as death. His lips shaped "No!" in a soundless cry. Then habitual distrust rushed in on him, and he narrowed his eyes in contemptuous unbelief. "This is some new trick of the king's to break me. He wastes his time. I *know* this cannot be true."

"It is true. Do you think I would come to you with so vile a lie?"

"No," admitted Richard in a breathy whisper. "No, you have not lied to me. Except as all this persecution has been one great lie. Has he, then, gone the one step further, and murdered her? That I could believe!"

Gilbert took him by the hands and held him hard. The shocked blue eyes looked through him and very far away out of this dim and none-too-warm room.

"Child, you know better than that. Whether we have done well or ill in this matter, this has been none of our doing. It's your pain that cries out against him, and God knows who dare blame you, certainly not I. But believe me and accept it: She is dead. Neither you nor I can change it now."

"You swear to me?" said the boy, and his thin hands turned and gripped feverishly in the hands that held them. "It is truth?"

"It is truth. I swear it!"

Richard was stone-still for a long time. Then he asked, in a voice level and toneless, "What happened to her?"

"She caught cold, and went into a bad fever. And though that passed, she had not the strength left to recover."

"And she is really dead?" Still unable to accept the finality of loss, he peered desperately into Gilbert's eyes, but found nothing but help-less pity there. "Yes . . . she's dead," he said dully. "How is it I did not feel her go?"

Nothing left to wait for now, nothing to fight for, all the valour and obstinacy and pain of this past year gone into thin air, wasted like unprofitable smoke from a fire abruptly quenched. Now he began to believe in it, even to understand what had happened to him, by the awful ease that crept through all his sinews, acquitted now of all effort, by the lassitude that sucked out all his energy and resolution, for which he had no longer any need, by the amorphous indifference that clouded his mind, now that all his prowess of mind and body could never be brought and laid at the altar where they belonged. Soon the pain would come, as it comes to frost-bitten members when the thaw sets in, but as yet all he felt was the abhorrent languor, the loathsome relief.

"Go now," he said in a quiet, reasonable voice. "Leave me alone. Oh, you can, I shall be safe enough."

Gilbert was not happy. He looked back twice before he ever reached the door, and then came back to frown down doubtfully at the boy, who sat and endured it without complaint or encouragement.

"Richard, you should not stay here brooding any longer. The king will give you your freedom if you will submit to him, and fall in with his plans for you. Will you let me go to him, and tell him you're ready to obey him?"

"Why not?" said the boy, lifting indifferent brows. "Let him do what he likes with me. What does it matter, now?"

14

January, 1238: Westminster.

On the day following the end of the Christmas feast, in the king's private chapel at Westminster and in the king's presence, Simon de Montfort, earl of Leicester, was married to King Henry's sister, Eleanor, in a ceremony devoid of all the usual display and extravagance. No one else had been consulted, no one else was aware of the occasion until it was over, except the king's closest officers. Henry was elated at the prospect of having his own way in the matter of one marriage, and had allowed his exuberant optimism to persuade him to countenance another. He felt able, successful, beyond challenge. He was fond of his sister, and had listened sympathetically to her pleas, he had a close and warm friendship with the earl, and was glad to think that two people dear to him should be happy.

There remained, of course, the reaction of the archbishop to be taken into account, but that was not primarily his concern.

"I myself," said Eleanor firmly, "will tell the archbishop what I have done, and why."

"*We,*" said Simon, equally firmly, "will tell him what *we* have done."

"*You* have broken no vows," she said.

"I have broken yours," he said with joy, and kissed her.

Archbishop Edmund Rich was gentle and kindly, and halfway to being a saint in his own lifetime, but saints can be very hard on ordinary men. They sought him out together, for the king's summons had gone out to all his magnates for the forthcoming council, and the archbishop was already in Westminster. Hand in hand they confronted him and made their confession.

The shock was profound and genuine. His distress drew tears from Eleanor, but only tears of regret at having so wounded someone she respected and admired, not at all tears of repentance.

"Daughter, what have you done? Have you forgotten the solemn oath you took in my presence, of your own will? Is the obligation of such a vow to be shaken off thus lightly? You imperil your soul, dear daughter! Was not the life of chastity your own choice? Did I urge you to it against your will?"

"It was my choice then," said Eleanor firmly, "for reasons not perhaps so worthy as you have imagined, and I acknowledge myself a sinful creature of many faults, but in this matter I cannot feel guilt, even when I try. I think I sinned then, not now. I must and will tell you nothing but truth, and the truth is that I stand here filled with joy. I did fight long and hard against an affection that tempted me back to the world, but I have learned that I am meant for the world, and for affection, and for marriage, and here I take my stand."

"This cannot work to your happiness, lady, when you have entered into your marriage sacrilegiously. And you, my lord—was it well done to tempt her from her troth?"

"In my eyes," said Simon bluntly, "it was. And, with respect, though you did not urge her to her vow, I think it was incumbent upon you to do more than that, to make clear to her then the gravity of giving up the world and love at sixteen! You might—I say it with humility —have urged her *not* to bind herself so!" He was growing over-warm in his indignation over the few words that had kept his fate in the balance so long between gain and loss, but the happiness of the ending flooded him with goodwill towards all the world. Even the archbishop, in his sad disillusionment with humankind, found the young man's sudden flush and smile very engaging. "Forgive me, I have no right to speak so to you, my lord. But have you considered that God himself may change his plans for us? I cannot believe that so strong a love could arise between two people, and feel itself so justified, and not be God's work."

"Children, children," said Edmund Rich sadly, shaking his head over them, "you play with words. A vow is a vow. Even at sixteen you should have learned that. Here is a sacred obligation broken. Can that be pleasing to God? And worse it is that you, the elder, knowing of the Lady Eleanor's chosen state, have so persisted as to seduce her from it."

"Very well!" said Simon, burning bright with ardour again, "if there is blame, it is mine. I will take my guilt to the highest court, I will make the pilgrimage to Rome and lay my case before the Holy Father, and show him that ours is a marriage lawful, ordained, blessed. Look at us! Look at my wife! Was not she meant to live fully in this world, to be loved, to love, to bear sons as valiant and daughters as beautiful as herself? It is vile and mean to confine what is large and noble into the narrower ways of service."

Eleanor drew him warningly by the hand she held, though she glowed at hearing him. Such inconvenient audacity was not likely to convince the primate, however it might startle and disarm him.

"Father," she said, "since first I set eyes on this man I've married, I have prayed every night for guidance, knowing I loved him. Never was there any doubt of that. If my prayers had brought no other answer but to hold me to my vow, I should have passed my life hereafter barren and sad. But it was not so. Gradually I have been led to understand that love does not come without the blessed intent of benign providence. I went where I was led, to arrive at this place where now I stand. I entreat you, give me your blessing, or if I may not yet hope for that, pray for me, pray for *us*, for now I am a wife."

The archbishop's experience, wide as it was at second-hand, knew marriage only as it occurred in the world about him, shrewd, calculated, dutiful, arranged for reasons of estate and wealth, accepted out of custom, often maturing into love of a kind, but not this impetuous and turbulent splendour. He recoiled from it baffled and alarmed. Prayer he could promise them, but nothing more. A smoke of damnation hovered ominously close to them. If he could pray it away, he would.

But the woman was forsworn, and the man implicated in her sacrilege, and guilty of an insubordinate arrogance the more disturbing for being in its own fashion passionately devout. Archbishop Edmund withdrew from them in dejection, and with his own austere standards in some disarray.

"We are come to a sad pass," he said as he dismissed them, sighing, "when not even princes, having set their hand to the plough, can be trusted not to look back. I despair of human constancy."

"If ever you see any falling off of constancy," said Simon, stung, "as between us two and the vows we have made to each other, then call us to heel as sharply as you will, and let loose all the bans of the church against us, for we shall deserve it. But I think neither your lordship nor your successors will ever live to see that day."

They went out from him hand in hand, as they had entered, to weather the first storm of a stormy life together; but neither of them looked back.

The summons to council came also to Hubert in Burgh, and in duty bound he obeyed it. Such burdens of state as still remained to him he never thought of laying down. But this time Margaret went with him to London, which was a mercy he had not dared to count on. Perhaps she went only to escape from the lamenting silence and emptiness within the house, perhaps because she, too, having set her hand to the plough, was never going to turn back from the furrow and leave the share to rust. Since Meggotta's funeral journey they had exchanged but few and arduous words, the common, necessary traffic of the day, and always with a resigned courtesy, as two incompatible people, forced to be together, carefully avoid the very friction of sleeves, for fear of pain. Nevertheless, she came with him to the city.

The orderly course of discussion at that council was violently shattered by the arrival of the earl of Cornwall, black-browed and furious, with a dozen other magnates at his back as indignant as he. King Henry, never good at foreseeing the results of his own actions, was taken completely by surprise and driven on to the defensive from the first bitter tirade. All manner of things he should have borne in mind occurred to him far too late: that his vigorous younger brother had for some time been raising dark objections to the mounting influence of aliens at court; that Simon might still be regarded as one of the aliens, being by birth and rearing French to his finger-ends, though he had ceased to think of himself in that way; that this marriage that Henry had so graciously patronized would be regarded not only as sacrilegious by the church but as clandestine and infringing their rights of consultation by the magnates, which was much more ominous; that it even offended against the terms of the general peace so laboriously worked out under the guidance of the bishops four years ago, when Henry had promised to act in concert with his council and nobles, and not arbitrarily at his own will. The sight of the earl of Cornwall's accusing face and substantial following also reminded him that his brother had gathered around him a very considerable party of like-minded barons, which could easily be turned into a dangerous faction.

Simon had foreseen the storm, and was braced to meet it, but he had expected it to fall all upon him, and instead the earl of Cornwall hurled his accusations at the king.

"This is not to be borne! Your Grace has torn up all those agreements to which you gave your pledge when the Great Charter was re-examined and defined, when you swore to rule not as a tyrant but always in consultation with all the powers of your realm, bishops, judges, and baronage, all who have a proper root in this kingdom of yours just as you have. What reliance can be placed on your word, after this? You have countenanced our sister's marriage in secret to the earl of Leicester, never consulting any man, never considering what great objections there might be to such a match, leave alone that our sister has broken a solemn vow. The earl of Leicester, like so many close in your favour—too close—is French, and though I say no word against his honest service and rights, like others he keeps from your side the true-born English barons on whom you should be relying."

Simon had flown to the king's side at the first sign of this attack, and stood a little advanced at his right, as though to shield him. His eyes opened wide in astonishment at this unexpected charge.

"My lords, I take objection to this dismissal of me as alien. When

I came to England, and the lord king received me graciously and gave me seisin of my lands, I put down roots here as deep—no, deeper than some of yours. What matter if I was born in France? Where I gave my homage I have given my loyalty and service, and here they stay, at the disposal of his Grace and of England, to the best I have in me."

"Yet it is not so long," Earl Richard rapped back fiercely, "since you were seeking a match with the countess of Flanders."

"Not since I have known the Lady Eleanor!" said Simon firmly. "Nor would that have made me less pledged to England than I am! But now I have confirmed my allegiance once for all, in sight of you all. . . ."

"Behind closed doors," countered Richard furiously, "and with the connivance of his Grace, whose coronation oaths and later pledges committed him, in so grave a matter, to consult with all his councillors before taking any steps. If my sister was to marry again, it should have been done with due regard to the immense value of such an alliance, and after proper thought. She is my sister, as well as the lord king's, and she is royal. . . ."

"If any man here desires to protest that the Lady Eleanor has been disparaged," blazed Simon, "I am ready to dispute the point with him as and when he pleases!"

"After the event! Your prowess is well known, but you made sure of the prize first, by theft! And in breach of a sacred oath!"

Simon controlled himself strongly; the issue was too important to be lost sight of under wilder and wilder recriminations. "I have already told the archbishop of Canterbury," he said, "that I intend to go to Rome, and submit our case to the Holy Father himself for judgement. If he grants dispensation, it is not for you to question. If not, it is not for me to complain. But I tell you this, my lords: I will use every art to keep my wife mine, against you and all the world, if need be. And whatever blame you find in what has been done, visit it upon me, not upon his Grace, who has done nothing worse than an act of kindness."

A dozen voices cried out together, returning stubbornly to the king's offence, which threatened their rights, and undermined the sound but still vulnerable order the archbishop had laboured for. Henry struggled to placate the growing resentment, for it was becoming frightening in its unanimity. Not one voice was raised in his support except Simon's. The earl of Cornwall had them all at his back, and meant to press the attack home.

"My lords, my lords, you have no just complaint. The Lady Eleanor had placed herself outside the consideration of marriage, and was not available to be matched with any prince abroad or lord here at home, so long as she held by her decision. You know it as well as I. For seven years there has never been question of her person being bestowed upon any man. What rights have you been deprived of? Discussion of her future never became a possibility. Only at her own express wish could she have quit the celibate life she had chosen. This was not a matter of discussing an important marriage but of granting or refusing my sister's petition to me, and that petition was not that she might return to the world and have a husband chosen for her, but that she might marry the earl of Leicester, and had that been refused, she would have remained as she was, and married none."

"It would have been more credit to her and to you," said his brother sternly. "But you make too little of the breach of charter and agreement. There are many of us here of one mind, and we say this shall end. We must have a better order, one that will be respected, and we will have safeguards for it that your Grace cannot flout at will."

"My lords," cried Simon, "I beg you to hear me, for I have been the maker of this discord. Whether I had a right to approach his Grace and ask him to countenance my marriage, that I leave aside. But surely *he* had a right to listen, and to be moved, when the Lady Eleanor and I came to him and told him simple truth, that we love each other, and have so loved now for some years. If it was a crime that I pursued her with my suit in spite of her vows, visit that upon me. She held out a great while against me, but love me she did and does, as you may ask her, and in the end, for us two it was marriage or a life without lustre or savour. We went together to the lord king and asked his consent. And he gave it, and we are married. What, is there no man among you will speak up for his Grace, when he has harmed none of you, but only had the goodness to make two people happy?"

The angry, rejecting murmur, like distant thunder, almost drowned out the single voice that said suddenly, "Here is one, at least!" But King Henry heard it, and turned to gaze, not immediately recognizing it. The earl of Kent came forward into clear view, and said again, more strongly, "Here is one!"

The foremost saw him, and fell silent, and the contagion of silence spread like ripples on a pond, into the furthest corners, until the whole hall was still. He spoke so seldom and so briefly in council, these days, and he was barely two months past his daughter's funeral, and here he stood up before them all, the sole voice raised against them, and on behalf of the king who had used him so ungratefully. He had still a presence; he stood straight, if he walked haltingly, he was fine and fastidious in his dress, and the dead-white hair and gaunt face and sunken eyes gave him a remote dignity. This once, at least, the deep eyes burned again.

"If there's none besides," he said, "let me at least declare myself in support of what his Grace has done. I say it was right and just to take into account the wishes of those two people surely the most concerned in a marriage, and not only the customary considerations of policy, rank, and possessions. Not that even these spoke against the match. The parties are well suited in rank, influence, and years, there is no disparagement here. But I count it a far greater thing if this union fulfils the dearest wish of two people who love each other, and secures them the happiness they surely deserve as much as they desire it. If the benediction of two lives is not a good deed, tell me what is!"

He turned his white head, and looked slowly round the whole circle of his opponents, and no one had a word to say. He looked at the king; the helpless remnants of old devotion were there in the look. "I thank your Grace for this mercy to one pair of lovers," he said. He looked at Simon, stricken silent like the rest, shining but humbled in his silence. "My lord of Leicester, I pray the blessing of God on your marriage, and wish you and your wife happiness. We too often make our plans and achieve them over the hearts and hopes of men and women," he said, his voice sinking. *"And children . . ."* he ended, but in so faltering a tone that perhaps no one heard. "My lord king, give me leave to withdraw. I am faint!"

"Do so!" said the king, in the soft, startled voice of a child. "I am sorry you are not well. Will one of you attend the earl!"

Hubert went out from the hall with terrible, solitary dignity, through the silence that no man was yet audacious enough to break, though the earl of Cornwall brooded and stored his thunder. In a quiet anteroom the old man sat down, and let the anger and bitterness slip away again out of mind. For some moments he was not conscious of his surroundings, then he became aware of someone who stood close beside him, and a steady young hand holding out to him a horn of wine. He looked up into Simon's face, a formidable face and irresistibly attractive, in its uncompromising planes both harking back to the old Norman vigour and searching forward into some shadowy, ideal future, better ordered than anything to be found in this present world.

"My lord," said the young man, low-voiced and hesitant, "what you have just done for me was more than I deserve. I wish to God I had now the means to requite you. My chance I let slip too easily. My wife has been so blessed as to have a voice to speak for her without fear." Still lower he said, with utter humility, "I am ashamed!"

What use would it have been now to answer "What is your offence, compared with mine?" Hubert merely took the horn from him, allowing his old hand still to be steadied within this vital young one, and drank.

"You have left your back unguarded," he said mildly. "Are they still thundering, within?"

"The earl of Cornwall is in earnest. And it was a breach of accepted form, I admit it. He has a grievance. He is threatening withdrawal from court, and all his allies will follow him."

"Don't trouble too much for him," said Hubert. "He is a well-balanced man, he will not push a disagreement like this into revolt. He wants forms to be observed, for good reason, but he knows the value of compromise. There can be reconciliation with Richard. He should have been the elder, he can always pull back from the abyss. But beware of the king."

Simon did not understand. He hovered, moved and troubled. "The king has my love, and has deserved it."

"He had my love, also. He has it still, only God knows how or why. But however he may stand by you now, for his own sake, this hornets'-

nest you've brought about his ears will have to be paid for some day. He will have it out of your hide, every sting. His dignity has been affronted, his actions called in question, his face blackened, things he never forgives. Be ready for him, for he'll turn on you and take his revenge for every embarrassment, sooner or later."

He saw that though his views were respected, he could not hope for them to be believed; the young man would have to learn by experience, as the old man had learned. But looking into this powerful and burningly honest face, he could not feel that King Henry would ever break the will and the integrity within.

"Shall I not have a litter brought for you," said Simon anxiously, "and see you safely to your house?"

"And leave your back unguarded still? No, no need, boy, I shall do well enough now. But you may lend me your arm to go back into council, if you will. If there are to be factions, it's well that it should be clearly seen where I stand, with you and with the king." He smiled, a little wryly, at Simon's doubtful glance. Such an ally was hardly likely to daunt the earl of Cornwall, if he really had it in mind to measure strengths with his brother. "I have forsworn arms," agreed Hubert with grim amusement, "but I have certain functions yet in this matter. I am the visible reproach that may stop a few mouths and change a few minds from pursuing you and your wife too bitterly. And I am the death's-head at the feast, reminding them they are mortal men, and had best keep their reckoning with God within bounds, while there's time."

Hilary came and passed, while King Henry kept an anxious eye on his brother's movements, and pondered a withdrawal to the Tower if the skies looked too threatening. The storm was to pass harmlessly in reconciliation, though not quickly. But at least the affairs of Richard de Clare offered a timely diversion, for the fixed date had passed, and there was no word from the count of La Marche. It seemed that he still felt that the future prospects for his numerous brood lay in France, and had no intention of jeopardizing them by a premature alliance with one of the highest magnates of England. The earl of

Lincoln was informed, accordingly, that his purchase of the marriage of the heir of Gloucester was duly accepted, and the marriage might proceed forthwith.

On the twenty-sixth of January, in the abbey-church of Westminster and with full royal splendour, the king's ward was married to Maud de Lacy. All the court was present in state; even the earl of Cornwall, though he had raised objections to this match no less than to his sister's, condescended to attend. It was an elaborate display and a lengthy feast, the king's opportunity to reassert his benevolent patronage and his domination of all things ceremonious and modish. He did not fail to look magnificent himself, and equip his ward equally splendidly.

Richard went through the long ceremony with stony composure, his face pale, his eyes wide and fixed. He had never seen his bride before, nor sought to, and he did not look directly at her now. Indifferently he was aware of a small, overdressed, glittering figure that stood beside him, and an almost inaudible voice, high and childish, that made the responses somewhat breathlessly. They had told him that Maud was just a few months younger than he, a most suitable arrangement. He was quite indifferent. It did not matter who stood here beside him, since she was not Meggotta.

His sense of grief and anger and loss had not abated at all in these long weeks, though no one could do enough to woo and compliment and flatter him now; all that had happened was that he had found ways of containing his pain. Not easy ways; they required this cold shell he had grown against all the world, which sometimes, in these last days, had suddenly frightened him by seeming rather a prison for himself than a fortress against others. But as yet he could not do without it. This sealed, immured creature within was dual; he was Meggotta's grave.

When he took the girl's hand in his at the altar, it was tremulous and small, with childishly plump fingers, and it startled him by first closing convulsively on his, as a scared child clutches at the nearest friendly grown-up hand, and then recoiling and hurriedly loosening the clasp, as the same child might do if repulsed. But he had not repulsed her. Why should he? It was not her fault. He stole a look at her then, for the first time acknowledging the presence beside him of another person. Rather small, as he had thought, and rather fat as yet, a plain girl with a round face and a great deal of soft brown hair. Nothing about her that could anchor and justify his desolation and rage. She looked as over-awed as she sounded, and was as assiduously not looking at him as he had been not looking at her.

Afterwards, at the banquet in the royal palace, she sat beside him mute and inert as a gold and white doll, saying hardly a word to anyone, and none to him, and speaking, even when she spoke at all, in a subdued whisper. Towards the end, when he had drunk rather more wine than he was accustomed to, Richard did wonder momentarily if she was as unhappy as he. But there were so many others about them ready and willing to do the talking that no one paid any attention to the silence of the bridal pair. And only the countess of Kent noticed, with a piercing stab of pain at her heart, that Meggotta's ring was still on Richard's finger, and took pride of place over his new wedding ring.

In the earl of Kent's riverside palace Hubert sat late in his chair, after Margaret had gone to their bedchamber. A long day it had been, the last memorial of a story that was over. This great house he had built when his star was high and his hopes for his child without limit was oppressive in its silence. He might give it, he thought, to some religious foundation, he had little use for it now, and his only heir would not need so grand a town-house, for he would never inherit the earldom of Kent. Only Margaret's child could have carried on that line. The title was as good as dead, like its holder.

Margaret came back into the room in her night-robe, her hair loose about her shoulders; the long dark cloud with the gleams of red had now other threads of grey in it, and there were brief, deep, upright lines between her straight brows. For a year they had gone about their lives with aching care, circling each other like creatures immured each in a bubble of glass, making cold, courteous gestures, uttering civil, alien words, unable to make any but the chillest of contacts, unwilling to make none at all. Now suddenly it seemed to Margaret that their twin islands of loneliness had touched, and the barrier between them was melting as she looked at him. What profit was there now in holding it against him that he had cast doubt on the truth of her word, and failed Meggotta in her most need? What help could it be to him to hold it against her that her desperate act had brought him into renewed danger and suffering, when his broken will could bear no more?

This old man is the man I have loved, she thought, and he is all I have left now, and he has nothing left but me. What folly, to reject the last of a fortune, because it is slighter than we hoped!

He stirred from a half-doze, abruptly, as old men do, and jerked up his head and saw her, standing with lowered head and grieving smile, looking at him as she had not looked for many months.

Gentleness and forbearance are not enough, where once there was passion, but they are something, at least—a means of living. She laid a hand on his shoulder, and he put up his own worn hand and covered it.

"Margaret! . . ."

"I am here," she said. "Don't sit longer, but come. It grows cold now the fire's low."

He had not heard that voice for a long time, nor had she truly been here beside him, as now she said she was. He held her eyes, and was afraid; but when they sustained his gaze with such resigned kindness, he rose, trembling, and took her into his arms. A charred log slid and cast sparks among the ashes. The fire had indeed burned low, but it was not yet out.

Richard wrapped his night-robe about his nakedness, and went into the bridal-chamber. He closed the door, and they were alone. The girl was already lying in the bed, in her white linen gown, stiff and straight and small beneath the covers, which were drawn up defensively to her chin. Her face upon the pillow looked white and pinched, and all the mane of brown hair was loose round her head. In a slanting light its colour was not quite drab, it had glints of lighter gold.

He felt nothing, nothing at all. This was his wife, the creature he was to live with henceforward; he neither wanted her nor minded her. As well this one as any other; at least she matched him in age, which gave the whole affair a less sordid look.

The January night was cold here, as cold as in Hubert's house, and the attendants who had prepared the bridal-chamber had left them a fire on the stone hearth. Richard stirred the embers, and added a couple of logs. He had nothing to say, and made no effort to find words where he felt none; he had spoken very little and very briefly since Meggotta's death. John de Lacy had wanted this match for his daughter; Richard was apathetically ready to supply what was demanded of him, but expected neither to give nor to receive anything more.

He was on his knees, staring abstractedly into the new splutter and glow as the wood caught, when he heard the small, convulsive sound from the bed, hastily suppressed. He turned and came to his feet in haste, staring. Her eyes were tightly shut, the brows drawn rigidly down over them, he saw the light glimmer along wet lashes, before she sensed his scrutiny and turned on her side, hiding her face from him. There was no more sound. He thought she was biting hard on her lower lip and holding her breath to prevent the next sob. How was it he knew so much?

"What's the matter?" he asked, startled and impatient. "Don't cry! What is there to cry about?"

"I'm not crying!" blurted the childish voice indignantly, and proved it with a huge sob that shook the bed. She curled into a ball, her back to him. "I know you hate me," she said from among the tangle of sheets. "My mother said you would, at first. You needn't pretend! She explained to me."

"She might have left that to me," said Richard, in the dry tone most people had heard from him since Meggotta's death, "if there's any explaining to do. I don't hate you. Why should I?"

It was not the most reassuring of voices, and it did not reassure Maud. She gave way and loosed her tears in a desolate flood, and when he sat down on the edge of the bed and laid a hand tentatively on her hunched shoulder, she flung round towards him, and showed him a contorted, child's face, not months but years younger than his own, and sobbed. "It isn't my fault! I didn't want to marry you!"

He felt something very deep within him wrung with a strange pang of pity and laughter mingled, and looked at her with yet another veil peeled from his eyes. She was alive, herself, a separate person, confused and torn with her own worries and regrets and fears.

"Didn't you, Maud? You don't like me—is that it? They don't ask us what we want. If we tell them, they don't listen."

"I didn't want to marry anybody," she gasped, and closed her eyes again upon despair, but not before he had seen how frightened she was, how deserted she felt by all those who had claimed to love her and then thrust her away into the arms of someone she must expect to hate her, how she clung to her threatened childhood, bereft so suddenly of its natural protectors. He felt something within him, very deep and very distant—a memory—break open and bleed. He stroked her shoulder, and teased back the tangle of hair from her temples. She shrank from his touch, and then was still under it. It seemed to him that she relaxed a little. Her eyes were large, clear, and sad, and watched him between wonder and apprehension; she was not altogether plain.

"Don't be afraid, I won't hurt you. I won't touch you, if you don't want me to. But I'm cold, out here," he said reasonably. "Let me in and I'll just lie by you, and you can go to sleep."

Resignedly she moved over in the bed, and lifted the covers to let him in beside her. He put out the small lamp, and they were left with the soft glow of the fire. The first sense of his nakedness stiffened her into distant stillness, but he lay remote and quiet, not touching her. His body was filled with longing, but not for her, and she did not feel or fear it. He shut his own eyes hard upon tears, but the dew was sparse and brief. For there she was, wracked and wretched and afraid, cast loose among strangers, and her need dragged at his heart.

After a while, since she went on softly weeping, and he felt her body quaking with the last tired spasms of sobbing, he put out a hand and found her arm, and stroked it gently. Perhaps she was half asleep then, for she turned and nestled against him, and he let his stroking hand fold round her shoulders and draw her close to his warmth. Her head found its way to the hollow of his shoulder. Distantly he heard a voice —surely not his own?—saying over and over, between the tremor of hope and the monotone of despair, "Don't cry! I'm here! You mustn't cry anymore. . . . I don't want you to be sad. . . ."

$\mathcal{T}$he main original sources for the details of Meggotta's story are the Calendar of Patent Rolls of Henry III, 1225 to 1247, and the Calendar of Close Rolls, 1227 to 1237, the former including all official documents issued open for general information, the latter those kept private. Several of the contemporary monastic chronicles also cover the story, notably Matthew Paris's *Chronica Maiora* and the *Annales Monastici* of Tewkesbury, Dunstable, and others.

All the material has been drawn together by Sir Maurice Powicke in a contribution to the *English Historical Review* (1941), "Hubert de Burgh's Daughter Meggotta." This is included as Appendix C in Sir Maurice's great book *King Henry III and the Lord Edward.*

The Close Rolls refer in 1232 to Meggotta's nurse as Alice. King Henry's letter to the Gloucester bailiffs, informing them of his commital of the heir to Hubert de Burgh, in accordance with previous agreement, is in the Patent Rolls, dated 1 November 1230.

The story of Simon de Montfort's visit to the earl of Chester at St. James de Beuvron, and the earl's championship of his cause and approach on his behalf to the king, was told by Simon himself years later, and is recorded in Charles Bémont's *Simon de Montfort, Earl of Leicester* (1884). Earl Ranulf's withdrawal of his forces from Painscastle is reported by the chroniclers of Tewkesbury, Chester, and Dunstable, though only Dunstable gives the reason as the earl's support of the Welsh claim.

There are various speculations as to who first proposed the compact of Bromholm. It may have been Hubert, struggling to protect his position, but it seems much more likely to have been des Roches, des Rivaulx, and the king, to disarm Hubert and put him off his guard until they received the papal letters and were ready to strike. Sir Maurice Powicke assembles all the material evidence in "The Oath of Bromholm," *English Historical Review* (1941). Papal letters of 10 January 1233 and 21 June 1235 refer to Henry's application for a dispensation from an oath on the grounds that it violated his coronation vows. The pope's letter dated 9 June 1232 provided the main ground for the first attack on Hubert.

The *Chronica Buriensis* records that Margaret sought sanctuary in Bury. An entry, dated 25 August at Kempton, in the Patent Rolls records the order of banishment to Hubert, drawn up but never sent. Matthew Paris in the *Chronica Maiora* tells the story of the bishop's refusal to interfere to prevent the mob's march on Merton, and Earl Ranulf's successful intervention. It is not stated that the earl was then already a sick man, but the Tewkesbury annalist records that he died on 26 October.

Both Roger of Wendover and the Tewkesbury annalist mention the secret marriage of Richard and Meggotta as taking place in September; the latter gives a definite date, 21 September.

The authority for the story of the smith of Brentwood and the ensuing siege is the Tewkesbury annalist. The order to the sheriff to arrest Margaret and take her to the Tower if she left sanctuary is in the Close Rolls, while King Henry's inventory of the treasures taken from Hubert's store in the Temple, and the king's published apologia for his actions, are in the Patent Rolls.

During the war with Richard, Earl Marshal, the Close Rolls record the king's diversion of his army against Usk, and the agreed surrender of the castle. Wendover and other chroniclers report how Earl Richard was intercepted on his way to the council at Westminster and warned that his life or liberty would be in danger.

The account of the rescue of Hubert, and of the activities following, is based on the flurry of official orders in the Close Rolls. The names of the two young men who befriended him are given.

Matthew Paris reports how the news of Earl Richard's death reached the king at Woodstock, while Roger of Wendover describes the scene in council, when the archbishop confronted the king with his own letters to Ireland. The action subsequently taken against des Rivaulx and his colleagues is recorded in the Close Rolls, which also mention the oath extracted from Hubert at Gloucester when peace was made.

The Tewkesbury annalist says that rumours of the secret marriage began to be circulated in the autumn of 1236, and certain magnates instituted proceedings against Hubert in the king's court when Henry was in the north. Hubert was summoned to join Henry at Eagle, in Kesteven. How the secret leaked out is not stated, but Gilbert, Earl Marshal, had married Marjorie of Scotland, and probably at about this time, suggesting a possible link. The account of the various hearings of Hubert's trial follows the Close Rolls, while the Patent Rolls record that safe-conducts were issued for Margaret and Meggotta to come to Kempton, the documents dated 14 October.

The king's concession to the earl of Lincoln of the marriage rights of Richard de Clare, conditional upon the count of La Marche's failing to take up his option by the following January, is entered in the Patent Rolls, dated 26 October 1237. The Tewkesbury annalist gives November as the month during which Meggotta died, thus showing that negotiations for Richard's marriage were resumed actively while his young wife was still alive.

Matthew Paris tells the story of the clandestine marriage of Simon de Montfort and Eleanor in his *Chronica Maiora*, and also describes the serious furor that followed it, mentioning Hubert as the only man who spoke up in support of the king's action in countenancing the match. Two or three weeks later, on 26 January, the Patent Rolls record the marriage of Richard de Clare to Maud de Lacy.